Hidden Revelations

THE THIRD BOOK
OF THE TREVU TRILOGY

By

F J WARREN

Other Books in The Trevu Trilogy

Broken Bonds
(ISBN 978-184685-208-4)

Familiar Strangers
(ISBN 978-184685-311-1)

Front cover design courtesy of Justin Hubbard

This novel is entirely a work of fiction. The names, characters and incidents portrayed in it are the work of the author's imagination. Any resemblance to actual persons, living or dead, events or localities is entirely coincidental. F J Warren asserts the moral right to be identified as the author of this work.

British Library Cataloguing In Publication Data
A Record of this Publication is available
from the British Library

ISBN 978-1-84685-689-1

First Published 2007 by
Exposure Publishing,
an imprint of
Diggory Press Ltd
Three Rivers, Minions, Liskeard, Cornwall, PL14 5LE, UK
and of Diggory Press, Inc.,
Goodyear, Arizona, 85338, USA
WWW.DIGGORYPRESS.COM

ACKNOWLEDGEMENTS

The author wishes to thank her family and friends for their encouragement before, during and after the completion of this work.

Particular thanks go to Joan, John, Jane and JT for all their hard work on my behalf.

Special thanks to Iris, Linda, Jennifer, Susan and especially Justin for his enthusiasm and invaluable assistance.

For JT

CHAPTER 1

THE light from the window of one of the small houses that boarded the narrow alley shone full into the face of a young man. He stood half obscured by a collection of empty barrels and kegs, which lay against the back wall of the grimy inn on the opposite side of the little walkway. Amidst the filth and squalor of the location his face appeared bathed in light and upon looking at him it was impossible not to believe that an angel appeared to be gazing attentively upon the scene before him. The solitary apparition stood as still as stone and was not in any way perturbed by the numerous shouts and guffaws of laughter that emanated from the houses, the alley and from within the hostelry. He continued to gaze, all unmoving, towards the end of the darkened alley which led down to the Seagull Inn, where most of the local fisherman preferred to sup their ale and other alcoholic beverages. The warm light that illuminated him threw into stark relief the classical beauty of his features when set against the ugliness of his environment. What such a young and innocent looking individual was doing, waiting so calmly and in such a place was not immediately apparent.

A sudden noise made his eyes widen as his ears registered the voice of the man he had come to find. Resolutely he took a deep breath, whilst desperately attempting to suppress the quiver of excitement that coursed through his body. Wiping his sweaty palms on the cloth of his coarsely woven coat, he took hold of the pistols that he had so carefully hidden in each of the coat's side pockets. Stepping back behind the stacked, empty containers, he was immediately hidden from view. The light from the window would now serve his purposes to a better degree; giving him sight of his quarry and enabling him to undertake the execution that he had dreamed of throughout so many of his young years. His annoyance on realising that two men appeared to be strolling through the alley, happily conversing with each other, quickly turned to worry. The one he sought was well known and instantly recognisable; there were few about of his height and looks after all. The voices grew louder as they approached him, trembling with excitement he withdrew his pistols and levelled them in the direction of the sound. Two men suddenly emerged from the darkness; both of them tall, and their long strides seemed to be bearing down upon him relentlessly. Desperate not to lose his advantage, he levelled his pistols but hesitated at the sight presented to him. His quarry was before him at last, but the stranger at his side was not the man he had expected to see. Suddenly the light emanating from the window disappeared as a rough curtain was drawn across it by the unknown occupant of the room. His proposed victim was dimly illuminated now but the two companions were fast approaching and he could not lose this opportunity. Stepping forward he squinted down his pistol, squeezed the trigger, and fired. There was a thunderous explosion, a flash of fire that lit not only his features but those of the two men, then darkness. If he felt fear before, he knew it now. As a sudden cry of pain rang out his mind was full with the sight of bright, cold blue eyes that had seemed to fasten upon him and hold him in an icy grip. The young man, aware that he needed to act quickly or else lose the advantage of what surprise there remained to his attack, squeezed his finger upon the trigger of his second weapon, and fired into the gloom. But even before he had loosed his second shot the sound of a man's voice, issuing orders, had reached his ears. The man he had managed to shoot was desperately shouting instructions to his companion to desist from doing whatever it was that the individual was intent upon accomplishing. Fear froze his heart and paralysed the young man's body for the name that was used belonged to his quarry. Whoever had been hit by his first shot was not the person that he had so desperately tried to kill. His victim's repeated shouts were in vain, for his orders fell upon two sets of deaf ears: the one because he would not hear and the unfortunate other because he could not.

At the sound of the first shot, the area had been stricken into silence, but when the second one shattered the peace of the night, doors flew open; curtains were dragged back from windows. The men from the hostelry piled into the alley, holding aloft lamps and looking around warily as to what it was that had caused such a noise to be made in their normally quiet locality. Against the far wall leaned the tall figure of the injured man, holding his left arm above the elbow whilst blood welled up between his fingers and dripped into the filth that lay so copiously on the cobbles. By the empty stack of barrels stood another man, standing astride a third, who lay on his back in the mud. They edged forward warily, fearful to see the sight that they knew was about to meet their eyes. The light from their lamps served to illuminate the face that stared in surprise back at them. They caught their breath at its angelic appearance, shuddered at the red, weeping gash across its neck, and slowly, almost as one lifted their own faces to look fearfully at the man who stood so resolutely before them. With his bloodied knife still in his hand, he stared impassively into the face of his victim before he turned away from the body and moved towards his injured companion. Making a cursory inspection of his friend's wound; he sighed with relief and said succinctly, "'Tis only a flesh wound, brother, you'll live." Removing his handkerchief from his pocket, he helped his shocked companion to remove his bloodied arm from his coat and, ripping open the sleeve of his shirt, proceeded to bind his wound.

"Is he ...?" the injured man attempted to ask, almost too shocked to speak.

"'Ess." replied his companion nonchalantly, before turning to the group of disbelieving men and telling one of them to go for the doctor to attend upon Mr Trevarthen.

"Bring 'en to Chapel Street," he said, quietly but authoritatively.

"What 'bout 'e?" asked one of the group boldly, pointing a shaking finger at the prostrate young body.

His killer regarded his victim dispassionately before advising the growing assembly to notify the authorities, informing them they were not to remove any items from on or around the body. His cold glance swept over them and they trembled as one as he said quietly but viciously, "I knaw everyone of 'e, so don't 'e go think to do anything thas' goin' make Joey Bolitho angry, understand me?" Nodding heads and mumbled affirmatives answered him. With one last sweep of his cold blue eyes across their frightened faces, he took his brother's arm and walked from the scene without a backward glance. By the time he had reached his home, the streets and alleys of Penzance were ringing with the news that Joey Bolitho had returned to his old ways after all and had killed again.

Joey Bolitho led his brother into the small dining room before ordering him to sit in the chair by the fire. The tall man sat down mechanically on his brother's instruction, still in a state of shock, and when presented with a glass of brandy, thoughtfully provided by his host, drank it down in one gulp. He coughed and tried to speak but no words came so he endeavoured to gather his scattered thoughts before attempting speech. His assailant's own shock at his appearance could be laid at the colour of his skin, for unlike his half brother, Paul Trevarthen was a man of mixed race parentage, and his dark skin was set at variance with his brother's lighter colour. The two men shared a father but whereas Joseph Bolitho was the son of a prostitute, Trevarthen's mother had been a mulatto. The dark skinned baby's appearance into his father's life had been traumatic. However, once the initial shock had passed he had been accepted and adopted into his father's family, mainly on the insistence of his father's childless wife, Penelope, who had refused to allow the poor abandoned waif to be sent to an orphanage. Joey Bolitho, on the other hand, had remained unknown to his father throughout Captain Trevarthen's life, growing up disadvantaged and underprivileged because of it. It was little more than two years since the brother's relationship had been established. Although they shared many qualities, Trevarthen had almost from birth had privilege thrust upon him, whereas his brother, from a pitifully young age, had been forced to steal and kill to have any chance of remaining alive. Paul Trevarthen, who resembled his father, inherited wealth from both the Captain and his real mother, who had become an accomplished businesswoman. Joey Bolitho had inherited his mother's blue eyes and many of her features, along with the grinding poverty in which they had struggled to maintain their existence. Murdered by a drunken lover, her son had avenged his mother's death, and set forth upon a life of petty crime in order to stay alive. When rescued from this existence by a benevolent smuggler and his wife he had grown up to become Cornwall's most famous and notorious smuggler. His ability to silence any number of the agents that were set upon him and his gang had instilled fear into many hearts, but upon his recognition by his brother and his subsequent marriage his life had completely changed for the better. Eighteen months previously, Joey Bolitho had married his beloved Sarah-Jane, the woman he had fallen in love with on first sight when he had been the young accomplice of the smuggler Barnaby Rickard. Her indifference to him, occasioned by her own love for his then unknown brother, Paul, and her distaste for Bolitho's occupation, had lasted for almost twenty years. She came to realise that the man who had continued to love her so steadfastly and had been determined to save his brother's life, even if he would have to sacrifice his own in the act, was worth her own love and, finally, Sarah-Jane had agreed to marry him. If her husband regretted their years of lost love he had never mentioned it to her. But his wife never failed to look upon each day of their marriage without a twinge of guilt; because of her foolishness, she had denied both of them the joy that they now shared so completely. Paul Trevarthen, while still a young man, had become a feted and successful author. He had fallen in love with the daughter of a man who had captained slave ships, but had married a different young girl on the understanding that he loved another. His stupidity in persistently loving another had produced his own love child, Daisy. But his own dear wife, Chloe, had forgiven his infidelity, as his beloved stepmother had forgiven his father on Paul's own appearance, insisting that the motherless child be brought up with their own family. Triumphs and disasters had tested their marriage but it had survived them all and their love had grown through it. Now, into the two men's settled existence, had erupted the evening's unlooked for attack and the death of their unknown assailant.

Paul, the younger of the two brothers, sat and watched in amazement as the ex-smuggler calmly regarded the drink in his own glass. Still struggling with what he had witnessed, he opened his mouth to speak.

"Who was he, Joey?" he asked worriedly.

"Dunno," replied his brother enigmatically and shrugged his shoulders. Paul knew his brother to be a killer, had known of it before they had even begun to meet with each other in the company of Paul's late friend, Bert Pendray, but until that evening Trevarthen had never been a witness to the act Joseph Bolitho was capable of committing without so much as a qualm.

"Why ... why did he attempt to kill us? He must have had a reason, for God's sake!" he cried, but his brother merely shrugged his shoulders again and sipped his brandy. "He was so young, Joey, with such a cherubic face. An innocent face, Joey," he continued accusingly, "could you not have overpowered him, and not have ... have ... killed him?"

" 'Tis instinct, Paul," Bolitho replied quietly. Lifting his eyes to his brother's face he frowned at the expression of outrage that lay across it and said with barely suppressed anger, " 'Tis 'ow I learnt to stay alive, Paul, an' if someone is goin' try kill me," and he paused before adding emphatically, "or you, then I 'idden goin' wait to ask 'en why."

He turned sharply as the dining room door opened suddenly behind him and looked into his wife's distraught face as she stood in the doorway. Hearing the news from a servant that her husband had returned home with his brother she had thought no more of it and had decided to leave them to their talk. However, when the servant returned to her room with the news that had come, blazing up through the town like a fire through the furze, she had rushed to find them immediately. That her brother-in-law had been injured, and in such a way, was traumatic enough, but her husband's actions had shocked her still more, though she had always acknowledged that in his previous existence those self same acts were committed to save himself from the hangman's grasp. At the sight of her, Joey Bolitho's cold, arrogant demeanour underwent a dramatic change. His expression softened, he dropped his glass onto the table and moved swiftly towards his wife with his arms extended. She fell into his arms and gasped the words, "Tell me it is not true, Joey, please," against his broad chest. Sarah-Jane felt him gasp briefly before his soft voice whispered his repeated apology brokenly into her curls.

A voice in the hallway announced the arrival of Dr Dunstan, and they heard Janey, their serving girl, leading him towards the dining room. Quickly, Sarah-Jane lifted her chin and smiled bravely at her husband before taking out her handkerchief and hastily drying her eyes before the doctor was admitted.

"Well, gentlemen - what's this I've been hearing? Attacked on your way home. Lucky to be alive for the fellow was well armed, so I was told, and had lain hidden to ambush you," said Dr Dunstan, all the while busily attending to

8

Trevarthen's injured arm. "Shouldn't give you any trouble, Paul," he pronounced expertly, "Might feel a bit feverish if you have indulged heavily on alcohol this evening, but apart from being uncomfortable for a day or two 'twill soon mend." He finished applying his bandage and helped Paul back into his coat before packing up his bag and turning his attention to the elder brother. "Have you sustained any injury, Joey?" he asked quietly, his calm expression staring serenely into Bolitho's inscrutable one.

"No, Denzil, I'm perfectly fit, thankee," replied Joey, impassively, and picking up another glass he filled it with brandy before passing it over towards the doctor. The doctor smiled his thanks and took a sip of the liquid, his face lighting up in appreciation of the quality of the drink he had just received. Trust a wine merchant like Bolitho to have the best quality in his own household, he reasoned. More voices from the hallway made the occupants of the dining room turn their heads towards the door. Sir Arthur Tregurthen was shown into their presence and, after briefly bowing to Mrs Bolitho, he too found himself the recipient of a glass of brandy. After ascertaining that Mr Trevarthen had not sustained a serious injury, he turned his attention to Joseph Bolitho and attempted to fix him with a stern eye. Like his father before him, he was a tall man, although not of the same stature as the two brothers. His love of food and intense dislike of exercise had caused him to put on weight and even his elaborately tied cravat could not hide his heavy jowls, nor could his corset completely disguise his corpulent figure.

"An explanation, if you please, Mr Bolitho, of the events that led to Paul's injury would be most welcome," he boomed in an authoritative manner. His host regarded him with an expressionless face, before requesting both the doctor and his latest visitor to avail themselves of a seat.

"Me an' Paul was on our way 'ome from Josh Pascoe's after spendin' an evenin' with the boys," said Joey, quietly. "We was nearly up by the back of Kendall's kiddlywink when we was shot at an' Paul was 'it in the arm. Another shot was fired at we but I see'd 'en from the flash from his first shot and 'ad put 'en goin' afore 'e could do any more damage," he concluded dispassionately.

"I . . . I see," said Sir Arthur, somewhat taken aback by Bolitho's brief description of the events and the calm way in which his tale had been delivered. "Have you any idea why this man should wish to kill you, either of you?" he asked, looking at each man in turn. Paul shook his head vigorously but his brother merely shrugged his shoulders. "Is the . . . I mean . . . was the fellow known to you, perchance?" But again both men indicated that they did not know of him.

Tregurthen sighed and took a sip from his glass, staring at the carpet meditatively. He raised his flushed face to Bolitho's and stared into his cold eyes. Something about the man unnerved one so, he thought to himself. In spite of his strong accent and scandalous past, Bolitho had an annoying habit of appearing to be completely in command of any situation in which he happened to find himself, and in his presence the peak of society felt themselves to be ranged slightly beneath the man, such was the aura about him.

"Well," he announced, with as much authority as he could muster, "I'll make enquiries round about and see what information I can ascertain as to what name the fellow went under. Not very old by the sight of him. Difficult to tell 'tho', such an innocent look as he had about him. Still, he had his pistols lying by his side and 'tis a well known fact that you, Bolitho, have never carried a pistol whenever you were upon your . . . I mean . . . 'tis not your ..." he spluttered and came to an ignominious conclusion. Fortifying himself with another sip, he announced it was best he was on his way. He would have to confirm that his instructions as to the safe disposal of the body had been carried out, he would then write a description of the events that had occurred that evening.

"I am informing Sir Reginald Bonython of course, Bolitho," he said apologetically. If he had expected the impassive expression to alter, he was to be disappointed. So, finding nothing more to add to the discussion, he finished his drink, nodded his farewells to the little gathering and found himself shown from the house by his host, whose face still wore its unaltered mask and whose cold eyes regarded him so blankly.

Outside in the cool night air, he shivered involuntarily, pulled his cloak tight about himself, and hurried from the house, feeling a share of sympathy for the failed murderer who lay on a bare trestle in a side room of the Customs House, with his angelic expression staring at the ceiling. No-one would disturb the body there and he had a man already on his way to Sir Reginald's with the news of the events surrounding Joseph Bolitho. For considering Bolitho's past, perhaps the best person to deal with that evening's strange occurrence would be the head of the Customs Service himself. The previous scandal involving Bolitho, Trevarthen and Gerald Hudson, the town's late Preventative Officer, had never fully been explained to him. In common with the rest of Penzance, he had been informed that the felon Leviticus Skewes, who was Bolitho's lifelong companion, was presumed to have killed Hudson when that gentleman had paid a call on Paul Trevarthen at his home. As Skewes had shot the Preventative Officer, Hudson's own gun had gone off, accidentally, and that this shot hit Bolitho, almost killing him. "Damn fairy tale," he muttered to himself as he walked quickly towards his own home. "Where the hell did Skewes disappear to? That's what I'd like someone to tell me!" and he puzzled even more to himself as to why Joey Bolitho should even have been in Paul Trevarthen's house that night. After all, he had been barred from ever going to Trevu again when Trevarthen had mistakenly believed him to be having an affair with his wife. At that time, the town had been buzzing with the scandal for months. Then suddenly, whilst Bolitho lay badly injured at Trevu, everything had changed and it was announced that Joseph Bolitho was the unknown bastard son of Captain Redvers Trevarthen and that his brother wished that full knowledge of this fact should be known around the town. Tregurthen's own mother had been the first to be informed. Probably, Sir Arthur surmised, because Paul Trevarthen had presumed she would be capable of spreading the news about the town faster than the loudest of town criers. Still muttering to himself the sudden thought occurred to him that perhaps Bolitho had not been the intended victim of the fellow with the angelic face after all and that Paul Trevarthen was the one the youth had attempted to kill. Perhaps there was a whole gang of ruffians attempting to murder members of the cream of Penzance's society. If this was the case then he himself could be a target of some unknown assassin. With this horrifying thought bringing beads of sweat out on his brow, Sir Arthur Tregurthen indulged in a form of exercise that he had not attempted since his early youth, and ran the rest of the way home as fast as his rotund legs could carry him.

Meanwhile, back in Joey Bolitho's dining room, Dr Dunstan was enjoying his second glass of brandy. He had advised Paul to spend the night at his brother's for it would be foolish to return home after the incident that had so recently occurred. Should he require medical assistance then it would be much easier to attend upon his patient in Penzance than to have to go all the way to Trevu.

"I don't think I shall require further assistance tonight, thank you, Denzil," Paul told him quietly. But Joey assured Paul that if a message was sent to Chloe informing her that her husband was not capable of returning to his home that night, she would merely conclude that Paul had succumbed to temptation and had imbibed too freely, deciding instead to spend the night at his brother's house. On a very few occasions during the past year this had been the reason he had been forced to convey to her to account for his staying in Penzance and she would not be unduly alarmed by such a disclosure. As he had been prevailed upon to stay the night, Sarah-Jane had left the men talking quietly together and went off to organise the spare bedchamber for their unexpected guest.

" 'Tis a most strange thing to have happened, because I sincerely believe the fellow is not known to you, Joey," said the doctor to Joey Bolitho, who sat staring impassively into the fire.

"I never seen 'en 'fore, Denzil an' thas' the truth," remarked his host in a soft voice.

"Perhaps he wished to kill you both to rob you?" suggested Denzil Dunstan brightly. His suggestion was dismissed as being impracticable by Bolitho. No robber in his right mind would attempt to commit such a deed behind one of Penzance's busiest hostelries. To kill two men and steal from their bodies before anyone in Kendall's had decided to investigate the sound of pistol shots, would seem too great a risk.

"True," agreed the doctor, momentarily disappointed that his suggestion should be dismissed so efficiently by Joey. Looking up, Denzil then noted the tired look on Paul Trevarthen's face.

"Best I should put you to bed, Paul. Methinks you are not accustomed to such sights and experiences as you have suffered this evening," he said and standing up, opened his bag again and produced a bottle. "Laudanum," he announced and laughed at the expression that swept across Paul's countenance. "Come on, my friend. I can guarantee that you will sleep like a baby with this inside you," he chuckled and taking Paul by his sound arm, persuaded Paul to go with him to his bedchamber. Sarah-Jane met them on the stairs and smiled brightly at them both, though neither man could fail to notice the sadness in her face. Proceeding down the stairs, she crossed the hallway and entered the almost deserted dining room, closed the door behind her and stared at her husband who was pouring himself another glass of brandy. She sighed and took a seat by the fire so recently vacated by Paul, staring into the flames as if in a daze. Her husband stood to drink his brandy, then returned his glass to the tray and crossed the room to stand in front of her.

"I dunno why 'e should try to kill me or Paul, Sarah-Jane," he told her quietly, "but I knawed no other way to save ourselves. I didden 'ave no way a knawin' if 'e 'ad more pistols about 'is person and 'tis the only way I do knaw to deal with a situation like that. Paul is disgusted with me 'cos 'e think I should 'ave overpowered 'en but I never learnt protect meself that way, Sarah-Jane. I promised 'e I'd never go back to my bad ways an' I 'ave not broken my word I swear. I did what I did 'cos I thought 'e was about killin' Paul, an' promises or no I'll kill any man thas' tryin' to put 'e goin'." He thought she was too angered to make a response, but after a short silence she sighed and raised her hand to him. He grasped it quickly and planted a kiss on her fingertips, before falling to his knees before her and hiding his face in her lap.

The following morning, at breakfast, the two men eyed each other warily across the dining room table. Paul Trevarthen, suffering the effects of a slight fever, stared sullenly at his brother, but Joey raised his chin defiantly and would not change his statement that he had any opportunity to do other than he did during their ambush of the previous night.

"Jes' 'cos 'e looked an innocent, Paul, didden make 'en one. I knaw plenty a people who look like they would'n do nawthin' wrong an' they be the biggest criminals in the county. Can't go by looks, Paul. You of all people should knaw that," he told him.

"I am not a criminal!" bristled his brother sharply.

"No, but people 'ave thought you was not as good as they often 'nuff jes' cos' of yer colour," Joey reasoned.

Both men got to their feet as the door opened and Mrs Bolitho came into the dining room. Paul watched with satisfaction to see the smile that crossed his brother's face whenever Sarah-Jane appeared before him. It gave him great pleasure to realise that his own brother should have such a happy marriage and the fact that his oldest friend returned her husband's love with equal regard lent extra warmth to his smile. However, that particular morning, he would have to be a fool not to have noticed that, although she was trying hard to disguise it, she appeared to be agitated. Responding to her question as to the state of his health, he informed her that he felt perfectly well. Sarah-Jane then took her seat, turned her attention to her husband and divulged that a message had been received from Sir Reginald Bonython. That he expected to be in Penzance by noon and that he wished to call upon Joey immediately upon his arrival in the town, for he had a matter of great importance that he wished to discuss with him. Joey received the news in his usual calm manner but his brother asked worriedly what conclusion ought they to draw from such a bold statement.

"Shan't knaw the answer to that one 'til Bonython arrives, Paul," his brother told him equably. Pointing out that as it would appear that Sir Reginald had no wish to see him, he advised Paul to return home to his wife before any person from the town should chance to call at Trevu and describe the previous night's events to her. Struck by the significance of this alarming suggestion, Paul hurriedly finished his meal, thanked his hostess and informed his brother that if his assistance would be required at his meeting he was to send for him immediately.

On the doorstep, he turned anxiously to Joey and said, shamefacedly, "I owe you thanks again for my life, brother. 'Twas the shock of what you did blinded me to my obligation to you."

"I knaw, Paul," responded Joey tranquilly, but he laughed at his brother's expression and they hugged each other briefly before Paul dashed across the yard towards the stables to collect his horse. Slowly, Bolitho retraced his steps to the dining room and encountered his wife's concerned face as he entered the room.

"It was you that the attacker wished to murder, Joey! Why else has Sir Reginald asked only to see you and not Paul also?" she asked him apprehensively. For answer, he smiled at her, grasped her hand in his firm grip, and squeezed it gently.

"Sweet'eart," he whispered softly, "Stop yer worryin'. We'll knaw soon enough what Bonython wishes us to be told."

Sarah-Jane smiled resignedly, knowing well that her husband was trying to relieve her mind of care. For the rest of the morning, although she busied herself about the house, she jumped at the slightest noise. When the servant announced the arrival of Sir Reginald, on the stroke of noon, her eyes flew to her husband's face nervously.

On being shown into the elegantly furnished withdrawing room, Sir Reginald Bonython greeted them both with his usual friendliness but apologised to Sarah-Jane most profusely that the matter he wished to discuss with her husband would have to be undertaken in private. On being asked if he had lunched, he shook his head and accepted with alacrity her suggestion that he should dine with them. Not only had Joseph Bolitho married an extremely fine looking woman, she was renowned for always providing excellent meals in her hotels and he had assumed, quite correctly, that she would ensure the same standard in her own home. Smiling calmly at his wife, Joey Bolitho closed the door behind her and turned his impassive face towards his guest.

13

CHAPTER 2

"Sit down, Joey." said Bonython, firmly. "'Tis a long story and I'll need information from you before you leave this room. However much you may prefer not to divulge it, divulge it you must if you wish to stay alive." If he expected to have shaken Joseph Bolitho, he was to be disappointed for no emotion crossed the man's face. Instead, calmly, Bolitho poured them a glass of brandy each and invited his guest to a seat by the fireplace where a small fire burned in the grate. Taking a seat on the opposite side of the fire, he lifted his head and waited patiently for Sir Reginald to begin his tale.

"Two names, Joey," he stated, without anymore preamble, "Tell me all you know of Archibald Rowe and Septimus Calloway and their sudden disappearance somewhere around the middle of May, 1804."

His face unaltered, Joey collectedly stated that Rowe ran a smuggling operation for many years from the port of Polperro and that Calloway was his henchman. As to their disappearance, he had no knowledge that he was able to impart to him.

"Yes you damn well have, Joey!" snapped Bonython, suddenly, "For my agents knew you and Rickard to have been in the locality of Mevagissy the day before they disappeared! And you had no cause to trade in those parts, man, for well I know that Rowe ran all the smuggling in that area!"

"If you say so, sir," responded Joey, with a hint of arrogance.

"Don't talk so to me, Joey!" Bonython stormed. "Best for your household's safety if you can give some account of yourself that gives me the information I need, for I have not travelled all this way to be fobbed off with your insolence," he continued angrily, a tide of crimson rushing into his cheeks as he glared belligerently at the inscrutable face of his host.

There was a long silence, but finally Joey relented, slowly relating the events of that fateful night so many years ago. He told of the meeting off the Saint's Head on Rowe's boat and how the smuggler's crew had set upon both himself and Rickard in an attempt to murder them so that Archie Rowe could operate across the length of the county. He told of his blow to the head and also admitted, unemotionally, to killing Rowe, but at this he paused and seemed to lose his way.

"Did you kill Calloway, Joey?" enquired Sir Reginald, his bright blue eyes fastened on Bolitho's frowning face.

"I . . . I can't remember sir," he faltered and ran his hand through his curls in consternation as he tried hard to order the jumbled images in his mind's eye.

"Surely you cannot forget if you have killed a man?" scoffed his questioner in disbelief.

"Somethin' 'appened, Sir Reginald. I know somethin' 'appened but . . . but I 'ave no idea what transpired after Calloway knifed me. Only that I awoke in the af'noon of the following day in a strange 'ouse that Barney 'ad taken me to so 'is friend could provide me with medical assistance, fer I 'ad lost a lot of blood from me wound."

Sir Reginald let out a long sigh and shook his head before asking Joey if his former companion, Rickard, was still alive. Bolitho nodded but did not furnish him with any further information.

"Best you should contact him for two reasons, Joey. The first being that Rickard might find himself the victim of an assassination attempt, although I consider it unlikely for 'tis you upon whom suspicion has fallen. And the second, it would seem to me, would be for you to know the circumstances that led to the death of Septimus Calloway if, as you state, you cannot remember what happened," Bonython informed him seriously.

"An assassination attempt? Who is it wishes to see me dead?" asked Joey.

"The boy you killed last night was Archie Rowe's son, Isaac," explained Sir Reginald moderately. "He was brought up to think you his father's killer and from what you have told me he was in the right of it to believe so." He noted Bolitho's look of surprise.

"Never!" exclaimed Joey in disbelief, "That lad 'ad no look of 'is father about 'en. Rowe was an ugly lookin' bastard an' could never 'ave fathered a boy with a face like 'e 'ad."

"But he did, notwithstanding. The boy had his mother's face as you, so I've been led to believe, have yours. Rowe took a wife as part of a debt owed to him by the girl's father, some innkeeper I seem to remember. The poor soul lived long enough to bear him a son but died of typhus before the year was out. Due to your violent actions last night we cannot question him as to what he intended, but from what has come to our ears in the Customs Service, it seems there is a plot afoot to murder you. However, it is not him we have to concern ourselves about but the other fellow," he continued.

"What other fellow?" asked Joey.

"Isaac Rowe, being orphaned, was brought up by the Calloway family. Septimus' father, old Luke Calloway, believed that whatever happened to the boy's father, you were presumed to be the cause of it. From the time he could walk that lad was taught to hate you along with Septimus' own son, Matthew, who was a lad of about nine years of age when his father disappeared. The smuggling gangs in that area fragmented after Rowe's disappearance and because of it, the Calloway's lost a great deal of their income. Luke, being infirm and of too advanced an age to take over the gang led by Rowe and Calloway, had his hatred grow with his diminishing financial circumstances and constantly repeated until his death three years ago that the cause of his distress was to be laid at your door. Matthew Calloway gradually took control of two small gangs, forming them into one larger unit, which plagued us for a long while. Last month we managed to capture a boat laden with brandy off Polperro. Along with the cargo were two members of Calloway's gang and these men were, . . . ahem, induced to give us certain information concerning their friends. Due to their confessions, we have successfully rounded up all but two of this group. The two members we could not find were Isaac Rowe and Matthew Calloway. We needed them apprehended most particularly, Joey, because we had been informed by the prisoners that a plot had been hatched by these two to find and murder you, to avenge the deaths of their fathers." Sir Reginald watched with interest to see the effect his tale would have on Joseph Bolitho. Bolitho's impassive mask stared back at him.

"This Matthew Calloway is presumed to be in Penzance?" asked Joey, placidly.

"From information I have extracted from the officers and my agents he was, until last night. Upon hearing the news of Rowe's failed attempt at murder, he was seen heading for Newlyn. A ship named the Pomme d'Or left for France on the morning tide and on board, I have been told, was a young man whose description exactly matched that of Matthew Calloway," Sir Reginald informed him, and took a satisfying sip of his brandy.

"Best I keep me eyes about me then," observed Joey, "fer 'e'll be back, no doubt."

"No doubt! Whilst he sojourns in France perhaps your henchman, Skewes, could be informed and he would, in his capacity as an old friend, no doubt be willing to search out Calloway for you, don't you think?" he asked, his eyes fixed shrewdly on Bolitho's face.

Bolitho regarded his old adversary acutely for a long while before he pronounced, quietly: "Perhaps."

"If Leviticus Skewes is in France then you must think me the biggest fool to have walked the earth, Joey! I believe him dead!" he blurted. "No trace has ever been found of the man since Hudson's death. As the presumed murderer when I implied that he got away you never contradicted me, but since that time, with no reports coming back to me of his whereabouts, I have been given to wonder if he was indeed the man in Trevarthen's garden who fired that shot. Did you lie to me back then, Joey?"

"I told 'e what you wanted me to tell 'e, Sir Reginald. I saved yer neck an' the reputation of the service with me words, an' you d' knaw it," replied Joey, insolently.

Bonython frowned in frustration, "Touché, Joey. Still to my mind, there would appear to be another murderer afoot, desirous of shooting preventatives," deduced Sir Reginald, incisively.

"Not so, sir," replied Joey, evenly. "Only someone, who by 'is actions saved yer precious service from being exposed by 'Udson's activities in tryin' to defame me brother." Joey fixed Bonython with a cold, uncompromising stare.

Sir Reginald let out a long sigh, knowing it would be useless to enquire more, and lowered his gaze to his now empty glass. Joey Bolitho allowed himself a grim smile, then stood up, fetched the brandy bottle and poured his would-be mentor another drink.

"I 'ave friends in France with whom I do business. They sell their goods freely, to smugglers an' merchants. A word in the right ears will not go amiss. What do Calloway look like?" Joey asked softly, using a more conciliatory tone.

"Calloway, unlike Rowe's son, looks like his father." replied Bonython. "He even sports earrings just like that blaggard Septimus always did," he added with a snort of disgust.

Bolitho paused in the act of filling his own glass.

"Earrings?" he enquired sharply, furrowing his brows in concentration. "I can remember an' earring, a gold one. Jes' like the ones that me m. . ." but he stopped in mid sentence and seemed to stare unseeingly into the far distance.

"Just like?" prompted Sir Reginald. But Bolitho, recalled to the present, merely shook his head and would say no more. There was a long, awkward silence and both men sipped their brandy reflectively. Sir Reginald felt well satisfied with the answers he had received, for he had probably discovered more than Joseph Bolitho would have told him were it not for the prospect of being the object of a murder attempt. Then he considered that this was an unfair assumption. Bolitho, as usual, cared not for his own safety, it would be his wife and his brother that would cause him the most concern. Quite rightly too, surmised Sir Reginald, for unlike the ex-smuggler who stood before him, he presumed that Matthew Calloway, because of his accumulated hatred, would not quibble to murder those dearest to Bolitho if the man himself did not appear in his sights.

A bell sounded in the hallway and upon being informed by his host that this was the sign for lunch, Sir Reginald beamed delightedly, downed the remnants of his brandy and followed Bolitho into the dining room. Here he was pleased to see a table had been laid with dishes that to his mind would do justice to the King of England. Appreciatively consuming his lunch he made small talk with Mrs Bolitho but, although she tried hard to disguise it, her nervousness was most apparent and he felt great sympathy for her. After his luncheon he thanked his hosts and made his goodbyes, telling Joey on the doorstep that if more information came into his possession he would ensure that Bolitho received it. He did not expect to receive the same response from his host and was not to be disappointed. Bolitho had no intention of providing Bonython with any more intelligence of his past life than he had already given him.

Returning to the dining room, Bolitho caught his wife's eye but resumed his seat and stared at his wine glass in silence. Sarah-Jane waited patiently but nervously. When finally Joey raised his eyes to hers he smiled calmly and began his explanation.

" 'Tis as you said, dearest. Paul was not the person the attacker wished to kill," he related, and on hearing her catch her breath reached out his hand and clasped hers gently. "There is another, but Bonython says 'e 'as took fright an' 'as left the country, so there is nawthin' fer 'e to worry your pretty little 'ead about, my sweet'eart."

"He will come back, Joey," she whispered worriedly and unable to control her emotions began to sob quietly. Immediately he got up, crossed to her side, and placed his arms consolingly around her, soothing her with his soft endearments. However, even in his calmness, Joey Bolitho felt the gripping hand of retribution clawing at his soul.

When Mrs Chloe Trevarthen was shown into her sister-in-law's withdrawing room she found Sarah-Jane sitting on the settle with a damp handkerchief clasped in her hand. The two women embraced each other consolingly and Chloe took great pains to point out that she was exceedingly grateful to her brother-in-law for saving her husband's life. She hoped that her words would bring some comfort to Sarah-Jane for her appearance gave the impression of a woman labouring under a burden of great distress.

"Thank you, dear Chloe," she whispered. "Joey cannot show. . . show his emotions but I know him to be deeply disturbed by what has happened. Paul's reaction to what . . . what took place was only natural for he could never abide to see another hurt. I can assure you, Chloe, that my husband is suffering for what he did but it has transpired from the little he has told me that someone is set to murder him. Another ruffian got away and has left the country but I am afeared that he will return, although Joey tells me not to

17

despair and assures me that he is perfectly safe, for being forewarned he will take great care in future." Her voice wavered and tears fell down her cheeks and her sister-in-law spent the next hour giving her what comfort she could, but when she left Sarah-Jane, Chloe had been unable to allay her fears.

On her return to Trevu, she informed her husband of the details that Sarah-Jane had given her and agreed that there was obviously a lot more that they did not have knowledge of. Aware of the secretive nature of Joey Bolitho, Chloe knew that he would not divulge to them just what it was that Bonython had told him.

"Obviously, it is someone from his past who has a grudge to settle with him. It would be best that when next you see him, Paul, you show a more conciliatory attitude to what happened, for with another laying in wait for your brother it cannot be at all pleasant for him," she observed, sagely. He concurred with her statement and informed her that he would be more accommodating to Joey when next he should see him. In this he could not fulfil his promise, for when two days later he visited his brother he was informed that Joey had left for Hampshire the previous day.

Arriving in the house in Chapel Street he had been surprised to see a larger number of serving men in and around the stables than was normal. Strange, rough looking men appeared to be sitting around and about the yard and stables idly whittling sticks or tying knots, but were not actively involved with the care of the horses. On being admitted to the house he found himself scrutinised by a burly individual who sat by the door on a chair in the hallway. His dress did not belie that of an indoor servant for he wore a rough, serge coat and had a slovenly tied neckerchief. The smell of the sea emanated from his person and he was an imposing fellow. On catching sight of a pistol protruding from his pocket, Paul Trevarthen was left in no doubt that, although his brother might not be at home to protect his wife from harm with his physical presence, provision had been made most carefully for her welfare.

Upon greeting Sarah-Jane he noted with due relief that she appeared less nervous than when last they had met. He succeeded in making her laugh when he made reference to the sudden rise in the number of her servants. Leading him to the settle she explained that her husband had insisted that these gentlemen should be employed in her establishment to set his mind at rest whilst he was away from her and unable to protect her.

"If you could have seen Joanna Penrose's face when she came to call this morning, Paul, you would have collapsed into fits of laughter yourself. I doubt not that the poor woman has ever come across such an individual as Ezekiel Holman ever before," she chuckled. Noticing Paul's look of surprise, she explained that this was the name of the large gentleman sitting in the hallway. "I know not where he comes from or what profession he normally follows, but he regards Joey in the light of a saviour and is quite prepared to lay down his life for him. The others that are so busy about the yard and stables hold your brother in similar esteem so I have to admit that, although they look somewhat incongruous, I am most relieved to have them around me. I only wish that Joey would have taken a companion to travel with him but like you, Paul, he can be the most obstinate of men," she said, then laughed in good-natured scorn at his protestation that he was in no way stubborn.

"Pooh!" she exclaimed, "Ask your dear wife if you do not believe me, for Chloe and I have often remarked upon the similarities between you."

Paul smiled ruefully at her words and then felt compelled to ask after his brother's whereabouts, for it worried him to think he should so foolishly travel alone.

"He told me that he had to go to see Barnaby Rickard. I did ask him if it was related to what happened the other night but he gave me only his smile and said it was not a matter for me to worry about. I must admit I would prefer to know, but Joey has spent his life being secretive and it is most difficult for him to alter his ways now," she said with a sigh.

Paul concurred with her words, but like his brother before him told her not to worry, for if there was any man capable of looking after himself it would be Joey. Sarah-Jane agreed, the trace of a fond smile playing on her lips.

"Joey paid for the burial of that poor boy, you know," she informed Paul soberly. "I did not question him but he did tell me that he felt compelled to do it. He is a complex creature is he not, Paul, for the lad did his best to murder him, after all?"

"He puts me to shame with his open-heartedness, Sarah-Jane, for he will do things for others that it would not occur to me to do. I felt so sorry for the poor fellow for the way he looked and angered that my brother should do what he did. Then he undertakes to see him properly buried. I had not considered to do such an act myself." Sarah-Jane could not fail to notice that Paul felt a glimmer of pride for his brother in spite of the circumstance. They continued their conversation and Paul, not wishing to heighten her fears, continued his reassuring remarks about his brother's ability to look after himself. Sarah-Jane's obvious gratitude for this inspired Paul to relate some tales of his children's exploits in an attempt to relieve her mind still further. Eventually, informing her that he had need to visit the library whilst he was in town, he made his goodbyes, but insisted that if she had any cares or worries she was to get in touch with him immediately. She agreed to his request but he acknowledged to himself that, because of his brother's arrangements, Sarah-Jane was well protected and consequently he was able to leave his brother's house without fear for her wellbeing. However, for his brother he could not help but to have some trepidation. He might have told his oldest friend that she need not worry over her husband's safety but Paul could not help but fret to himself, particularly as it seemed to him that his brother's past life was transpiring to bring him down. Such cruel fate it would be, he considered, for his brother to have reached a peak of happiness that the poor fellow had never known before, only for him to be brought down by the consequences of the crimes of his past.

When a tired, dusty traveller knocked on the door of Barnaby Rickard's house, the young serving girl who greeted him looked at the visitor with disdain. He was indeed a fine looking man, she considered, but when people came to call upon her employers they arrived in a far more presentable condition then this strange gentleman. And they did not arrive with barely an hour to spare before dinner was to be served, at least not unless they had been invited. Leaving the man in the hallway, she went off to find the mistress of the house and could not believe the reaction of Mrs Rickard when she was told the name of the gentleman who had called. The lady in question had been dozing tranquilly by the fire when the maid's raised voice brought her abruptly awake. Springing from the settle and not stopping to pat her grey curls into place or even to set her cap properly, she rushed from the room. Then, upon catching sight of the caller, she shouted his name in excitement and rushed towards him, flinging herself into his outstretched arms. The servant, bemused by her mistress's reaction, was told off most soundly for allowing the caller to kick his heels like a stranger in the hallway. Before the poor girl could apologise for doing such a thing she found herself sent on an errand to the stables, to bring the master and Billy to the parlour at once. Barnaby Rickard, conversing with his adopted son about their latest foal born that morning, spun on his heel at the mention of the name on her lips and almost ran from the yard. He entered the house and lost no time in making his way to the parlour. Upon throwing upon the door he espied his erstwhile companion. His face breaking into a broad grin, he rushed forward with open arms and proceeded to hug Joey Bolitho with delight. The gangling boy, Billy, on entering the room was told to greet his former abductor. That he did so as warmly as he did was due in no small measure to his understanding of how lucky he was to have been kidnapped by that gentleman and brought to this place. His life had altered so immeasurably for the better because of it that he would continue to be grateful for the change in his fortunes until the day he died. With the Rickards talking volubly and excitedly to him at the same time it proved difficult for Joey to speak above the babble of their raised voices, but after a while he succeeded in making himself heard. The strain of the last week was still etched on his face, but he had no wish to state the reason for his appearance. Phoebe Rickard, with the presence of mind of a born homemaker, directed the servant to prepare a bath for their visitor, and to take the overnight bag he was holding in his hand and to see his clothes pressed and cleaned, ready for him to put on so that he could dine with them. Excusing herself she bustled off in the direction of the kitchen. Availing herself of an apron, she seriously disconcerted her cook by proceeding to feverishly make up pastry, and to set some lamb to fry on the stove. Then she directed the kitchen maid to prepare more vegetables, so desperate was she to ensure that her dear boy should once again have the opportunity to eat one of her pies, of which he had always such a fondness.

"Damn me, Joey!" exclaimed Barney with a smile, "You could have written to tell us you intended to call, you rogue, for see the pelter you have got Phoebe into with your sudden arrival?"

"I'm sorry, Barney, but events 'ave come upon me so fast I 'ad no time to send off a letter," apologised Joey, quietly. Barney studied his impassive expression for a while and noted the strain in his eyes. He knew his friend well enough to understand that, whatever those happenings might be, Joey would not disclose them until they were alone, so he sent him off to make himself more presentable and went in search of his wife. When he ran her to earth in the kitchen he had to smile at the sight of his normally serene and neat wife; with her excited, flushed cheeks, floured hands and a smut of soot on her nose from the now considerably overworked stove.

"Is it not typical of Joey to turn up like that with no warning!" she exclaimed happily, layering her pie dish dextrously with the meat and vegetables.

"Yes, my dear," agreed her husband and then proceeded to advise her that he wished to have a quiet discussion with Joey after supper about a matter that was worrying their former employee, so she was not to keep him talking all evening.

"Something is wrong, dearest? Has he suffered a failure with his business or, heaven forbid, troubles in his marriage?" she asked worriedly.

"I don't know the answer to that, my love, but knowing him as I do, I can see he is troubled," he told her, "and the sooner Joey feels able to tell me the better it may be for him." Then, smiling at his concerned wife he remarked, "Troubles or no, 'tis wonderful to have our boy back with us again, don't you think, dearest?" He smiled again as she nodded her head vigorously in agreement.

At supper, a considerably cleaner Joey Bolitho set Phoebe's mind at rest by informing her that his business was running smoothly and that his marriage had made him the happiest of men. Reaching across the table she clasped his hand and squeezed it delightedly in her pleasure.

"You'll stay 'til the end of the week, Joey?" she asked hopefully, but was disappointed to hear that he would have to leave on the morrow, and early at that, for he had urgent business to attend to that might involve a trip to France. His diplomacy in telling Phoebe that even his dear wife, a renowned cook, could not produce a pie to equal one of hers made her go pink with pleasure. He even exchanged words with young Billy on the subject of horses, a passion that the young lad was quite prepared to talk about at great length. But when they had finished eating, Joey noted that with a sign from Barney they were soon left alone. His host poured liberal amounts of brandy into two glasses and crossed the room to a pair of well-upholstered chairs, set on either side of the fireplace. He sat himself down and cordially invited his companion to do the same. Sipping his drink calmly, Barney waited for his friend to begin the conversation. Without preamble, Joey informed him of the events that led to his appearance in Barney's home and of the information that Sir Reginald Bonython had divulged to him.

"I don't want worry 'e Barney an' Bonython did not think that you are one of Calloway's targets. Because 'e bin brought up to think of me as 'is father's executioner 'tis me 'e 'as in 'is sights," Joey informed him.

"I see. 'Tis a problem indeed, Joey, but I have to agree with Bonython that it is not me that Calloway's lad wishes to kill. However, was it just to warn me that you have come all this way," he remarked acutely, lifting his head to look his former protégé directly in the eyes, "or have you more to tell me?"

"Not to tell 'e, Barney, but to ask? I 'ave no memory of what 'appened to Calloway. Try as I will nawthin' comes to me about the fight after 'e knifed me, so I 'ave come to ask 'e to tell me what you knaw. Truth to tell I don't even knaw if the man is dead although I 'ave always presumed that to be the case," said Joey. Barney could not fail to note the worried look on his normally enigmatic face.

Barney averted his gaze and stared solemnly into the fire. Joey, watching him intently, waited patiently for his response, surprised at the time it was taking his former master to explain the events of that fatal night long ago. Eventually, Rickard cleared his throat and to Bolitho's further surprise, began his reply with a question.

"Joey, my boy," he declared sympathetically, and sighed heavily before asking how much of his friend's former life he could remember before he came into the Rickard's household.

"Enough," replied Joey, guardedly.

"Can you talk of your . . . your mother yet, Joey?" he enquired gently.

"When you came to us you refused to speak of it, so we stopped questioning you because we realised you would not talk to us about those times," he explained quietly.

"I don't speak of it, Barney, you d' knaw that," came the cold reply, after a long pause.

"I understand, but something of your past was known to me, for I had made it my business to ascertain just who it was I was considering taking into my home and into my employment. I learnt of your stealing ways, the conditions you had been brought up in and what had happened to you to leave you homeless and constantly starving as you were when you attempted to rob me all those years ago. I was informed that, a few months previous to our meeting, after being from your home all night you returned the following morning and discovered your mother's . . . your mother's body," he remarked carefully, noting the way in which the listener had flinched at the sound of his words. "I'm sorry, Joey, but I have to continue with my tale in order for you to understand what happened to you," he apologised gently. He saw his companion nod his head solemnly so he cleared his throat and explained, as delicately as he could, that the body of Sally Bolitho had been badly beaten around the head and that, were it not for her clothes and jewellery, she would have been unrecognisable. His companion's hand was gripping the chair arm so tightly that his knuckles were white, even in the glow from the candles, but he merely stared at Barney, his face inscrutable, and gasped out for him to continue with his story.

"It was always understood that you found and killed her attacker after he was released for lack of evidence and that your old neighbours, the Nance family, stood up for you by saying that you had been with them when the murder . . . no dammit 'twas no murder! When the execution took place. That was a part of your past before I knew you, but now I must tell you something it was never my intention to divulge to you and I would ask your forgiveness for what I am about to do," he said regretfully, noticing a puzzled frown appear between his companion's dark brows. "When we boarded Archie's boat that night there was a brief amount of talking and then Rowe's men, as you had warned me, set on to put us going. You had killed three of the crew, single-handed, before Calloway laid you out with an oar. I thought you dead, Joey, such was the blow you received, but you came back to life and killed Archie Rowe before attempting to do the same to Calloway. Can you remember that?" His companion nodded, so helping himself to a large mouthful of brandy, Rickard swallowed hard and then continued. "Calloway knifed you and although you were doing your best to fight back, you were badly injured and had begun to weaken. I picked up Rowe's pistol, which he had taken out to despatch me with, and aimed it at the blaggard who was attempting to kill you. Not wishing to hit you with my shot, I aimed for the devil's head and not his body. I fired and the man fell back, pulling you with him. What you saw next was the result of my handiwork, Joey, not yours. I'm not going to describe it, my friend, but what you witnessed turned your mind. You believed yourself back at the time when you discovered your poor mother's body. At first you were sick, but I thought that due to the blow you had

22

received to your head." Here, Rickard paused for consideration, then plunged on, "But when you began to scream and call for your mother to respond to you, I knew full well what sight it was that you thought yourself witnessing again."

He heard Joey's sharp intake of breath, saw his whitened face and knew what pain he had inflicted on his friend, but he had told him this much and knew he had to continue. Therefore, he related how he had thrown the bodies overboard and had got the boat ashore, that he had stolen two horses and headed off in the direction of Probus in order that his friend could give Joey assistance.

"You collapsed when we got there from your injuries and lack of blood and were insensible for almost a day, Joey. I thought you had lost your mind and had great fear for you but when you woke up you could not remember seeing Calloway dead, so I decided never to tell you of what had happened for fear of what the knowledge would do to you. Sorry I am, my boy, that I should have to tell you all this, for I can see in your face the pain my story has brought back to you," he concluded sadly.

Joey stared at the fire and then shut his eyes tightly in an attempt to blot out the image from his mind that he could now envisage so horrifically. The two bloodied, disfigured faces came together as one, with one body lying in all its tattered finery upon her crumpled bed and the other on the bare deck of his master's boat. He saw again the gold earring dangling so incongruously and swallowed hard on the sickness he felt welling up inside of him. Beads of perspiration dotted his brow and he found himself breathing heavily in an effort to control the panic he felt rising up within himself. Tears began to fall unheeded from his eyes, but he could not stop them and would not, had he the ability to do so. His friend determined that he should not fail him in this, his moment of dire need, so he talked to him in a gentle, subdued tone, helping him to bring his troubled mind back to the present. After, he placed the brandy bottle on the table at Joey's side before returning to his own seat, but he continued to regard his former associate worriedly. They sat in silence for a long while, until Joey lifted his lowered head, cleared his throat and began to speak, the tears on his cheeks glinting like diamonds in the firelight.

"If I . . . if I 'ad stayed I could 'ave saved 'er, Barney. 'Twas my fault that 'e killed 'er. I always tried to be there to see 'er safe when she was . . . was gin soaked. I should not 'ave run away but the ugly bastard began to . . . he began . . . he pulled at her fine dress an' . . . an' ripped it . . . an' . . . 'Twas all my fault . . . mo . . . mother died. I should 'ave stayed with 'er, Barney. 'Twas I that killed 'er, not that drunken bastard she brought 'ome that night an' if I 'ad the . . . the courage to stay with 'er . . ." he whispered brokenly. But his friend interrupted him and told him to stop torturing himself, for he was not to blame for his mother's death.

Barney sighed heavily before stating gently: "There was nothing you could have done, Joey. When your dear mother was . . . was about her business you were barred from the house, for I heard the tales of how she would not have you around when her customers were with her and how you were left to wander the streets alone. That night was no different from many another, my boy. If you had stayed, as thin and puny as you were back then, Joey, he would have killed you too. Lucky for a great many people; ourselves, your brother, your wife, and especially our dearest Billy that you should have lived. If there are to be regrets, then they should come from me, for I should have done with you as I have been overjoyed to do with our Billy and taken you for my son. Back then I wanted only a helpmate in my business so I trained you up with no thought for you and your problems," he acknowledged sadly, and raised his hand to silence Joey who had opened his mouth to protest. "If there is any man to blame 'tis me, Joey, not yourself, for I was given the opportunity to make a great man of you and I let you down and used you for my own selfish purposes. I shall always regret that, my dearest friend, always," he concluded and sniffed loudly before pulling out his handkerchief and blowing his nose, wiping his eyes and then taking another grateful swig of his brandy.

The two old friends sat long into the evening with their brandy and their sad recollections. When they got up to retire for the night, Joey, of his own volition, hugged Rickard to him and said in a soft voice, "You were the nearest I ever 'ad to a father, Barney. You fed me, clothed me, paid me, an' saw to me needs. Without you I knaw well I would 'ave bin 'ung from a gibbet years ago. I shall remain always grateful to 'e and to Phoebe, Barney, fer all you did fer me back then, an' . . . an' fer what you've bin an' done fer me tonight. 'Twas a brave thing to 'ave me remember and I thank 'e fer it."

Joey's companion sniffed loudly, whispered his thanks and pleaded that Joey should stay one more day, for his dear Phoebe's sake at least. He would have refused him, for he wanted to be off to pursue his pursuer, but fondness and gratitude made him capitulate and so he agreed to his old friend's request. When he had climbed into his bed for the night the effects of the brandy and a strange sense of what he likened to relief allowed him to sleep more peacefully than he would have thought possible. It was well for him that he did, for on the morrow young Billy's boundless energy ensured that he was given a tour of the stables and proudly shown the youngster's various horses, including the spindly-legged foal that the enthusiastic horseman was convinced would one day prove a champion steeple chaser. When released from the youth's presence he was immediately set upon by Phoebe, who talked incessantly and walked him around her beloved garden to show him the work she had in progress there, for she was most proud of her flowerbeds and the little grotto that she had instructed Barney to have built for her. Joey smiled to himself, imagining how the ex-smuggler had been cajoled into providing her with everything she had required to make the formerly plain little garden into such a magnificently opulent site. With his former master he rode around the estate and noted how satisfied Rickard was with his present life and the pleasure his situation gave him. The couple's delight and love for young Billy gave him more joy than anything, although it was tinged with sadness that fate could not have transpired to have given him the same opportunity. Then he considered philosophically that he first met the woman who was to become his wife when he was a criminal, delivering illicit goods to her employer's home. For her love he would have quite happily dragged himself through hell itself and he acknowledged that in some strange way his lawbreaking past had played an important part in his life. So on the morning of the following day he bade his farewells to a tearful Phoebe, an ever-smiling Billy and to Barney, to whom he felt more bound than at any previous time in his life. Promising to return again and to bring his wife with him when next he came to visit, he waved them goodbye and set off to his home possibly a more complete man, certainly the jagged wound he had always carried so secretly in his heart had begun to heal. Even the nagging problem of Matthew Calloway did not seem such an issue as it had done before. France would not hide the fellow forever and Bolitho would be hard on his heels now, determined to lay another ghost from his dark past.

CHAPTER 3

THE summer sunshine filtered through the tall window and cast its rays over the middle-aged woman who had seated herself purposely with her back to the light. Joanna Penrose, eldest daughter of the late Inez Carter, had no wish to have the harsh light of day point out any discrepancies in what had been, in her youth, a most fine complexion. She gazed at Mrs Chloe Trevarthen, seated in the full glare of the sun, seemingly completely oblivious to any such qualms. But Paul's wife was the younger and - she noted with a touch of chagrin - everything about her was as youthful as ever. If her waist was a little thicker than it had been when Trevarthen took her for his bride it was only natural. 'Eight children, five still alive and still she looks like a young girl,' she noted angrily to herself. However, she had not visited to admire Mrs Trevarthen's appearance or fecundity, and having chatted idly for a few minutes about children, the new fashions, and life in general, she began to relate the events that were causing her such annoyance. Like her mother before her, she considered that the members of the higher strata of society should endeavour to set an example to the lower classes, for how else would those poor unfortunates know their place? Drawing a deep breath, she began her narrative. Before she was halfway through her tale, Chloe Trevarthen was experiencing great difficulty in keeping a smile from her lips. The previous evening, Joanna stated crisply, Mrs Trevarthen's sister-in-law was on the point of leaving the church after evensong when all heads were turned towards a galloping horseman making his way towards them. Mrs Penrose smoothed down the silk of her dress in aggrieved agitation as she related how this gentleman had swooped down upon Mrs Bolitho, dismounted from his horse in one athletic leap, pulled her into his arms and kissed her soundly in full view of the assembled congregation.

"My dear Chloe, Mrs Roskilly and myself knew not where to look!" she exclaimed, two spots of colour blooming on her cheeks.

"Well, I believe Joey to have been away from Sarah-Jane for well over a week. I expect he could not forbear but to greet her so after such a while, for he does love her dearly," remarked Mrs Trevarthen soothingly.

"Chloe, I can understand a man's desire to greet his wife after his absence but to do it in such a way, and in front of the church! An institution that he never attends, I might add, in spite of the prominent position he now holds in society," she retorted tartly, "it was quite . . . well, I can only use the word disgusting."

"Surely not, Joanna?" queried her companion.

"Disgusting!" repeated Joanna distastefully. Taking another breath, she continued in the same vein, although allowing that Mr Bolitho had, out of politeness, greeted the little gathering. However, she recounted, he then lost no time in remounting his horse. Then, removing his dirtied and dust covered coat, he threw it across his horse's withers and then leaned down and lifted his wife up before him before turning his horse back the way he had come, whilst holding her in his arms. "He had even removed her bonnet, the better to kiss his wife!" she announced in an outraged tone.

"I'm sure Sarah-Jane was equally delighted to have sight of her husband again, Joanna," remarked Chloe placidly, "for the recent attempt on his life has given her great worry."

"Far be it from me to remark upon the manners of any member of your family, dearest Chloe, but I can only relate that Mrs Bolitho positively threw herself at him! She laughed when he pulled her up before him although she did point out to him that it was only a short step to their home and she could quite happily walk at his side. Not that the man had any intention of letting her do that!" she snapped.

Mrs Trevarthen, struggling to control her features, attempted to explain that, as the couple had remained unmarried for so many years and were now able to show their love for each other, perhaps it was only to be expected that they should conduct themselves with less propriety than other members of society, and she remarked again upon their recent troubles. "I expect, knowing Joey, he would not listen to anything that Sarah-Jane had to say to dissuade him in any case," added Chloe reasonably, before biting her lip firmly.

"You are quite correct there, Chloe! Standing so close as we were, Sophia and I could not fail to hear what was said," she acknowledged. Then, leaning forward - the better to impart her most shocking news – she whispered: "He spoke with that strong accent of his, and in that soft voice he has he told her that his dearest love would not walk when he could hold her again in his arms, for he had missed her like the . . . like the very devil!" She gasped and sniffed in displeasure.

Mrs Trevarthen, stifling a giggle, was about to continue her attempt at placating her outraged visitor when her husband entered the room. He strode forward and greeted Joanna Penrose in his normal friendly manner and she took the opportunity of his entrance in retelling the events concerning his brother's reappearance in the town. Paul Trevarthen, immediately perceiving the humour in the situation and relieved at the news of his brother's return safe and sound, laughed aloud, but instantly reproved himself on catching sight of Mrs Penrose's inflamed expression. Launching herself into a speech, that reminded him forcibly of her late mother, Mrs Carter, she bemoaned the fact that manners and morality should be at such a low ebb. Unable to leave the subject of Joseph Bolitho's behaviour alone she noted disdainfully that which her husband, Manville, had observed; that Bolitho's attitude had a lot to do with the female companions he had previously escorted.

"I'm sure you do not need me to tell you the sort of female to which he was referring, Paul," she intoned forcefully. Mr Trevarthen dutifully nodded, but kept his lips clamped firmly together, for in his own youth he had availed himself of the delights offered by so many of those same ladies. "Manville says that he often caught sight of Joseph Bolitho dangling one or more of those creatures on his arms. My only hope is that his dear wife does not have cause to regret her marriage and that he reverts to visiting those loathsome women again," she concluded primly.

Joey's brother would have remonstrated with her but Chloe, smiling sweetly, interposed that, as she had previously remarked, Joey Bolitho was completely in love with his wife and that this both explained his behaviour upon seeing Sarah-Jane again and precluded any other activities with whatever female should cross his path.

27

"Let us hope so, at least," said Mrs Penrose, sharply, before adding in a more conciliatory tone, "Although it is only fair to say that certain females find him most attractive with those dark curls of his and those fine blue eyes. "Most attractive," she repeated, seemingly to herself. Then, getting to her feet, Mrs Penrose shook out her skirts abruptly and announced that she had best be going, for Manville wished to escort her to Lavinia Martin's afternoon gathering where her eldest daughter, Catherine, would be performing some songs by Purcell whilst accompanying herself on the piano. "My eldest daughters will accompany us, for I am sure that Jennifer and Loveday will be most entertained by the rendition," she recounted with pride, but added with annoyance: "Of course, Melior is far to young to attend, but then what that dratted child could possibly gain from the event I am sure I have no idea. One can only hope that time will improve her disposition. Of course, Manville will not hear a word against her, so besotted with her as he is. I ask you, Chloe, what is a mother to do with such a wayward child?" She sighed elaborately before adding that, when the time came she could only hope that some eligible young man would be able to discern some finer qualities in her youngest daughter than any she had been able to find. Mrs Trevarthen suggested that possibly Melior's attributes might develop as she grew older but that, in her own opinion, she had always found her a delightful child. Mrs Penrose merely sniffed derisively and raised her eyebrows in disbelief. She made her farewells, adding that she hoped to receive a visit from them in the not too distant future. Paul, flashing a despairing look at his wife on receipt of this unlooked-for invitation, dutifully escorted her to her carriage. However, when he returned to the withdrawing room, he burst into laughter and his wife joined in, for Mrs Penrose had unintentionally given them much entertainment.

"I suppose that it has not occurred to Joanna how it comes about that her 'dear Manville' should have such information of Joey's past amours. To my certain knowledge Manville Penrose, when a youth, frequented every house of ill repute he could find. I would not put it beyond him still to indulge in such pastimes," pronounced Paul, a gloating expression on his face. "To be married to such a frosty character as Joanna must be more than the poor man could be expected to bear!" His dear spouse wickedly pointed out that he seemed to have a more than fair knowledge himself of the goings on of particular ladies of the night. Caught in a trap of his own making, his expressive face immediately registered discomfort and his wife went off into a peal of laughter at his expense. After a moment's hesitation, Paul found he was unable to keep from laughing at himself and he joined in.

"Relieved I am to know Joey safe home again, my dearest," announced Paul, after their mirth had subsided. "Methinks if I have the time I will go at once to Penzance to see him, to discover how he goes on and if he has any more information concerning recent events." Taking out his pocket watch, he looked at the time and advised his wife that he could ride to Penzance and be home again before the luncheon hour. Chloe counselled him that such an action would inevitably mean that he would overtake Joanna Penrose's carriage, for she habitually had her horses travel at no more than a sedate trot, and that he would have very little time to converse with his brother even when he had arrived in Penzance. At this, Paul changed his mind; as always, his wife was quite correct and so he did not venture forth to the town until after he had dined.

Sarah-Jane, her face alight with a happy smile, met Paul at her door and informed him that her husband was in the small library - that he also used as his office - for some letters had arrived for him whilst he had been away and he was occupied in replying to them. Upon the answer to his knock, Paul strode into the room and advanced towards the desk at which his brother sat. Joey Bolitho, not as demonstrative as his brother, greeted him with a nod of his head but flashed a smile in his direction. Paul, grinning broadly, told him how pleased he was to have him home again. They chatted companionably about Bolitho's visit to his former employer and how well the erstwhile stable lad, Billy, was progressing. Attempting to thank his brother once more for saving his life, Joey brushed aside his gratitude and proceeded to thank Paul for calling so frequently to ensure that his wife was safe.

"My pleasure, Joey. Although you had made provision for her safety I considered that it would not go amiss if I called upon her. The . . . er . . . gentlemen that you had set to guard her seemed most capable of fulfilling their appointment," he said, laughing at the wry smile that crossed his brother's face. There was something different in his brother's manner but for the life of him, he could not fathom what it should be. Perhaps that Calloway fellow had been apprehended and there was no further need to worry about the likelihood of an attack upon his brother's person, but upon enquiry, he discovered that this was not the case. Another knock at the door caused them both to turn their heads. The caller was their old friend, the fisherman, Seth Mankee. He greeted them both warmly and then produced a letter from his pocket, which he handed to Bolitho with the comment that Pascal's boat had at that moment docked and he had orders for the letter to be delivered immediately. His face impassive, Joey opened the single sheet and read its contents at speed. He smiled grimly before thanking Seth for his trouble and enquiring after his wife and family. They chatted for a short while before Mankee announced that his wife required his assistance at home, for they had purchased a new bed and he would be needed to help assemble it. With much laughter and the brothers' ribald comments ringing in his ears, he waved them farewell and left for his home.

Paul, intrigued, glanced surreptitiously at the letter and blinked in surprise as he realised that it was written in French. Carefully, so as not to offend his brother, he offered to provide a fair translation of the contents for him, then shifted uncomfortably in his seat as his brother's cold glance came to bear upon him.

"Brother," he crisply informed Paul, "I would thank 'e fer yer offer but 'tis not necessary. I 'ave bin visitin' France since afore I 'ad a man's voice, five or six times a year. Not only can I speak the French, I can read an' write it as well. Truth to tell I probably 'ave more knowledge of the language than you d' do yerself." Joey's voice was not without a trace of annoyance.

"I beg pardon, Joey," muttered his brother, much disconcerted by this information. "I should have realised, for I knew that because of your . . . er . . . activities you had much cause to go to that country. It was most stupid of me not to realise that you would have to have a knowledge of the language in order to conduct your business." He studied the polish on his riding boots for

29

a while before asking in a humbled voice if the news his brother had received concerned information regarding Calloway and his whereabouts.

"Perhaps," replied his brother coldly.

"Joey!" urged Paul, "You can tell me, for God's sake!"

His brother studied him shrewdly for a long while, which discomforted him greatly for it always reminded him of his father; Redvers' eldest son had the same way of putting him out of countenance. He thought his brother would not reply, but finally Bolitho announced that the name of Matthew Calloway was known to the author of the letter. However, at this present time, he had no certain knowledge of where the man was residing.

"When 'tis known my friend will inform me," Joey told him then folded the letter and placed it in his pocket. Trevarthen correctly interpreted this action as a signal that he wished for no further discourse on the matter. Something troubled Paul, but for the life of him he could not fathom what exactly it was. Seeing his puzzled frown, his brother asked him what it was that was disturbing him.

"Something you said, Joey, is puzzling me, but I cannot remember what it was that has so intrigued me," he muttered. Suddenly, the image of his father arriving at his home from his final journey to Penzance, wrapped in another man's cloak, came into his mind's eye. He jumped in astonishment as the significance of Joey's words registered with him before shouting out, excitedly, "It was you! It was you, Joey, for Mr Murdoch said it came from France!"

It was now his brother's turn to frown in puzzlement and he enquired as to what exactly Paul was referring.

"Father!" gasped Paul in his excitement, "Just before he died. Father came home from Penzance on horseback too ill to have made the journey alone. Wrapped about him was a cloak, obviously put there by his fellow traveller and benefactor. After . . . after father had died I tried to discover the owner but no one knew to whom it belonged. The ostlers at the stable had seen no one but Mr Murdoch knew from its cut and the quality of the material that it came from France. But I knew of none of our acquaintances that would purchase such a garment there, for we were still at war then. After all these years, I believe I know who it could be now! It was you, Joey, for you could go to France, and indeed you have just told me that you made the journey frequently!" A smile trembling on his lips, Paul swallowed hard and enquired boldly if it was indeed his brother that had seen their father safe home.

Joey regarded him calmly and then nodded his head by way of reply. At once, Paul's face lit up in delight. Reaching out he took his brother's hand and shook it warmly, whilst informing him that he had always wanted to thank the man who had shown his father such consideration, for well he knew Redvers would have been too unwell to get home alone.

"Saw 'im to the farm gate after comin' on 'en stopped on the road," Joey recounted softly. "Shiverin' brave 'e was so I wrapped 'im up 'gainst the wind 'cos 'twas some bitter, an' then I led 'im back to Trevu at walking pace." He smiled reminiscently as he cast his mind back to that day. "Told me 'e knew me from somewhere but couldn' place me." Joey's blue eyes stared seemingly at nothing, as he again saw that day in his mind's eye.

"Perhaps he knew you for his son at the last," breathed Paul in wonderment. But at his words his brother shook his head, a sad smile resting on his lips.

"No, Paul, 'e didden knaw me. I told 'en 'ow 'e 'ad rescued me years afore in Penzance, an' that I was returnin' the favour 'as 'is due," Joey told him in a gentle voice.

"Rescued you?"

" 'Ess, rescued me. I'd stole a loaf of bread an' the damn baker caught me, was goin' 'ave me 'ung, or so I thought anyway," chuckled Joey, his eyes gazing into the past. "Redvers offered pay fer the loaf but the bleddy swine wouldn' take no money. So Tregenna, the baker, dragged me off an' I thought me time was up fer even if I didn't get 'ung I wouldn' goin' enjoy what was goin' 'appen to me. Anyway I get away from 'en 'gain an' id under a stall in front a shop window next to where Redvers was standin' with you in 'is arms. When the sod comes a runnin' an' a yellin' down the street father pointed to the 'arbour an' off 'e went to look fer me there. I couldn' believe Redvers didden try to give me up fer I knawed 'e saw me! No man 'ad ever done the like fer me afore. Then he threw a 'andful of coins on the ground where I was 'id. Never forgot 'en fer doin' that, either." Joey's voice was full of respect.

It was not only Joey Bolitho that was transported back to his youth, for his brother also could remember the scene; the impoverished, tattered wretch with the bright, blue eyes, desperately clasping the dirty, crushed bread to his thin chest.

"You!" gasped Paul in disbelief, "That was you?" His brother nodded and smiled grimly.

"The first time that I ever remember encountering you was when you were with Barnaby Rickard, riding into town on a grey horse. Father told me Rickard was a smuggler and that I was to have nothing to do with him. I believed you to be his son, but Father said that you were not. I was puzzled because I thought I recognised you but I could not place you," said Paul, still amazed. "God, Joey! I cannot believe that we met all those years ago. You looked so different then. All your clothes were ripped and hung about you in tatters and you were so thin and . . . and so filthy. I can remember I cried because I was afraid for you. I believed the baker was really going to hang you." Paul noted the way his brother's hand clenched. Then another image came to him and he smiled at the memory. "Some years later it was you that knocked down that boy who used to call me names. I can remember I waved to you and we smiled at each other whilst he lay in the mud. My God, it's all coming back to me now!" Paul was breathless at the tide of memories which had suddenly washed over him.

Looking up, he caught his brother's sad expression and wondered at the reason for it. Softly and slowly, Joey recounted the tale of how his mother had been killed that very night. He described the event briefly, unable, Paul realised, to tell him more, for the memory was too traumatic for him to go into detail. Soon afterwards, Joey recounted, he had been rescued by Rickard and set out on the smuggling path that he had led until his life had changed completely on being recognised for who he was.

"Joey," whispered his brother, so disturbed by his memories that his tears hung on his lashes, "If Father had known I know . . . if he had recognised you .

31

. . Trevu would have been your home, there is not the slightest doubt in my mind of that."

Bolitho's expression remained inscrutable, but Paul could not fail to notice that his blue eyes glimmered with a watery sheen. " 'Tis all in the past now, brother. Best not speak of it 'gain," he said with a slight tremor in his voice.

"As you wish, Joey," he concurred. Feeling considerably shaken by the revelations that had come to both brothers during their talk, Paul announced quietly that, if it would be in order, he would call again on the morrow with young Jack, for the little scamp had been pestering his father to allow him to visit his uncle for the whole of the past week. His brother announced that he would be delighted to receive a visit from both of them. Still stunned by the details of their talk, Paul said his farewells abruptly and let himself out of the house. Collecting his horse he made straightway for his home, for he had great need of his wife's compassion; she would understand like no other how poignant it was that, in spite of all their meetings, neither Redvers nor himself had recognised the young Joseph Bolitho for who he was.

Meanwhile, back in the little library, Bolitho sat with his head in his hands. Sarah-Jane entered the room quietly and went to his side. Then, placing her arms around him, she caressed him affectionately. Reaching for her hand, he took it to his lips and placed a soft kiss on her fingers. Softly, she asked for an explanation, but he merely shook his head and promised to tell her one day, "When 'tis not so sharp in me 'eart, dearest love," he whispered.

"As you wish, Joey," she intoned softly and reassuringly, "As you wish."

CHAPTER 4

SUMMER had gone and the first chill winds of autumn were beginning to sweep up the valley, moaning and crying around Trevu's sturdy walls. In the back parlour, a cosy fire blazed in the grate where two women sat chatting companionably to each other. Although they had known each other for a little over three years as sisters by marriage, they had become most attached to each other. Their affection was genuine and they took great delight in each other's company. On this day, however, the elder of the two could not completely hide her sadness, though she was trying most valiantly to do so.

"When will this one be born, Chloe dear?" asked Sarah-Jane, her smile as bright as she could make it, considering the sorrow she felt.

"Denzil says at the beginning of April, but I believe him to be wrong and think it nearer to the middle of the month," she confided happily, "and I believe my estimation will prove correct for I have vast experience in these matters, you know." She burst into a gurgle of laughter that bubbled forth like a spring from the ground.

Sarah-Jane smiled again, but in spite of her own happiness, Mrs Trevarthen could not fail to notice that her good news had not been received with the delighted pleasure that she had thought it would have engendered.

"My dear," she said softly, "What is the matter? What is it that troubles you so?"

"Oh! 'Tis nothing. Mere silliness on my part," replied Sarah-Jane tersely.

"Sarah-Jane, dear sister, please! I can feel your sadness. Please tell me my dear," Chloe coaxed, in a gentle tone.

For a while it looked as if Sarah-Jane would keep her determined silence, but then she remarked bitterly: "Denzil says it is . . . He says I may be past the age when . . . I have tried all sorts of potions but we have been married almost two years now and still . . . still I have not conceived!" Unable to control her emotions any longer, Sarah–Jane burst into tears. Immediately Chloe got up, went to her side, and hugged her compassionately, whispering soothingly as she did so.

"Every Sunday at church, I pray for God to forgive me all my years for treating my dear so coldly and denying him the love that was so justly his. Chloe, if only I had taken him for my husband when first he had asked me to be his wife it would all have been so much the better. He had given up the smuggling for me, but like a fool I was blinded with the love I thought I felt for Paul and spurned him. Now, God is punishing me and will not let me bear him a child," she sobbed, and buried her face in Chloe's shoulder.

"Sshh ...my dear," soothed Chloe, "Do not punish yourself so. Sometimes it is not meant to be. After all, you had no children with your first husband either," she concluded gently.

Wiping her eyes angrily, her sister-in-law informed Chloe that it would have been impossible in any case, for Captain Polmear wanted a nursemaid, not a wife. "He was an elderly gentleman as well as sick and feeble, Chloe. A kind and considerate man, yes, but certainly he had not the health to . . ." At this, Sarah-Jane paused, unable to continue as a fiery blush stole across her face. Finally she announced boldly: "Joey has been my only lover, Chloe!"

"Pardon dearest, I did not mean to pry," said Chloe, a flush of pink flooding her own face. They sat in silence for a long time whilst Sarah-Jane attempted to compose herself. Their husbands had gone to spend the afternoon shooting on the estate and Joey's wife had no desire to show her dearest love a tear stained face upon his return.

Clearing her throat, Chloe tentatively pointed out that perhaps the problem was not entirely due to the female in this case, but she was rounded upon most abruptly for her insinuation as to Sarah-Jane's husband's ability in such a matter.

"After all," announced Sarah-Jane, sharply, "his brother has only to look at you and you are immediately with child," and she promptly burst into tears again and sobbed an apology into her sister-in-law's shoulder for her rudeness.

"Joey says he wants only me and does not care to have a child, but I know it is untrue for you know how much he loves your own children, Chloe," cried Sarah-Jane, speaking fitfully between sobs. "He never remonstrates with me for my coldness to him in past years. Always he tells me I have made his world perfect. But a man should have children, Chloe, and surely he will turn from me as his father did from his own wife and look elsewhere?" For answer, Mrs Trevarthen grabbed her by the shoulders and gave her sister-in-law a firm shake.

"Stop that at once, Sarah-Jane!" she exclaimed robustly. "I thought never to hear such stupidity from you! If you cannot see that your husband worships the ground you walk upon then you are the biggest fool in the county. Why, the man adores you, has always adored you, and has never looked to take another woman for his wife as you know well. Come now, sister. Less of this silliness if you please. Time and God will decide if you are to have children. This behaviour will not give you issue, but perhaps some patience and less distress on your part will prove a better solution to your troubles!"

Her firm tone did not go unheeded by her companion, who immediately sought forgiveness for losing her temper with her dear sister and for acting in such a foolish way. Taking out her own handkerchief, Chloe began to wipe the tears from Sarah-Jane's cheeks. In spite of her own happiness, she could not help but to react to her dear sister's sadness and could not refrain from shedding a tear on her sister-in-law's behalf. Sarah-Jane glanced at Chloe and once more burst into tears, so that when the two men entered the room they were met by the sight of their respective wives crying heartily in each other's arms. For explanation they were told that the news of the forthcoming happy event had brought forth tears of happiness, which remarks produced a proud smile from Paul Trevarthen and a furrowed brow from his brother.

That night, on their way home in their carriage, Joseph Bolitho gently enquired of his wife if all was well. Sarah-Jane promised him that it was, but after some more prompting from him she could no longer deceive her beloved spouse and blurted out her unhappiness at not being able to conceive.

"Sweet'eart," he crooned, " 'ave I ever told 'e that I wanted a child?"

"No! You never have, Joey," she whispered. "I know well that never once since our marriage have you ever mentioned the subject, but it is my duty to give you a son, for you deserve one for the love you bear me. I am sorry to have failed you, my dearest, for it must be the greatest disappointment to you," and at this, Sarah-Jane began to sob quietly. Reaching out his arm, Joey pulled her to him and consoled her tenderly.

"I 'ave me 'eart's desire in me arms, dear love. I 'ave bin made complete, an' I ask not nor wish fer more than what I am cradlin' to me 'eart at this moment," he murmured gently.

"Oh Joey!" she breathed, ecstatic at his words. He wiped away her tears and told her he wished to hear no more of such silliness on her part. "Do 'e understand me, Sarah-Jane?" he asked firmly. Against his chest he felt her head nod and heard her whispered affirmative. Holding her in his warm embrace, he felt the tension in her body slowly dissipate as she began to relax in his arms.

"Anyways, me dearest love, when we d' get 'ome I shall do of me best to provide 'e with a baby," he told her provocatively, unable to keep a mischievous smile from hovering on his lips, for he was aware of what his wife's reaction would be to his words.

"Joey Bolitho!" she cried in a shocked voice. Joey gave a throaty chuckle. Her husband well knew, even in the darkness of the coach, how becoming the blush would be on her face and how her eyes would be sparkling at the boldness of his remarks. Placing his hand under her chin he tilted up her face to his and murmured, his voice throbbing with his ardour, "Kiss me, beloved, kiss me," and she responded to his request with as equal a passion as that which he was exhibiting to her.

Seth Mankee ran from the harbour towards the Seagull tavern as fast as his legs could carry him, the letter clutched firmly in his hand. Nat Roscorla had told him that Paul Trevarthen was seen heading in that direction and it was quite likely that he had arranged to meet with his brother there, for they often drank at the inn of a Friday. Puffing with exertion, he arrived in the little yard and plunged into the smoky atmosphere of the small inn. He heard Josh, the landlord, call him from the bar, but he shook his head and peered into the gloom as his eyes adjusted from the bright sunshine that he had just left to the darkened interior of the inn. Spotting his quarry, he hailed him and strode towards him, his hand holding the note extended towards Joey Bolitho. Immediately the two brothers stopped talking and, taking hold of the letter with a word of thanks, Bolitho broke open the seal. To read it he had to turn towards the solitary candle that burned brightly on the bar. When he had finished his perusal he smiled grimly, before turning toward Seth and enquiring what he would like to drink.

" 'Tis a cold day, Joey, a bit a rum wouldn' go amiss," replied Seth hastily. Joey ordered him a large drink and passed it to Seth, who thanked him hastily before smacking his lips together and imbibing the liquid with delight. Joey Bolitho turned back towards his brother and informed him quietly that he would be leaving early, for he had some business to undertake. He met his brother's direct gaze boldly but his face remained as inscrutable as ever. Trevarthen informed him that he would leave with him, for he had more to say to him and they could talk on their way back to the house.

"Fair 'nuff," remarked his brother dispassionately and, wishing their group of friends farewell, they left the inn and walked back stride for stride towards

Chapel Street. Upon reaching a short cut through an empty courtyard, the younger brother determined to know what news was in the letter that it should curtail their convivial afternoon in the Seagull inn.

"You have news from France again, Joey?" enquired Paul.

" 'Ess," he replied, but vouchsafed no further information. His brother drew a deep breath and pressed on regardless. No matter how intimidating Joey Bolitho could be, Paul would have an answer.

" 'Tis about Calloway, I presume, else why the haste to leave Josh's inn?" he queried, obtaining no reply. Convinced that his conjecture was correct, Paul, frowning all the while, announced his determination to go with his brother to France to be of assistance to him. He had an answer of sorts this time, for his brother stopped in his tracks and turned a face on which an expression of disbelief was writ large. When Joey began to roar with laughter at the serious look on Paul Trevarthen's face he had to bite back his temper, for he did not enjoy to be laughed at in such a fashion.

"An' what will 'e do to assist me, Paul?" Joey quizzed, after he had managed to stop laughing.

"Well, I . . . I could guard your back. Make sure you are not followed and . . . and," he stumbled. But by this time his companion was laughing uncontrollably. Paul, thoroughly annoyed by his brother's reaction, lost his temper and began to shout that it was unfair of Joey to taunt him so, for he was involved in the matter as deeply as his brother.

"Paul, Paul!" gasped his brother, " 'Ow come? 'Ow come yer involved? Matthew Calloway be nawthin' to 'e."

"If you care to cast your mind back, dear brother, I was the one who was shot that night!" fumed Paul, thoroughly nettled by Joey's attitude.

"Shot?" laughed Bolitho, "You call that bein' shot? My God, Paul, I got a great 'ole in me shoulder! Thas' bein' shot, not that tiddley liddle mark you got on yer arm." Paul had heard enough and, thoroughly incensed by what he considered to be Joey's insensitivity, swung back his arm to hit his brother. Expertly, Bolitho caught his brother's wrist and twisted it, turning Trevarthen around as he did so. Holding him tight by throwing his arm around his chest, Joey spoke soothingly into Paul's ear. "Thas' nuff now, Paul. Calm down. No good losin' yer damn temper with me, brother, fer I can't take 'e with me. You'd be a liability to me, Paul. I thank 'e fer yer concern fer me, but I should 'ave spend me time lookin' after 'e instead of what I 'ave to do."

"And what is that, Joey? Killing another poor soul I suppose. Will you never leave behind your damned evil ways?" he cried.

Angered by his remarks, Joey Bolitho released his brother and pushed him away. Paul stumbled awkwardly, but regained his footing and turned again to confront Joey with a furious expression on his face. "Best not to take me, Joey, after all," Paul shouted angrily. "'Twould be no good if I should get in the way of your murderous plans!"

"Paul, this man I be after d' think I killed 'is father," explained Joey, patiently. "Well, I didn't, Barney did. Now would 'e 'ave me go to France an' tell 'en 'e got the wrong man? What's goin' 'appen then? If 'e don't believe me 'e's goin' try to kill me in any case, an' if 'e do believe me 'e's goin' try to kill Barney. Well you might look down yer nose at Barnaby Rickard but 'e saved me life twice over. First time 'e took me off the streets an' the second 'e killed Calloway's father to stop 'en from killin' me."

"Capture him and hand him over to the authorities, then!" pleaded Paul in desperation.

"What do I tell 'em?" asked Bolitho, his eyebrows raised.

"Why, that he wishes to murder you! No. That won't do for they could not arrest him for that," Paul muttered to himself. "There must be something you can do that does not involve killing the fellow!"

"I promise not to kill 'en if at all possible. Does that make 'e feel better?" Joey asked him calmly. His brother nodded his head, unable to speak. "I warn 'e 'tho, Paul," he continued grimly, "If 'tis goin' be 'e or me I got a wife to think of now. The woman I spent more than 'alf me life wantin' to 'ave fer me own. I idden goin' lose what I got now fer some liddle bastard thas' 'appy 'nuff kill me as soon as look at me. Understand me, Paul?"

"Yes, Joey," mumbled his brother. "I'm sorry, but I will never come to terms with your attitude to killing, for to me you appear so cold-blooded. It is as if the taking of a life means nothing to you."

"I 'ent proud of meself, Paul, but I was taught to be that way an' it kept me alive all these years. Fer yer sake I'll do me best to find a solution without killin' 'en, an' thas' the best I can offer 'e," he said in a soft voice.

The Master of Trevu breathed a sigh of relief. "Thank you, Joey, thank you," said Paul. "I know you think me a fool to be always on at you, but I know you for a fine man and, damn you, I would have you stay that way," he told his brother earnestly.

"Compliments an' curses, brother," smiled Joey and threw his arm around Paul's shoulders. "Now, come on 'ome with me an' lets get some brandy inside of 'e. Can't be sendin' 'e 'ome to Chloe with a face like you got on 'e," he said and laughed as his brother smiled sheepishly. "Thank 'e 'gain fer yer proposal to come with me. 'Tis much appreciated, Paul, but I'd rather you d' stay 'ere an' keep an' eye on me beloved fer me. She's a bit upset at this present time on account of yer missus bein' with child again." he confided.

"I know, Joey, for Chloe did mention it to me, saddened as she was to see Sarah-Jane so distressed. We hope most fervently that you will be blessed with children, brother, for you would make the most wonderful parents, you know," Paul informed him.

"I got me share of 'appiness, Paul. More than I d' deserve, so I am content," said Joey, squeezing his brother's shoulders reassuringly, but keeping his own anxieties to himself. Not about the possible consequences of his visit to France: his thoughts lay with how he was to console his wife, for well he knew how upset she would be. Day after day, Sarah-Jane had waited in dread of the information arriving to take him away from her and, although she had pleaded with him not to go after the man, she knew he would. His past would not leave him be. But surely, this time, if he could stop Calloway from pursuing him further, his life at last would be free from all cares and worries, for he was content to have and hold that which it had taken so many years of his life to attain.

CHAPTER 5

IN THE feeble moonlight the ship rocked lazily from side to side, the waves lapping quietly at its sides. Less than a mile offshore, in the sheltered bay that lay to the south of Trebeurden on the coast of Brittany, the mate placed his telescope to his eye and scanned the water inshore. When he had spotted what he had been looking for, he tapped his companion on the shoulder and offered him the telescope, but the tall man had caught sight of the object he was pointing at and nodded silently. They waited without a word until the little rowing boat had pulled alongside the Belle Marianne. Then, shaking hands with the mate, the man slung his bag over his shoulder and made his way, hand over hand, down the rope that had been suspended over the side, the end of which was held fast by the single occupant of the boat. He greeted the rower silently and, picking up the spare pair of oars, took up his position with his back to him. Then, silently, they pulled away from the ship and into the darkness. When they had reached the shore they beached the boat and climbed out, then dragged it up the sand. Once clear of the water they lifted it up and placed it, upturned, on their shoulders, transporting it away across the beach. At the bottom of the cliff, they carried it into a small cave and walked sure-footedly in the dark to the back where the rocks lay tumbled in profusion. Taking care and moving as silently as they could, the boat was hidden from view, though few of the locals would dare to visit the cave; legend had it that it was haunted by the ghost of an old, drowned sailor who would send mad anyone who entered into his domain. Retracing their steps, they made their way to a path at the bottom of the cliff face and steadily climbed their way to the top, crossed the short stretch of green sward and were soon on a rough track that led inland. Half an hour later, the shorter man opened the door of the largest house, that lay on the outskirts of the little village in which he lived, and motioned his taller companion to come in. The door was closed and bolted behind them and they moved into the room, lit only from the soft glow of the embers from the fire.

Taking a taper to the fire, the man lit the candles on the mantelpiece, then went to a large cupboard and produced two glasses and a bottle of wine. Expertly removing the cork with his teeth, he spat it into the fire, considering that they would have no other intention than finishing the contents of the bottle. Pouring the ruby liquid into two large wineglasses, he passed one to his silent companion and smiled.

"Oh! My friend! It is just like old times, no? When you would come to do the smuggling and no one would know if you were on French soil or at home in Cornwall!" he exclaimed, his smile lighting up his tanned, round face with its seemingly permanently jovial expression.

"It is indeed, Jean-Pierre, and I do most sincerely thank you for your trouble in my time of need," replied the tall man with a swift smile, speaking fluent French.

"Joseph! Joseph! You must not thank me. For you I would do anything! See my fine house, and all my beautiful furniture and possessions. Even better, upstairs in the bedchamber I have a fat wife who keeps me warm at night and cooks like an angel, whilst in Lannion I have the most delightful mistress, the so charming Nicole, who obliges me whenever I feel the need to call upon her. I know well that I would have none of these things were it not for the excellent trade we carried out together, first between my father and Barnaby and then with you. I have made myself a rich man through your custom. I do not begrudge you this small matter in return." He smiled magnanimously and raised his glass to his guest's good health.

Turning to the fire, he carelessly threw some logs onto the flickering flames, then motioned to his friend to avail himself of a seat at the side of the slowly awakening fire, informing him that, once they had finished the wine, he had procured an unbelievably fine brandy for him to try.

The tall man lowered his long limbs into the well-upholstered armchair and took a sip of his wine. He rolled it over his tongue, swallowed, smiled appreciatively, and then said, "My God, Jean-Pierre, this is a very good wine!"

"Good? Good?" his companion almost shouted in disbelief. "It is magnificent! You must indeed have a terrible worry on your mind if you can only describe this little treasure as good. Now I look at you, and knowing you as I have done for over twenty-five years I can see you have a worry even with that face of stone you carry. Never mind, once you have killed this Cal'way you can go home to your wife and lose yourself in her arms." He smiled mischievously. "Pascal has seen her and he says she is very fine. A trifle old perhaps, but magnificent for all that," Jean-Pierre observed happily.

Joey Bolitho would not have tolerated such an unflattering description of his wife from any other, but he had known Jean-Pierre since he was a young boy and did not take offence at his remarks. In a sense they had grown to manhood together, had frequented all the inns on the coast, shared drinks and prostitutes in equal measure. Fought together as a team against any group of drunken men that attempted to curtail their pleasures, got drunk themselves time out of mind and generally misbehaved as much as Jean-Pierre's father and Barnaby Rickard would permit. Dragging his mind away from his reflections, Joey smiled at his friend's cheery countenance, and asked if Calloway was still in the locality.

"But yes! Of course, he goes around openly because he thinks no one knows him, but he does not blend in and he likes to drink. Unlike you, my friend, his French is very poor and when he is drunk it is even worse. He has a poor head when it comes to wine." Shaking his head in disgust, he leaned towards Joey with the bottle in his hand and refilled his glass.

"Does he know you for my friend, Jean-Pierre?" Bolitho asked softly.

"Perhaps," replied Duchamps with a shrug of his shoulders, "but never mind, Joseph, for I presume you will not leave him alive long enough to bother you."

Joey Bolitho gave a long sigh. "Unfortunately, Jean-Pierre, neither my brother nor my wife wishes me to kill the fellow," he explained, softly. "As you can imagine this imposes a restriction upon me, but I have pointed out to them both that if it is my life or his, then I will have no choice but to see him put out of this world."

"Naturally, my friend, but do not worry. I will kill him for you. An old friend like yourself, it is the least I can do, is it not?" he reasoned philosophically, a broad grin on his face.

Even Joey had to smile in return at Jean-Pierre's simplified solution to his problem, but by this time his old friend had returned to the cupboard and was searching amongst its contents. After some swearing he found what he was looking for and, returning to the table with two more glasses, almost filled them to the brim with his cherished brandy. 'Damn' thought Joey, 'better not stay drinkin' too long, else old Jean-Pierre will 'ave we too drunk to think straight.' None of this showed on his face, however, and he accepted the drink being passed to him with a grateful smile, this time being careful to praise the potion more than adequately. Feigning tiredness after his third glass of brandy, he succeeded in cutting short their drinking session and after emptying their respective glasses, Jean-Pierre led his guest to the bedchamber that Joey always stayed in when on a visit to France. Unpacking his bag, he undressed and put on his nightclothes. Then, settling into the large bed - with its excellent, soft mattress - he was soon fast asleep.

Sir Reginald Bonython sat at his desk, regarded his second in command and sighed with exasperation. The young man had a downy growth on his top lip, which he was hopeful of turning into a fine moustache, but Bonython considered it would be many years before Felix Philpotts' wishes were to be granted. He considered ruefully to himself that he must be getting old indeed if his subordinates all looked so extraordinarily young. However, Philpotts' news had been of some interest, he acknowledged.

"So, Bolitho is not in Penzance, and no one is aware of his location at this precise moment?" he asked in a measured tone.

"Yes sir! I mean, no sir!" stammered the blushing youth.

"Well, man, which is it?" bellowed Sir Reginald, so loudly that the poor youth jumped.

"Well, sir. Harvey says Bolitho is not at his home, but all his horses are in the stable because his cousin is a stable boy there and told him so when he took him for a drink to celebrate his wife being delivered of a son, and . . ." His explanation was cut short by Bonython's shouted request to spare him the unnecessary details.

"Yes, sir! Well, it is understood that no carriage has left Penzance and neither has the stage had the man as a passenger. The only form of transport that was available at the time of his disappearance were two ships which left for France on the high tide on Friday night. But neither of them carried Joseph Bolitho on board, for only one passenger was known to have boarded at Newlyn," he said, his young face a mass of red embarrassment.

"The passenger that boarded at Newlyn, I presume, did not resemble Bolitho?"

"Yes, sir! Actually, I mean . . . No . . ." he began before catching his commander's eye and informing him that the man was most certainly a Frenchman, because he spoke the language all the time. He wore a large hat, was heavily cloaked and walked with a stick due to a shocking limp - possibly from the war, enthused the irrepressible Philpotts. However, his enthusiasm for his conclusion was to be dampened by his commanding officer.

Sir Reginald Bonython regarded the quaking young man with a jaundiced eye before asking him if he imagined Bolitho could not speak the French.

"But of course he can't, sir," he replied with a swift smile. "Surely you know, sir, that the fellow never attended school. Where would he learn to speak it like a native, sir, were it not for a good education? And then he would have forgotten the half of it as the years have passed. I should know, sir, for I had six years of it myself and can remember but two or three words of it at the most," he explained, smiling condescendingly.

"Philpotts, far be it from me to decry your most excellent education, but Joey Bolitho has been visiting France every year since he was little more than a boy. For someone of his intelligence it would not take much effort to acquire another language. To my certain knowledge he has never had any difficulty in making himself understood in that country, for I have heard often of the tall Cornish man and his exploits in France. It was always much more difficult to find him leaving the country or returning to it, but when he was abroad, sufficient information would come back as to his whereabouts," Bonython informed him scathingly.

"You don't say, sir. What, even when we were at war with the Frenchies?" he enquired, wide-eyed.

"Philpotts!" said Sir Reginald in exasperation, "There is always a way of getting information if you are prepared to pay the right price for it!"

"What, sir? I say, do you mean spies, sir?" enthused the young man, his brown eyes sparkling with excitement.

Sir Reginald appeared to be having some difficulty in swallowing, but after a while he thundered: "Yes, you damn fool! Of course I mean spies!"

"Gosh!" breathed Philpotts, much struck by this explanation.

"Well, I have to presume the fellow with the limp was Bolitho, so find the exact destination of that ship, and the other one and best to check that no rowing boats have gone missing in the locality, just in case," he ordered.

"Rowing boats, sir?" enquired the young man, much perplexed, for he could not imagine that Bolitho should attempt to row himself to France.

"Yes, man. You heard me. 'Tis a favourite trick to row a boat offshore and board a ship at sea at a prearranged time," he explained patiently. "They abandon the boat if they have nobody to row it ashore again, you see."

"Gosh! Yes sir. Clever idea, what?"

"Very!" fumed Bonython.

"Well, sir, as you believe him to be in France it won't take long for your spies to find him, don't you know," said Philpotts with a beaming smile.

"Enlighten me, Philpotts, if you would be so kind?" said his commander, with thinly veiled sarcasm. "Why should it not present any difficulty?"

"Well, sir. A tall man, wears a large hat, cloaked and walks with a limp. Should be easy to spot, should he not?"

Sir Reginald availed himself of a deep breath and studied the paperwork on his desk before he saw fit to speak.

"Philpotts?"

"Yes, sir?"

"Did your dear father have to pay for your education?"

"Yes, sir! And worth every shilling, so he told Mama," he answered with pride, drawing himself up to his full height.

"When next you write to your esteemed parent, advise him from me that he would have been better employed to have frittered away his money gambling,

41

than spending his income on instilling some learning into your poor brain," Bonython informed him scathingly.

"Yes, sir! But it would have been impossible for him to have done that sir," the earnest young man informed him seriously.

"I see. He has an aversion to gambling, perhaps?"

"Yes sir!" Philpotts replied proudly, "He's a man of the cloth don't you know, sir. Rector of the Parish of Sepperton by the Wold."

The head of the customs service sighed heavily whilst regarding the innocent cherub standing in front of his desk, smiling inanely at his commander, before apprising him softly: "That information, my dear Philpotts, explains everything that I think I will ever wish to know about you. Dismissed! And don't forget to enquire about any missing rowing boats!"

"Yes, sir!" replied Philpotts briskly and rushed from the room, intent on attending to his commander's orders immediately.

Getting up from his seat, Sir Reginald moved towards the window and looked out across the sea. It would not be fair to say that Bonython had not a care for Bolitho's life as he had a great admiration for the man. Sir Reginald fervently hoped Bolitho failed in his attempt to get rid of Calloway; the felon could be used as a threat to keep the ex-smuggler towing the line. He had given up his criminal past, it was true, but a man with a history as damnable as Bolitho's? There would never be a guarantee that he would remain law abiding. Aside from that, Calloway had the names of the contacts that handled much of the distribution of the illicit goods that were coming into the county. Bonython's men were getting more proficient at catching the rogues that engaged in the smuggling trade, but as usual they had little enough to go on. It would not take much of an inducement to make Matthew Calloway divulge all he needed to know. Threatening him with putting Bolitho on his trail would be enough, judging by the way the man took to his heels as soon as he knew Isaac Rowe had failed in his attempt to kill his quarry and paid for it with his life.

"So, Joey, you've found him for me, have you? I want Calloway as much as you do, but which of us will get to him first, I wonder?" he mused softly, turning on his heel and gazing blankly at his desk. "For Calloway's sake it had better be me," he observed, "for the felon is more use to me alive than as you would have him be."

After his lunch, Sir Reginald Bonython closed the shutters and enjoyed a most pleasant nap, as was his custom. When he awoke over an hour later he sat up, rubbed his eyes and slowly focused on the letter sitting atop his desk. Recognising the writing, he swore loudly and broke open the seal. When he had read all he needed to know, he swore again and went off in search of the unfortunate Felix Philpotts, berating him most forcibly for not awakening him when the letter arrived. Mr Philpotts attempted to remind his enraged commander that the last time he had inadvertently awoken Sir Reginald it had put him out of countenance with him for nigh on a week, and he determined never to make the same mistake again. Sir Reginald vented his temper on the unfortunate young man and called him a great many names - most charitably of which was 'blithering idiot' – and, grabbing his hat, headed in the direction of the harbour, affronting several ladies as he went with the loud oaths that were still issuing from his unguarded mouth.

Meanwhile, in France, Joey Bolitho kept himself indoors during the day and went forth only at night and always heavily cloaked. He watched with interest the antics of the gentleman with the flashing gold earrings, but made no attempt to approach him or to have speech with him. It was impossible to talk with him after he left the little village hostelry that he liked most to frequent, for he was invariably drunk, but it was possible to follow him to his lodgings and to watch his inebriated attempts to open the door to the dwelling. On the fourth night he failed completely to gain admittance to the house and slept the night against the wall, snoring loudly. It would have been the work of a moment to cross the little street to the garden and to despatch the man there and then, but it would not have been practical, for Bolitho had no wish to commit a crime on French soil, and in front of a witness. The muffled figure that Joey had spotted on his first night of tracking his main quarry was still completely oblivious to his presence. Bolitho was having the task of watching two men at once made somewhat easier by the fact that, whoever this stranger was, he was just as determined as Joey to know of the whereabouts of Matthew Calloway. Consequently, although the stranger looked about frequently and always kept himself well hidden, he was as unaware as the inebriated Calloway that he was being observed. On the sixth night, Joey's drunken quarry again had recourse to spending the night on the grass beneath the window of his lodgings. Bolitho waited patiently, knowing well that Calloway would not rise from his slumbers until late into the morning when Joey would be safely hidden in Jean-Pierre's house. Well before the dawn began to break, the muffled man, that had kept watch so steadfastly during the night, came to the same conclusion, so he melted away and headed off towards a small farm that lay down a long lane to the north of the village. When he reached the door of the farmhouse he knocked loudly on it. After a moment a light appeared in an upstairs room and then disappeared, only to reappear at the downstairs window next to the door. When it was opened it was impossible to see the figure within, but at the very English exclamation of "Damn and blast! Have you any idea what hour of the clock it is, man?" Bolitho, who was watching the scene from the shadow of a small barn, froze as if he was made of stone. Joey listened intently as the muffled figure that he had so painstakingly followed explained in his broken English that he had watched most carefully, but had only seen the Calloway man.

"Blast the fellow! Where the hell is he? I know he is around and about here somewhere, I can feel it in my bones!" he shouted angrily. They conversed for a while longer, quite unconcerned that they might be overheard. With a final recommendation that the man was to keep his eyes peeled at all times, for his quarry was a most wily fox and it would take all his expertise to find him, he was handed a purse of money and departed up the lane the way he had come. Inside the house, the disgruntled man made his way back to his bedchamber, pushed open the door and headed to his disturbed bed, muttering to himself all the while about the bad luck that he was experiencing. Placing his candle on the small wooden table by the bed, he heaved himself under the covers and leaned forward to blow out the light. Fear sucked the breath from his body as he heard a voice he knew well say softly: "I believe 'e be mindful to see me, Sir Reginald?"

CHAPTER 6

SIR REGINALD BONYTHON, his nightcap all askew, spun around in his bed and stared in horror towards the door, where a tall man stood at his ease leaning with his back against the wall. Obviously he had been hidden from view behind the door when Bonython had returned from talking with his accomplice, but how had the fellow got himself into the house, for he could not have come through the front entrance?

"Damn you, Joey! How the hell did you get into my house?" he blustered, feeling ill at ease, for Bolitho did not look best pleased to see him.

"Your house, Sir Reginald?" Joey asked, his eyebrow raised sardonically, then he smiled coldly and pointed to the single window. A shudder of icy fear ran down Bonython's spine as he realised that, all the time he had been talking at the door, Bolitho must have been nearby and had probably heard most of their conversation. If that was the case, then his visitor was well aware of both his desire to see him and at least part of the reason why.

Bolitho moved from his position and crossed the room. Availing himself of a chair, he placed it at the side of the bed and seated himself in it, seemingly not in the least concerned by the presence of the head of Cornwall's customs service in the bed before him. Bonython struggled to keeps his nerves under control in the face of the ex-smuggler's imperturbable manner. He had never been placed in this position with Bolitho before, for when he had met with the fellow in the past he had always been in total control. Few knew of his presence in Brittany, for Bonython had purposely kept himself hidden from view. He had left no details at his office as to where he had so hastily departed, for he had no wish for that fool, Philpotts, to tell all and sundry about his whereabouts. He kept his eyes on Bolitho's expressionless face and hoped that he himself was not showing the fear that he was actually feeling. Joey Bolitho was an imposing figure of a man but it was his manner that Sir Reginald was most in awe of. Bolitho gave the impression of being completely in charge of the situation, which in truth he was. Bonython, in his nightclothes, sitting in his bed, looked insignificant compared to the cool, self-possessed man regarding him so calmly.

"You . . . uh . . . you have been keeping an eye on me, it would appear Joey," he said apprehensively, "but when I discovered that you had left Cornwall I was most concerned for your . . . um . . . safety, so thought it best to follow you here. Wouldn't want any disaster to befall you, you know," he concluded, attempting a laugh that sounded rather hollow in the face of the man's enigmatic presence.

"Kind of 'e to show such concern fer me welfare, Sir Reginald, but I bin' lookin' after meself fer many a long year an' I reckon 'e be well aware of that. You idden 'ere fer me, but fer yerself. An' pardon me rudeness, but afore I leave 'e to yer slumbers yer goin' tell me zackly why yer lying in a bed in a French farmhouse, instead of 'ome in yer own mansion," said Joey, frostily.

Sir Reginald attempted a blustering denial, but Bolitho lifted his chin and in the face of that resolute, ice cold stare, Bonython found his words drying on his lips.

44

"Like I told 'e, Sir Reginald, yer goin' tell me," said his visitor firmly, "an' I'm a man that don't like be kept waitin'."

"Now, listen here Bolitho, best not to threaten me you know!" he protested. "There are several back home in the county are well aware of my visit here and they would be concerned if I should suddenly disappear. Methinks you should know that they have been told where I am situate for I have left details of what I am about and where I am to be found should I need to be contacted," Bonython lied with as much bravado as he could muster. Bolitho, looking into Bonython's flustered face, smiled. Sir Reginald shuddered involuntary and found an instant empathy with the many agents that he and others had instructed in past years to hunt the man down; all of whom had never been able to make a final report on their success.

Joey Bolitho studied Bonython calmly and then spoke in his soft voice, but his calmness did nothing to soothe the nerves of the listener. "Isaac Rowe wanted kill me, Sir Reginald, I'll give 'e that but Matthew Calloway wouldn' no part of it. 'E might 'ate me but 'e would 'ave bin' with Rowe that night if 'e 'ad it in 'is 'ead to kill me. Thought it strange the boy was left do the job all on 'is own. I dunno' but I d' believe that boy thought to ambush me all by 'iself an' that Calloway 'ad nawthin' do with it. Perhaps you caught Rowe an' you put it to 'en to kill me in order that 'e could go free if 'e put me goin'," Joey stated, his eyes never leaving Bonython's worried face. Sir Reginald shook his head hastily. "When Calloway 'eard what 'appened to Rowe 'e fled to France fast 'nuff but 'e bin' down the south a' the country all this time. 'E only bin' back 'ere fer less than three weeks. You told me a pack a damn lies 'cos you couldn' find Calloway as fast as I'd be able to, so I was told a tale so I'd go after 'en, jes' like you knew I would. Calloway bin' a damn nuisance to 'e 'cos I d' knaw 'e was settin' up a fair size smugglin' trade. An' in the smugglin' trade the most important piece of information the preventatives want above everythin' else is names; names a' smugglers, names a' ship's captains, names a' buyers. With a name, 'e got somethin' go on an' can find an' arrest more people. A boatload a' gin idden goin' tell 'e no names, Sir Reginald," he concluded.

Sir Reginald Bonython gulped and ran his tongue nervously around his lips, but remained determinedly silent. Bolitho serenely removed his knife from its sheath, slowly turning and twisting it so that it shone and sparkled in the candlelight. "I'm waitin', Sir Reginald," he whispered placidly.

"Joey . . . I . . . Listen man, there's no need for you to do anything rash," he spoke hastily, his words tumbling from his lips. "I have to keep this smuggling in check, I've got the authorities on my back, for God's sake! When you stopped your criminal activities I breathed a sigh of relief. Yes, there were small pockets of it still going on, but nothing compared to what you were able to undertake when you followed that occupation. Then Matthew Calloway's operation started to get bigger and luckily for me I managed to catch some of the gang. Young men, easily threatened. You know what I mean, Joey." But still his visitor's face remained impassive. Swallowing hard, Bonython plunged on with his desperate explanation. "It did not take long to persuade them that it would be in their best interests to tell me what I wanted to know. You know how well it is to be before a Cornish jury for they will not convict a smuggler. I promised each and every one of them that I would get them such a jury." Bonython attempted a tentative smile, but to no avail, for there was no response. He breathed deeply and continued his tale: "Within a week, Calloway's gang was finished but its leaders were proving more difficult to catch. Then Sir Arthur's message arrived on my desk. His description of your victim's face could belong to no other than Isaac Rowe. My luck had changed at last, Joey, and I hatched my plan when I discovered that his companion had been seen with him in Penzance, but had left immediately for France on hearing of Rowe's disastrous attempt on your life. I told you the truth about their wish to kill you, for they had often talked about it in front of their men, but they had no plan. They had gone to Penzance to get away to France because they knew my men were after them. In his excitement, Rowe must have found out by chance that you were in the town that night and thought he had a good opportunity to despatch you on his own, so I worked a story around the incident and made out that Calloway had planned to kill you as well. It was fortunate that you were with your brother that night and that he was shot, for I know well what you would undertake to safeguard his life; you damn near killed yourself the last time you saved him. I believe Matthew Calloway does want you dead and also that he will come for you one day but, unlike Rowe, he will have a plan, for he will not attempt to go against you without one. I had to get the information I wanted from him first and to do that I was prepared to promise him my protection from you. If you kill him, Joey, the smuggling will slowly take hold again, but if I can get the names I want from him I can close so much of it down that it will never have the same power to corrupt the county again. To find Calloway, so as to put my plan into operation, I needed your expertise. Yes, I have agents in France but you can see the sorts of idiots they are. No news was coming back of Calloway's whereabouts and my agents in Penzance were having a hell of a job trying to keep track of you. You might have retired from the profession, Joey, but you still have the old traits of a smuggling man," he remarked with another smile again eliciting no response. Trying to stop his voice from shaking, and with one eye on his visitor's knife, he continued: "I had the harbours watched because if I set a man on to you I feared he would not have lasted a week. Believe me, Joey, I have no wish for the honest and lawful achievements you have gained in recent years be taken away from you. It would not suit my plans for Calloway to kill you, so when it was relayed to me that you were no longer in Penzance I was desperate to discover your destination. I presumed, correctly it seems now, that you had information on Calloway's whereabouts and had set off after him. Whilst enquiries were being made about your disappearance, chance dealt me a good hand again; news came back from a man I use in this locality that an Englishman, wearing gold earrings, had appeared and was drinking in the inns in this locality. I got here as fast as I could and arranged the hire of this - " and he raised his hand palm upwards, before continuing: " - humble dwelling, for I needed to get to you before you had killed Calloway. I set my man on to Calloway and told him to keep a lookout for you because I was convinced you were hereabouts, but the damn fool could discover nothing except that Matthew Calloway has no head for drink." Bonython watched his old adversary's face intently as he narrated his tale, but it told him nothing, for Bolitho's expression was as inscrutable as ever. Throwing what he felt was his last coin onto the table he said, softly and persuasively: "If you kill Calloway then I will be unable to discover the information I need, to terminate the bulk of the illicit sales that are being made in the county. Think of it, Joey, just think. With the smuggling shut down, how well will your own - legitimate - business prosper then? The people that bought from Calloway will have to buy from you." Now Joey's impassive mask fell away, but the expression that replaced it was not as Sir Reginald would have wished. The sneer of disgust on the other man's face instilled him with renewed fear, for he realised that the former smuggler did not agree with his sentiments; in fact, thought rather badly of them. There was a long uncomfortable silence until Bolitho, his knife in one hand, slowly reached out with the other and snuffed the candle, plunging the room into darkness. The last thing Bonython saw before the light was extinguished was a pair of glittering blue eyes staring icily into his sweating face.

"Joey, Joey, old friend!" he cried in terror. "Don't be a fool, man! Please! Don't kill me, please! For God's sake, Joey, have mercy!"

Jean-Pierre looked across the table where he was sitting and waited for his companion to speak. Not ten minutes before, Joseph Bolitho had come into the house, his expression of anger most apparent. Jean-Pierre had poured him some wine but Joey declined the bread and cheese that his host offered him, so he took a seat instead and waited patiently for what Bolitho had to say. Joey drank his wine but made no comment about its quality, indeed, he appeared not even to notice what it was he was drinking. Duchamps had seen this temperament in his companion before and from hard-earned experience had learned to keep his mouth firmly closed.

"It was all a plan to get me here, my friend. Calloway did not try to kill me that night. He was in Penzance in order to flee from the man who heads the customs service in Cornwall. When I killed his companion; the boy, Rowe, he left all the quicker, so the chief of the preventatives set me on to find him by telling me my wife and brother were in danger. It does not sit well with my conscience to discover that I, an ex-smuggler, have been used, not only to discover Calloway's whereabouts for them, but to be hung over his head as a threat so that he will talk the readier," Joey said harshly.

Shrugging his shoulders, Jean-Pierre merely said, "C'est la vie, Joseph!" and filled his companion's glass again. There was another long silence until finally, Bolitho revealed all that had happened that night, his anger with Bonython growing the more with every word he uttered. Jean-Pierre nodded sympathetically.

"You killed this heathen . . . er . . . this Sir Bonniton, I presume, Joseph?" he enquired dispassionately.

After another period of silence, Joey lifted his eyes to his friend's face and said, acrimoniously, "I wished to, Jean-Pierre, but I did not. I left him pleading for his life like the coward he is and came back here, so sick with disgust that I can barely come to terms with it."

"Well, will you kill Cal'way then?" Duchamps asked him quietly. "If you leave him alive then surely he will come after you and if you do not kill him, he will be captured by this man and will tell everything and all your old friends and accomplices will be taken. You have only the two choices, my friend." said Jean-Pierre philosophically.

Joseph Bolitho regarded his old friend with cold, blue eyes before saying, shrewdly, "I believe there is a third, but I will have to wait for Bonython to make his next move. Knowing the fright I have given the bastard tonight I am of the opinion that he will not wait overlong before he acts. He will wish to get himself away from my presence as fast as he possibly can. However, as fearful as he is, Sir Reginald will keep his head, and if he undertakes to do what I think he will do I have to be prepared to put my head in a noose at last," Joey said, a grim smile on his lips.

Worriedly, Jean-Pierre reached out his hand and clasped his friend's arm. "Joseph, I will do anything to assist you, you know that. But please, my friend, I beg of you, be very careful. You are like an angry snake at the moment, but beware, for like the snake you are looking only at your target. Guard your back, my dear Joseph, guard your back!" he urged him passionately. But that stony expression had set hard on Bolitho's face. Jean-Pierre sighed heavily and silently cursed God for making his friend so obstinate.

The following evening, the sloop that was tied up beside the harbour wall waited patiently for the little party to come aboard. A rather corpulent gentleman led the way, walking quickly and making furtive glances around all the while. He was followed by two men, who in turn held tight to a third who was being dragged along with his head down and his hands bound behind his back. Hurriedly, as if they had little time to lose, they walked up the gangway and disappeared from view. Silently, a small boat, its oars muffled with sacking, pulled alongside. One of the occupants hung a blanket over its side, so that if it knocked against the ship's wooden hull it would not make a noise on contact. The larger of the two men in the small craft stood up, grasped a knotted rope with a grappling iron attached to one end and threw it expertly up and over the side of the ship. Having ascertained that it had obtained a purchase by pulling strongly on it, he turned to the other man and hugged him silently. Then picking up his bag, he slung it over his shoulder and climbed up the side of the ship. Heaving himself on board, he pulled up the rope and hid it from view between some boxes stowed on the deck. Then, moving with the stealth of a hunting cat, he headed towards the hatchway that led to the lower deck. Once down below, he had no difficulty in finding his bearings. He flattened himself against the wall of a dimly lit passageway at the sound of a loud English voice, shouting instructions to someone that he wished to leave immediately, the man presumed that someone to be the captain. The captain explained, in poor English, that they had to wait for the tide and that would not be for at least another fifteen minutes. The Englishman swore in disgust, turned on his heel and stamped angrily away. He passed within feet of the intruder, but he had concealed himself well and was not seen. The hidden man waited a short while, then judging the way to be clear he began a methodical search of the ship. On peering around the corner of another passageway, he espied one of the men that had been seen leading the bound man onto the ship and smiled to himself. This gentleman, well built and with a determined expression on his face, stood with his arms folded resolutely across his chest, barring the way to a doorway immediately behind him. Reaching into his pocket, the interloper removed a coin and tossed it against the wooden planking on the far side of the corridor. Startled, the guard turned his head to see what had caused the sound. There followed a soft thud and the surprised sentry collapsed slowly to the floor. Immediately, his inert body was dragged into an adjoining cabin, where he was hastily gagged, then bound, hand and foot. Still insensible to the proceedings, he was left alone to recover his senses at leisure.

Matthew Calloway sat with his head bowed, any activity on his part impeded by the tightly bound rope and the remains of a hangover in equal measure. 'Bleddy fool I am, to let meself be caught like this' he thought to himself, sighing in disgust that he could have been so easily taken, and by only two men. He looked up as the door opened, expecting to see one of the men who had captured him, or perhaps the man who had already attempted to interrogate him. His eyes opened wide in shock as he recognised the face that regarded him so impassively. He swore, loudly, then asked: "What you doin' 'ere?" The intruder swiftly put a finger to his lips and closed the door silently behind him, then crossed the room to his side. The little cabin was lit by a solitary candle fixed firmly into a glass sided lamp. The only furniture it contained was a single bunk, a rough table and two chairs. As Calloway occupied one of them, the tall man availed himself of the other. Moving it alongside the prisoner, he sat down and fixed him with a cool gaze. Calloway swallowed convulsively and thought swiftly. Bonython, he presumed, in spite of all the promises that he was making, had intended all along that he was to killed by this man after all. Joey Bolitho regarded Calloway with his inscrutable expression and began to speak in a soft voice. As he talked, Calloway's eyes opened wider still in shock. "Once Sir Reginald 'as 'ad all yer information, my friend, you'll be 'angin' from a gibbet, 'cos yer nawthin' to 'e. I got two choices, Matthew. I can kill 'e now, or set 'e free an' give 'e money an' a place to go, if you'll promise me you'll never set foot in Cornwall 'gain."

"What'll 'appen to me if I do go 'ome?" the young man asked, although he knew the answer before even Bolitho had significantly drawn his finger across his own neck; a silent description of the action that would follow on from such a rash visitation. Bravely, Calloway raised his head, looked directly into the eyes of the other man and said firmly, "You killed father, Bolitho, an' I'm sworn to kill 'e fer that. I'll make 'e no promises, you bastard!" A flicker of admiration crossed Joey Bolitho's countenance before he replied, softly, "I idden the one who killed 'en."

"Rickard?" enquired Calloway swiftly, his brows raised.

Slowly, Bolitho shook his head. "In the smugglin' trade you can't afford trust any man, Matthew. You should knaw that one by now. 'Twas Archie Rowe," he informed him without a trace of emotion in his voice or on his face.

"I don't believe 'e. Yer lyin'!" Calloway spat, derisively.

"Rowe was lookin' to get rid of me an' Rickard along with yer father. Good man at the smugglin', yer father. One of the best, certainly better than Rowe an' that bastard knew it. If he could get rid a' me an' Barney an' then yer father 'e'd 'ave all the trade an' money fer 'imself. When we all met on the boat that night he set his crew on to kill me an' Barney, an' so yer father knocked me out cold. Some strong man, yer father, 'cos no one else bin' able do that afore or since. Then, thinkin' me dead, they went to attack Barney 'cos he was unarmed. Yer father 'ad 'is knife about 'en so Rowe shot 'en first an' then turned on Barney. Comin' back to me senses I saw it all, but I couldn' get to 'en fas' nuff. That bastard Rowe shot yer father in the back, an' then turned to shoot Rickard. Thas' when I killed 'en," Bolitho lied calmly.

The young man regarded him in shocked amazement, but before he could completely take in all that he had been told, Bolitho took out his knife and began to cut through the ropes that were binding him so tightly. His chance of liberty had come, but he wavered, for he had spent his life hating the man who was now giving him his freedom. Yet the possibility of a better life lay before him, for he had little family left to go back to and certainly would not be able to live openly, as he would have preferred to do.

"You'll 'ave be quick an' follow me 'cos there idden much time left," hissed Joey in his ear.

"I 'aven't made 'e no promise," said Calloway staunchly. "Why should I trust 'e? You jes' told me not to trust anyone in this game."

"Yer fergettin', my friend. I idden in this game no more," the tall man said, flashing a wicked smile. Taking Calloway's silence for consent, he informed him that in the small boat alongside was a fellow called Jean-Pierre Duchamps, a rich wine merchant in the locality and an old friend of Bolitho's.

"Duchamps 'ill see 'e safe. Keep 'e 'idden away fer a while. Teach 'e better French than 'e got at the moment. But I warn 'e now, be careful of 'en," he told the younger man strictly.

Calloway raised his eyebrows in silent enquiry.

" 'E do think the world a' me, so don't 'e change yer mind an' come after me, young man, 'cos you'll never make it past the rocks. An' the other thing you'll 'ave watch out fer is Jean-Pierre is a 'eller to drink. 'E'll 'ave 'e so you'll not knaw if yer comin' or goin if 'e 'ent careful, understand?" he said.

Matthew Calloway nodded solemnly, but he was still puzzled. " 'Ow come yer doin' all this fer me?" he asked, "I thought yer intention was to kill me?"

"I got a grudge 'gainst Bonython," said Joey, his face betraying nothing, "but I 'aven't got none with 'e. I don't smuggle no more but I wouldn' be worth nawthin' if I would stand by an' see a smuggler put down by that damn man now, would I?" A smile broke out across Calloway's face. Self-consciously and solemnly, he held out his hand to the man that he had sought so long to kill, and shook it warmly. Allowing himself a swift smile, Bolitho reached into his pocket, producing a roll of bills and a leather purse, which he placed into Calloway's shaking hands. The young man's attempts to thank him were swiftly silenced by Bolitho, who advised him not to spend it all on drink. "I'll knaw if 'e do 'cos a lot a me business 'is with Duchamps, so bear me words in mind!" Bolitho told him strictly. As Calloway nodded in agreement, his arm was seized and his rescuer quickly led him to the side of the ship. Ascertaining that all was clear, Joey helped to lower him down to Jean-Pierre's boat, which bobbed gently on the rising tide, using the knotted rope he had retrieved from its hiding place for the purpose. When Calloway had reached the little boat safely, the rope, having no further use, was thrown down behind him. The two strangers greeted each other in silence and wariness. Both, however, had reason to trust each other on account of their individual knowledge of Joseph Bolitho. They turned as one and raised their hands in silent farewell to Joey as he looked down into the little boat, then took up their oars and began to pull away from the sloop. With equal silence the erstwhile smuggler made his way back to the deserted cabin. Placing his bag underneath his head, he lay full length in the bunk and, having now been awake for well over twenty-four hours, promptly fell asleep, a soft smile playing on his lips.

The next morning, a bound man stood in front of Sir Reginald Bonython's desk, seemingly impervious to the stream of oaths that was being directed against him. The man appeared to have been in a vicious fight, for his face was badly cut and bleeding. There was a large bruise forming on his left cheekbone, bruising around both his eyes and the blood, which poured from the cut to his lips, ran down his chin and dripped onto his white shirt. However, his bound hands were neither cut nor bruised, so it was obvious that he had either not defended himself or had perhaps been tied up before the attack upon his person began. Felix Philpotts winced at both the picture the man presented and the language being uttered by Sir Reginald. Nevertheless, he performed his duty, as directed to do by his commander, and waited patiently with Bonython for the prisoner to give an account of himself.

"My business in France was finished, so I came 'ome," the prisoner answered simply.

"And what business would that have been, Bolitho?" thundered Bonython.

"Sampling some wines an' brandy that a wine merchant 'ad procured, to see if I 'ad a wish to buy some of it," he replied calmly. His blue eyes, in spite of the heavy bruising surrounding them, twinkled in amusement.

"I don't believe you, Joey! So don't damn well lie to me," shouted Sir Reginald, savagely, secure in the knowledge that this time Bolitho was not in a position to inflict any injury upon him. "What have you done with him, you bastard?"

"Who would that be, sir?" replied his prisoner innocently.

"Calloway, who the hell do you think I mean?"

"Didden see nobody sir," avowed Bolitho quietly, "Jes' boarded the ship an' went straight to me cabin."

"Your cabin!" Bonython roared, almost lost for words at this statement.

"Yes, sir. Me cabin. Can't arrest a man fer that, can 'e, Sir Reginald?" he asked with a grin.

Sir Reginald moodily studied his prisoner's damaged - but still wickedly grinning - face. Everything had been going so smoothly until he had been awoken in the early hours of the morning by one of his men, who informed him that he had been attacked and tied up. Only when his companion had come to relieve him his watch had the fellow been released. Worse news followed, for he was told that Matthew Calloway was nowhere to be found. The cabin in which he had been placed was not empty, however, for it now contained the sleeping form of Joseph Bolitho. Amazed at the man's revelations, Bonython thought at first to go with him to ascertain the truth of his words. Then, remembering what had transpired when last he was in Bolitho's company he gave orders for the fellow to be overpowered and bound. Then the new prisoner was to be guarded turn and turn about until they had reached the harbour. 'Now,' thought Sir Reginald, 'the damn man has the audacity to tell me he had passage home on the same ship as myself! Well, he's not going to get away with that trick.'

"Get the captain of the ship, Philpotts," barked Sir Reginald, "and we will have the truth of this once and for all. You will not lie your way out of this, Bolitho!"

51

"Ship, sir?" enquired Philpotts, totally lost by the unexpected request.

"The ship that brought me back from France, you damn idiot! 'Tis called L'Hirondelle," he shouted.

"Yes, sir!" he answered quickly. Then, bethinking himself of something to add he enthused, proudly, "That's French for swallow, sir. The bird - not what you do. . ." Sir Reginald's thundered interruption instructed him to bring the ship's captain to his office at once. He turned on his heel immediately and fled the room, but not before he had heard a chuckle from the prisoner. His face red with embarrassment, Felix Philpotts headed down the stairs and out into the street that led to the harbour.

"You may laugh now, Joey but this time you have gone too far. You have obstructed me in my duties and I will not allow that," announced Sir Reginald in his most officious manner.

"Yer duties are performed 'cross the channel in France are they, sir?" asked Bolitho, a smile still curling his damaged lips. Sir Reginald, his face red with fury, stood up, rushed from behind his desk, and dealt another blow across the prisoner's damaged face. Breathing heavily, he hissed viciously, "I never understood how Gerald Hudson could hate you so much to do what he did, but I do now, you bastard!" Still, Joey Bolitho would not stop smiling.

"I didden realise 'e was allowed go France an' kidnap people, Sir Reginald, or 'aul law abiding passengers before yer jurisdiction. The government passed a new law while I bin' in France 'ave they, sir?" he asked softly. Bonython, white hot with fury, hit him again, then turned away and began to pace the room in evident frustration. A while later, Felix Philpotts led a rather small and wiry middle-aged person with a heavily weather-beaten skin into the room. If this individual confirmed that Bolitho had no right aboard the Hirondelle when it sailed, Sir Reginald would have some reason for holding the man, even if it was only as a stowaway. Bonython concluded to himself that, clever as Bolitho was, his tale would be easily disproved. He felt his confidence growing within him again.

"Capitaine Lebrun, est ici," Philpotts announced grandly in his best French, before adding hastily, "Sir!"

Sir Reginald bluntly asked the Captain if the man before him had right of passage on his boat for the previous night.

Captain Lebrun regarded Joey Bolitho with his shrewd grey eyes before announcing in broken English, "But of course. M'sieur Bolito bought a . . .ah . . .a ticket,"

Sir Reginald Bonython's confident manner diffused like a pierced pig's bladder. "He bought a what?" he shouted in disbelief.

"A ticket. That is what it is called, is it not?" explained the captain again.

"I don't believe you! What was he doing in that cabin when you knew I had reserved it for someone else, eh? Tell me that?" thundered Sir Reginald.

"I do not know. Perhaps he was lost," the captain said, shrugging his shoulders.

Turning away from him in disgust, Bonython regarded his prisoner with an expression of acute repugnance writ large on his face. As if Matthew Calloway's disappearance were not enough, now his case against Bolitho, feeble as it was, had begun to disintegrate around him. He could not hold prisoner a man who had legally bought himself a passage home. All his schemes and plans lay in tatters around him as he realised he had no cause to hold Bolitho now. With Bolitho's known criminal past and the fact that he had appeared to be illegally taking a berth on the sloop, some sort of case could have been concocted against him. With the man in custody perhaps someone, anyone, would have stood witness against him. No need to fear the fellow after all once they had got him safely behind bars. Suddenly, Sir Reginald looked up, a gleam of hope in his eye, and a malicious smile began to spread across his lips.

"If he bought a ticket, he should still have it in his possession," he said slowly. "You!" he ordered the guard, "Search his pockets and find me this ticket that he is supposed to have bought, if you can." Bonython leaned towards Joey and smiled menacingly at him.

Unfortunately for Sir Reginald, it took the guard very little time to find the appropriate document and he passed it to his chief with little attempt at keeping the grin from his own lips as he did so. Snatching it from his hand, Sir Reginald gave it a cursory glance, but it was in written in French. Bonython passed it angrily to the captain and asked him if the piece of paper was indeed the ticket that had been purchased.

"Bien sur," said the captain, with a nod of confirmation. "See, here is my name where I have signed at the bottom. C'est moi - Capitain Pascal Lebrun."

Breathing heavily, Sir Reginald turned and gazed out of the window in blank despair, unable to look his prisoner in the face for he had no wish to see the gloating smile that he knew was being directed at him. "Untie him and let him go," he said quietly, and then added viciously, "for I want never to see his damn face again!"

Later that day, on Joseph Bolitho's arrival at his home, his poor wife did not know whether to laugh or cry, so delighted was she at his safe return and so shocked at his appearance. She caressed his damaged face and, despite his protestations that his injuries should be of no great concern, she insisted on cleaning his cuts and salving his bruises herself.

"Oh, dearest! Your poor face!" she crooned as she deftly wiped the blood from his cut lip and applied some lotion to his bruised and swollen cheek. "I have instructed Janey to prepare a bath for you at once. Have you any bruising to your body?" Sarah-Jane asked with concern.

"I might 'ave. Shall we go to the bedchamber an' see if we can find any?" he replied irrepressibly, then laughed as she hit him gently on his shoulder for his wickedness at making fun of her solicitude. Then, sighing with relief, she hugged him to her again, only then allowing herself to ask him the question that was burning into her soul.

"Joey, dearest, did you . . .?" she began, her voice trembling. But he lifted her face with his hand and promised her that he had killed no-one whilst he had been out of the country.

"Truly, dearest?"

"Calloway is not dead," he assured her, softly. There then came a knock at the door and Janey appeared to inform them that the master's bath was ready.

It was not until they sat down to dine that her husband was able to tell his wife of all his adventures whilst he had been away from her. She looked shocked at the deliberate way in which Sir Reginald Bonython had attempted to entrap her husband, but laughed when he explained how he had been able to extricate himself from his difficulties.

"Jean-Pierre got a message to Pascal, so 'e wrote me out a ticket an' sent it back to me. Sir Reginald would 'ave a job to arrest me fer bein' a stowaway in any case," he said, smiling. "but knawin' as I do now 'ow 'e operates, I knew 'e wouldn' goin' be best pleased to find Calloway gone an' me in 'is place, so I knawed I 'ad be careful what I was about."

"He had no right to beat you so badly, either," she said crossly, "and to think he came to our wedding and has dined in this house!"

"Sir Reginald expressed a wish never to see me face ever again, beloved, so I don't think you'll 'ave to lay a place fer 'en in the future," he laughed. Reaching out his hand, he caught up hers, took it to his lips and kissed her fingers. "The past, beloved, the past be all be'ind us now. Never 'gain will we 'ave to worry about it, fer we 'ave the future to look forward to. The future, with all the 'appiness me dearest 'ave brought into me life," he told her solemnly. She squeezed his hand in relief and smiled into his blue eyes that regarded her so warmly. They talked happily and contentedly whilst they continued to eat their meal. Sarah-Jane shook her head when her husband enquired if she had sent a message to his brother that he had returned home.

"No, for if I did I feared Paul would immediately take horse to come and see you with his own eyes. An' I should imagine, sir, you would not wish to have to spend the greater part of the night retelling your adventures to him," she suggested coquettishly.

"Damn right, me lady!" he swore. He stood up immediately, plucked her from her seat and lifted her with his strong arms. Then he turned and walked purposefully towards the door.

"Joey!" she laughed, "We can't leave the table with our meal half eaten, you mad fool! Put me down at once!" But, presuming her husband had not the slightest intention of following her instructions she obligingly reached out to open the door for him as, she reasoned, it would be quite impossible for him to do so while he was holding her so firmly. In the hallway, they met the startled gaze of Janey. Sarah-Jane blushed scarlet with confusion, for she had no idea how to explain their sudden reckless conduct in front of their serving girl.

Her husband merely remarked, with aplomb, "Thank you, Janey. You may clear the table, fer the mistress an' I 'ave decided to retire early fer the night." The servant stared at them both with astonishment. Undeterred, Joey Bolitho strode across the hallway and ascended the stairs, seemingly deaf to his wife's half-hearted protests at his behaviour.

CHAPTER 7

JONAS HAMPTON, the estate manager, brought the news to Trevu that Joseph Bolitho was home from France and his brother lost no time in racing to Penzance to ensure that no harm had come to him. He found Joey on the point of rising from his breakfast but obligingly Bolitho sat down again, poured Paul a tankard of ale and informed him of all that had transpired during his absence abroad. Paul's relief at Calloway's survival was evident and his disgust at the way Sir Reginald had acted was written all over his expressive face.

"Damn the man! You could have been killed through his actions, Joey, although it would have been most unlikely that Calloway might have had the opportunity to murder you," he said angrily.

"True, brother, true." agreed Joey calmly, "but it 'as turned out better than I could 'ave 'oped. When I left, Jean-Pierre promised 'e will keep a close eye on Calloway so I don't worry 'e'll return 'ere. I wouldn' be surprised if 'e don't turn to 'en fer 'elp with 'is work, fer Duchamps, although fairly rich, is a smart man fer takin' advantage of an opportunity. Fer many years 'e bin' after me to help 'en run 'is business."

"Then why did you not give up the smuggling and go?" Paul asked in amazement.

"Sarah-Jane," Joey answered simply. "I wouldn' be where she was not an' I'd said years ago I would marry 'er, no matter 'ow long I'd 'ave wait fer 'er."

"You shame me, Joey, with the honesty of your love for her. 'Twas not the same with me, for poor Chloe was informed that I loved another before ever I asked for her hand in marriage. When I think back on those times, I cannot believe that she has put up with all my failings down the years and yet still loves me," he said contritely.

"Don't be so maudlin, Paul," smiled his brother. "I fer one 'ave no complaint with the world this mornin' an' I refuse to let 'e sit there with that sad look on yer face. We be two lucky men an' I, at least, am grateful fer that."

Paul Trevarthen gave a chuckle at his brother's proclamation and after some slight consideration, found he had to agree with the justice of his words. A sudden thought struck Paul, he raised his head and asked his brother when he had been born.

"Dunno," replied Joey unabashed.

Shocked, Paul asked if he had not even a vague idea about the date of his birth and his brother shook his head, his eyes still dancing with merriment. Obviously, Bolitho was the elder of the two men, but by how much it was difficult to say. Paul could remember his brother as a young boy when Joey had been the taller, but as he had been of such a thin and starved appearance his age had been difficult to ascertain. Paul announced his attention of finding out, for he reasoned there must be some record of his brother's birth.

" 'Tis of no importance, Paul." said his brother, who then turned in surprise as the door shut with a loud click. The two men rose to their feet at once as Sarah-Jane, a most becoming blush on her cheeks, walked towards them.

"And what, pray, is of no importance, husband?" she enquired, an eyebrow raised and a twinkle in her green eyes.

Her brother-in-law explained that they had no idea of the date of Joey's birthday and that he, for one, wished to discover it.

"And so you should," she enthused warmly, "for on the anniversary of my own birth, Joey insists on piling my arms full of gifts and I have never been able to repay him in the like manner." She turned and directed a smile of such warmth towards her husband that, in spite of all his bruising, a blush could be seen spreading across his face.

" 'Tidden no more than 'e deserve, sweet'eart," he told her simply, returning her smile with one of his own.

Considering it an opportune moment to take his leave, Paul stood up and announced that he had to call in at the library to see Mr Pawley, for they had to make a list of all the books that had gone missing and he was wishful to publish an account of the lost books in the local gazette.

"It might not suit, but if it stirs one person's conscience I shall have had some satisfaction at least," his brother said with some annoyance.

"Brother, you poor fool. Who do 'e knaw with a conscience in Penzance, fer goodness sake?" asked Joey, a mischievous twinkle returning to his eyes.

"You!" replied his brother promptly. Picking up his hat, Paul wished them both farewell and left the house, a smile of satisfaction on his lips, for it was rarely the case that he was allowed to have the last word when jesting with his brother.

Sitting at his desk in the library office, Mr Pawley regarded the neatly written list in front of him with increasing trepidation. Admittedly his heart had filled with joy when old Mr Sampson had returned Boswell's Life of Johnson to the library that morning, but it had not led to an influx of similarly penitent individuals clutching their overdue copies. He sighed, scratched his head and wondered just what Mr Trevarthen's response would be when he caught sight of the long line of titles that it had been his duty to record. His wedding, not a month previously, to the Widow Hudson had brought much joy into his life, but the question of just how many books had disappeared from the library's shelves during his sojourn as librarian forever nagged at him. Mr Trevarthen had the most forgiving of temperaments, but Mr Pawley's guilt-ridden conscience convinced him that even he would be appalled by the vast number of books still residing on the shelves of various subscribers to the library. Studiously wiping his spectacles, the librarian responded to the rap at the door nervously before hastily replacing his glasses and blinking owlishly into his employer's stern face as he strode into the room. After greeting his visitor he hastily handed over the list, along with a tumbled explanation as to his lack of perception in not realising that such a large number of tomes would disappear so rapidly. A silence ensued as Mr Trevarthen studied the paper he held in his hand and when his eyebrows rose in disgust, Mr Pawley felt for the man, knowing that to have lost possession of their only copy of Fairfax's translation of Tasso's Gerusalemme Liberata would cut into him deeply; his employer was especially fond of that particular work.

Mr Trevarthen finally finished his perusal, then lifted his eyes to Mr

Pawley's tortured countenance and smiled resignedly. The librarian felt the tension melt from his body in an instant, but endeavoured to give an explanation. He had been at great pains to identify the culprits but had met with no success. Elias Sampson had returned his book, but for no other reason than that he had discovered it that morning amongst his four volumes of Wesley's Works. Mr Sampson had confessed that an illiterate maidservant had replaced it on the bookshelf in that position purely because the binding was of a similar hue, but Thomas Pawley could not hope for similar discoveries amongst the other members who had taken out the missing volumes.

"Well, Thomas," remarked Paul, kindly, "I know well how hard you have worked to make this establishment such a success, so I have no words of reproach for you. If I am saddened it is because so many people assume that it is quite in order to retain these books in their homes, thus denying others the pleasure of reading these works." He sighed heavily. Then, requesting paper, pen and ink sat down opposite to his librarian and between them they composed a suitably worded notice, listing the missing books along with a request for their return. It would be sent to the offices of the local gazette in order for it to be included in the next edition of the paper.

"Let us hope that some, if not all, of these volumes will find their way back to the library in due course," said Paul. They continued to discuss topics relating to the library and Mr Pawley was gratified to receive his employer's consent to purchasing further copies of the some of the most popular because, as he pointed out, certain volumes were becoming rather worn with use. He bravely requested again that Mr Trevarthen would allow him to purchase some of his own writings to be placed on the shelves but Paul, as ever, gently refused.

"It is a shame, Paul, for they are so frequently requested. Although I know it not to be the case, some of the subscribers have pointed out that perhaps you would rather your works were purchased than borrowed," mentioned the librarian, artfully, in the hope that this strategy would finally enable him to place his employer's works in his own library at last.

Mr Trevarthen looked suitably embarrassed, for he had not considered the possibility that such an idea would be drawn from his determination not to put his own books in the library.

"Is that what people have been saying?" he asked, worriedly.

Mr Pawley, emboldened by the concerned expression on his employer's face, nodded and fixed Paul with a direct look.

"I had not considered that they should so think of me," Paul mused. After a moment's thought, he agreed that perhaps it would be for the best if they should be included.

"I can have a special section for them, Paul," enthused Thomas, delighted with the results that he had achieved, but Mr Trevarthen shook his head and informed him that he would be most annoyed if he noticed that any particular attention was to be made of their inclusion.

"Do you understand me, Thomas?" he asked, his eyebrow raised.

"Certainly, Paul, certainly," he replied. "It shall be as you wish, of course, but I think you will find that, once it is known hereabouts that they have been included, then their popularity will be ensured," and Mr Pawley gave a knowing smile.

F J Warren

Their meeting drew to a close and only now did Paul bethink himself to ask Mr Pawley if he would know the best course for Paul to follow, to enable him to discover his brother's date of birth. The librarian's suggestion that Paul should look in the Parish register met with approval and he left to find the nearest Church to his brother's place of birth, convinced that he would find the answer he sought relatively quickly. However, he was to be disappointed and when the vicar tactfully pointed out that, as the birth was illegitimate, perhaps Sally Bolitho had not seen fit to have her son baptised, he realised that his quest would not be so easy to undertake as he had imagined. Struck by the idea that Likky Skewes' mother would have some idea of the date he sought, he hurried to her house, but met with disappointment yet again. Although she was able to state that her son's friend was the younger of the two and that, as Leviticus was born in the spring of '82, Joey must have been born in the summer of the same year. She could not, however, remember any particular date.

"Ol' Sally never did make much of 'im, Mr Trevarthen, sir. An' as to mindin' 'is birthday," she added with a wry smile, "Well, 'er was always too gin soaked knaw much 'bout anythin' most times."

Paul smiled grimly and was about to thank her when she pointed out that a few years back, she believed that his brother did have a cousin in service at the Hudson's for a while, before she had taken up employment with the Penberthy family over to St. Erth. With his usual enthusiasm he determined to visit this family. Realising, with the lunch hour almost upon him, it would be more appropriate to arrive in the morning, he determined to return to his home and to set off early on the morrow in his curricle. Thanking Mrs Skewes and wishing her well most warmly, he returned to his home, disappointed but still hopeful of success. Taking a stable lad to act as his groom, he left Trevu early the following morning and, keeping to the better roads, arrived at his destination in the middle of the morning. At first, Mrs Penberthy was unwilling to meet him for her servant's description had made her rather wary; dark skinned gentleman being a most uncommon sight in that area. However, upon perusing her caller's card once more, realisation dawned upon her that the person who was waiting patiently in her hall carried the same name as the famous author of whom she had such a fondness. She received him formally and grandly in her best parlour, but on discovering Mr Paul Trevarthen was indeed the same writer she so admired her disposition mellowed considerably. The information she was able to impart, however, was not what Paul had hoped to hear. Taking care not to inform her of his reason, other than that he wished to discover the whereabouts of the servant that had worked for the Hudson's during their time in Penzance, he gave the impression, as was indeed the case, that he had no knowledge of the girl other than her name. She confirmed emphatically that his brother's cousin had indeed been in her employ, but had formed an attachment to a miner from Redruth. This gentleman had decided that America would give him a more advantageous living than the one he had previously survived on, especially when embarking upon matrimony, and had set sail for the former colonies full of confidence. Upon arrival and after establishing himself in a carpentry business, he sent for Rachel Bolitho to take ship to join him. Her cousin from Penzance had apparently given her a substantial dowry, she informed Paul, and so the dear

58

child had left her employ and set off on the greatest adventure of her young life. Upon arrival, the happy couple married immediately and within a twelvemonth, Rachel presented her husband with a son and heir. Upon receipt of Rachel's letter informing her of the happy event, Mrs Penberthy had replied with a small gift for the child and her best wishes for her former servant.

"A most kind and diligent girl, Mr Trevarthen," she remarked, having recourse to her handkerchief. After she had recovered herself, she proceeded to inform him of the tragedy that enveloped the young family before her token of affection had even reached its destination.

"Typhoid!" she announced, dramatically, then repeated, "Typhoid, Mr Trevarthen! Young Mr Maddern, Rachel's husband, survived, but the dear girl and her poor innocent were taken. Her devastated husband had a letter written on his behalf and despatched to me with the sad news some months later. I do not know of anything that has upset me so much since the loss of my dearest Cedric three years ago."

Upon receipt of this disastrous news, Mr Trevarthen's expressive face recorded his disappointment as he realised that all avenues to the information he was seeking had been closed. He was not prepared, therefore, for the details that Mrs Penberthy divulged in her next statement.

"Of course, I informed her family for I was well aware that it would be my duty to tell Miss Leah Bolitho under the circumstances. Yet another tragedy to afflict that poor family," she said, with a disbelieving shake of her head and a heavy sigh. She added, contritely, "I was unable to notify her relative from Penzance, of course, but as he had kept in contact with Rachel whilst she had worked for me, I should imagine that he must be well aware of the terrible disaster that befell them in America."

"I beg pardon, Mrs Penberthy, but you mentioned a name that I have never heard of. I beg you, would you be kind enough to enlighten me as to whom you were referring. A Miss Leah Bolitho, I believe you said?" enquired Paul, almost unable to believe that another door had been opened to him.

"Why yes, Mr Trevarthen, Rachel's mother, Ruth, was one of the Bolitho's of Trevanoc," she advised him. "Married beneath herself, unfortunately, but that was after her father and mother took up with the Methodists so strongly."

"Trevanoc!" cried her visitor, then hastily remembered himself. "I beg pardon, Mrs Penberthy, but I am astounded that he . . . I mean . . . she would be a member of those same Bolitho's! Why, they are one of the biggest landowners in the hundred, surely."

"I know, Mr Trevarthen, I know. It came as quite a shock to me, but you have only to consider what has happened to the family down the years to understand why Ruth's daughter should be reduced to finding employment amongst menials," she confided in him.

"I am afraid you will have to enlighten me there, Mrs Penberthy, for apart from the name and the estate I have little knowledge of them. I think my father arranged to buy some oxen off their home farm many years ago through his estate manager, but in all other matters I have little recollection of them," Paul told her.

"Well," began Mrs Penberthy, her eyes sparkling with excitement that her honoured guest should require her services in such a way. Smiling benignly at

Mr Trevarthen, she related the history of the Bolitho family from well before the restoration of the monarchy. She spoke with such authority that Paul had the distinct impression that the lady could have provided the same information on half the grand families of the county. Although the family had had many interests over the years, including fishing, mining, and farming, they had consolidated the farming side of their business and sold off their other enterprises in order to buy more land. Trevanoc, although a well-known estate, was not the largest in the locality. Hardly more than a well-appointed farmstead in reality but the Bolitho ancestors had bought good farms as they came on the market, and built up their properties in this manner. Consequently, although large landowners, they did not have one large estate, more a combination of smaller tenanted farms from which to derive their not inconsiderable income. Mrs Penberthy, thoroughly enjoying herself, talked with great authority on the various farms and lands that had been brought into the estate over the years by this enterprising family. His interest was fairly sparked however when, finally, she arrived at Hugo Bolitho, for with some mental calculation he realised that this gentleman had to be his brother's grandfather.

"Old Hugo Bolitho was such a handsome man; well above medium height, always bewigged of course, as they mostly were in those days, and with the most wonderful pair of blue eyes. And Patience, his wife, was considered a most suitable addition to the family and not only because of her beauty. Hugo and Patience settled down to family life and had five children, four of whom grew to adulthood." Mrs Penberthy then began to list their offspring on her fingers: "Leah, the eldest girl. Zachariah, the son and heir. Ruth, who was my dear Rachel's mother and the youngest, another girl, Miriam. She was the one that resembled her father most closely and was, regrettably, her father's favourite. Patience was a most God fearing woman and named all her children from the bible. Unfortunately for the family, she became a devout follower of John Wesley and converted her husband to the new religion. After their conversion they became most exacting with all their children and insisted that they follow the strictures of Methodism to the letter. The eldest complied most dutifully with their wishes but the others were most put out, for they had not been brought up to expect such a turn of events in their lives. To be hemmed about by the strictures of such devout parents began to irk them greatly and they did not take kindly to the impositions that their parents wished to place upon them. What with Mrs Bolitho praising the virtues of her Lord from sunrise to sunset and her husband complying with her every word, the three youngest rebelled against such sentiments. Zachariah availed himself - I shall not say stole, for the poor boy deserved a great deal of sympathy - of the money he thought owed to him from the estate and set off to buy himself a commission in the army. Hugo was devastated, naturally, but worse was to follow for the poor lad was to lose his life in a most terrible accident. A munitions store caught fire, and being placed next to the stables all available soldiers were attempting to remove the terrified animals whilst detonations and carnage erupted all around them. Zachariah was seen to go into the fire with a detachment of men, but unfortunately the blaze had reached the powder kegs and store and stables were blown apart with a terrific explosion. Ten men lost their lives and a considerable number of horses were killed. When the news of their son's death was brought to Trevanoc it almost did for poor Hugo, for he had a great fondness for his only son. Patience, glowing with her Christian fire, seemed not to notice," she said, and sniffed with disapproval, "but within a month of receiving the news the effects of the consumption that was to kill her became apparent and she had to take to her bed. Her husband, dutifully continuing to follow her every command became most severe with all the girls. Ruth became distraught at having to continue to live in such a solemn house and ran off with a coachman who worked in Marazion. The family disinherited her immediately, on Patience's insistence of course, but the young couple married and, after some years, dear Rachel was born. They had little money, but Rachel's father was an excellent man with horses and they managed tolerably well. Miriam it was that broke her father's heart finally, though, for she was found in the stables with a . . . with a . . . I am sorry but I don't know how to phrase this exactly, but she had taken a local tradesman to a . . . to the stables and a . . ." At this point, Mr Trevarthen broke in to save the poor lady further embarrassment, informing her that he understood the situation completely. She smiled with relief and went on to inform him that young Miriam had been thrown from the house that very day, on her mother's instructions, with only the clothes she stood up in. Staring directly at her guest, Mrs Penberthy remarked that, under the circumstances, it would have been difficult for the family to have avoided this action after having set themselves up as the arbiters of Methodism in that locality. She pointed out, however, that to turn off their daughter without a penny to her name was not her idea of Christian kindness. Paul nodded in agreement, whilst the redoubtable matron drew breath and continued: "Well, Miriam, made her way to Penzance and soon became part of a low company of women, who spent their time and earned their income from a way of life that . . . " but here she seemed disinclined to add further details. Her guest spared her blushes once again, nodding to indicate that he deduced to what occupation she was referring.

"Some years later," sighed Mrs Penberthy, "I was informed that she was most brutally murdered in some hovel. A woman with that surname and her description - and she was a most notable looking girl Mr Trevarthen," she emphasised, "was killed. It was always believed to be young Miriam, although this person was not known by that name for she used another - Sally. Apparently that's what she called herself in her new . . . ah . . . her new..." Once again, her words ground to a confused halt and she appeared to consider before continuing with the lives of the other family members instead. Rachel's mother and father lived a quiet but happy life together, she informed him, but both died during a great sickness that had swept through the Penzance area some years before and this left the young girl to fend for herself. Miriam's illegitimate son, on discovering his relationship with Rachel, helped to find her employment. In due course she came to work for Mrs Penberthy, whose husband had dealings with the fellow, as he was a . . ." and here she lowered her voice and mouthed the word, 'freetrader', and boldly stared Mr Trevarthen in the eye.

"My husband, although normally law-abiding, had no time for such exorbitant taxes as honest people were supposed to pay, for he said they were only put upon the poor people to make the king even richer and to pay for his stupid wars," she informed Paul defiantly. "Of course, the freetrader no longer follows that profession, for he has come into great wealth, so they say, through his father's side of the family and has also married a widow with a considerable fortune." She smiled at Paul in a conspiratorial manner and whispered coyly, "I saw him once, you know, when he was talking to Rachel in the kitchen. Such a look of old Hugo about him I could not believe it! And so tall that his head touched the beams. Not that I believe you would be taller, for you have a great height about you, Mr Trevarthen."

Paul smiled, politely. Then, noting the time, considered it best that he took his leave, lest Mrs Penberthy should think him an ill-mannered oaf as well as a giant. He had not completely wasted his afternoon but could not see how he would be able to continue making further enquires into his brother's past, as it appeared to him that all the avenues that he wished to go down had been barricaded to him. Paul began to thank his host profusely for her time and help and she in turn blushed rosily and requested, rather in the manner of a schoolgirl, if he would be so kind to sign his book of poems for her. He agreed to her wishes and flashed his most charming smile. Mrs Penberthy left the room, returning a few moments later with the book and breathless with excitement. Paul sat himself down at her writing desk and penned a few words of thanks on the flyleaf under her name, then added his own signature. Smiling broadly, she informed him that the ladies reading circle would have much to discuss when next they met. However, Paul politely refused her invitation to hold a talk, explaining gracefully that, so occupied was he with his writings, he had very little time to devote to such things. He was about to take his leave of his smiling hostess when he felt compelled to ask one final question.

"The eldest Miss Bolitho is no longer alive, I presume?"

"Dear me, Mr Trevarthen, certainly she is! She never married and looked after her parents until they died, you know. If anything she has become a more devout Methodist than poor Patience could ever have been. Still, 'twill be of no avail, for she had no children and on her death the estate will pass to her next of kin. I should imagine that thought alone will keep her praying until Gabriel blows his trumpet," she informed Paul with a mischievous smile.

"I beg pardon, Mrs Penberthy, I'm afraid the significance of your remarks is lost upon me," Paul replied with a puzzled frown.

She giggled with delight and informed him bluntly, "Miriam's boy, Mr Trevarthen. The freetrader! For all her devout ways 'tis Miriam's boy stands to inherit the whole lot, and knowing Leah's devoutness that fact must cut her to her saintly soul!" At this she allowed herself a chuckle of pure spite at the unfortunate Miss Bolitho's predicament.

"Paul, have some sense!" observed his exasperated wife. "You cannot go to your brother and bluntly tell him that you have been probing into his background and lay all your discoveries in front of him. He will not be receptive to such boldness from you, as you well know!"

"I did not probe into his background, madam!" retorted Paul, stung by her condemnation. "I was merely attempting to discover the date of his birth and, well, one thing led to another. As soon as Mrs Penberthy began her tale it was impossible to put a stop to her flow! Once I had been informed of the death of his cousin I presumed that my enquiries would come to an end, for there would have been no one else able to give me the information I required. How on earth was I to know that the blasted woman would be capable of giving me the particulars of her servant's family with such detail?"

"Let the matter drop, Paul, and do not take it any further. In the fullness of time perhaps Joey will be informed of his relationship to this Miss Leah Bolitho. But if you, in your usual haphazard manner, blunder about in his life as you are like to do you will only serve to annoy him most particularly. Consider for one moment, what likelihood is there that his aunt would have knowledge of his birth?" observed Chloe.

"Mrs Penberthy gave every impression that Joey's aunt was well aware of his existence," replied Paul.

"Well," retorted Chloe, "even if she has knowledge of it, she is most unlikely to wish to contact Joey! Let the matter drop!" She fixed him with a straight stare and raised her eyebrow. Paul, recognising the look, beat a hasty retreat to his study and passed the rest of the afternoon ostensibly translating a speech of Cicero, but he could not get the thought of his brother's unlooked-for relative out of his mind. He spent the next week worrying at the problem like a terrier with a rat, until finally he took pen to paper and dispatched a letter to Trevanoc. After introducing himself and informing Miss Bolitho of his relationship to her nephew, he asked that, should she have the knowledge he sought, he would be most grateful to receive it. He impressed upon her that he had no wish for any further acknowledgement on her part of the existence of Joseph Bolitho if she had no desire to do so and, that if no reply were to be forthcoming, he would not contact her again.

He admitted to his wife the action he had taken only when the letter had been safely despatched. Her derogatory comments about his lack of sense rattled him somewhat. But Chloe considered that, as he had the foresight to inform the lady that he would not press her for further information, then in all probability they had heard the last on the matter. In such naivety, Paul and Chloe went about their pleasant life together, oblivious to the volcano that was about to erupt in their midst.

CHAPTER 8

GEORGE TREVARTHEN, Paul's eldest son, stepped out of the carriage, stretched luxuriously and took a deep breath of the bracing, frosty air. The leaves had left the trees since last he had been at home, but he liked the starkness of the place at this time of year for, in spite of the privations of the damp and cold, there was always an air of excitement about Trevu leading up to Christmas tide. Having a birthday to celebrate on Christmas Day had always made him feel rather special in an excited, childish way. He warmly greeted their old servant, Davy, noting that he seemed to be moving more slowly than was usual. But he waited patiently for his shuffling approach, for he had no wish to disappoint the veteran by avoiding the ritual of their greeting.

"Master George, I believe 'e be taller by six inches since last I seen 'e," announced Davy, delightedly.

"Possibly Davy, but you are the same as ever I see. Just as sprightly! How do you do it?" George lied, kindly, ignoring the fact that, if he had grown as much as the old servant always insisted he had, he would by now probably be almost as tall as the house itself.

"Good food an' 'ard work, Master George, thas' 'ow!" retorted Davy proudly, but hastily arranged for the young man's heavy trunks to be carried by one of the stable lads, for age had diminished his strength. Not wishing to be retired, he had pleaded with Mr Trevarthen that he should be allowed to continue in his post as a sort of head groom and general factotum about the yard. Paul, noting the look of fear in his old servant's face at the prospect of refusal, had agreed, only on the condition that he was to do no heavy lifting. Further, if his exertions proved too much for him, he was quite at liberty to return to his cottage at any time of day. Davy acquiesced to the arrangement, although his wife called him a silly old fool for wishing to continue to work when the Master had suggested that perhaps the time had come for him to retire.

"An' well 'e d' knaw Mr Paul would see we right! We'd 'ave no fears 'bout bein' turned out the cottage 'cos Mr Paul 'eddon never done such a thing in 'is life to any of 'is workers," his spouse lectured him crossly.

"Aw, shuss'up woman do!" retorted Davy angrily. "Paul says I'm t' do as I d' wish an' I knaw 'e'd be 'ard put to find another as good as me at the job." Mrs Pascoe raised her eyes towards the heavens but tactfully decided not to make any further comments. She reasoned, philosophically, that her husband's belief in his continued abilities kept him from under her feet for the greater part of the day, so perhaps it was to her advantage, after all. She then smiled fondly to herself as she recognised that, by keeping him in employment, their dear Mr Paul had succeeded in making her poor fool of a husband forget his increasing infirmities.

Davy saw Master George to the door, receiving both his thanks and that kind smile that mirrored his father's so precisely. He then made his way slowly back to the stable block where a warm fire blazed in the off-room reserved for his use. A young stable lad swiftly presented him with a steaming bowl of tea. Davy thanked him briefly before pointing out in a severe tone that the Master's tack appeared rather dull and the boy had best clean it properly this time, else he would have words to say about it up at the house. The admonished boy scurried away to correct the fault and proceeded to polish the offending items until they shone like gold. Returning to Davy's cosy little room, he offered up the saddle for inspection and received a gruff, "Tidden bad, fer a youngen," by way of acknowledgement for his efforts.

Meanwhile, George had found his mother in the withdrawing room and covered her face with kisses, so pleased was he to see her. Chloe, in turn breathed a huge sigh of contentment and hugged her eldest son happily. Their reunion was abruptly cut short when the door suddenly burst open. Startled, they both looked round to see who could have broken in upon them in such a rude fashion. On the threshold, a crumpled piece of paper grasped tightly in one hand, stood Joey Bolitho. He was breathing heavily and his face wore a thunderous expression never before seen by either his nephew or his sister-in-law. Dispensing with formalities, through gritted teeth, he uttered only one question.

"Where the bleddy 'ell is 'e?" he raged, in a tone of voice that did not bode well for the person he sought.

"Uncle Joey!" exclaimed George, a scowl crossing his face, "How dare you speak so in front of my mother. Apologise at once, sir, for I will not have such a thing!"

His mother turned to George, surprised to hear her son speak in such a fashion, for of all her children she would not have considered her beloved George to address any man, let alone his uncle, with such authority. Facing their visitor once again, she noted that his face had suffused with colour. Looking contrite, Joey began an apology, but it was obvious that he was doing so under considerable strain.

"Please to come in, Joey," advised Chloe, gently, "and inform us as to what has happened to cause you such distress."

Breathing heavily, her brother-in-law closed the door firmly behind him and strode into the room, before thrusting toward Chloe the paper that he clenched so tightly.

"This! This is what I'm on about!" he stormed.

Taking the proffered paper from his hand, Chloe was about to read it when the door opened once more and her unsuspecting husband stood framed in the doorway. His appearance had a dramatic effect upon his brother, who turned on his heel and, before anyone could stop him, grabbed Paul by the lapels of his coat and pushed him back against the wall. Once again, Joey began to swear and was on the point of drawing back his arm in order to deliver a well-aimed punch into his brother's face, when he was stopped immediately from entering into an affray by the sound of a woman's voice from the doorway.

"Joey! Stop that at once!" cried Sarah-Jane in a frightened voice. Looking extremely agitated, Joey's wife nonetheless stood her ground. Her intervention had its desired effect, for her husband suddenly released his brother. Sarah-Jane noted, however, that Joey's hands remained clenched and an angry scowl still lay across his face.

Chloe, with admirable control, suggested that perhaps it would be for the best if the two men should not attempt to brawl in her withdrawing room and directed them to take a seat. Paul, still fuming at being accosted in such a fashion in his own home, strode past his brother without a glance and stood beside his wife. Sarah-Jane caught hold of her husband's hand and led him to a seat directly opposite and, with some hesitation, they took their places on the settle. George, unsure whether to go or stay, looked to his mother for advice, who smiled serenely before pointing to the seat by the small table, so he crossed the room and sat down quietly.

"Well," said Mrs Trevarthen briskly, "having had a brief chance to look through this letter," and here she directed a telling look at her brother-in-law, "I presume that your anger has been aroused by my husband's lack of tact in interfering in your private family affairs. For that I would apologise on his behalf, for I presume he will not have the wit to do it for himself." It was now Paul's turn to scowl but before he had a chance to speak, Sarah-Jane interjected, requesting an explanation of the argument that had suddenly erupted between the two men. She hurriedly explained to her sister-in-law that she had been breakfasting with her husband when the mail had been brought in by the maid. Upon reading the crumpled letter, which was now residing in Chloe's hand, Joey had erupted into such a show of temper as she had never seen before and left the house, informing her that he had every intention of killing his brother. She had ordered up the carriage and had followed him to Trevu immediately.

Chloe gave a brief explanation of her husband's stupidity in writing to his brother's only known living Bolitho relation, without asking his permission or informing him of what he proposed to do.

"Bolitho relation!" exclaimed Sarah-Jane, and turned to her husband to say, "but I thought that, Paul aside, you had no other relatives, Joey?"

"I 'ave an aunt," Joey replied tersely.

"You knew of her?" cried Paul in surprise.

"Course I did!" snapped his brother.

"Why did you never tell me?" Paul asked.

"Cos I'd no reason to think she'd want anything do with me," he answered in angry tone. "An' anyways, I never 'ad any recognition from that side of the family an' neither did . . . did mother. If they didden want knaw us fore I didden want nawthin' do with 'em," His wife squeezed his hand sympathetically and he glanced at her, giving a weak, sad smile. Chloe, directing a withering stare at her husband, explained to the couple that her Paul had found out about the aunt and penned a letter to her in his attempt to discover his brother's date of birth.

"As a consequence of his actions the aunt, a Miss Leah Bolitho, has invited Joey to attend upon her on Friday of this week at her home. She has informed him that his brother is to receive a letter extending the same invitation to him for, and I quote: 'Without his kind offices on your behalf I would have not felt emboldened to attempt a reconciliation within the family.'"

A long silence followed her statement. It was eventually broken by Sarah-Jane, announcing in her matter of fact way that perhaps Paul's actions had not been so very wrong after all. Joey gazed at her blankly for a moment, then angrily rasped that, not only would he refuse the invitation, nor would he even acknowledge receipt of the offending document. If he thought this pronouncement would quell his wife into silence he was to be mistaken. She turned upon him and informed him robustly that he was not to talk such nonsense and that he would attend upon his aunt, along with his brother, should Paul so wish, at the appointed time.

"Damned if I will!" shouted Joey in temper, who got up from his seat and left the room immediately. The door banged behind him, the sound of the main door slamming with equal force followed shortly afterwards.

Immediately, Chloe crossed the room to sit beside Sarah-Jane and clasped her hand chafing it gently. "Dear Sarah-Jane, we have to acknowledge that as far as Joey is concerned, his aunt could have contacted him years ago, when, as I understand it, he and his mother stood in desperate need of her help. To receive such an invitation now is, in Joey's eyes, tantamount to an insult to himself and to his beloved mother. I consider him to be justifiably agitated and I can only apologise on Paul's behalf both to you and to Joey," she said, gently.

"Do not apologise," replied Sarah-Jane firmly. She gave herself a little shake and then turned and kissed Chloe's cheek. "You are not to be concerned, dearest," she announced with resolution, "for I will make that bull-headed husband of mine see sense. It will do his position in society no end of good if it is to be acknowledged that he has relations other than the Trevarthens. He is admired and respected through his own efforts and our dear Paul's determination to recognise him, but to be taken back into his mother's family will add to his consequence. If his aunt wishes to meet with him then he will attend upon her." She noted her sister-in-law's raised eyebrows and laughed roguishly. "He will do as I say. Never fear, Chloe." She stood up and shook out her skirts, apologised on her husband's behalf for his behaviour and informed them that she would be in touch before the proposed visit. Before either of them could say a word, she left the room and departed before Paul could gather his thoughts to see her from his house.

George took note of the fiery glance that was being directed in his father's direction by his mother and thought it a prudent moment to excuse himself from the charged atmosphere. He shook his father's hand in greeting and disappeared from the room, offering up the excuse that he wished to see his brothers and sisters.

"You idiot!" stormed Chloe at her husband, immediately upon their son's departure. "See what pain you have brought to poor Joey. He did not deserve that, as a result of your actions, he should find himself placed in such an invidious position."

"Sarah-Jane sees the advantages of this proposed reconciliation," he countered defensively, still annoyed by his brother's assault upon his person.

"Sarah-Jane is bound to recognise the advantage, Paul!" Chloe retorted. "She showed great courage in allying herself with a person of Joey's reputation and I can well imagine that it has not been easy for her. Penzance society, like all social circles, defines itself by the rules it sets for itself. No matter how great her love for him, her husband is known more for what he was than what he has become. Of course she will hope for an acknowledgement from his new family but you seem to forget, both of you, that Joey's beginnings were of hardship and degradation. He is bound to feel that the hypocrisy of his aunt's actions in wishing to meet with him now is more an insult than an overture of friendship."

"Well," announced her husband, somewhat pompously, "I think that he is viewing this development with too much sensitivity."

"Paul!" cried Chloe, "What an unfeeling remark to make! Surely, you of all people would understand his pain at this time. Did Penzance display such kindness to you in the past?"

He blushed and lowered his head in recognition of the acuteness of her observations. After a moment of reflection he apologised for his stupidity and thoughtlessness in causing such a disruption within the family.

"He's my brother, Chloe and I love him dearly, more now than any man before him. I wanted only to ascertain the date of his birth and knowing that his aunt was aware of his existence I presumed, wrongly, I now admit that if she would be willing to divulge it then that would be the end of the matter. How could I have foreseen that she would be so willing to arrange a meeting. Mrs Penberthy gave me the impression that she would, in all probability, have nothing to do with him," he said, and then added with conviction, "or with myself, for that matter."

"Paul!" cried an exasperated Chloe, "Of course she would wish to meet with him. He is her only living relative and your letter presented the opportunity for which she has waited so long. She could hardly contact him in his previous guise. Now he has attained respectability and as a law abiding member of society she would have no qualms about endeavouring to establish a link with him."

"I cannot believe it, Chloe! I was given to believe that she is a staunch Methodist. Surely she has not so much Christian kindness in her that she would be willing to countenance the admittance of a person of Joey's reputation into such a family?" he asserted, strongly.

"Miss Leah Bolitho, if I am not mistaken, has wealth and position in abundance. All that is as nothing if she had no one to inherit. Christian kindness, my dear husband, was what you were prepared to show to your brother, even though you were aware of how his past actions had affected your dearest Sardi and the resulting despair that this family suffered. Why should his aunt be any different? As I said, without a family she must be so lonely. I for one think it most understandable that she should attempt to be reconciled," she told him with conviction.

The rift that had arisen between the brothers over Paul's actions had hardly healed by the time the Trevarthen's carriage stopped at the house in Chapel Street. Sarah-Jane had demanded of her husband that he should attend upon Miss Bolitho as requested. For his beloved he would do anything, but his heart bled to have to leave again and so when the two brothers set off on their journey, hardly a word was exchanged between them. Paul noted that Joey was wearing his finest apparel and that his hair had been neatly trimmed. He presumed, correctly, that his Sarah-Jane had insisted that he should be well groomed. If he continued to keep the blank expression on his face that he wore to hide his feelings from the world, then so be it, but his aunt could not fail to be impressed by her nephew's appearance. They travelled in silence for the most part and studiously avoided looking directly at each other. A carriage was not the means by which either gentleman would have wished to travel the relatively short distance to Trevanoc, but both of their wives had insisted that it would not do to arrive at their destination on horseback, mud spattered and dishevelled.

When the carriage turned up the driveway towards the house, Paul could not contain his natural curiosity and looked about him with interest. The cottages set by the roadside were all well appointed and the land appeared in good heart. The crops were well maintained and when his eye alighted on the livestock grazing in the fields, he, as a farmer, could not fail to be impressed by what he saw. The cattle surveyed the carriage with a total lack of concern and at the sight of their gleaming coats and general appearance, Paul felt a pang of envy. 'Sheltered land,' he mused, but even this excuse did not detract from his admiration for the farming skill needed to produce such fine animals.

As their equipage rounded the corner the house came into view. A surprisingly large, modern establishment with steps leading up to the main door and with high, wide windows looking out over the front garden. Paul had expected something older, but his surprise at the sight of the house was as nothing compared to what he was about to witness. As the carriage drew to a halt, Mr Trevarthen was to receive the shock of his life as the door was pulled open and a grinning, black face looked in upon them with obvious delight.

"Good morning, Sirs," said the stranger, who then proceeded to let down the steps for them to alight. "The mistress is expecting you."

Paul stared in disbelief to see such a dark face and remained rooted to his seat. He would have stayed there if his brother had not unceremoniously kicked his boot. They both descended onto the driveway and were formally welcomed to Trevanoc by the smiling servant. This gentleman introduced himself as the estate manager, not the manservant that the brothers had presumed him to be. His name was Richard Nairn and he appeared as oblivious to Mr Trevarthen's surprised expression as he was to Mr Bolitho's aloofness. Guiding them to the front door, he preceded them up the steps and led them in to a large, brightly-lit hallway.

"The mistress is in the front parlour. I will arrange for tea to be served, gentleman. I expect you will be glad of some refreshment after your journey," he said. Obviously, thought Paul, Mr Nairn had a great deal of authority within the household if he could take it upon himself to undertake the commission of such arrangements.

The two men followed in his wake, experiencing different emotions; one full of curiosity and the other an all-consuming anger that was laced with fear. Mr Nairn stopped at a large door, knocked once and waited for an acknowledgement, before pushing it open and walking into the room. Paul was vaguely aware that his name was being mentioned, but he was by far too engrossed by the woman sitting in a chair beside the large fireplace. The elderly lady inclined her head to him as he made his bow to her, but in all other respects she completely disregarded him. She had eyes only for one person in the room and for this reason Paul had the opportunity to observe the lady at his leisure. Miss Leah Bolitho sat erect in her chair, one hand resting lightly on a black Malacca cane. Her light blue eyes were fixed firmly on his brother's face and her dimpled cheeks served to emphasise the smile on her lips, but it was the mixture of suppressed excitement and recognition that lay across her expressive face that surprised him the most. He had mistakenly assumed that Joey's features were to be replicated on his aunt's face but this was patently not the case. Admittedly, there was a family resemblance but it was slight. He shot a quick glance at his brother and noted the familiar enigmatic countenance. Immediately, he felt sorrow for Joey's relative that she should be confronted by this stern-faced individual who showed not a spark of human kindness towards her. He need not have felt such concern, however, for as the meeting progressed it was impressed upon him that he was in the presence of an extremely redoubtable character.

Smiling broadly, she invited the brothers to take a seat in a firm voice in which her dialect was particularly noticeable.

"Well, nephew," she said, turning her beaming face to Joey, "pleased am I to welcome you 'ome at last."

Joey Bolitho replied swiftly that he did not consider Trevanoc to be his home and continued rudely that he had no wish to move from his present abode to come to live in a house which, to him, held no appeal, mainly because its owner had never shown any interest in him before.

" 'Ave I not?" queried Miss Bolitho. "I'll 'ave you know I seen you afore, Joseph. Three times!" Bolitho's eyes widened slightly in surprise but his face remained otherwise unaltered. His aunt, completely unabashed by his icy stare, continued to inform him - and it was only to her nephew that her speech was directed - of small details of his past life of which he had never been told.

"I went Penzance to see you when news come back that my sister 'ad been brought to bed. Miriam wouldn't best pleased to see me and at first I thought she 'ad you 'id away somewhere, but the place was too small for that. You was 'cross the road with a neighbour, so I sent 'er to go and get 'e." She broke off her tale at this point and chuckled with glee at the recollection of her first sight of him. "Great long thing you was. All arms and legs and a great 'ead of black 'air. And 'owling fit to bust!" she enthused. At this, Paul laughed aloud, but on receiving a withering look from his brother he stopped immediately and asked for pardon. Miss Bolitho, however, seemed not to notice. She answered a knock at the door and a young serving girl came in bearing a tray of tea, a plate of well-buttered bread slices and a large fruitcake, which had been cut into generous portions. Paul's eyes gleamed with pleasure but Joey ignored the proffered refreshment, merely staring woodenly at his aunt. Undaunted, Mr Trevarthen partook liberally and then settled back in his chair to listen with interest to the old lady's narrative.

"The first time I come to see you I give Miriam some money, for 'er and you, 'cos I'd 'ad a look around when she went to fetch you and for the life of me I couldn't find much in the way of vittals or clothes in the house." For a moment her face hardened unexpectedly as she remarked, bitterly, "I kept sending money and writing letters but I 'ad no reply. I came again before the year was out but Miriam 'ad taken a liking to strong liquor an' was drunk out of 'er mind. As for you, you was in with your neighbour again. I thought to take you away but I couldn't do it. Mother was still alive and wouldn't 'ave allowed you over the threshold. Father would 'ave welcomed you with open arms tho'," she said and reached across to gently pat the back of his brother's hand. Joey snatched it away as if it had been soiled by the contact. Miss Bolitho smiled grimly then continued to recount her story.

"When I seen you next you was walking. No shoes and dressed in tatters, filthy dirty. You was a sight and no mistake. I'd bought a basket a food with me and when I offered you some you started eating so fast I feared you'd make yourself sick. Miriam didn't seem to care much for you, so I . . ." but here she was rudely interrupted by her nephew who shouted angrily, "That's a damn lie! Mother did care fer me!"

His sudden outburst did not discompose his aunt, however, who firmly repeated that his parent showed little concern for him. "You'll 'ave your own feelings, Joseph, naturally enough but Miriam 'ad been taken by the evil of drink and did not seem capable to look after you. Mother 'ad passed away not a month before and Father would 'ave wished it, so I took it upon myself to come for you, determined to bring you 'ome and away from that place. My sister was welcome to come back and live at Trevanoc, I told 'er. I argued with 'er, Joseph and tried my 'ardest to persuade 'er but she would 'ave none of it. I thought in my innocence that she would let you come. Let me take you away and give you a chance to grow up fit and 'ealthy amongst your family. She wouldn't 'ave it," she recalled flatly.

"Perhaps you'll believe me now when I say that Mother did care fer me!" snapped her nephew, a hint of triumph in his voice.

An expression of compassion crossed his relative's face, then she stated quietly the words that rocked her poor nephew to his tormented soul.

"She offered to sell you to me, instead."

There was a brief pause. Paul felt the tension rise in the room and saw his brother's face furious with anger.

"You bleddy liar!" he blurted.

Miss Bolitho, completely unabashed at being sworn at in such a manner, repeated her statement quietly and then continued.

"Of course, I couldn't do such a thing, tho' many a time since I know God would 'ave forgiven me if I 'ad. How could I, a staunch abolitionist, 'ave bought another. God did not make us to buy and sell our fellow man," she said with conviction. At this point she glanced briefly at Paul before turning back to Joey and adding compassionately, "Ask your brother, for he will understand my predicament above all others."

Paul did understand her meaning, but set against it was the knowledge that his brother could have had such a fine life in this house and not have had to endure the privations and hardships that he had endured as the result of living under his mother's roof. There would never have been the smuggling, the murders, the long years of waiting for his love to recognise him for the man of worth that he was. He turned towards his brother, then averted his gaze immediately; the pain in Joey's features was a sight he wished never to see again.

There was a prolonged silence before Miss Bolitho spoke again, but her voiced was laced with great pity as she recounted that she did not come to call again, but sent money. Of course, she had no way of knowing if her money had been spent on food for her nephew or drink for her sister. She could only hope it was used for him. Miriam never answered the many letters that she sent and it was not until news was brought of her death that she came again to the little cottage.

"I come for you then, Joseph," she told him with conviction. "You was to come 'ome but again I 'ad been thwarted by circumstances. News was slow to reach me of Miriam's sad demise and when I arrived you was nowhere to be found. The cottage was empty. Nothing left of you to be found. It was as if you 'ad never existed," she added with a sigh. "The only item left in the whole place was this," she said, lifting up her cane, "so I took it with me and determined to set about to find you. When I arrived 'ome I was met by the doctor and 'e told me Father wouldn't going to last the night. The first words Father said to me when I went in to 'im was of you, my dear. Wanted to see you for 'e was sure you would 'ave come 'ome with me." The old lady was leaning forward now and she had lowered her voice. "I lied for the first time in my life, Joseph. Told him you would be coming tomorrow." As she spoke, a tear trickled slowly down her face.

There was no response from her nephew, so she sat back and hastily wiped away the tear. "What a foolish old woman I am become? So many years ago and still so fresh in my mind," she said with a sigh. Then she smiled again and, leaning on her cane, rose from her chair. "Come along, now. Come with me and I'll show you around," and she caught hold of her nephew's arm in such a fashion that he had no choice but to allow her to hold on to him as they set off to walk to the door.

Once in the hallway, Mr Nairn bowed politely to them and whispered to the young serving girl at his side. She scurried off immediately to the kitchen and returned with a small band of her fellow workers. They lined up and curtsied or bowed as the couple passed between them. Paul, bringing up the rear, had ample opportunity to observe their faces. It was not just Miss Leah Bolitho that was pleased at the appearance of his brother in their midst. Some of the older members stared in disbelief at his face, the younger ones merely beamed in delight. Miss Bolitho stopped in front of the cook and thanked her for the lovely cake. A small touch, but it charmed Paul to think that Joey's aunt showed such kindness to those around her. Perhaps, in time, she would charm his brother in the same way, but there was something about the stiffness of Joey's demeanour that did not give him hope that this would be the case. He was also delighted to discover that hardly anyone took the slightest notice of him, for they had their eyes fixed firmly on his brother's face. An unusual occurrence for Paul, as at most times it was he that people habitually stared at when he came into a house.

The hallway reached to the ceiling with staircases at either side of it that led to a wide landing, off which lay the bedchambers. Off from the hall itself were various moderately decorated rooms, and Paul noticed with interest that the room nearest to the kitchen was the dining room. A well thought out touch, he reasoned, for he had often thought that the kitchen in his own home lay too far away from his dining room, resulting in extra work for his servants. By this time the little procession had reached the far staircase and began slowly to ascend the stairs. Joey's aunt maintained a flowing description of all that was to be seen around them. Her father, she explained, had rebuilt the original house in the last century, because he considered that it was far too inconvenient for the family to live in with comfort.

"He never could abide 'poky little rooms' as he called them - he was much like you are, Joseph, tall and well built - and anyway Mother came from Truro and thought the house old-fashioned. 'Tis a fine house, don't you think, Joseph?" she asked, but her nephew remained noncommittal.

By this time they were strolling along the landing. They came across a secluded alcove with a small settle set back against the wall, above which hung a large portrait of a young girl. She had a most serene expression on her face, but something about the way she stood denoted a determination about her. On being informed that it was Miss Bolitho in her youth, Paul was not surprised. Her youthful features were there for all to see, but although she had been an attractive young girl she could not claim to have been beautiful. Hung on the main wall were three more portraits: the first of Miss Rachel, the next of Joey's grandparents and the third of Zachariah Bolitho. There was a noted family resemblance between all of them but it was Hugo Bolitho's face that reminded Paul of his brother. All the children seemed more to have their mother's features and cast of countenance. Miss Bolitho stopped to regard her nephew, but he was looking at his grandfather with no trace of emotion on his face. "He was a 'andsome fellow too," she remarked, but after a moment they moved along to another alcove. Above another settle hung a fifth portrait, and this time the effect on Joey was volcanic. He moved forward and reached out his hand as if to hold again something that time had stolen from him. The young girl that looked down at them this time had none of the sobriety of the previous portraits, but she had all of the beauty. Her face glowed from the light of the facing windows and her eyes seemed to dance with excitement. The painting was so well executed that it seemed she could step down from the frame and be among them at any moment. Paul did not need to be told the name of this beautiful woman. Her son so resembled her it would have been hard for any man not to have realised that this was, indeed, Joey Bolitho's mother.

CHAPTER 9

"She was sixteen when that was painted. So excited to 'ave her portrait done that she could 'ardly keep still. Of course, when Miriam left, Mother 'ad it taken down, but soon after she died Father said I was to 'ave it put back and it's been 'ere ever since," his aunt informed him. She turned to her nephew with a gleam of satisfaction in her eye. "I am glad it 'as pleased you to see 'er again, Joseph. I 'ad 'oped for that at least," she remarked softly, and squeezed his arm gently with her hand.

Her touch brought Joey back to the present time and he fought hard to regain control of himself. It was a rare thing for him to give way to his private emotions in public and even in the midst of his closest family he could not allow himself to do it. Whilst he fought his demons, the two brothers were informed that Miss Bolitho had arranged for Mr Nairn to show them around the home farm, because she imagined that it might be of some interest to them. Paul imagined that Joey would be glad to get out of the house, and so it proved to be. But, whereas the farmer found plenty to see and admire, and asked the estate manager some very pertinent questions, the heir to the property said not a word. Mr Nairn proved to be a most entertaining and informative guide and Paul felt on such good terms with him that he politely enquired as to how he had arrived in Cornwall. Mr Nairn was very obliging and explained that his earliest memories were of a pageboy in a large house in London. As he grew older he had been retained as a groom in the stables because he had a good way with horses. When the family had made a visit to Cornwall he had come into contact with Miss Bolitho at Truro, where he had been sent to buy some harness for his master's carriage horses.

"There and then she offered me the position that I have now, Mr Trevarthen. She had no knowledge of me whatsoever, but told me I had an honest face," he told Paul, clearly still amazed at the change in his fortunes. "My master wasn't best pleased, as you can imagine, but he had never treated me with anything like respect, calling me names and what have you."

Paul nodded in sympathy. "I know," he said, remembering how often the names had rung out around the streets of Penzance and in the school at Helston. All a long time ago, but the cruelty had left its scars.

"That Miss Bolitho is a saint, sir," enthused Richard Nairn, "and I have come home to Paradise." He beamed at Paul, who laughed in return, but his brother rode on beside them cloaked in silence, his thoughts and feelings well hidden from his companions. As a farmer, Paul could not fail to be impressed by all he had seen and heard. He felt a pang of regret when the short tour came to an end and they were once more back at the house.

Lunch had been set out for them in the dining room and when they entered, Miss Bolitho was seated at the head of a long dining table. Places had been set for the two brothers on either side of her chair, so Paul lost no time in seating himself at the left hand side of the table. His brother paused for a moment but took the remaining seat, his face completely devoid of the anticipation that Paul's showed. When his aunt smiled and asked if he would wish to say the grace he shook his head and mumbled a refusal, so she and

Paul bowed their heads and she issued a short prayer. It was noted that her nephew stared resolutely ahead and neither inclined his head or closed his eyes. The meal that was served was, in Paul's opinion, one of the finest he had ever had presented to him. Honest, plain cooking and a plentiful amount of it. Naturally, he consumed his food with delight, but Joey picked at everything and seemed to have little or no appetite. The meal was notable for the two men in one other respect. Pitchers of water were placed on the table but there was a complete absence of any alcohol. Their host pointedly remarked that she abhorred alcohol and would not have it in the house.

"Quite understandable, Miss Bolitho," Paul remarked, "but this meal is so delicious it needs no embellishment."

"I presume," she said, turning to Joey, "that you would disagree with that statement?"

"I would refer you to St. John, chapter two, if you have any doubts about your Lord's attitude to wine," replied Joey and looked his aunt directly in the eye. She giggled, the reaction surprising Joey.

"Quite so, dear Joseph, but it does not mention that our dear Lord partook of any, even if the guests at the wedding did," she countered, looking pleased with herself at the anger that flashed across his face.

Complimenting her nephew on his knowledge of the scriptures, she went on to say that after lunch she would be pleased if he would follow her to the library, where the family bible resided.

"I am sure you will both find something of interest in it," she told them, playfully.

This was indeed the case for, once in the library, the one name that Joey Bolitho had never expected to see in such a book was his own. Even more surprising was the fact that he appeared to have his grandfather's name as well as his own. His date of birth was recorded as well and Paul made a mental note of it, for the one reason that this strange meeting was taking place at all was to obtain this single piece of information.

"Miriam told me to include Father's name, for she had always a fondness for him," she said, before adding without a tremor of jealously, "and he for her." The date and details of his marriage had also been included and a line drawn down from his and Sarah-Jane's name so that their children could also be recorded. Joey realised at once that his aunt must have had knowledge of his existence for many a long year.

"You seem to 'ave known of me all my life. How come you never sought to take me away from the Rickards?" he questioned suspiciously. "All this show of me name in the family bible and so on. You are so fond of me as you make out to be. What was to stop 'e from coming for me there?"

Miss Bolitho sighed heavily before replying in a resigned tone, "It was a few years before I even knew of your . . . your association with the man. He 'ardly advertised your existence with the people I came into contact with, Joseph. I 'ave often wished that I 'ad shown more strength of character and gone to 'im to take you away, but I 'ad a great fear of the man and could not bring myself to meet with him, such a dreadful reputation as he 'ad. I 'eard tales of your reputation too as you grew to manhood. I feared for you and your immortal soul and thought you lost to me. As time passed I gave up 'ope of ever meeting with you, but I remembered you in my prayers each and every day. God must 'ave listened, Joseph, because he took you away from that life and gave you a new and better one." It was stated so simply, with both contriteness and conviction, that Joey was completely taken aback. Paul heard his sharp intake of breath then, suddenly, his brother reached over and slammed the book shut.

"There stands the man who changed my life fer me, not your precious God!" he shouted viciously, pointing to his brother. He stared into his aunt's eyes with a fierce expression on his face, but she did not flinch and merely gave him a sympathetic smile. Her attitude inflamed him the more; thwarted, he turned on his heel and headed for the door. He ordered his brother to follow him but Paul hesitated, not capable of displaying such ill manners. Turning to Miss Bolitho, Paul offered his sincere apologies for his brother's behaviour, but if he expected to find the poor lady distraught with the rudeness of her nephew's reaction he was surprised to find that it was not the case. Instead, she smiled up at him, quite unabashed by Joey's words.

"I am not discouraged, Mr Trevarthen, and I thank you sincerely to 'ave brought 'im into my life again. To see 'im in this 'ouse at last 'as given me such 'ope for the future. I shall not despair now," she told him.

Joey called from the hallway, his anger apparent in his voice, and on hearing it, Leah Bolitho laughed out loud and took hold of Paul's hand, shook it and then wished him farewell. "Best not to keep 'im waiting, his grandmother had just such a way with her," she said with a gleeful laugh.

On their return journey, Paul attempted to rebuke his brother for his manners and behaviour in his aunt's house, but Joey would not say a word. He sat with his arms folded across his chest, staring at the opposite side of the carriage, his face expressionless but his eyes burning with anger. Nothing would change his demeanour so, after a while, Paul lapsed into silence and they continued their journey without a word being exchanged. When they arrived in Penzance, Joey alighted and went into his house without so much as a farewell.

The Christmas Eve party at Trevu was to take place as usual, although most of the people who were to attend were well aware that a serious rift had arisen between Redvers Trevarthen's sons. Few, if any, of Penzance society felt much sympathy for the ex smuggler for their attitude held to their belief that Paul had acted correctly in contacting Miss Bolitho. Most of their acquaintances considered that Joey Bolitho should have shown gratitude to his brother for the action he had undertaken on his behalf. Their society had evolved through acquiring good connections, family or financial, but the former were considered the more desirable because a blood line could not be taken away. However badly he had transgressed in the past, in society's eyes Joey had been redeemed by his actions to a certain extent, although mainly for having the same father as Paul Trevarthen. But now that he had become heir to Trevanoc he was considered by many to have attained a higher strata of social class, even to have surpassed the Trevarthen line in status.

This novel position did not impress Sarah-Jane's husband but the lady herself was clever enough to realise that, if now the connection had been established, he would retain the link to his family. She would then be considered as having married into two well-respected local families, rather than being looked upon, as was sometimes the case, as the wife of an ex smuggler. Sarah-Jane knew that she loved her husband for who he was, but she had been brought up on the Trevu estate and was wise enough to realise that position in society carried with it many advantages. She understood that when she believed herself in love with Paul, a part of her craved the life of ease with which his position could endow her. All her life, John Williams' daughter had accepted the gifts that had been passed to her by her betters. She had received a good education through the kind offices of the Trevarthens, found genteel employment because of it, but as she continued to improve her position in society she craved recognition. However, it was her marriage to a scion of the Trevarthens that had finally seen her admitted into their circle.

Joey Bolitho had always been aware of his wife's attitude. Even if she had not been in love with another when they had encountered each other at the Tregenza's, all those years ago, her attitude towards him then had always been one of disdain. When he had offered to change his way of life for her it was in vain, because the object of her affection at that time held such a high position in the local area. Admittedly, she had grown to love him, but at the back of his mind he wondered if perhaps the link he had to the Trevarthens had not played some part in her acceptance of his proposal. He had achieved status through his notoriety as a smuggler, but he was being made well aware by the attitudes presented to him from acquaintances at the party that he had risen far above anything he could have attained as the recognised illegitimate son of Redvers Trevarthen.

"My dear Joey," exclaimed a voice at his side, "what a serious face you wear tonight!"

He turned to see his aunt, Mrs Caroline Crebo, smiling up at him. She was most finely attired in a dress of lavender silk that seemed to froth with the addition of much black lace at the neck and elbow. He greeted her with a brief kiss on the cheek and told her he hoped to find her well.

"Tolerable, my dear, tolerable, but unlike yourself I am giving the impression of enjoying this festive occasion," she said. Then, with a chuckle, added: "and indeed I will admit that, to travel to Trevu for the Christmas is a far more pleasing prospect than to have to spend any time with my own family. Strange, is it not, that I should have worked so hard to have found respectable partners for my children, only to be so irrationally bored by their company?"

"Paul an' 'is family could never be classed as boring, aunt," admitted Joey softly.

"Quite! I hear he has been busy on your behalf," she remarked suddenly, turning to look him boldly in the eye. "You have Redvers' look on your face. He was most discomforted when first Paul appeared on his doorstep. I imagine that the shock of what your brother has done still rankles with you but you had best forgive him, for he has managed, albeit by accident, in lifting you higher in the ranks than ever you could have foreseen." His aunt waited for a reply, but none was forthcoming. Her eyes were then distracted by something that she had spotted across the room and she exclaimed, "Good grief! Whoever made that poor woman's dress? And to put her in puce! With that complexion! Heavens! Oh dear, now the dratted woman is beckoning to me!" She muttered her excuses quickly and set off towards the lady. However, in spite of her previous remarks, Mrs Crebo was bearing down upon her with what appeared to be an expression of rapturous delight on her face. "My dear Mrs Rodda, how delightful to see you again and what an exquisite gown. Locally made, I presume?" she enquired artlessly, but the poor woman was so overawed to be greeted by Mrs Crebo that she completely missed Caroline's barb and gabbled on at some length about her newly found seamstress that had become such a treasure to her.

At the sight of this amusing diversion, and for the first time that evening, Joey Bolitho felt a smile settle on his face. It froze when he realised that his brother had left his wife's side and was heading purposefully in his direction. They had exchanged a brief greeting earlier in the evening but since that time, Joey had studiously avoided the Master of Trevu.

"I thought it best we appear to be on speaking terms as we are in the view of so many of Penzance's notables," said Paul wryly.

"Makes no difference to me, brother," replied his brother curtly.

"Your attitude is making everyone well aware of that," observed Paul, "however, I cannot abide that we should be at odds like this. I apologise wholeheartedly for my actions, Joey, but I cannot alter what has passed. I was foolish in the extreme, but you have to believe that I never intended any harm or hurt to you." He looked his brother boldly in the eye, but not by so much as a flicker of an eyelash did Joey betray any emotion. There was a long silence in which Paul attempted a wary smile.

Joey regarded him blankly, but he had to admire anyone who, knowing that he had angered a man of the ex-smugglers renowned temper, could attempt a reconciliation in the midst of Trevu's seasonal party and in front of his, for the most part, prying guests. Their interest was now well and truly caught by the sight of the two brothers, in conversation for the first time since they had met at the door of Trevu. The little boy who had shed tears for him all those years ago when the baker threatened to have him hung had held a special place in Joey Bolitho's heart from that moment on. And now, he found it in his heart to forgive Paul for interfering in his life; for making him relive a past that he had tried to forget and discovering that his adored mother thought no more of him than as an object that she could sell. That realisation had torn his life apart. He could not bring himself to talk of it, not even to his beloved wife, but the anguish gnawed at him day and night.

"I'll fergive 'e, brother, 'cos you 'em got no idea 'bout what a terrible thing you bin an' done."

Paul's smile widened, though hesitantly, and mixed with the expression of relief was a look of pity. "My grandfather was considered good enough to be sold. Twice, that I know of, Joey. It didn't lessen him in my eyes or dear Sardi's," he informed him, softly.

His statement was met with a surprised look. Joey could not believe that his brother could be so acute though, given his history, it was the more understandable in him than in any other.

"Your mother never tried sell 'e!" He rasped unguardedly.

The scales fell from Paul's eyes then. That his dear mother could think to sell the son who loved her so dearly. He knew well how much that would have hurt him.

"My mother abandoned me. Growing up, I never thought of her and when I met her it was so hard to forgive what she had done. Perhaps your mother was testing her sister. She came from a house where she had been imprisoned like a caged bird, chained about with her family's religious beliefs and practices. I saw her portrait, Joey: I never realised that she looked like that; so full of life and passion. If Leah Bolitho could have forsaken her beliefs, taking you on your mother's terms, perhaps she would have let you go, but I do not believe it. I imagine your mother set your aunt a test that she knew she could not pass. Escaping from that grey tomb, as she saw it, do you think she would want to send her only son there, to suffer as she had done? I think she thought to save you from that hardship, whereas my mother, who I had to struggle to love, preferred to leave me with another because she thought she would find it impossible to look after me. I learned to love her as a son should love his mother only at the end of her life, Joey. You have always had the advantage of me there," he concluded, his voice little more than a whisper at the end.

Joey Bolitho had lowered his eyes before Paul had finished speaking. He felt the compassion in the speech and felt eased by his words. He would give thought to what his brother had said; drink had always befuddled his mother's mind. But there were moments - not many, he knew - when she had told him of her love for him. That they were so few made them the more precious. He imagined a dried up Methodist like his aunt would never know of a love like that.

"I'm goin' up Bristol next week," he said, softly. "Be glad if you'll keep an eye on Sarah-Jane for me."

Paul was not surprised that his brother should make no reference to what he had said. Like his father before him he would do his best to keep his personal grief to himself.

"Of course, we will. Chloe will be pleased to have her company," said Paul, relief in his voice and a twinkle in his eye. In his heart he believed he had told his brother a lie; even old Edwin Nance, who had always admired Sally Bolitho and knew her well, had always maintained that she had no time for her son. If Paul had been dishonest, he was not ashamed of it, because he hoped it had eased his brother's tortured mind.

After Christmas, Joey set off for Bristol by horseback. It was his preferred mode of travel and meant he could cover the distance between his home and Bristol the quicker. He had no wish to spend long away from his wife as she had been upset by his reaction to his visit to Trevanoc. Joey was well aware that, to her acquaintances, he was considered a fool for his determination not to cultivate a friendship with his relative. 'Perhaps,' he mused, as his horse broke into an easy canter on leaving Penzance, 'it's time I thought of delegating some of the business. I'm making a fair amount and 'ave no wish to travel away from 'ome and me wife as much as I 'ave to do. 'Tis best fer me be 'ome, else Sarah-Jane's goin' 'ave her ideas made by a damn passel of women I wouldn' 'ave over me threshold if I 'ad me own way.' On the road to Bristol he gave the matter much thought and, when he arrived, it was not long before his proposal was being considered by various of his staff employed in his wine business. One would be appointed to be in overall charge, with the responsibilities that such a change would entail, but others in the business would see their positions expanded and all would have an increased remuneration. The matter was discussed openly with the appropriate staff and an agreement was reached that suited all parties. Therefore, when Joey Bolitho began his homeward journey a week later he was in a far better mood than when he had left.

Whilst he had been away, Sarah-Jane had received a letter asking her to visit Trevanoc and she hesitated only briefly before accepting. Well she knew that her husband would be angered by her actions, but few people in Penzance would think she was in the wrong for calling on his aunt. When the two women met they took an instant liking to each other and spent an enjoyable day together. Miss Bolitho considered that her nephew had married a sensible and well brought up woman. After lunch, the two ladies withdrew to the parlour and spent the afternoon discussing Joseph Bolitho. Miss Bolitho expressed the wish that he would, in time, become a regular visitor to Trevanoc and his wife promised to do all in her power to see that this would come to pass. When Leah touched upon the subject of children, she realised how badly Sarah-Jane was suffering from the effects of being childless.

"They are a gift from God, Sarah-Jane. You cannot force his 'and," she emphasised, patting Mrs Bolitho's own hand sympathetically as she spoke.

"I know, my dear friend," she sighed, tears appearing on her lashes, "but it grieves me so that I have not given him a son. You should see him with his brother's children. He is a loving and devoted uncle and never a word to me of blame that I have not provided him with a family of his own. Indeed, he says he does not want children, but I cannot believe this. He speaks so as to make my failure weigh less heavily on me."

Miss Leah appeared to struggle for a moment but then said, resolutely, "As a Methodist I should not encourage this, but I 'ave 'eard that a raw egg beaten into a glass of port and taken before you retire is considered most efficacious in the matter. Farmer Boskenna swears by it because his wife was brought to bed of seven children; five of the male gender. And when she stopped drinking the mixture, they 'ad no more!"

Sarah-Jane informed Miss Bolitho that she would make up a potion that very night. Leah, with an amused twinkle in her eye, pointed out that, as her nephew was still in Bristol, it would be perhaps best to wait for his return. The two women maintained their composure for almost half a minute, but by the time the servant brought in the tea tray they were both howling with laughter and continued to break into giggles for the rest of the afternoon.

"Well, my dear," observed a cheery faced Leah, "if God had not meant us to laugh, he would not have given us the ability to do so."

When Sarah-Jane left, it was with much regret and she promised to come again as soon as she was able. Kissing Leah affectionately on the cheek, she made her farewells and travelled home to Penzance, determined that her husband would accompany her when next she made a visit to Trevanoc. Quite how she was to accomplish this feat, she was not certain, but she was a capable and determined woman and Joseph Bolitho's largest failing, as she well knew, was his blind, besotted love for his wife. She convinced herself that, with a little cajoling on her part she would get her way.

CHAPTER 10

WHEAL SANKEY was, as always, a hive of activity; mules laden with ore, horses pulling carts with coal for the mine engine, bal maidens slaving over their work, miners coming off their shift and others beginning their day. When Jimmy Jarvis arrived for his turn of work at the engine house, Henry Furniss looked at him suspiciously, for the man appeared to be unstable.

" 'Ave 'e bin drinkin' Jimmy?" he enquired, but received only a toothless grin and a knowing wink for his answer.

"Ya bleddy fool!" swore Mr Furniss, though he knew all the men drank to a certain extent. Despite the strong smell of gin about his person, Henry merely shook his head disapprovingly and said no more. Though there were rules to be followed, most of the workers flouted them to some degree. Why, that very morning, Dicky Johns had brought his boy in with him, a strapping twelve year old, and was even now preparing to take him down the mine with him. They all knew that Mr Trevarthen expressly forbade that children should work in or near the mine, but with two pairs of hands at work more money could be earned; many of the men had large families to feed and could not afford to be too particular. Anyway, Sankey was the safest mine in the area. Mr Trevarthen would have only the best equipment and what was worn was immediately thrown away. He had purchased the latest pumping engine at great expense and had it installed to pump out the water that constantly flooded the mine. The returns on his investment were not so high as in the past, now that the blockades were over and Britain could trade abroad again, but Wheal Sankey was not worked out and could still furnish an income good enough to justify the instalment of such an engine.

Not unduly worried by Jarvis's appearance, he picked up his bag and coat and set off for his home. He crossed through the spoil heaps, made bright with sturdily growing gorse, and worked his way around the old shafts that littered the landscape, until finally his feet took him down the well worn path that led to the little line of mine cottages where he had lived, man and boy, for thirty-five years. There would be a pie baking in the cloam oven and he licked his lips in anticipation of the hearty breakfast he was to enjoy. His hand was on the doorknob when the ground seemed to shake beneath his feet and a huge explosion rent the air. A shaft giving way would not make such a noise, but he knew just what it was that would. He turned, a silent prayer on his lips, to see the engine house that he had so recently left seemingly split apart, with great pieces of brick and machinery flying through the air as if they were birds. Immediately, dropping everything, he turned and ran back the way he had come, heading towards his place of work. The sound of the explosion could be heard all over the vicinity. Farmers' boys dropped their shovels, blacksmiths downed their tools, wives left their washing, all the local inhabitants left off their various occupations and, as one, ran towards the mine. He was almost at the mine entrance when he was overtaken by a man on horseback, who came thundering up from the road that led down to Trevu. With the sun in his eyes, Henry could only make out his silhouette, but he knew exactly who it was that rode at such a furious pace towards the mine.

Some people were laid out on the floor of the yard, coats placed over their faces. By some of the bodies, women knelt, keening desperately, other corpses lay alone and discarded. The living called for help or moaned softly, unable to move from where they fell. The more fortunate staggered about with blood pouring from their injuries. Mr Furniss knew that only an explosion of the high-pressure steam engine could have inflicted such damage. By shattering with such force the engine house that enclosed it, anyone unlucky enough to be in the vicinity would be pelted by the debris that was blasted outwards. And that which was hurled skywards became a lethal rain of masonry. Anyone hit by such would be severely injured, if not killed on the spot. He spotted Mr Trevarthen running towards the destruction and rushed after him to stop him.

"Mr Trevarthen, sir! The gynjy idden safe sir! Wait, sir!" he screamed in panic. But to no avail, for Mr Trevarthen was climbing over the rubble and disappearing into the steaming, smoking wreck. Mr Furniss followed as recklessly as had the mine owner and when he got inside he searched around in the gloom, trying to recognise the inside of the building that he had so recently left. The top half of the boiler had been blown completely off and was nowhere in sight, and its sides were pushed out as if they had been made of paper. Beams and bricks lay tumbled about all over the place, large sections of the walls had been blown away and the roof had gone. At first he thought that the body of Jarvis must have been thrown out through the building and was even now one of the corpses in the yard. Then he saw him, or the main part of him. His left arm had been blasted away above the elbow, but the rest of his body appeared to be slumped over the remaining portion of wall. Mr Trevarthen reached him first and, catching hold of the back of his shirt, pulled him off the wall, then let him go again with a cry of revulsion. Henry Furniss stopped just short of the body but he saw, as the mine owner had just done, that the body lacked a head. It was only to be expected; Jarvis had been in the engine house and would have caught the full force of the explosion. That there was so much of him left as there was, surmised Henry Furniss, was to be considered a miracle in itself. He heard the sound of a man retching in the corner. He waited respectfully before going forward, then taking hold of Mr Trevarthen's arm he gently led him back out the way they had entered.

"Gone in a second, sir," he observed prosaically, " 'E wouldn' knaw a thing, sir. Don't you fret yerself 'bout that."

Mr Trevarthen nodded in agreement, but his shocked face now turned to survey the scene of carnage that lay strewn about him. In his innocence, he thought some of the corpses were merely stunned by the force of the blast, but slowly he realised that they were dead and were left uncared for in the need to assist the living. With Mr Furniss to help him, he set about having the dead identified and removed to one of the sheds, then gave instructions for them to be washed and made as presentable as possible before they were to be conveyed to their respective homes. The mine doctor had already been called up from Penzance and when he arrived, he set about bandaging and splinting, enlisting the help of some of the bal maidens and miners to assist him. Some, although physically uninjured, could help no one. A few sat on the ground in a dazed state, the others ran around crying and screaming; there was no one to help them, for all the efforts now were being concentrated on the injured and deceased. Paul sent men to local farms to borrow carts and wains, anything with which to transport the injured. Just as he thought the hell he had found himself in could get no worse, a cry went up from a group of miners standing by the head of the shaft.

"She's floodin'!" came an excited cry. Paul and a group of men ran over to the shaft but the miners were coming up, one at a time, scrambling up the ladder with all speed. He got to the group and asked breathlessly, "Are they all safe?"

"All but Dicky Johns and 'is boy," one of the men told him, holding his side and catching his breath as he did so. "The boy was coming up behind we an' 'e slipped an' nearly knocked Dicky off the ladder. I 'eard the cry and the splash an' then Dicky went down after 'en." Paul pulled off his coat and was about to climb into the shaft, but the more able men stopped him. A short, wiry man pushed passed him, excusing himself, and took his place on the ladder. He disappeared from sight with great speed and it was not long before they heard a single word echo up through the shaft: "Drowned!"

A kibble was thrown down and they braced themselves to take the strain. Paul pulled alongside the men and after a while the kibble, now containing the body of Dicky Johns, swung into view. One of the miners leaned over the lip of the shaft and called down to ascertain if any other bodies remained.

" 'Ess," came the reply. Once more, the kibble was thrown down the shaft and when it returned for a second time, Paul felt the sting of tears as he gazed upon the fresh - faced boy who lay in it. The men lifted him out and laid him beside his father, in whose hand was clasped a part of the young boy's shirt, the ripped and soaked remainder of which still clung to the son's body.

"He has family?" enquired Paul, in a hollow voice.

"A missus an' five maids," said one of the miners, "Paul's 'is only boy."

"Paul?" Mr Trevarthen whispered.

" 'Ess, sir. Named 'en after 'e, sir. Proud work in yer mine, sir. Best in the county, Dicky says . . . said," he amended. Then he continued, briskly, "You can't do no more 'ere, sir. Best t' go 'ome. We'll clean up they two and take them over to Bessie's, don't 'e worry, sir."

"No!" Paul barked, "I'll do it! They worked for me and I will be the one to take them to their family." They were washed like the others, but had not yet been moved to the cart when a woman's scream filled the shed where the bodies had been temporarily laid out. Hearing the explosion, she had rushed over and now she knelt over her boy, crying like an animal in pain and calling him by name, over and over. The Master of Trevu left her to lament with the other women, unable to stand the cries of agony and despair that echoed all around him. He stood outside in the fresh air but could not rid himself from the feeling of complete and utter helplessness that had befallen him. He turned to Mr Furniss, who again assured Paul that he would take care of the terrible duties that lay ahead, remarking that Mr Trevarthen looked barely able to stand. Paul, however, insisted that he remain to help as best he could. So for the rest of that day, he took home the dead and wounded as need be, consoling the families as far as he was able. He spoke with various officials that travelled from Penzance. An engineer examined the engine, but it was so badly damaged that it was difficult to ascertain precisely what had happened. However, this venerable gentleman hazarded a guess that possibly a foreign object had blocked the steam release valve, or that perhaps there was no water in the boiler, something of that manner, and with the resulting increase in pressure the boiler had blown. Enquiries were made as to Jarvis's condition when he had arrived at his place of work that morning. Several of the miners and bal maidens who had seen him remarked that he was walking unsteadily and when questioned, Henry Furniss said that there was a strong odour of gin about the man. He lowered his eyes to avoid seeing the mortified expression on the mine owner's face.

When there was nothing more to be done, Paul mounted his horse and made his way back to Trevu and to his wife, who had received barely a word from him all day. Jonas Hampton had given her the details of the disaster; the explosion had been heard at Trevu and further afield, and various people had called in during the day to pass on more bad news as the details emerged. Chloe avoided questioning her distraught husband as he was clearly in no condition to speak of his experiences of that terrible day. She arranged a small meal for him in the parlour, but he seemed disinclined to eat and merely stared at the flames in the fireplace. He stayed there for most of the night. Not until the early hours did Chloe awake drowsily as the covers stirred and Paul crawled into bed beside her. She placed her arms around him but, after placing a brief kiss on her head, he lay immobile, staring at the ceiling. When the first rays of the morning sun began to peep in around the curtains, he arose, washed and dressed himself and left the bedchamber.

Mrs Gurney heard him close the door to his office and took it upon herself to prepare him a pot of tea and take it to him. She, like every member of the household, was aware that he had suffered terribly following the horrors of the previous day and should be paid particular attention. He smiled at her gratefully when she placed the tray on his table, and thanked her again for her kindness. She left him to his labours, but was saddened to see her master so worn and tired.

Later, Paul came to breakfast with his wife. He informed her that he preferred not to talk of the previous day's events and she was wise enough to maintain her silence over the matter. They spoke instead of the children, the farm, the forthcoming Penrose's ball, anything other than the event that had disrupted their community so tragically. When he returned to his office he took up his pen again and began to write furiously. When Jonas Hampton came to see him a little later he found that Paul was still engrossed in his writing and that various sheets of paper lay scattered across his desk. Again, at Paul's request they did not discuss the mining catastrophe but talked only of farming matters. During that long day, Mr Trevarthen was seen only when he took a break for his meals; even the children were kept from disrupting him, for their mother knew his mind was so set about with what he had to do that their presence would not be welcomed.

After that day, Paul's life was consumed by a round of funerals. He took it upon himself not only to attend every one of them but also to pay the costs. He had already arranged that money should be distributed amongst all the mining families; for those that had lost members of their household and those who had not, for with the mine being inoperative there would be no income generated for the miner's families. A report appeared in the local paper, giving a vivid picture of the disaster but praising Mr Trevarthen's concern and kind actions on behalf of the work force. As he read, a look of derision set into his features. In his opinion, he had done nothing and the greater part of him believed that in some way he had been responsible for the disaster.

Notices were issued, to be delivered to all who had connections with Wheal Sankey, either as workers, customers or suppliers. As Paul owned the mine and he was the sole financier, he had no adventurers to inform. All the expenses were laid at his door, as were the profits. The printed notice advised that a meeting was to be held at the Wheal Sankey Count House, on the Tuesday of the following week at eleven in the morning, asking all those notified to be present or, if unable to attend in person, to send a representative. Paul visited the town to see his bank manager and solicitor and what he had to tell those gentlemen made the colour drain from their faces. Despite their efforts to dissuade him, his mind was made up. He swore them to secrecy so as not to spread undue alarm amongst the populace and business community.

On the following Tuesday, at the appointed time and place, Paul Trevarthen stood in front of a packed audience in the Wheal Sankey Count House and announced that from that day forward the mine would be closed. There was a stunned silence, immediately followed by a tremendous uproar. The mine owner, standing alone on the raised dais at the end of the building, swallowed hard and in the face of the angry cries that were being directed at him called for order, which took no little time. However, his self-possession in the face of such an incensed crowd finally subdued them. And when he cleared his throat and began to speak, slowly and deliberately, there was not a person in the room who did not understand the sincerity of his words.

"My dear friends," he began, looking directly at each and every person around the room as he spoke, "I cannot explain to you how much it hurts me to have to close this mine. Wheal Sankey has been a part of my life since I can first remember. Some of you here will remember Captain Williams, a mine captain who worked here back in the eighties and nineties. John Williams was the first mine captain I ever knew and I shall always remember his belief in this mine and his never-ending enthusiasm for the lodes he was convinced it carried. However, irrespective of whether the mine is worth the working I can no longer allow it to continue to function in my name. The scene of destruction and despair that I witnessed last week will be forever embedded in my mind. I cannot continue to profit from your endeavours on my behalf; my conscience will not allow me to do it."

"Yer conscience won't feed we!" cried an angry voice from the back of the room. The crowd picked up his call and they rose as one, all shouting at him, some even shaking their fists at him. One man was so infuriated that he rushed towards him and, if it were not for his work-mates catching hold of him and pulling him back, Mr Trevarthen would have been dragged into their midst and thrown to the baying multitude. However, Paul would not be intimidated by them and he waited patiently until they became quiet before continuing with his speech.

"I am aware of the financial implications to all of us in this terrible time but I can assure all of you, from the youngest to the eldest, that monetary reparation has been set aside to provide you with an income comparable to that which you would have earned in a year," he resolutely announced.

This statement provoked another silence. No one in the room had ever heard such a thing before, yet more was to come.

"Those of you who live in the mine's cottages may continue to do so, for as long as you wish, without payment of any rent. If you find alternative employment and if you wish to remain in your home a fair - and I do mean fair - rent will be set upon the property," he expounded. "The injured will receive compensation relative to the injuries they have sustained. The widows, orphans and other dependants will receive a pension. A trust fund has been set up that will enable these payments to be made. Details of these arrangements will be given to you at the beginning of next week. Furthermore, within a short time I am seeking to found a training establishment, enabling those of you who wish to take advantage of learning a new skill to be given the opportunity so to do. To my suppliers, obviously I have no choice but to end my contracts with you, but a singular payment will be made in recognition of your services over the years. I cannot give my customers the same remuneration but I trust and believe that you will be able to find other mines that will wish to do business with you. No doubt, many of you will wish to discuss what I have had to say today amongst your families. But before you leave: I have arranged a small payment in lieu of this week's salary for the workers from Wheal Sankey, which may be collected from me. In conclusion, may we please have a moment of silence to remember all those who so sadly lost their lives here in the recent tragedy," and so saying, he removed his hat and bowed his head. The people gathered before him stared at him in wonder before joining him. When it was over, Paul walked over to a table set on one side of the dais and sat down behind it on the chair provided. He then took a key from his pocket, inserted it into the lock of a wooden box that sat directly in front of him and pushed back the lid.

At first, no one moved towards him. Then the miner who had attempted to pull him off the stage advanced towards the table and was the first to line up for his payment. Mr Trevarthen asked for his name and upon being given it, he made a mark against some writing on a long list of paper that he had removed from the box. He passed over a small leather bag and the man immediately tipped the contents into his hand. A quantity of coins tumbled into his palm and he quickly calculated their worth.

" 'Tis two pound, boys. Two pound!" he cried enthusiastically, his anger forgotten at his delight in receiving such a payment. From then on a steady stream of people came to Mr Trevarthen to collect their money. Some thanked him, others pulled their forelocks, widows shed tears and two women caught hold of his hand and kissed it. Slowly, the crowd disappeared from the room until at the last stood a group of three girls, holding hands and staring at him with large eyes. The tallest moved forward towards him and he asked the name of the person they represented.

"Dicky an' Paul Johns, Sir" replied the girl, staring at him in awe.

Paul's eyes became momentarily unfocused as he again saw the man and his son, lying soaked and dead in the dirt of the yard.

"Ah, yes," he said gently, "Mrs Johns' girls. And what are you called?"

"I'm Chloe," answered the tallest, who then roughly pulled forward first the girl to her left and then to her right, "an' this is Grace an' this is Daisy. Penny, she's the eldest, Penny's 'ome looking after Mother an' the baby." She paused

86

briefly before continuing, "An' the baby's called Sardi." Unbeknownst to Mr Trevarthen, Dicky Johns had taken the names from female members of Paul's family and given them to his girls.

Taking command of his emotions, he passed over two leather purses to the girl named Chloe, who thanked him. The next tallest of the three girls, her eyes still wide with wonder, asked, "Do it wash off?" but was at once silenced by her sister.

Paul smiled and replied, "No, it doesn't, Grace. My skin will always be this colour." Having been threatened with severe retribution by her elder sister for saying any more, she only nodded in response. But the youngest girl now plucked up some courage of her own and proclaimed in a shrill voice, "I d' like it. I fink 'e look . . ." but here she had to stop as she was given a shaking by the domineering Chloe. Paul held up his hand, signalling her to stop.

The youngest girl flashed her a look of triumph, took a step forward and finished her pronouncement by saying, "Pretty! I fink 'e look pretty!" At this point, Chloe quickly mumbled an apology on behalf of her sisters, then dragged them off the stage and hurried them away to disappear through the open door.

A smile slowly spread across Paul's face, but in time, like the girls, it disappeared. He looked around the now - deserted room. This mine had enabled his father to find the funds for his education, whether it was appreciated by Paul at the time seemed irrelevant now; it had allowed Redvers to invest in his farm, for Paul to divide his Trevu finances between himself and his half brother and to give them all a sound financial backing. The strain of the events of the past week had taken its toll and he found that tears were pouring down his face. There was nothing he could do to stop them, so he let them fall. They trickled down his face and splashed on to his tightly clenched hands. He then dropped his head on his arm and began to sob uncontrollably, the sound of his distress echoed around the deserted building and out into the yard.

Henry Furniss, standing alone by the open door, wondered if he ought to go in to console him, but he thought better of it. "Poor beggar!" he murmured softly to himself, then turned on his heel, walked out of the gate and along the familiar path to his home.

CHAPTER 11

THE door to the house in Chapel Street closed behind the tall man, who took off his soaking cloak and proceeded to shake it violently so as to remove the rain that was clinging to it. Janey rushed up from the bowels of the kitchen towards him and he flashed a smile at her as she took his cloak and hat. He did not receive an answering smile, which was unusual, but he presumed that she may have been busy in the kitchen and found it difficult to break away from her chores to come to his assistance. Joey had always felt slightly uncomfortable at having servants do the things for him that he knew he was perfectly capable of doing for himself.

"The mistress is in the withdrawing room with Mrs Penrose," she announced nervously, knowing full well that the Master detested the lady.

"Blast!" he uttered, unceremoniously, but he desired above all else to see his beloved and Joanna Penrose's presence was not going to stop him, so he strode resolutely towards the withdrawing room.

The ladies were taking tea when the door burst open. Mrs Bolitho's face broke into a delighted smile, and completely forgetting the presence of her guest, she got up from her seat and rushed towards her husband, who was advancing towards her with both arms outstretched. She disappeared in his crushing embrace before yielding wholeheartedly to a prolonged kiss. Mrs Penrose coughed pointedly and loudly, bringing a blush to Sarah-Jane's cheeks and a wicked smile to her husband's lips.

"I see you are returned, dear Mr Bolitho," she remarked in a brusque tone and fixed him with a hard stare of admonishment.

"Oh! Do forgive us, Joanna, but he has been away for ten whole days and I have missed him so," apologised Sarah-Jane, somewhat breathlessly.

"Quite!" she replied, curtly. She then fixed her eyes on Mr Bolitho, who returned her stare enigmatically. She considered him rude and uncouth, but most of all she thought of him as probably the most desirable male she had ever set eyes on, and had done so since first catching sight of him sauntering around Penzance in his smuggling days. Her dear mother had expounded at great length on the evil character of the man and Joanna knew she should always look upon him with disdain, but she found that as difficult as it was not to look at his wife without a stab of jealousy. Manville, her dolt of a husband, could in no way match up to the splendour of the man who stood before her. She admired his brother as well but that was for his money and charm as much for his handsome looks. It was the image of Joseph Bolitho that had always given rise to an uncomfortable sensation in the pit of her stomach.

"My apologies, Mrs Penrose, if my behaviour 'ave offended 'e," he said, but the smile that flitted across his lips implied that he could not care less what she thought. Even the slight bow he directed at her did not convey any sense of respect. She raised her eyebrow and looked him up and down, from his muddied boots to his dishevelled curly brown hair. When her eyes settled once more on his face, he grinned at her in a most unforgivable fashion and her bosom rose indignantly as she turned her face away in disgust.

"Dear Sarah-Jane, it has been so pleasant, as it always is, to sit and talk with you," said Mrs Penrose, making her farewells. Such a refreshing change from others of my acquaintance," she added, a glassy smile on her lips. At this point she rose from her seat and shook out her skirts. "I must not leave it so long before I call again, my dear, and indeed I long to hear more of your visit to . . ." Here she paused, looked at Joseph Bolitho's inscrutable face, and almost spat out the word, "Trevanoc!"

It was not rare for Mrs Penrose to disconcert people, such a cutting tongue as she had, but to see the angry look that settled on Mr Bolitho's otherwise inscrutable face was a personal triumph. She moved towards the door but neither the husband nor his wife went to open it for her, they both seemed rooted to the spot. Sarah-Jane stood with her hand over her mouth and a frightened look in her eyes, whilst her husband glared at his spouse with a look of such anger that Joanna Penrose trembled to see it. At that moment, Janey opened the door and, noticing that Mrs Penrose was advancing towards her, she dropped her a curtsey and took it upon herself to see her off the premises. She then returned to the tea tray that she had placed on a small table by the doorway, entered the room and set it down for her mistress to pour the master a cup of tea.

Mrs Bolitho was seated on the settle with her head bowed, twisting a handkerchief round and round in her hands. Janey had caught sight of the master's face and quickly left the room without exchanging a word with either of them. She rushed for the kitchen to inform the other servants that Mr Bolitho looked as if he was about to commit a murder.

"Won't be fer the furst time," observed the stable lad, laconically. He then helped himself to a hefty slab of cake and began to munch noisily. The cook, Mrs Nancarrow, caught him deftly around the ear with the end of the cloth that she was holding and sat down abruptly to converse with the other females in the room on the subject of Mr Bolitho's infamous temper and the imagined ructions that were taking place in the withdrawing room at that very moment. They sighed in sympathy for their poor mistress, but none would be brave enough to attempt admittance to retrieve the tea tray.

Joanna Penrose's naming of his aunt's house had so annoyed Joey that he was having a hard time in not laying hands on his wife and shaking her. In spite of Joey's formidable reputation, it was not in his nature to hit a woman, any woman, so his wife had no fear of being assaulted. She knew that he had been deeply wounded by the revelation and it was not as she had wished for him to discover the news of her visit.

"Well?" he thundered at her, "I'm waitin' fer an explanation, Sarah-Jane!"

She winced, then suggested tentatively that he sit down, to which suggestion he unloosed another blasphemous torrent. Doing her best to ignore him, Sarah-Jane poured a cup of tea with shaking hands and held it out to Joey, who took it and threw it, cup and contents, against the wall. Sarah-Jane jumped, then bowed her head and began to sob. Tears had always had a mitigating effect on his temper in the past, but today they did not seem to be calming the situation at all.

"I'm still waitin'!" he shouted.

Sarah-Jane steeled herself before explaining about the letter and how she could not possibly be so rude as to refuse the invitation. She asked defiantly what harm there was in going to see his aunt? Miss Bolitho had been so kind to her and had invited them both to call whenever they wished. At this announcement, Joey gave a groan of anger and dismay, then advanced towards her. She screamed in fright as he stopped beside her, for his face was so full of fury. Plucking the tray and its contents from the table, Joey sent it flying into the fireplace, causing Sarah-Jane to scream again. Now her husband was at the door and had wrenched it open.

Half rising from her seat, she stammered, nervously, "J..Joey, where are you going?"

"Out!" he flung back at her before slamming the door behind him. She heard his footsteps march across the hall, then a bang as the front door was violently pulled shut. Sarah-Jane sat back in her chair and gave way to her tears.

The merry crowd in The Seagull were stunned into silence when Joey Bolitho strode into the room. Most of them had known him all their lives and though they had not seen him in such a foul mood for a long time, they were wise enough not to question him. He tossed back four brandies in quick succession, then swept a fiery glance around the room. As one they bowed their heads and set to studying their ale or contemplating the non-existent polish on their boots and shoes. He threw down a quantity of coins on the counter, shouted to Josh Pascoe, the landlord, to 'buy 'em a drink' and left as angrily as he had come in. Returning to his home, he avoided the house, made directly for the stables and began to saddle himself a horse. A young stable boy offered to do it for him but was told, using a wide variety of expletives, that Joey Bolitho was perfectly capable of saddling his own horse. Outside the rain continued to pour down, but by now he was soaked already and could not care less if he was to get even wetter. He led the horse outside, threw himself across its back and sped out of the yard. At first he had no idea where he was going, but eventually he found himself on the road for Trevu. Upon entering the familiar yard he jumped down, gave up his horse to a young lad from the stables, and ran up the steps. Lizzie answered his frenzied knocking and was shocked by his appearance. She would have been a fool not to realise that he was in a furious temper, so she bravely took it upon herself to tell him that he was not to accost Mr Trevarthen.

"Why the 'ell not?" asked Joey angrily.

"On account of the disaster," she told him.

"What disaster?" he snapped.

"Wheal Sankey's boiler bin' an' blawed up," she replied firmly, " an' sixteen people killed."

This information stunned him into silence, allowing Lizzie to continue with the further news that Mr Trevarthen had closed down the mine because, he said, he would not be responsible for such a catastrophe again.

"Where is 'e?" asked a quietened Joey.

"In 'is study," replied Lizzie and asked if she should go and get him.

"No . . . no thank 'e Lizzie," he told her quietly. He took a deep breath and assured her that he had calmed down now and would not lay a finger on his brother.

"I'll fetch 'e up a cup a' tea," she told him, adding that he looked like he was in need of some. Joey, meanwhile, climbed the stairs and walked along the passage to the room that Paul used for his writing.

Joey knocked softly on Paul's door and upon opening it, Paul seemed as shocked at Joey's appearance as Joey was of his. They talked quietly for a while, then Paul sent him off to change his soaking clothes whilst he stoked the fire in the grate. Lizzie arrived with the tea and set it down on Paul's desk. She had had the foresight of putting two bowls of steaming broth on the tray along with some bread rolls. When his brother returned, they both turned their chairs to face the fire and consumed their food. Paul recounted details of the disaster to Joey and explained his reasons for closing the mine. His brother nodded in understanding, before relating with some difficulty that, on his return, he discovered his wife had been a visitor to Trevanoc whilst he had been away.

"Seems to 'ave taken a quite a shine to Aunt Leah," he muttered acrimoniously, "an' she to 'er."

Paul sighed and said that the longer he lived, the less he would understand the female sex, to which his brother agreed wholeheartedly. They continued to sit for a while in companionable silence, regarding the fire blazing in front of them. Lizzie entered the room to remove the tray, replacing it with another, which sported a bottle of wine and two glasses. As she set it down beside them, Paul politely asked if she could make up a bed for his brother.

"Already done it, sir," she informed him. She then told Joey that a stable lad had been sent to tell his wife not to worry, for he was staying the night with his brother and would return in the morning.

" 'Ow do 'e knaw I'll go tomorrow?" Joey demanded, peremptorily.

"Yer missus mean more to 'e than anybody walkin' this earth," replied Lizzie wisely, "an' yer as big a fool fer she as Paul 'ere is fer 'is missus." She then notified him that his clothes would be dried and pressed ready for him in the morning, before leaving the brothers to continue their interrupted discussion.

The following morning, after he had breakfasted he returned home, and it was a subdued Joey Bolitho who apologised to his wife for his behaviour on the previous evening. Sarah-Jane was relieved that her husband seemed to have forgiven her and sobbed into his lapel so copiously that he considered his coat might need drying again. He assured her that he would not refuse permission for her to attend upon his aunt, but added that he would not be escorting her and that she was not to encourage his aunt to believe that he would ever have reason to call upon her. Indeed, he was convinced that he had made his one and only visit to Trevanoc with his brother and that no situation would arise whereupon he would need to do so again

Joey had already informed his brother that he had altered his own business arrangements so that he would not have to spend so much time away from his home and, when he informed his wife of what he had done, she was delighted to hear of it. The thought struck her that she could make similar arrangements with regard to her hotels. She had employed managers to run them, but she was often called upon for advice. She found, as did her husband, that being away from her home so often did not suit her. She suggested that she broach the matter with her brother, William-John, as his eldest son, Simon, was a most estimable young man and she was sure he would be capable of taking over the running of her hotels, without detriment to either the business or to the customers. Joey agreed that this was an excellent suggestion. To arrive back from being on his business visits only to discover that his wife was staying the night at one of her hotels was always a disappointment to him. Sarah-Jane determined to visit her brother and to set her plan before him the very next day so, after breakfast the next morning, she gave her husband a loving embrace and set off in the coach for Falmouth. Left to his own devices, Joey took himself off to his library and began to sort through the assorted papers that had built up on his desk since his departure.

A short while later, his ruminations were abruptly cut short by a resounding crash, causing him to look up sharply. Before him stood a very distraught Janey, who had quietly entered the library carrying a tea tray for him, which she had dropped upon the wooden floor before she had reached his desk.

"Oh, sir!" she cried, "I'm some sorry, sir." But instead of picking up the broken crockery as Joey assumed she would attempt to do, she sat on a chair, hid her face in her apron and began to cry.

"My dear Janey, 'tis no matter," he soothed. "I bin an' broke a load of crockery meself this week. 'Twas an accident, I shan't make 'e pay the cost of 'em." But the servant only cried the louder.

"Oh! Mr Bolitho, sir," she sobbed, "I 'ave sinned. What's goin' 'appen to me now?"

"I dun a fair bit a' sinnin' meself, Janey," he began, still attempting to stem the tide of the poor girl's tears, "an' I'm still . . ." but Joey's voice trailed off as he took a closer look at Janey's face. The girl looked heavy-eyed and exhausted. Joey recalled Mrs Nancarrow's recent angry comments; that of late the stupid child seemed to be all fingers and thumbs. A thought then struck Joey and he closed his eyes, considering that perhaps this might be a matter best dealt with by his spouse. With a sigh he reconsidered: given the probable nature of Janey's distress his wife was, in fact, the very last person to whom this problem should be delegated.

"You in . . ." he began, hesitantly. He then coughed in embarrassment and began again, "You in trouble, Janey?" She nodded, trying hard not to sob aloud.

"I sinned with a man I met at Crowlas feast day, sir! 'E said 'e loved me, sir an' I kept to meetin' 'en on me days off. But 'e got took up for stealing, sir. An' now 'e bin sent off t' be transported," she sobbed, beginning to rock herself back and forth on the chair as she cried.

"I see," said Joey, slowly. He sat, pensive, for a while, then suggested to Janey that, as she had no family and provided she had no objection, then perhaps a suitable man could be found to take her to wife and accept responsibility for the child.

Janey shook her head and cried, "There 'idden no man goin' want this baby, sir."

"Of course there'll be somebody, dussen be s' silly," Joey began to tell her. But she put up her hand to stop him, saying that it would be impossible to find someone to stand as father for the child.

"My shiner, 'e worked the fairs an' feastins like I said, sir, but 'e was different, sir. 'E's a mulatto, sir!" and on saying the word she began to howl again.

This revelation shocked Joey Bolitho to his very core. Easy to explain away the fact that your servant had got herself pregnant by a fellow from the fair, easy to say that the fellow had been transported. How did he explain the colour of the forthcoming baby when his own brother was a mulatto? His brother, who so often stayed in his house when he had gone out upon the town, consumed too much alcohol and had to spend many a night under his brother's roof. Who would believe that the child was not Paul's? Very few in Penzance. They would love another scandal to be laid at the Trevarthen's door and what would the cruel gossip do to his brother and family? He thought for a moment before taking out his handkerchief and passing it to Janey.

"Now, Janey, dry yer eyes an' stop yer worryin'. I'll get somethin' sorted out fer 'e, don't 'e fret," he told her and gave her a confident smile.

She sniffed and attempted to smile back at him through her tears. He advised her to go to her room and wash her face and then to lie down for a while. Mrs Nancarrow would be informed that she had tripped while carrying the tea tray and had fallen badly that he had ordered her to her room to rest.

When she had left the room, Joey gathered up the broken china, placed it on the tray and carried it down to the kitchen. Mrs Nancarrow was appalled at the sight of him carrying his own tray, but Joey assured her that Janey was not to blame as she was currently unwell and was not be reprimanded in any way when she returned to the kitchen. Upon realising that Mr Bolitho had not even had the opportunity to drink his tea, Mrs Nancarrow hastily prepared him another cup, which he drank whilst sitting at the kitchen table, a habit of his that Sarah-Jane had been unable to break.

The tea refreshed him and gave him time to ponder, so when he had finished it he returned to his room, took out a sheet of paper and struggled to word a letter. When he had completed it to his satisfaction he gave it to his stable lad with an order to convey it to its destination. The fellow looked at him wide-eyed, then pushed the letter into his pocket, saddled his horse and set off as he had been directed. Upon his arrival he cantered up to the door of the large house, dismounted and handed over the message. He was invited in and sent to the kitchen, but was disappointed to find they had no alcohol. However, the quality of the food he was given to eat went some way towards alleviating his disappointment. Just after luncheon, he was called to the hallway where he was greeted, to his surprise, by a Negro of above medium height who handed him a letter, which he was instructed to convey to his master. Once again he set off for Penzance and carried out his task, after which he retired to the kitchen, where he told his fellow servants that he thought 'Mr Bolitho 'ad gone funny in the 'ead'. He then proceeded to inform them all where he had been that day. Their astonishment at his tale guaranteed him some excellent slices of the cook's fruit cake and as much ale as he could drink.

Meanwhile, his master read the reply to his letter. Finding the contents were as he wished them to be, he sat himself down in his withdrawing room to await the return of his wife with growing trepidation. He could swallow his pride and write to his aunt, asking her for a favour, but to tell his wife that their servant girl had fallen so easily for a child when Sarah-Jane was trying so desperately to conceive her own, he knew, would come close to breaking her heart. Her heartache in private was shared only with her husband. It mattered

93

not that he repeated what he had told her so many times before, that he was happy with his wife and had no need of children in his household. However, the more he told her that this was the case, the more convinced she became that her husband was suffering greatly because of her lack of fecundity. When Sarah-Jane returned, he put Janey's predicament before her as sensitively as he could. It was as he feared: after the shock of hearing the news, his wife raged that Janey should so easily conceive when all her attempts had been met with disappointment, but she had a kind heart and did not take out her grief and anger on the girl herself. She agreed with her husband that it would be impossible for their servant to remain in their household, with his brother such a frequent visitor. Paul must never know the precise details, for how would he feel when he realised that his brother had acted to ensure, in the greater part, that no breath of scandal should attach to the Trevu household?

Sarah-Jane retired to her bedroom, feeling unable to bring herself to talk to her servant with regard to the arrangements that had been made for her future. On closing the door, she fell face down upon her bed and began to sob uncontrollably. The injustice of the situation weighed down upon her and her heart ached that Janey, by her own gullibility, found herself in a condition that Mrs Bolitho was so desperately trying to emulate.

Meanwhile, her husband told Janey that, if she was agreeable, on the morrow he would convey her to his aunt's house, his aunt having stated that she could remain there as long as she wished to do so. He had stipulated that she was to suffer no recriminations regarding her condition and he had been given his aunt's word that this would be the case.

"She wen't mistreat 'e, that I knaw. But if 'e do agree to go, she will 'ave to inform 'er staff of yer predicament, 'cos she got a Negro who do work for her an' 'twouldn' be fair on 'e if when . . . when yer time do come 'e should be taken fer the father an' . . ." He paused, unsure of how to continue. Janey solved his problem by rushing across the room, catching up his hand and planting a kiss on the back of it. When she raised her face a delighted smile lay across her lips and her eyes were brimming with tears.

"Oh! Dear, dear Mr Bolitho!" she cried and began to sob. "You an' yer missus always bin so good t' me, an' now I brought this trouble t' yer 'ousehold you 'ent goin throw me out on the street, all on me own, an' I . . ." but Joey held up his hand and told her to stop.

"I can write t' me aunt sayin' 'e be willin' t' go?" he asked. She nodded through her tears and Joey presented her with another handkerchief, telling her to dry her eyes. He informed her that he would merely tell the household that she was moving to another establishment to work, in order to be near a long lost relative that she had recently discovered.

"There'll be a mite a' talk, Janey, but no matter," he observed. "I'll tell the staff now if you d' agree."

Janey blew her nose loudly, took a deep breath and then said, " 'Es, sir." She waited to be dismissed, and disappeared to her room for a while to take in the implications of how her life was about to change completely.

CHAPTER 12

AT THE top of the cliff, a man sat with his back against a rocky outcrop, staring out over the sea. From his vantage point he could see across the expanse of water known as the Mount's Bay. The tide was out and various people were making their way to and from the Mount by way of the causeway. Further out to sea, large sailing ships sat at anchor, awaiting the turn of the tide so that they could come in to the various harbours dotted along that coast. The numbers coming into Penzance were greater now than when he had been a boy. The town itself had an increasing population and was beginning to grow accordingly.

The winter sun shone pure in a cloudless sky and although it had not the warmth of summer, it was an enjoyable place to while away some time, sheltered as he was by the rock and the fact that the wind had eased. He often came here to sit and think and today was no exception. After all, the man faced a quantity of problems. However, his solitary contemplation was to be cut short. Hearing his horse give a whinny, he turned his head to see another rider on the point of dismounting and lifted his hand in greeting. The rider joined him and sat down with him in the lieu of the outcrop.

"Af'noon', Paul," said Joey.

"Good afternoon to you, Joey," greeted his brother, a smile on his face.

" 'Tis unusual see you up this way?"

"I called in to your home and your cook said this was where you would be, so I thought I would follow you here," Paul said.

"I come 'ere now an' again," Joey told him, then turned to face him when his brother enquired as to what had happened to his usual servant, Janey.

"She bin' an' brought some trouble on 'erself with the 'elp of a wayward man," he replied truthfully, "An' was thought bes' she left me employ."

"You did not throw her out, surely?" asked Paul, shocked.

"No, I didden!" replied his brother, indignantly, "but I could 'ardly keep 'er under my roof with me reputation bein' what it is. Sarah . . . Sarah-Jane's a bit upset by it all, what with 'er a tryin' fer children and then Janey fallin' fer one so easy, so all in all 'twas best she went away."

"Yes, yes," confirmed Paul, "I quite understand."

Joey Bolitho turned back to watching the scene before him. He waited patiently, knowing full well that his brother's natural inquisitiveness would lead to more questions. His supposition was soon to be proved accurate.

"Where has she gone, for she has no family and no one to take her in?" his brother enquired.

Bolitho stared steadfastly out to sea again and bit his lip; it would be best to tell his brother where Janey had gone, for although he would be unlikely to go to Leah Bolitho's again, there was always the possibility that he might.

"Trevanoc," he replied.

Paul was busily unscrewing the top of his hip flask as the word was uttered, and his brother's pronouncement made him fumble with his flask and almost lose the top over the cliff edge.

"You are not serious?" he expostulated. His eyebrows snapped together suddenly as he asked why she should be sent to his aunt's and who had arranged it. He could not, for one moment, believe that his brother had made submission to Leah Bolitho for Janey to reside with her although, knowing the lady, she would certainly be kind-hearted enough to take her in.

"I wrote me aunt a letter explaining the maid's predicament. See 'er fellow, well, 'e couldn't marry she 'cos 'e's on 'is way to Botany Bay by now. Like I told 'e, she couldn't stay with we so I made up a tale she 'ad found relatives out that way an' off she went, an' . . . thas' what 'appened," he concluded, hoping he had said enough, but knowing he had not fully slaked Paul's thirst for information.

"But who took her to Trevanoc, for surely she would not have travelled to a strange house unaccompanied?" asked the ever enquiring Paul.

Joey sighed, closed his eyes and said bluntly, "I did." At the precise moment his brother made this announcement, Paul was taking a sip of his brandy. The shock of what he had heard made him open his mouth in surprise, with the inevitable result that he consumed rather more alcohol in one swallow than he had intended. His brother was forced to slap his back to help ease the fit of coughing that ensued. He waited until Paul had regained his breath and had wiped his streaming eyes before continuing. He recounted that he had no choice but to take his servant, as he could hardly have despatched the poor girl with the stable lad all unknowing and he would not put the strain of the journey upon his beloved wife. "Sarah-Jane 'ave took it bad, Paul," he explained, "an' I was the one who asked, so 'twas only right I should be the one to go with her to meet me aunt."

"What did Miss Bolitho say to you? More importantly: what did you have to say to her?"

"She started to 'arp on about the Good Samaritan, but I told 'er I'd rather not 'ear it an' . . . an' I thanked 'er fer what she had done an' I gave 'er a purse of money fer Janey," he ended in a rush.

"What happened then?" asked Paul, agog with the story he was hearing.

"She . . . she thanked me," said Joey, not wishing to tell his brother that his aunt had insisted on catching hold of his hands and pronouncing that he was a living saint for his care of another. Of a certainty, he was not going to disclose to him that he also submitted to be kissed on the cheek by her. "An' then I come 'ome," he said flatly, giving his brother a warning stare.

After a moment, Paul shut his mouth, which had been hanging open, and took note of his brother's expression. Past experience warned him that he would be wise to change the subject. He considered, prudently, that he was too close to the cliff-edge to question his brother further whilst he wore that expression on his face.

"Most commendable, Joey," he firmly announced and pushed the open flask towards him. His brother took a large swig of the contents for, after that difficult explanation, Joey felt in need of it. If Paul wanted to imagine that the Bolitho clan had been reunited, so be it. Joey would not be the one to divulge the rest of the conversation with his aunt, during which he had firmly informed her that, although he was indeed grateful to her, he saw no need to visit her again, in either the near or distant future. The disheartened expression that had fallen across the old lady's face disconcerted him somewhat and had come back to play upon his mind since. It was for that reason he had come to this point on the cliffs, his favoured place, where he came whenever something had occurred to agitate him and he had need of the calming effect of solitude.

"Best be goin' on," Joey abruptly announced, pointing to the clouds that had suddenly built up towards the southwest.

"Yes, of course," agreed his brother, "I thought to head back by way of Gwavas. Would you wish to accompany me?"

"Might as well," agreed his brother and in a short space of time, the two men were making their way along the lane towards the small village. Their attention was drawn to a notice pinned to a gate, whereon nearly every word had been misspelled The sign warned that the 'turnaps' in the adjoining field belonged to the farmer and anyone stealing them would be arrested. Their grins disappeared immediately as they heard a loud shout and looking over the hedge they spotted the farmer, Percy Eustace, with his shotgun in his hands. He was oblivious to them, however, and as they watched he suddenly levelled his gun at something that moved amongst his crop of vegetables. Bolitho, following the farmer's line of sight, spurred his horse towards a gap in the hedge below the gate and jumped into the field. Whatever it was the farmer could see, Joey espied it, too. He set off across the field, his horse's hooves committing much damage to the turnips as it galloped towards the farmer. However, Eustace, on realising that he had a trespasser on his land, now turned his gun towards the horseman. His finger squeezed the trigger, but then relaxed as he recognised the rider. Immediately, he threw his gun to the ground, closely followed by his hat and began to shake his fists with impotence. Joey Bolitho was unconcerned with his own safety and would have continued to ride straight at the farmer if he had not lowered his gun. However, now that the danger had passed he turned his roan and headed down the row towards a crouching figure, trying to hide between the rows of vegetables. A small boy with a shock of bright ginger curls stood up, holding some turnips in his hands, and catching sight of the horseman careering down upon him, turned and ran as fast as he could towards the hedge. The young lad was somewhat hampered by a severe limp and in his arms he was trying desperately to contain the vegetables that he had acquired in the field. Two terrified eyes, set in a filthy face, were turned towards Bolitho, who was now upon the lad. Bending down from his saddle, he caught hold of the thief by his shirt and hauled him up into his arms. Joey was surprised at how light the boy was and concerned to feel the bones under his clothes. He held him as firmly as he could without hurting the child, but the fear felt by the lad made him struggle. His booty of turnips had been lost when he had been plucked from the ground, all except for one. In an attempt to make an escape, he held on to the foliage and swung the hard, round root at his attacker. The turnip thudded into the side of Bolitho's left temple, quickly followed by a small fist, which delivered a blow to his nose, bringing tears to Joey's eyes. The child, whose arms were free to defend himself, then launched into a frenzied attack upon his captor, delivering all his puny muscles would allow. Joey, on the other hand, was attempting to remain seated on his horse and to control his struggling captive at the same time. He failed, however, due to the unprecedented attack to which he was being subjected and realising he was about to fall, held on grimly to the child as he fell from his roan's back, landing with a thump on the earth. His horse took off but Paul, who had followed his brother into the field and was by now at the end of the row, caught the animal by the reins before it could make its make way home. Getting up from his ignominious position in the mud, Joey, swearing profusely, wrenched the offending weapon from the child's hand and tossed it away. The farmer, swearing with equal ferocity, rushed up to him and began to berate Bolitho for galloping all over his crop.

"You 'ent no farmer, Bolitho, 'cos' yer brother managed ride 'is 'oss roun' the 'eadland but you bin' an' ruined me crop!" he stormed.

" 'Ere!" shouted Joey, trying to feel in his pocket for some money whilst hanging on to the human eel. He threw some coins at Percy Eustace. "That will cover the cost a' the damage," he said angrily. "An' what was 'e a thinkin' of? I seen 'e! Goin' shoot the little beggar!"

"I thought 'e were a fox!" returned Farmer Eustace, much red in the face.

"Fox me a . . ." began Joey, but was cut short by his brother, who had arrived on the scene and advised him to watch his language in front of the child. Paul automatically held out his arms for the struggling infant. The poor unfortunate took one look at the dark man before him and recoiled in horror, then threw his arms around his assailant's neck and hung on for grim life.

"A devil!" he shouted, and then screamed, "Git away you!"

Paul's brother gave the frightened child a shake, telling him not to be such a stupid fool, but it hurt him to have to witness the expression on his brother's face at the ignorant insults that had been directed at him.

"What's yer name?" Joey asked his captive.

"Boy Nicky," replied the child grumpily.

"Nicky what?"

Here the farmer supplied the vital information, "Thas' Nicky Nankivell. 'Is mother's gone as a ladies maid up country an' left 'im with 'er brother an' 'is wife 'bout a year since. Then they went to go for Amerikee, an' not 'avin' any family left 'ereabouts they brought 'im up 'ere to live with 'is grandmother, ol' Mrs Glasson. Well, she's 'spose be 'is grandmother on account of 'er boy, Nicky, was 'spose marry 'is mother, Lucy Nankivell, 'cos 'e got 'en on she, but then 'e went an' . . ." Here, Percy Eustace paused for a moment, before bravely looking Joey in the eye and concluding, ". . .'e went an' disappeared."

Joey Bolitho's face registered nothing but his brother gasped, unable to stop himself. They both stared at the bright ginger curls that lay all over the little boy's head and each saw in their mind's eye the nervous, ginger-haired youth with the withered hand and the golden guinea that had tumbled to the floor.

After a short silence, Bolitho asked for the grandmother's direction, as he thought it best to return the boy to her care. The farmer pointed to a run-down cottage set on its own at the end of the village, warning them both that Mrs Glasson was silly-headed.

"Either she's out runnin' round in the middle a' the night with 'e in tow shoutin' fer Nicky to come 'ome or else she idden seen fer days. Queer beggar she is, always 'ave bin'," he said, stooping to retrieve the coins that Joey had tossed him. Counting them, he smiled to discover what largesse he held in his hand, then turned away from the men and walked back to where he had left his hat and gun.

"What . . . what are you going to do, Joey?" asked Paul, in awe.

"Take 'im back to Mrs Glasson's," he said quietly, avoiding his brother's eyes. With this intention, he set off down the field, still clutching the child, and headed towards the corner gate that led into the field from the road. Paul retrieved the horses and caught up with him. When they were safely out on the road, Joey strode out purposely for the property that the farmer had indicated.

Once there, Joey knocked on the door. The child gazed at him, before informing him that Nana would not reply because she was sleeping.

"How long 'as she bin' asleep?" asked Joey, a shade of concern in his voice.

"Dunno," replied the lad, studying with fascinated interest the red bump that was beginning to form on the side of the man's head.

Pushing open the door, Bolitho knew at once why Mrs Glasson should still be in her bed. His brother, with his usual, almost childish innocence, asked what the sweet, sickly smell was. For answer, Joey walked across to the bed that contained the old woman and flipped the meagre blanket over her head. The room had precious little in the way of food; some flour on the floor had the marks of small fingers running across it, as if a little hand had tried to scoop it up. A tallow candle lying on the table had been gnawed, some pots lying on their side had been scraped clean. One of the pots had been broken and the contents had spilled across the floor; coins of every denomination lay where they had rolled. The room itself was cold, but unburned sticks had been pushed into the dead embers of the fire as if an attempt had been made to keep it ablaze.

The man, holding the child, turned on his heel and left the house at once, heading towards the nearest cottage. Paul, sensibly, retrieved the money that lay on the floor, for it had belonged to Mrs Glasson and by rights should belong to her grandson. Meanwhile, Joey, who had arranged payment of the same money to the old woman since the disappearance of her son, made his way, with a stony expression and a troubled heart, towards the first cottage set by the roadside. There the neighbour, a ruddy faced middle-aged woman, confirmed that Mrs Glasson had not been seen for over a week. This was not considered uusual, she explained, as Mrs Glasson liked to keep herself to herself, so she had not called upon her to ascertain if all was well. Joey felt again in his pocket but having no coins remaining, asked his brother to purchase some soup or milk for the boy from the woman in the cottage. A cup of warm milk was procured, which the starving waif drank in such haste that he succeeded in spilling a fair amount over the collar of the man's coat.

"We'll take him back to Trevu," announced Paul, authoritatively, intending that the boy should stay with him for the time being. Joey, however, told Paul he would be grateful if he would, instead, inform the authorities, as he intended to take the boy to his own home. Shocked, Paul advised him to consider the possible consequences of this proposal.

"What will you tell Sarah-Jane?" he asked incredulously.

"Dunno!" snapped Joey. Then, still holding tight to his captive he mounted his horse and headed back to Penzance with his brother riding at his side, querying all the time the sense of his proposed actions. They parted company at the constable's house and Bolitho rode on to his own home. The dirty little waif nestled against him and yawned unconcernedly, the warm milk had made him tired and the man had unbuttoned his coat and lapped it around the child; the warmth from the fabric and the man's body was most enjoyable. He had missed being cuddled by his grandmother and could not understand what he had done that had made her so angry, that she had stopped wrapping her arms around him at night and keeping him warm.

The stable lad gawped when he was passed the sleepy, filthy infant to hold. The mud clinging to his master's clothes and the large contusion on the side of his head caused his jaw to drop further, but he lowered his eyes when Joey stared directly at him and passed the child back without a murmur into Mr Bolitho's waiting arms. Inside the house, Mrs Nancarrow could hardly believe her eyes, but she set about at once to arrange a bath for the filthy scrap of humanity. The child, however, was now awake and would not leave go of the man who had given him the warm milk. In his mind, a saviour had appeared who fed him and held him tight to keep him warm, and he wanted no other. Once in the bathroom, this vision of a saint rapidly vanished, but between the two of them the adults managed to remove his sparse, ragged clothes and the screaming, fighting child was carefully placed into the sweet smelling, warm water. It was obvious, when they removed his clothes, that he had badly damaged his foot at some stage, so they washed the cut carefully and removed some of the dirt that was in the open gash. The rest of the child's body was scrubbed until it shone pink, a circumstance that the boy clearly did not approve of; his howling and wailing rent the air in the entirety of his immersion.

Once it was considered that the child was clean enough, he was removed from his torture and wrapped in a large, soft cloth. He was then subjected to a vigorous wiping before being placed in a shirt that Mrs Nancarrow produced from the linen press.

"I'll send out fer some clothes fer 'en, Mr Bolitho, sir, but this shirt of yours will do fer now," she announced, deftly placing the child in the garment. She wrapped the ties around his tiny wrists and at his neck and when she had finished, all that was to be seen was a large amount of white material with two small hands and a head of ginger hair sticking out of it. The child, now sitting on Joey's lap, was still bawling but with less conviction, it was noticed.

"I'll send Minnie to air the spare bed," she told Joey briskly over the head of the crying child and disappeared, only to appear in a trice with a bowl of hot milk in which were soaking some pieces of bread. Immediately, the crying stopped and two hands shot out towards the bowl, but the man held it by the rim for him whilst Mrs Nancarrow placed a spoon in one of his hands. He was a young child and not adept at handling the utensil so once again, Mr Bolitho was to find himself liberally spattered with some of the contents of the bowl. The rest disappeared into the ravenous boy in a very short space of time.

Once the bedroom had been prepared, a very sleepy infant was placed between the warm sheets and, after his exertions of the day, was soon fast asleep. Joey, clearly relieved, asked if it would now be possible to bathe himself. Mrs Nancarrow assured him that she had put more water to boil as soon as he had come in, as he was clearly quite filthy himself. He briefly explained some of the details concerning the child's appearance into his household, assuring her that the stay was a temporary one until they could trace the child's mother and return her son to her. His housekeeper nodded, having no wish to query his explanation and, once his bath had been prepared, she left him alone. Once washed, Joey dressed himself and stared into the mirror, regarding the bruise to the side of his head with a rueful grin on his face.

"The little beggar's a fighter, I'll say that fer 'en," he murmured to himself. Suddenly, the door was flung open behind him, causing Joey to swing around, sharply. His wife stood on the threshold, her eyes blazing with anger.

"How dare you, Joey! How dare you!" she cried. She made his heart melt when he saw her, so beautiful did she look in her anger. This was not the time to tell her so, however. He assumed, correctly, that Minnie had informed her about the uninvited guest slumbering unconcernedly in the bedroom and she had great difficulty in controlling her emotions in front of her servant. There was no need to adopt such control in front of her husband, however, so she ran across the room and dealt him a hard slap across his cheek.

"You should have asked me before you brought your by-blows in to this house, husband!" she blazed at him, before bursting into tears and running from the room. For a moment, he stood still, shocked at her assumption, but then he realised it would be a natural mistake to make. He had hardly behaved in the manner of a monk in earlier years, after all. Running after her, he was halfway along the corridor when he heard the door firmly shut and the key turn in the lock. Never in their marriage had such a thing ever happened to him. Knocking on the door and calling out to his wife with a string of endearments produced an answer, but not the one he wanted. Aware that he was no longer alone, he turned to find Mrs Nancarrow at his elbow, bearing a tea tray.

"There's a tray set out fer you in the parlour, Mr Bolitho, sir," she informed him, in a firm, no-nonsense tone. "Off you go now, sir, an' if I 'ave any messages fer you I'll bring them myself." Joey had no intention of leaving, but Mrs Nancarrow nodded silently at him, then inclined her head in the direction of the stairs. "Best let a woman reason with a woman, sir," she advised him in a whisper. Joey, shaken and bemused, retraced his steps along the corridor and headed down the stairs towards the parlour.

Fifteen minutes later, his wife threw open the door and rushed towards him before he had the time to get out of his chair. She cast herself upon his chest and sobbed for his forgiveness for her false accusations.

"Mrs Nancarrow explained all to me! I should have realised, for you are such a kind and caring man. Of course, you could not have left the poor child there with his dead grandparent and who else would take him into their home as you would do, apart from Paul, of course? Such a thing as he called Paul tho'! I will explain to him that he must not say such things to people, but I expect that . . ." but she got no further, as Joey required nothing more. He kissed her into silence, then lifted her on to his lap and held her in his arms, a smile of complete contentment on his face. Yet, at the back of his mind lay a problem: the identity of the child's father. However, once he had succeeded in finding the whereabouts of Lucy Nankivell, her son could be packed off to her, along with a box of good clothes and some money, at which point his life would return to normal. Demanding another kiss, Joey almost crushed his wife with the strength of his passionate embrace, blissfully unaware of the consequences that sleeping child would bring upon the household.

101

It was the morning after young Nicky had entered his household and the doctor had been called to examine the badly damaged foot. He had sucked in his lips and shaken his head after making his examination. The flesh around the wound was beginning to putrefy and he could think of no way to save the foot with the medicines available to him. Without removing it, his patient would be doomed, for it would soon cause poisoning of the blood and in such an undernourished child his chances of survival were slim. Admittedly, the shock of cutting off the foot could just as surely kill the boy, but at least this measure was an attempt to save him. To leave the wound untreated would condemn the infant to certain death.

"What 'e mean?" demanded Joey of the doctor, "It can't be saved." The young boy who lay on the bed regarded both men with a worried expression. His foot lay uncovered and the two men were staring at it with concern.

"If it had received treatment earlier, Joey, perhaps something could have been done," determined Dr Dunstan, "but I fear that it will poison the blood now and he will not survive." He placed his hand on Bolitho's shoulder and said softly and with concern. " 'Tis for the best, Joey, and if he survives he will learn to manage with only the one foot." Revolted, Joey shook Denzil's comforting hand away, "No!" he cried, "I will not 'ave it done to 'en. 'E's suffered 'nuff. I'll fix 'en meself," and with those words he marched from the room, slamming the door behind him.

Joey strode through Penzance, a determined expression on his face. The thought that, after all the poor child had suffered, he was now to be subjected to such an operation that the consequences would probably kill him, he could not accept. Something he had read in some long-forgotten book had crept into his mind and he determined that he would prefer to try this method of healing, rather than submit to any of the procedures that Denzil Dunstan would wish to use. Turning a corner, he marched into Frederick Annear's butchery establishment and stood foursquare in the tiny shop.

A couple of local woman, baskets on their arms, looked in surprise to see him there. Freddy Annear himself scowled at Joey, his memory still vivid of the day he had been knocked to the ground as a youngster by Bolitho, merely for calling the Trevarthen mulatto names. Over the years, the grudge had festered and he had no intention of being polite to the man; the circles that Joey Bolitho now moved amongst did not contain the sort of clientele that would deign to set foot in his shop. Swatting aside a persistent bluebottle, he enquired, rather rudely, as to how he could be of service.

"Will you be wishing to pay fer the goods, Mr Bolitho, sir, or will 'e steal it, like 'e always used to when Father 'ad the runnin' of the place?" he asked in a surly voice.

Unabashed and seemingly oblivious to three more customers that had entered the small room that served as a shop, Mr Bolitho merely smiled and announced in a loud voice that he required half a pound of Mr Annear's best maggots. The ladies uttered shocked cries of disgust at his statement and Mr Annear's red cheeks now deepened to purest crimson. Struggling to maintain his composure, he snarled that he did not harbour such creatures on his premises and he would prefer that anyone who said such a thing should take their custom elsewhere.

"I would, if I could be sure of gettin' what I'm after," announced Joey, with a derisive curl to his lip, "but in my stealing days, 'twas always the meat from this place that I 'ad fight the maggots over." Two of the customers, identical expressions of disgust on their faces, removed themselves from the shop and its vicinity as fast as their legs could carry them. The remaining customers, looking decidedly unsettled, continued to watch this altercation with interest. At once, the butcher realised that, disreputable as he was, Joey Bolitho's word would carry more weight in the community than his own.

"Ladies," he purred, "of course, when 'e didden 'ave nawthin' in 'is young years, poor Mr Bolitho 'ere 'ad do 'is best to feed 'iself with whatever means 'e could. 'E was forever goin' roun' the back an' stealin' from me yard, where any bad meat be put," he emphasised loudly. At this point, he appealed to Mr Bolitho for assistance. " 'Idden that so, sir?" he asked, the desperation in his voice obvious to all.

"Of course, 'tis true, Mr Annear," confirmed Joey, unabashed at the change of tone in the butcher's voice and smiling graciously at the remaining customers. "Mr Annear is most particular that 'e should sell only the best to such discernin' ladies, I can assure you. Anythin' that is not of the 'ighest quality is discarded at once, an'..." he paused at this point and directed his most charming smile at each of the ladies in turn, before continuing smoothly, "...if it were not fer that fact, I would not 'ave bin' able to maintain my existence. Now, ladies, consider this," and he paused again for dramatic effect. "If I d' look like this from stealin' meat Mr Annear 'ere would not dream of sellin', what will the result of eating 'is good meat be on your progeny?" The customers gazed in wonder at the tall, well built man before them, who glowed with health.

Mr Annear, taken aback by such a compliment, was momentarily stunned by his adversary's words. However, he recovered himself quickly and invited Mr Bolitho to come through to his back yard, where the 'discarded' meat was kept. They passed through to a high-walled area, where various carcasses swung from hooks attached to the beams of a shed with a low roof. The smell was enough to turn the stomach of most people and even Joey Bolitho, made of sterner stuff than most, almost gagged at the foul aroma. Mr Annear, beaming in anticipation of the increase in sales that Mr Bolitho's unlooked-for proclamation of the benefits of his wares would produce, busied himself with procuring the man's requirements at once. Espying a side of beef that appeared to be heaving with the creatures, he picked up a small, wooden box that lay discarded on the bench and proceeded to sweep a quantity of maggots into it. Ever the businessman, he carefully levelled the top, found a dirt encrusted piece of sacking and bound it around the box so that its contents would not spill out. Turning to his new customer, he presented him with the carefully wrapped container and announced with a complete lack of irony, "Four pence 'apenny, if you please, Mr Bolitho, sir."

"Cheap at 'alf the price, Mr Annear," replied Joey, unabashed, then tossed a coin in his direction. "An' please to keep the change." Clutching his purchase in one hand, he tipped his hat at the butcher and turned to retrace his steps through the shop, bowing politely to the admiring ladies as he did so. Mr Annear wiped the remaining maggots from his hands, slapped the rump of the decaying carcass with glee and returned to confront his customers. "Now, Mrs James, what will it be for you today?" By the end of that day, so quickly had word spread of Mr Bolitho's commendation of the efficacious effects of eating this particular butcher's meat, that all that remained on his premises of the revolting side of beef was the hook from which it had hung. The remaining maggots now writhed over a particularly revolting lump of putrid beef in a large pot, placed carefully at the side of the shed. A strange request indeed, considered Freddy Annear to himself, but perhaps Mr Bolitho might require more and he would not wish to disappoint him.

When Joey returned to his home, he immediately set Mrs Nancarrow to melt him one of her tallow candles and then, carefully carrying the box and a pan containing the melted wax, made his way up the stairs to the spare bedroom. When he arrived, Dr Dunstan was still present, for he had taken it upon himself to explain to Mrs Bolitho that, in his professional opinion, nothing could be done to assist the child other than to carry out the operation that he had previously recommended to her husband. All eyes turned to the door as Joey entered. He advanced across the room and placed the box and the pan down on the table at the side of the bed.

"Now, me lad," he said breezily to Nicky, "let's see what we can do fer 'e." The wax was allowed to congeal, before Bolitho carefully moulded it into an oval shape and placed it around the edge of the wound. The child clamped his lips together firmly when the hot wax touched his skin, but he had complete trust in this man and did not utter a sound.

"Thas' a good fellow," Joey encouraged. His wife, however, gasped with revulsion when he untied the sacking from the box.

"My God, man!" exclaimed Dr Dunstan. "What are you thinking of? That practice is antediluvian! I must protest..." but he was cut short by Mr Bolitho, who advised him that he had no need to stay as his services were no longer required. Denzil Dunstan, like the child, clamped his mouth firmly shut. A healthy man like Joey Bolitho might rarely require his services, but his wife was a frequent visitor to his establishment and had purchased all manner of potions in her desperate attempts to get herself with child. He had no wish to lose the custom of this particular household, so he maintained an exasperated silence.

Carefully, the amateur practitioner placed a quantity of the smallest maggots into the hollow formed by the wax and politely requested a length of bandage from Dr Dunstan. He bound the boy's leg, enclosing the maggots, wax and wound carefully in a soft cocoon of lint. Then, well satisfied with his efforts he explained to the boy that, in a few days time, they would unwrap the bandage and look to see what had happened. The boy smiled brightly at him, but upon being told that he could not leave his bed and would have to stay there for the duration, his face fell.

"I want go fer a look roun'!" he protested loudly.

Joey sighed, but repeated his instructions. A mulish expression settled across the boy's face. "I wen't!" he pronounced, angrily.

"Don't 'e cross me, me 'ansome, else I'll slap yer . . ." A loud cough from his wife halted his words before they could slip, unguarded, from his tongue.

"I shall send at once for some books and toys for you, dear," she brightly announced. At these words, the boy's face immediately broke out into a beaming smile.

"Fank 'e missus," he said with delight. He knew well enough the meaning of the word 'toy' but what he was supposed to do with a book, he was less sure.

However, he had never been given much in his young life, so he was grateful for any gift.

During the next few days, the child demanded almost constant attention as he lay imprisoned in his bed. It was during this time that Joseph Bolitho attempted to discover the whereabouts of the boy's mother and, when he ascertained the name of the family she worked for and their direction he despatched a letter immediately. It was unfortunate that the girl should no longer reside in the county, but he assumed that it would not be long before she was to be reunited with her son. In the days that followed, he discovered just how much time and energy needed to be devoted to a child of Nicky's age in order to keep him amused. Joey read all of the stories in every book he could obtain that was suitable for a young boy and had sent to Trevu in desperation when he had exhausted his supplies. A box arrived by return, carried by Mr Trevarthen himself and, although Nicky regarded him with trepidation, the contents of the container filled him with delight. There were brightly painted carved animals of every description, a large boat and some carved people as well. The top of the boat could be removed so that all the animals and people could be placed inside and when he shook it violently they made a loud, rattling sound, which gave him immense enjoyment. There were books, too, with pictures of all sorts of things inside them: animals, birds and so many pictures of objects that he had no idea what they were called. Perhaps, reasoned the child, Mr Trevarthen was not a devil after all just as the kind lady had told him? His demands that someone should read to him or play with him were always met with a smile, even though, on occasion, the people he asked appeared to be wishing themselves somewhere else. His best friend, the man with the strange name, was his favourite playfellow because he seemed to pay him more attention than any of the others. He never seemed to tire of reading to him or of playing with the toys; he had even mended the wheel of the little wooden cart, which fell off because the little boy had banged it with too much enthusiasm on the bedside table. All in all, to have to be confined to his bed was not so very bad as he had anticipated. He had received a variety of appetising bowls of food at regular intervals and he marvelled that the supply should appear as if by magic, without his having to do anything. He had his own little night-shirt, too, which did not scratch his skin as his old clothes had done. In fact, when the day dawned upon which his bandage was to be removed, Nicky felt a high degree of disappointment, as the horrible thought occurred to him that he was now to be totally ignored.

Dr Dunstan had asked if he could attend, in order to witness the outcome, as he had a professional interest in the results of Mr Bolitho's intervention. Sarah-Jane did not wish to be present, for although she had great faith in her husband's abilities, she was worried that he could not possibly be successful in this instance, having had no medical training whatsoever. When the lint binding was rolled away, Joey carefully set about displacing each maggot with a tweezers. When this was completed, he stared at the pink, healthy flesh that lay exposed in the wound. Dr Dunstan asked to see the result and stared at the injury in disbelief, even going so far as to study it further with the aid of a magnifying glass. After a moment, he replaced his glass before holding out his hand unreservedly to Bolitho.

"I should not have believed it, Joey, if I had not seen it with my own eyes. You are to be congratulated, and this young lad here will thank you his life long for your efforts on his behalf," he said, shaking Joey by the hand and indicating the patient with the other. Young Nicky, smiling happily, was not at all sure what this strange man was talking about, but he beamed at his friend just the same.

Mr Bolitho gave an embarrassed cough, "Thank 'e, Denzil. Now whas' to be done with it? Can't leave it like that."

The doctor announced with authority that it would be best for the wound to be sewn together so that the healing process could be completed. Mr Bolitho nodded in agreement and then explained to the little boy that this time he would have to be very brave indeed. The boy looked wary, for he had discovered that when grown ups talked about being brave, it invariably led to a painful experience on his part. His friend moved across the bed to his side and proceeded to hold him tightly.

Sarah-Jane, downstairs in the parlour, dropped her book and placed her hand over her ears so as not to hear the poor child's screams. Tears cascaded down her face, both in sympathy with the poor angel's distress and because her husband had obviously failed to improve the condition of the wound. After a while, the screams subsided to a sobbing, then stopped completely. She then heard a man's footsteps descend the stairway, but they did not belong to her husband; it was to be a little while later before she heard Joey's tread on the stairs. He looked sombre upon entering the parlour, causing his wife to burst into tears before he had a chance to open his mouth. He came towards her and comforted her, then laughed when she remarked how terrible it was, that the lad had lost his poor foot in spite of Joey's efforts.

"What 'e talkin' bout, sweet'eart? Denzil sewed up 'is wound, thas' all. Got a powerful set a' lungs, that lad," he added with conviction, his ears still ringing with the sound.

"Has he not had his foot removed?" she asked, her face brightening immediately. Joey nodded and she hugged him in relief. Her husband went on to explain that Nicky had been given a potion to make him sleep, as it was thought best that he should rest after his experiences of the morning. Sarah-Jane gave a sigh and allowed herself to be cradled in her husband's strong arms. After a while, they set to talking about the young lad's imminent return to his mother. They could not imagine, either of them, any event that would not lead to the little boy being sent to stay under his mother's roof. Of course, they determined that money should be made available for Lucy Nankivell, to enable her to care for him properly and also to purchase a quantity of clothing suitable for a lad of his age and size. Joey was prepared to travel with the boy to ensure that he arrived safely, though he did not relish the prospect.

It was, therefore, a matter of great consternation when, a week later, a letter addressed to Mr Joseph Bolitho from Miss Nankivell's employers arrived, to inform him that his own letter had been returned. The unfortunate young lady had caught a severe chill and expired just before the Christmas festivities. When Joey informed his wife of what had happened to the boy's mother, the colour drained from her face.

"The sweet innocent," she said, with a heavy heart, "What is to become of him now?" Joey opened his mouth to speak, then a vision of the young man with the withered hand appeared before his eyes and he kept silent.

"Perhaps, dearest," Sarah-Jane began cautiously, "we could take him into our own household, for he is a delightful child and has no one to care for him. Mrs Nancarrow has explained to me that, with his head of hair and those light blue eyes, he could be mistaken for no other than a Glasson, for they have always that particular colouring. No-one could lay the blame for his existence at your door, dearest," she concluded. It was not the young boy's existence that so disquieted her husband. The disappearance of the boy's father had more to do with Joey Bolitho than he cared to admit to his wife, and not a few of his acquaintances were all too aware of it. How on earth could he tell her such a thing? His dearest love would be revolted by such an admission on his part. Announcing his intention of giving the matter some thought, he decided that he had best inform Nicky that his mother, like his grandmother, had gone to sleep and would not be coming back. On being told the news, Nicky shed a few tears, as he had seen grown-ups do, but he was far more preoccupied with the fact that Dr Dunstan was coming to remove the stitches in his wound. Remembering the pain he had suffered when they were put in, he could not believe that their removal would be in any way less traumatic. In this, he was pleasantly surprised. Mrs Nancarrow then crowned his delight by presenting him with a delicious sticky bun that she had made for him for being a good boy. Munching his way through his treat, he considered that it was not at all bad to get hurt occasionally, because of the benefits that one accrued as a result.

At Trevu, Joey sought urgent discussion with his brother as to what to do with his young charge. Paul and Chloe, aware of his predicament, suggested having the child adopted by a suitable couple, or even, as a last resort, sending him to an orphanage, anything other than the solution that was staring Bolitho in the face. Joey stoutly maintained that he could not have him in his own home but, the more he thought of the alternatives, the more his conscience plagued him. The disasters that had fallen upon the boy's family had sprung, in no small part, from his own actions. If he had not killed the father, perhaps the child would, even now, be living out his life in his own home, surrounded by his loving parents. That, in all probability, Joey would have been hung at Bodmin for the crowds to gawp at as a direct result of failing to act against the nervous young agent, he also considered. The problem remained unsolved and, tormented by his reasoning, he made his way to his home, his heart heavy and his head full of tortured thoughts.

CHAPTER 13

JACK TREVARTHEN held on tightly to young Nicky Nankivell for fear he should run off again. The young man had offered to show him the newly born piglets. At first, the little boy was most impressed with them, but he soon became bored with simply admiring them. The moment Jack had turned his attention away, Nicky had climbed the wall and scampered across the sty in an attempt to catch hold of one of the squealing litter. The sow took exception to the intruder's attempt to abduct her young and if it were not for Master Trevarthen's quick presence of mind, a serious accident could have occurred. Leaping over the wall, Jack grabbed hold of the runaway and extricated himself before the sow could attack them both. Annoyed, Jack told the youngster that he was not to do such a thing ever again, as sows that had just farrowed could be very dangerous. Nicky nodded solemnly, but as soon as he was put on the ground he caught sight of a very large, tethered cow. At least, the little boy assumed that it was a cow. Giving a loud whoop, he set off towards it at a run. He was caught by the back of his coat, whisked up into his companion's arms and told not to annoy the bull, for they were the most dangerous animals on the farm. Once again he was returned to the ground and Nicky now thought to chase the ducks. Upon apprehending his charge for a third time, Jack held him fast, determined to get him back to the nursery as soon as possible. Miss Clavering, the nurse, was forever telling Jack that as a young boy he would get up to all sorts of pranks and tricks, but he was sure that he could never have been as badly behaved as this young devil. Frowning, he marched into the house, stamped up the stairs and deposited the disappointed Nicky into the nurse's care.

"Don't you dare tell me again that I took delight in annoying you, for I cannot possibly have been as bad as he is," he told her in disgust. Then he left the child with her and hurried away, lest she should call him back to look after the rascal. He retreated to his room, picked up his pens and drawing book and headed out and away from the house to the river, to do some drawings of the riverbank. Meanwhile, in the confines of the nursery, Miss Clavering allowed herself a smile. Taking Nicky over to a large wooden castle, she sat him on the floor and advised him to play with Samuel, who was contentedly setting out his wooden army. The two boys looked at each other suspiciously. Then Sam, a good-natured boy, offered some of his soldiers to Nicky and they were soon playing together quite happily, if rather noisily. Miss Clavering moved her chair to a strategic position in front of the door and sat down to attend to her sewing. Long years of looking after young Master Jack had made her wary, so if this little scamp thought to escape her, he would be in for a surprise.

Downstairs, in the withdrawing room, the four adults were talking quietly together over afternoon tea. Two of them appeared to be ill at ease, one gave the impression that she was suffering from severe stress and the fourth stood, his face impassive, seeming to contemplate the far distance as if he was not in the presence of the others at all.

"Why?" cried Sarah-Jane despairingly, "Why cannot Nicky be taken into our home, Joey? What is so wrong with that?" There was a silence. Paul and his wife would not catch her eye and instead hung their heads, staring at the carpet.

"Tell me, one of you! There is something you are all hiding from me! What is so wrong with the boy, that you tell me it would be better for him to be sent away?" she cried in despair. Her husband tried hard to remain detached, but could not bear to see his wife so distressed.

"Nicky is not at fault, Sarah-Jane, 'tis me," he announced quietly. "Nicky's father was an agent fer Hudson an' I . . ." but Sarah-Jane stopped him with a shrill cry. She knew what it was he would say, knew very well just what her husband had been prepared to do and what he had done to save himself from being arrested by the preventatives in his former life. She shook her head in disbelief, not prepared to believe the truth when finally she had heard it. Chloe, heavily pregnant, heaved herself up from her seat, crossed to her sister in law and put her arms around her.

Mrs Trevarthen seemed to be lost in thought, as she remained silent for a long while. "There is no need to tell the little boy any of this," Chloe reasoned. "If dear Sarah-Jane and you, Joey, can take him into your home, knowing what you do, then take him in and give him a family that will love and cherish him. To abandon him to the coldness of an orphanage would surely be a fate that Nicky does not deserve after all he has suffered. You do not need to tell him of the past, surely? What good would that do?"

Another long silence followed until finally, Joey said, softly, "There are people who can guess at what 'appened to Nicky Glasson, although I 'ave never admitted it."

"Can they prove it?" she queried sharply. For one moment, Joey appeared off guard. His face expressed shock at the boldness of her words. "N...no," he confirmed in a startled tone. For reply, Chloe levelled a steady gaze at him, her eyebrows raised questioningly. Sarah-Jane struggled to regain her composure. Taking a deep breath, she raised her head and stated that her sister in law was correct. "If my punishment from God is for me to remain childless, then it is only right that we take into our home the son of that poor man, who died as a result of my husband's actions," she announced, a slight quiver in her voice. All eyes turned to Joey.

"It is no punishment for us not to have a child, Sarah-Jane," he pronounced, softly, "but to take Nicky into our home will not erase my past. I cannot give him back his father."

"Then stand in his place," advised Chloe, staring boldly at Joey as she spoke. Her brother-in-law gave no reply, instead abruptly announcing his return to Penzance.

"I'll go an' get Nicky if e' would be so kind to ask fer the carriage, Paul," said Joey, sharply, before turning and leaving the room.

Sarah-Jane blew her nose determinedly, stood up and embraced Chloe. "Always the wisest, dear Chloe, and you, dear Paul, forever the kindest," she told them in a voice that barely rose above a whisper.

After being removed from Miss Clavering's care, Joey and the boy returned to the hallway. Nicky, whose future was causing such heart searching amongst the adults, was complaining loudly that he wanted a puppy. Paul, Chloe and Sarah-Jane exchanged smiles when they heard Joey inform him that he was not to have any animal in their house. A remark that was immediately countered with the inevitable reply: "Why?" To save her husband from further badgering, Sarah-Jane caught up Nicky's little hand and led him over to the Trevarthens, telling him to thank them for letting him come to play in their house. Nicky obliged, but expressed his gratitude with a sulking voice. He considered it most unfair as his new friend, Samuel, had told him that he had lots of puppies and dogs in his home. Nicky admitted to having none and considered this circumstance to be most unjust. Once in the carriage, he complained at length about this inequity and was still complaining when they reached home. He had resolved to grumble for the rest of the evening, but upon arrival in Penzance he was handed over to Minnie, who took him down to the kitchen, the cook having taken advantage of his absence to prepare some delicious biscuits. With a cup of warm milk and a plate piled high with these delicacies to satisfy his ever-present hunger, he proceeded to hold court on his experiences that day.

The Bolitho's sat in their withdrawing room and talked until the dining hour. After dinner, Joey retired to the young boy's room to read him one of his favourite stories until he fell asleep. It was a habit that had developed almost since the day that Nicky had first entered the household. When, finally, Nicky's eyelids closed and sleep took him, Joey remained in his seat. It was here that Sarah-Jane found him, when she came to make sure that the child was safely tucked into his bed and to give him a goodnight kiss, as she did every night. Joey caught up her hand and planted a kiss in her palm, then they sat together in silence and gazed at the child for a long while.

The following morning, Joey Bolitho arrived at the office of his solicitor and announced his intention to adopt the orphan, Nicholas Nankivell, formerly in the care of Mrs Emily Glasson, deceased.

Manville Penrose stared into space, envisioning himself in the arms of the voluptuous Meg Jacka, the notorious prostitute, who held court in one of the less salubrious inns that were sited in Penzance. His wife, completely oblivious to his presence, was talking animatedly to Mrs Sophia Roskilly on the subject of the forthcoming ball, that the Penrose's were to hold in the middle of the next month.

"Sir Reginald has promised to attend if at all possible but, of course, much will depend on whether poor Lady Bonython will be well enough to travel. So sad that she should be so afflicted, dear Sophia, for she always appeared to have such a good constitution and she is of no age to speak of," Joanna Penrose proclaimed. The two woman continued to discuss the absent lady's complaint but, after a while, Joanna could not resist divulging her hard work in the planning of the forthcoming event; the elaborate decorations that were to be used in both the dining room and the ballroom, some of the dishes that were to be served and, most importantly of all, the names of the people who had accepted her gilt-edged invitations.

"The Squire and his wife, Sir Reginald and Lady Bonython. The Trevarthen's, although poor Chloe is growing close to her time and may not be able to attend. The Bolitho's, of course, and..." but here, Mrs Roskilly suggested that, perhaps, Joseph Bolitho would not wish to meet with Sir Reginald.

" For 'tis well known that they no longer meet socially. Such a row as they had last year, don't you remember, dear Joanna? Sir Reginald thought to use him to obtain information on those ghastly freetraders but the silly, proud fellow would not give him any assistance. Such a thing to do, for surely he is not of such a high standing that he should dare to behave in that manner? Those dreadful smugglers deserve to be hung ,every one of them, for they are drawn entirely from the lower orders and could hardly be considered worthwhile members of society. 'Hang the lot of them', dear Mr Roskilly, is forever declaring," gabbled his spouse, "and who is Joseph Bolitho to think himself so high that he can afford to behave with such temerity?"

"Well," replied Joanna silkily, "he is the heir to Leah Bolitho, whether he likes it or not, and in due course he will inherit a substantial fortune."

"Trevanoc is not such a large estate, Joanna dear," Mrs Roskilly pointed out, disdainfully.

"True, dear Sophia, but Leah Bolitho has acquired large numbers of farms and smallholdings from the Lizard to St. Agnes Head, including those in Crowan. I am not versed in the mathematical arts, but in acreage alone I calculate that she owns more land than Paul Trevarthen. Am I not correct, Manville?" There was a long silence, so Joanna loudly repeated his name. Mr Penrose jumped in his chair, his vision of the sensual Meg disappearing from his sight immediately. He compounded his wife's disapproval of him by making it blatantly obvious that he had not heard a word of her conversation, by guiltily enquiring, "What's that, m'dear?"

Cowering under her frosty glare, he listened attentively when she asked him to confirm that the Bolitho lands were greater that those owned by Paul Trevarthen.

"Quite so, m'dear," he agreed, nodding wisely. For a few moments more, Joanna continued to direct a withering stare at her husband, during which he squirmed in discomfort. She then turned back, with a smile, to her friend.

"As I was saying, the fellow will be a veritable King Croesus when his aunt dies, dear," she pronounced with satisfaction.

"But what will it avail him, dear Joanna, for he remains childless?" Mrs Roskilly retorted, sporting a satisfied smile of her own and determined not to lose the argument, "for surely, that waif he has brought into his household will not stand to inherit all. 'Tis only the progeny of the Glasson's and Nankivell's, after all. Hardly the sort of family one would want elevated to that position." Sophia Roskilly lifted her eyebrows questioningly, unable to resist a smirk of triumph. Joanna, like her mother before her, would not wish to have the wrong sort of family in her coterie. Paul Trevarthen and his half brother had only entered her portals by dint of being the sons of Redvers Trevarthen, and Joseph Bolitho's wife was admitted through marriage only.

Joanna fumed inwardly but was not to be outdone. "Mrs Bolitho may not remain childless, it has been known!" she snapped, somewhat ruffled by Sophia's pertinent remark.

"Quite so, dear Joanna, and, if I may lower the tone somewhat, it is remarkable that they remain childless, for one must admit that the Bolitho fellow cannot keep his hands off his wife. Why, whenever one meets with them it is most noticeable that he regards her with such a look in his eyes. If my dear husband should dare to gaze at me in such a fashion I do believe I should not know how to suffer the embarrassment," continued Sophia silkily, enjoying a brief reign of superiority.

"My dear, do not think of it for, for knowing your husband as I do, I am sure that the possibility of that happening will never arise!" trounced Joanna with alacrity. As she made this triumphant statement, a loud snoring rent the air from the vicinity of her husband's chair and a pained expression flitted across Mrs Penrose's face. A vision of the ex smuggler, with his handsome face and athletic stature, swept into her mind but she resolutely forced her thoughts back to the present.

She inclined her head in the direction of Mr Penrose and informed Mrs Roskilly, with just a touch of chagrin, that her poor husband was always so set about with managing his various business acquisitions that he frequently found it necessary to rest throughout the daylight hours. Sophia Roskilly was well aware, as was most of Penzance, just what kind of activities Manville Penrose spent most of his time indulging in, once he had escaped his wife's hawk-like gaze, but she was far too well brought up to allude to them. Her own dear husband would frequently tell her that he had caught sight of the unfortunate fellow with various females, who plied a trade that a lady should have no knowledge of whatsoever. It was most annoying, she reasoned, that in view of that fact she could not in all politeness point out Mr Penrose's failings to his wife. Mrs Roskilly did not think to question why her own spouse should have such an intimate knowledge of Manville's activities; it had never entered her mind.

Silently calling a truce, the two companions then went on to discuss at great length the apparel they would be wearing, alluding with pride to the expense of their garments. Manville, awake once again and in a misguided attempt to redeem himself in the eyes of his wife, brightly informed them that, no matter what expenditure they made on their own dresses, they could not hope to emulate the quality of the clothes that Paul Trevarthen and Joseph Bolitho could provide for their respective wives. Two withering gazes came to rest upon him and he suddenly remembered a most pressing business engagement that he had to attend. Excusing himself as graciously as he could, he left his house and headed for the nearest drinking establishment, where he was a frequent customer. Relieved to discover that his friend, Sophia Roskilly's husband, William, was also present, the two men acquired their drinks and retired to a quiet corner to bemoan their lot.

On the afternoon of the day of the ball, Joanna was in her bedroom, resting from her exertions. She had covered the ballroom and dining room with baskets and sprays of flowers, arranged swags of greenery to decorate and enhance the walls and spent a small fortune on candles so that the room would sparkle and glow like a jewel. She had also completely replaced the dining service with the latest offering from the Wedgwood factory and invested in a small, but select, orchestra to provide the musical entertainment for the dancing. When the bills were deposited on her husband's desk the colour had drained from his face and he swallowed convulsively. His wife had succeeded in spending almost a quarter of his annual income on one evening's entertainment. However, he fervently hoped that, as two of their daughters would be formally presented to society at the ball, then perhaps the cost might well be offset by the possibility that one, if not both, would soon be residing under some other family's roof, provided their marriageable qualities were allowed to shine. A loving smile brightened his countenance as his thoughts turned fondly to his youngest daughter, Melior. He would be sad to lose that sweet child from his household, though she was but thirteen and there would be plenty of time before she was to set out on the path towards matrimony. As if summoned by his thoughts, the door to his office opened quietly and the beloved child herself poked her head around the door. He regarded her indulgently. Melior Penrose would never be as handsome as her elder sisters, but she had a charm and vivacity that set her apart from their cold, haughty beauty. Auburn hair, large brown eyes and a small nose were set in a face that radiated laughter. Smiling brightly, she bounced into the room, ran to her father and delivered a loving kiss on his cheek.

"Mama says that if I am good I may observe the dancing from the balcony. Won't that be exciting? All the gentry will be there, gawking at each other and trying to establish who has spent the most on their respective dresses. They need not bother, for the Trevarthens will win that contest and Mrs Bolitho will look as beautiful as ever. Do you know her husband had three whole trunks of dresses brought down from Mr Trevarthen's fashion emporium in London for her? Mama's maid, Cissy, told me because she had it from her cousin Minnie, who has gone to work at the Bolitho's. You should have seen Mama's face. She went green with envy," she enthused and went off into such a peal of laughter that it infected her father who, in spite of everything, himself gave way to mirth. "If my sisters think to acquire any proposals this evening they will first have to learn to show some interest in the opposite sex, for they are far more concerned with how they look. I doubt that either Jennifer or Loveday will have enough wit between them to raise the slightest spark of interest in even one man, let alone a roomful!"

"Mel, my little puss, don't be so cruel," instructed her father with a smile, "I am sure your sisters will acquit themselves admirably."

"Oh yes! In a horse race," nodded his daughter, completely unabashed. She thought for a moment and then considered, sombrely, "But that is all it is when one thinks about it, isn't it Papa?" A thought struck her, and she brightly announced that she intended never to marry in order that she could spend her life looking after her adored father instead. Manville smiled indulgently at her words. In truth, they gave him untold comfort. Suddenly she released him from her embracing arms, kissed him again and announced that she had to attend on Jennifer, who was having gold ribbons threaded through her hair and wished for Melior's opinion on the effect. Manville's youngest child pointed out to her father that Jennifer did not need Melior's thoughts on the subject at all, but wished instead to show herself off in front of the one member of her family who would be unable to attend the event, thus raising a spark of jealously in her. "Well, she will be out of luck, dear sweet Papa, for I shall tell her she looks like Medusa! Won't that proud face of hers look a picture then?" and with another gurgle of laughter she was gone. Manville shook his head at her antics, but she held his heart in her hands and had done so from the day of her birth. Despite knowing of the disruption she would soon be causing in her sister's bedroom, he returned to his paperwork with the smile she had placed on his face impossible to remove.

When the eagerly anticipated ball took place, Joanna Penrose took the opportunity to bask in triumph as the recipient of the many approving remarks made by her guests. Indeed, her preparations had the desired effect and the house did look most impressive though, curiously, in spite of all her efforts, it did not feel at all welcoming. The Penroses stood side by side to greet their guests; Manville, as always, cowed into obedience and Joanna, frostily correct. When Mr and Mrs Bolitho arrived, Joanna's abundant use of candles only served to emphasise the quality of the jewels that Sarah-Jane wore. A golden band, set with exquisite diamonds, had been placed in the thick brown curls of her hair and a matching necklace, earrings and bracelet caught the light and sparkled and shone with impunity. Not that the jewels were in any way ostentatious, even Joanna had to admit, but they were of far higher quality than any in the room. Sarah-Jane's dress was exotic in its simplicity: A plain turquoise gown of the finest silk, trimmed with gold ribbon and worn with a lace shawl delicately embroidered in gold thread depicting tiny lovebirds. The cut and workmanship was there for all to see. She looked so elegant that Joanna could not help her bosom swelling with indignation at the sight of her.

"Dearest Sarah-Jane," she enthused coldly, with a swift kiss of greeting, "and our dear Joseph, as well." Mr Bolitho's well-known inscrutable expression struggled to remain set when presented with such effusive posturing from Joanna Penrose. He found himself offered her cheek for him to kiss and could not dishonour his hostess by refusing to oblige. His nostrils were revolted by the overpowering smell of the perfume that she habitually drenched herself in. She trembled when he kissed her and he concluded that it would have been sensible for her to wear a garment of a thicker material, in order that she should not feel the cold draught from the open doorway. The couple passed on their way into the dining room and Joanna turned to greet her next guest, delighting in the shiver that she had experienced from the kiss she had just received.

The tables in the dining room groaned under the weight of the accumulated dishes that lay on top of them. Sophia Roskilly's lips tightened in annoyance when she noted that her friend had acquired new, expensive tableware. At her side, Mrs Dennis enthused about the many candelabra that had been set on every conceivable surface, with all their candles glowing brightly.

"Is it not so fine, dear Sophia?" she gasped, breathless with wonder.

"Quite blinding!" snapped Mrs Roskilly, rather too briskly.

In one corner of the dining room, Paul had found a seat for his wife. He was relieved that he should not be called upon to dance, because he would have the excuse of having to attend upon Chloe for the evening. Joey strode towards him, the ever-elegant Sarah-Jane at his side. There would be no need to fear his brother taking to the dance floor, either, but for an entirely different reason. In the past, Paul had explained to Joey that perhaps some lessons in dancing would prove beneficial. Their efforts were not helped by their wives, who could do no better than collapse with laughter to see Paul attempting to instruct his brother in the steps. The men gave up in defeat when Mr Trevarthen pointed out, with good humour, that Joey had inherited another trait from his father: Redvers Trevarthen's dancing accomplishments were considered minimal, even amongst the most charitable of his friends.

Consequently, although Joey squired his wife to a great many entertainments, he always resisted the temptation to involve himself in any of the dances and would spend the evening talking to acquaintances and sending admiring glances to his beloved wife. They were smiling at each other when the names of Sir Reginald and Lady Bonython were announced, but whilst Mrs Bolitho looked momentarily dismayed, her husband merely raised his eyebrows briefly and continued to gaze lovingly into her eyes.

The entrance of this couple caused an increase in the hubbub of chatter in the room, for Lady Bonython was being carried in by one of the Penrose's taller servants; her disease had made her joints most tender and to be touched at all was very painful for her. She was set down gently in a chair by the fireplace and her husband solicitously passed her an ebony cane, which she used to help her walk about when presented with a level floor. Ascending and descending from a carriage or attempting to climb any form of staircase had become quite impossible for her. Yet, despite her persistent suffering, she continued to survey the world with a sweet and tender smile. Sir Reginald, carrying a soft blanket, proceeded to place it over her legs and to tuck it solicitously around her. When he turned to review the room, amongst the first faces he noted was that of Joseph Bolitho's, whose eyes showed a great depth of sympathy for the couple, despite his enigmatic expression. The two men merely bowed to each other in recognition, but made no effort to speak.

The evening wore on interminably for Joey; the meal in the dining room was lavish in the extreme, but Joanna had relied heavily on sauces to embellish any of the meals that lacked flavour in their own right and consequently Joey's appetite had lessened accordingly. To add insult to injury they were served a wine that was well below the merchant's standards. He would not have sold such a poor vintage, let alone serve it to his guests. Having sold to Manville some wine and a particularly fine brandy, responsibility for the poor quality of the drink at the gathering could only fall upon Mrs Penrose. The woman even had the barefaced cheek to attempt to inveigle him into taking to the dance floor with her. During the interlude the orchestra retired to a side room, where ale and a cold collation had been laid out for them. But Mrs Penrose wished for even more music and Jennifer, her eldest daughter, was marched to the piano, whilst Loveday was called upon to sing. The pianist attacked the piano as if it were her sworn enemy. Her sister attempted to follow her notes with some vocal ones of her own, but they appeared to be performing at cross-purposes; the one thumping out some extremely strident chords and the other with a voice that wavered on the point of being inaudible. When they had completed their rendition, there followed an embarrassed silence, which was, after a moment, abruptly shattered by a trilling peal of laughter. Joanna Penrose lifted her eyes to the balcony and caught sight of her youngest daughter, convulsed with laughter. The young girl put her hand over her mouth to stifle the noise, but even the basilisk stare from her mother could not contain her amusement. However, catching sight of Mr Bolitho's blue eyes, she abruptly stopped laughing and stared at him. He was looking directly at her and his stony expression had fallen away, revealing obvious amusement. Her mother turned her gaze back to the assembled company and thanked her guests for their polite, if slightly belated, applause. She then took to the piano herself, convinced that in her skilful fingers lay abilities that would so impress the room as to render them speechless with admiration. She played all the notes of a simple piece by Bach, but her style was forced and awkward. A collective sigh of relief rippled across the assembled company when Joanna finally withdrew her fingers from the keys. Amidst more polite applause, she swept the crowd with her most condescending smile and noted that Paul Trevarthen, though clapping politely, appeared deep in conversation with his brother. Her indignation knew no bounds that they should be rude enough to talk to each other during her applause, so she called Paul's name loudly and beckoned him to the piano. Mr Trevarthen, his face darkening with embarrassment, made his way self-consciously across the room.

"Do play for us, Paul, for you have such a delightful touch. Perhaps your brother could also impress us with a piece?" she said, turning her gaze to Mr Bolitho, who was still standing by his wife's chair on the other side of the room.

" 'Ardly, Mrs Penrose, fer I do not play," he announced, coldly.

"Oh dear!" she sighed elaborately, "Such a shame that you have no accomplishments."

Profoundly insulted, Mrs Bolitho stoutly defended her spouse by announcing that he had the most wonderful singing voice. Her husband felt no desire to sing in public, but the guests, along with the hostess, were much intrigued by this statement. And so Redvers' other son, amidst much vocal encouragement, was called to the piano to accompany his brother.

Paul hastily flitted through some sheets of music and, when he found one that Joey knew, began to play. Mr Bolitho had no need to read the words, for he had often sung the piece to his wife in the privacy of their own home. It was not deluded pride that had led Sarah-Jane to maintain that her husband was a good singer. He had a light baritone voice and his rendition captivated his audience, though it was directed to just one person. Paul, as always, played beautifully and when the piece was finished, a roar of approval went up from the audience. Joanna beamed to think that, through her efforts, they had been so royally entertained. She thanked Mr Bolitho and held his hand - rather too tightly, he thought. He was greatly relieved when he noted the orchestra making their way back to their seats and he escaped with his brother back to their respective wives.

In the middle of the second dance, the brothers noted that Manville appeared to be beckoning them to follow him. They excused themselves and allowed Mr Penrose to lead them out of the ballroom and across the hallway, to an open door set back in the corner. They descended the stairs and soon found themselves in Manville's wine cellar. To Joey's discomfort, Manville had also invited Sir Reginald, but he seemed not to notice the cold chill between the two men and proceeded to pass around some glasses, before pouring out a copious amount of his favourite brandy into each of them. Manville, away from his wife, was a delightful host and the brothers were to see another side of him, which surprised and impressed them still further. The assembled party turned in unison at the sound of footsteps on the stairs and suddenly, Melior Penrose appeared, seeming to fly into the room. She stopped in surprise when she saw the four men, but only for a moment. She dashed across to her father and threw her arms around him, then turned to Sir Reginald and, calling him 'Sir Buttons', proceeded to kiss him as well.

"Now, now my little puss," said her father, smiling indulgently, "You know you should not be here. Mama will be most displeased."

"Pooh!" shrugged the child, grinning gleefully, "as if I care!" Joey Bolitho stared in amazement to see the effect her appearance had on her father. He looked so carefree when in the delightful child's presence, for she seemed to draw the best out of him. Her comic rendition of her sister's singing ability along with a demonstration of Jennifer's playing almost reduced the men to tears of laughter. This was followed by her tale of Loveday's despair when Thomas Rutter, an ungainly giant of a boy, stood on the hem of her dress and ripped it. The poor boy then compounded this disaster by attempting to wrap the loose piece of material around her. Loveday, in a furious temper, stamped off but Thomas, - 'with a face like a beetroot' stated the young girl - hung on to his piece of cloth and there was an even louder ripping sound.

"Never mind, dear Papa, for the dress looks so much finer now than it did before and having such red cheeks has improved Loveday's complexion immensely," she concluded, laughing.

"Forgive this little madam, gentleman, I beg of you," said Manville fondly, before planting a kiss on her curls. "Now, my sweet dove, you have entertained us long enough. You had best away before your mother finds you. Perhaps she will not be best pleased with you, for I heard you laughing at your poor sisters and so, I think, did everyone in the room."

"I clapped when you sang, Mr Bolitho and when Mr Trevarthen played the piano," she said earnestly, but then her irrepressible giggle burst forth again. "Did you see Mama's face, Mr Bolitho? When you were singing, she looked positively stunned!" She would have gone on to say more but her father advised her to leave the cellar, as the men wanted to drink in peace. On his instruction, she immediately delivered another kiss on Sir Reginald's cheek and gave her father a joyful hug and kiss. Then she was gone and a silence descended on the room.

"I will not apologise, gentleman, for my daughter, for in this house she lights up my life, as I think you can well imagine," he announced. In fact, he was so different from the fellow that normally trailed despondently in his wife's wake, that Paul and Joey warmed to him. Sir Reginald also looked most avuncular in the child's presence. Joey considered it a strange thing indeed, that a child could have such an effect upon people. But then his thoughts turned to Nicky and he smiled ruefully to himself, as he considered the effect that particular little lad was having on his household since his arrival.

CHAPTER 14

NICKY NANKIVELL had never had new boots before and so he beamed with delight as he strode from the shop into the street. He held tightly onto Joey's hand as the street seemed to be full of people. Now that his wound had healed completely, he had been taken to have his feet measured and Mr Eddy, the cobbler, had made his boots especially for him. His previous footwear had been borrowed from the Trevarthens, as it was thought best that his injured foot should heal completely before he was fitted with the correct size of boot. His expressive little face temporarily lost its delighted look, however, when he was told that he could not jump into the puddles as he wished.

The man and the boy continued along the street and upon entering the greengrocers, Nicky's smile grew wider as he gazed upon all the produce displayed. While Mr Bolitho was paying for his purchases, he surreptitiously reached out for a rosy red apple that had caught his eye but to his frustration, he discovered that he could not reach it. He stood on tiptoe, but to no avail, so he grabbed at the nearest object he could find and hastily hid an onion under his jacket.

"Nicky!" called Mr Bolitho, "Come up 'ere to me so I can buy yer onion fer 'e." Nicky frowned, annoyed that he should have been found out. In truth, he should not have been surprised, as his guardian always appeared to be one step ahead of him. At the counter, he handed over his onion and Mr Bolitho solemnly paid for it, then passed it back to the little boy. As they left the shop, Nicky's eyes wandered to the display of tempting apples, he was still exasperated that he had not been tall enough to reach them.

Instead of returning to their home as he had thought they were to do, they walked down to the harbour and sat on a low wall to watch the fishing boats lying at their moorings. Seagulls screamed and swooped above him and a dog ran along the quay with a large fish in his mouth, having procured it from a basket when the fisherman who had brought it in was not looking. Out of the corner of his eye, he watched as Mr Bolitho took out his knife and asked for the onion. Nicky passed it over without a word. Swiftly, the skin was removed, the top and bottom cut off and the white flesh was returned to him, the milky liquid just beginning to run from the cut surfaces.

"Eat it!" demanded his companion.

Nicky lifted astonished eyes to Joey. "No!" he said, defiantly. The man pressed on, his expression remaining unaltered. "You stole it, Nicky, so you goin' eat it." The little lad's lip quivered, but in the presence of this intimidating man, he gave in and attempted to take a bite. A horrible burning sensation filled his mouth and he screwed up his face, shook his head and passed the pungent tasting vegetable swiftly back to Mr Bolitho. However, Joey was determined that the boy would learn his lesson and promptly returned it to the young lad, repeating his instruction. If this had been any other person, Nicky would have taken the offending vegetable and thrown it in the sea. This, however, was the one grown up that he had tried to defy on numerous occasions, without success. He attempted another bite, the taste was now worse than before, but still the man would not allow him to stop. By the time he was halfway through the onion, his stinging eyes were flowing with tears and his nose had begun to run. Unceremoniously, Joey took out his handkerchief and performed the operation of wiping his nose for him. Eventually, the poor child could manage no more, his mouth was so sore and red. Solemnly, the remnants were despatched to a watery grave and without a word being uttered, the dejected Nicky was led back to the house in Chapel Street, all the while sniffing and sobbing, much to the amusement of passers-by. However, Nicky realised that, if he could not defeat the man who had been so cruel to him, there was another who could. On coming across Mrs Bolitho when they entered the house, Nicky let out a wail of enormous proportions and it was not long before Sarah-Jane had discovered the truth, admonishing her husband for being so cruel and unthinking to the poor, sweet child. Much to the child's delight, honey was liberally applied to his sore lips and Nicky, rapidly licking it off, managed to consume a fair quantity of it. Soon, the little boy's mouth was feeling a lot better. But he was wise enough to know that it would not be to his advantage to admit this, so he continued to cry, loudly and dramatically.

"I was teachin' 'en not to steal!" protested Joey, to no avail, for Nicky was now clasped in a pair of protective arms and Mr Bolitho was the recipient of a severe scolding. Unfortunately, Nicky's smirk of triumph at witnessing the admonishment of his mentor was short lived. Mr Bolitho had promised to take him to Trevu to play with his friend, Samuel, that afternoon. But his wife was convinced that, after such a traumatic event, the little boy's mouth must be badly burnt, for he had cried so bitterly it was obvious he was in great pain. It would be best if Nicky should stay at home that day, she told him, and probably a restful afternoon in his bed would be much better for him than to go out in the cold air, where the wind could chafe his damaged lips. The effect of this pronouncement from Mrs Bolitho was dramatic. Nicky stopped crying at once and announced, "I'm all better now." Alas, his attempt to place Mr Bolitho in the wrong had been only too successful. Mrs Bolitho, annoyed that her husband should have treated the poor innocent so roughly, scooped the infant up in her arms and whisked him off to his bedroom. Nicky's last sight of Joey Bolitho was of him stamping out of the house and slamming the door behind him.

At Trevu, Joey had a sympathetic response from his brother, but scant approval from his sister-in-law.

"Children of that age have such delicate skin, Joey." she scolded. You should have shown more restraint." Nettled, he accepted with alacrity his brother's suggestion that they go shooting and by the time they had spent a pleasant afternoon amongst the rabbits, which had taken up residence in the lower meadow, he began to feel less annoyed.

"Didden want 'en be like me, Paul," Joey explained, sincerely. "I stole 'cos I didden knaw how else to get food." Paul nodded in understanding, but their conversation set him thinking. Ever since Paul had been a small child, he had regularly raided the kitchen at Trevu. He always felt a frisson of excitement to steal, first from under Hannah's nose and then from Mrs Gurney's, although both these ladies knew well what he had done. When he had been in the kitchen at his brother's house, Joey had always asked politely of his cook if he could have anything to eat, be it the smallest of biscuits. For the young Paul, who grew up in a house of plenty, stealing the food was thrilling, though he knew full well that he had only to ask and he would be given whatever he wanted. His brother, on the other hand, had been forced to steal to eat and his actions were born out of necessity. Stealing to Paul was an adventure in which he willingly partook, to his brother it had been a requirement to survive.

"I don't know which will prove the most effective, Joey. Nicky may learn not to steal because you made him eat the onion, or he will simply remember that if he does something to annoy you, then he is denied a treat," he surmised.

"I 'aven't laid a 'and on 'en, Paul, but 'e's a little devil an' I bin' sore tempted," admitted Joey, ruefully, which remark produced a loud chuckle from his brother.

That evening, Joey sat on the chair by Nicky's bed and read to him from his favourite book. Nicky smiled contentedly at him all the while, having been worried that perhaps he had behaved so badly that the man would not wish to keep him in his house. Without being asked, he affirmed that he would not steal again. He was not quite sure what the word meant, but he thought it had something to do with taking things from people. He had even told Mrs Bolitho not to scold Mr Bolitho, as he was his best friend. She had called him a 'dear sweet child' and burst into tears, so he could not be sure if she was still angry or not. After that day's experience, Nicky took great pains always to ask if he wanted something. It was not always the case that he got what he asked for - he still longed for a puppy of his own, for instance - but on the whole, his wishes were granted.

At first, the residents of Penzance were surprised to see the infamous Joseph Bolitho in the company of a small boy with a head full of ginger curls. Many people stared, though the child did not resemble Mr Bolitho. His cook, Mrs Nancarrow, had made it her business to inform the servants of other households, as well as the many tradesmen that she dealt with, of the child's origins and that the couple had adopted him out of the kindness of their hearts. Others in society smiled to themselves, contented to think that they harboured such philanthropists amongst them, although none of them felt the slightest desire to emulate their example. However, amongst Joey's former smuggling associates, the name of the boy's father had caused many raised eyebrows. The crowded room in the Seagull Inn was given over to much speculation regarding the ex smuggler's decision to take in the son of Nicky Glasson. Most were aware that the Glasson fellow had disappeared and assumed him dead, but none could say that it was Bolitho who had killed him and if they could, there were certainly none who would dare.

Oblivious to the gossip surrounding his appearance, young Nicky's life became a whirl of new experiences. On one day he would visit at Trevu, on another he would be on the beach at Marazion, searching amongst rock pools, or on the moors at Morvah. On another he would visit amongst Joey's old friends, all former members of his smuggling fraternity. And it was whilst visiting at the Mankee's that Seth's son, Charlie, with the innocence of youth, explained to the young boy just what it was that Joey Bolitho was believed to have done to his father.

After Charlie's exciting, but somewhat garbled, explanation about agents and smuggling men, Nicky, always enthralled by a good story, began to feel fearful. The narrative was reaching its climax and the name of Nicky Glasson had figured so prominently in the tale. The young storyteller, his eyes shining, reached the most terrifying part and gave full rein to his imagination. "An' then Bolitho grabbed 'im an' took out 'is knife an' then cut 'is throat from ear to ear!" enthused Charlie, "Like that!" and he drew an imaginary knife across the young boy's throat. Little Nicky, his eyes bulging, swallowed convulsively.

"An' then all 'is blood comed out an' runned all over the floor, an' then 'is eyes fell out an' then..." but here, his lurid version of events was cut short by his mother, calling to him to fetch his sister from their cousin's house.

" 'Ess Ma," moaned Charlie, sulkily. Annoyed that he had to stop his account at the most interesting part, he sloped off to collect his sibling. Meanwhile, Nicky sat on the steps outside the back door, staring at the dirt of the small yard. He could hardly believe that Charlie Mankee had been talking of his Mr Bolitho; this wonderful man, that he had grown so fond of, spent his life killing people! That was why, when he went out in the evening, Nicky had to stay at home. He always had his knife with him, so he could kill somebody as soon as he caught them! His head filled with thoughts of Mr Bolitho catching hold of people and cutting their throats as he walked about the town. Lost in his vivid imaginings, he jumped when he heard a familiar voice behind him. "Goin' 'ome now Nicky?" asked his guardian. Nicky raised worried eyes to Joey's face. After what he had just been told, he was not at all sure that he wanted to go anywhere with this man ever again, but he had nowhere else to go. Getting up from his seat on the steps, his legs seemed to be wobbling and he began to tremble.

"Whas' matter, me 'ansome? Cold?" Joey asked. Bending down and lifting Nicky into his arms, he shouted his farewells to Seth Mankee and his wife and made his way down the lane. The young boy had little to say that evening and seemed not to enjoy his bedtime story as he usually did. He did not complain of feeling unwell, so the Bolitho's assumed that he was merely more tired than usual.

In the middle of the night, Joey and his wife were awoken by a piercing scream emanating from the boy's bedroom. Sarah-Jane got up immediately and went to him, but the child seemed so badly disturbed that she thought it best that he should be brought into their room and placed in their warm bed. When poor Nicky discovered that he was now lying next to the person whose hands had just been dripping blood in his nightmare, he began to whimper and cry. Mrs Bolitho comforted him and gave him to her husband to hold while she went for some warm milk to calm him.

"No good be frightened, Nicky," Joey said softly. "Nawthin's goin' 'appen to 'e, don't 'e worry." In spite of all his fears, there was something in the tone of this man's voice that comforted him. Charlie Mankee had told him a tale to frighten him, he concluded. He was a nasty boy and not as nice as his friend, Samuel. Nicky decided that he did not want to go to his house to play with him ever again. Consequently, when Sarah-Jane returned, she was relieved to discover that the child seemed less disturbed. He drank his milk and then settled down into the crook of his guardian's arm. His last thoughts before he fell asleep were of Charlie Mankee, being made to eat an onion for being a very bad boy and making him cry.

"Paris!" Joanna Penrose almost screamed, her eyebrows high on her forehead in surprise. Sophia Roskilly smiled in delight; never in her life had she managed to so shake her friend's composure so successfully.

"Well, I believe that they will spend some time in London first, of course, but he intends to take her to Paris after that," she said with a condescending smile.

"But . . . but why?" spluttered Joanna, still dumbfounded by the news.

"Well, rumour has it, that with Mrs Trevarthen so near to her time, Mrs Bolitho was becoming more exasperated at not falling for a baby herself, so Mr Bolitho decided to whisk her away in order to give her something else to think about. They leave tomorrow and are taking that little boy with them, not that his presence has arrested Mrs Bolitho's desire for a child In fact, I can well imagine it has made the situation worse. Mrs Prout, the apothecary's wife, told me that poor Sarah-Jane has almost emptied their shelves, such is her desperation to give him a child, most particularly a son of course, and she is forever calling at Dr Dunstan's. But then, if it is not meant to be, what is the point of it all?" Mrs Roskilly rattled on, proceeding to describe her own fecundity in great detail. "Of course, I had only the one girl, fortunately," she said with an ingratiating smile and directing a pitying glance towards the three Penrose girls, who sat demurely on the settle. Jennifer and Loveday bowed their heads with shame, but the youngest merely stared rudely back and raised her eyebrows. 'Dratted child,' thought Mrs Roskilly, 'such boldness. She'll have to change her ways if she thinks to trap a man. No great beauty, either!'

"Jennifer has received an offer!" snapped her mother, "and we have reason to believe that Thomas Rutter will entertain hopes for Loveday."

It was now Mrs Roskilly's turn to raise her eyebrows, for it was less than a week since Joanna's extravagant ball. Mrs Penrose received with pride the compliments that her friend directed at her. No other matron had succeeded in receiving a proposal so quickly and if the Rutter boy could be brought up to the mark, then it would be a triumph indeed. Two daughters off her hands in the wink of an eye! Mrs Roskilly fumed, but took a deep breath and enquired as to who would be the lucky recipient of Jennifer's hand.

"The eldest Tregenza boy, Richard," announced the proud matron. She fixed Mrs Roskilly with a cold stare and waited to be congratulated once more.

"My dear, what a catch! The Tregenzas! Well, you are to be congratulated indeed. Why, they are the most renowned family in Penzance and they say Anthony will not live out the year, for his condition has not improved, you know," Sophia informed her, without hesitation.

"Yes, poor man. That young Richard should have to step into his shoes so soon. It is very grievous. But of course, it is only natural that Mr Tregenza would want his eldest son married with all possible haste, thus ensuring that the family name will continue," Joanna informed her, graciously.

"Naturally," Mrs Roskilly replied with a nod, and could not resist adding, "which goes a long way to understanding Mrs Bolitho's predicament. Still, to be taken to Paris! C'est formidable!" she sighed, longingly. Unfortunately, Mrs

Penrose had regained her composure and showed no intention of losing it again.

"I have no desire to visit France, my dear Sophia. It is not at all the sort of country to which I would wish to go and therefore my knowledge of the language is somewhat limited," she informed her friend, injecting just a hint of boredom into her tone.

"Mr Bolitho speaks perfect French," announced Melior, boldly.

All eyes were turned upon her in surprise. Taking their silence as her cue, she informed them that she had come across Mr Trevarthen with his brother in the lending library, where Mr Bolitho was translating a play by Moliere for him.

"First he would read a piece in French, and then in English and he did it with barely a pause. I thought it was the most wonderful accomplishment!" said the youngest girl, admiringly.

"How on earth does that rough fellow know such a language?" questioned Mrs Roskilly in amazement.

"Smuggling," replied Melior before anyone could stop her. "He has been going to France for years and still goes there, for where else would he go to purchase the wine he sells? He had to learn the language or else he could not turn a profit, for without a knowledge of it they could have sold him dear."

"Melior!" snapped her mother, in frustration. She addressed her speech to Mrs Roskilly, remarking smoothly, "She prattles on so, for she will spend too much time with her Papa. He fills her head with such rubbish," Turning to the talkative child, she advised her to attend more to her embroidery, for with her looks it would stand her in better stead when she set out to find a husband. The child seemed completely unabashed by this withering comment from her mother and stared brazenly at her. Suddenly, her expression altered and her face broke into a smile of delight as her father entered the room. He greeted them all with great politeness, but there was a special smile and a covert wink for his beloved daughter.

"I'm sorry I could not have been here before, my dear, but pressure of work, y'know," he said, nervously. As he had spent an enjoyable morning in the arms of the ever-obliging Miss Jacka, he was wary of appearing too relaxed, but he need not have worried. Joanna Penrose had spent the last half an hour being in turns infuriated, triumphant, despairing and elated. Her fool of a husband could not dislodge her from her pedestal of the proud mama, whose daughter had succeeded in catching the most eligible bachelor in Penzance. Perhaps, with some extra tuition from the governess, even Melior could manage to entrap some such equal luminary. Her mind wondered idly as she considered the young men that might fit that category and the youthful, handsome face of George Trevarthen swam into view. She sighed inwardly, admitting to herself that, when Paul's eldest set himself on the path to finding a wife, he had no need to look in the direction of her wayward daughter.

Later that evening, she chided her husband - in her usual robust manner - for filling his youngest daughter's head with useless information on business matters and such like.

"It is quite beyond the pale, Manville, that you should admire her so, for really she is the most objectionable child and has no sense of decorum whatsoever."

"My dear, do not be so hard on her, for she has great charm and that is an asset many females would do well to have," he replied with irony, a fond smile on his lips.

"Stuff and nonsense!" returned Joanna, sharply. She would have said more, but Manville informed her that he had a most terrible headache and thought it best to retire for the evening. The candlelight seemed to be affecting his eyes and perhaps rest would make him feel better.

"Go to bed if you must!" snapped his wife, "I am sure that I can well do without your company, for you never support me in anything I do or say, particularly if it concerns your beloved Melior!" but she had to shout the last as the door was closing behind him. He trudged wearily to bed and hoped that on the morrow he would not wake to find himself with a severe cold.

In a sparsely furnished room in a poor neighbourhood of Penzance, Meg Jacka lay abed alone. Not her usual practice at all, but a fever raged through her and she fought its demons through the night. They found her the next day, rigid and cold in the same bed where she had warmed and frolicked with so many men in her short life.

The horse stopped in the yard, as tired as its master and grateful to recognise the young stable lad who came running. Dr Dunstan got down wearily and entered his home, whilst his beast was led away to the stable. Never had Denzil experienced such a day before in all his working life. First he had been called to the most revolting hovel, where a young girl of about twenty years of age had been found dead in her bed. It was obvious that she had died of some form of fever but he had hoped that it would not spread about the town. It was a forlorn hope, for no sooner had he left her abode then he was called to a fisherman in Newlyn, in the throes of fever. He did what he could but knew that would be little enough. From then on it had been a series of visits about the town and its environs, the same symptoms being presented everywhere. He had no idea what had brought the sickness to the area, but immediately took the precaution of having the first victim's body removed for burial in a pauper's grave. He then ordered that all her clothes and bedding be burnt, in case the evil contagion lay trapped within them. He assumed, incorrectly, that the highest number of cases of the fever would be found in the young girl's neighbourhood, but it transpired that hers was to be the only fatality in that quarter. Indeed, the only case of illness. The other patients he had visited throughout that long day seemed to be spread about all over Penzance and he could think of no explanation as to why that should be. Some did not seem so badly affected, but they were in the minority. The majority succumbed to the contagion and quickly died, leaving anguished wives, grieving parents and numbed children. In some houses, whole families seemed to be suffering. In others, just one member of the household, usually a male.

Upon entering his front parlour, he almost fell into his chair by the fire and his housekeeper, having heard him come in, had ladled some tasty broth into a bowl and set it on the tray that she had prepared earlier. When she carried it in to the poor man, he thanked her, for he had had little time to stop and eat during that day. She enquired as to the scale of the disaster that had befallen the community and blanched when he informed her of some of the people who had breathed their last that day.

"I've just come from the Penrose's. Such a thing," he sighed and shook his head despairingly, "A healthy man gone like that and his poor daughter fighting to live. She won't, of course. But poor Joanna, widowed and now about to lose her youngest child, and all in the course of one day. It is beyond my comprehension, how she can appear so strong, for she has not shed a tear, you know, Maddie!"

"Oh! 'Tis terrible, sure 'nuff, sir, but you eat up now an' I'll go up to warm the bed 'gain," said Maddie, before adding, "Les' 'ope you'll be able catch a bit a' sleep."

When Maddie returned later, Dr Dunstan, exhausted, had fallen asleep in his chair, so she carefully covered him with a blanket and set about to keep the fire burning in the grate. Carefully putting out all but the one candle, she made her way from the room. Shortly afterwards, she climbed to the attic room that she inhabited and was soon fast asleep herself.

Jonas Hampton, the estate manager of Trevu, yawned and stretched and rolled over in his bed, finding an empty space where his wife would normally be lying. He sighed and closed his eyes, knowing well where Emily would be at this early hour of the morning. It seemed pointless to remain where he was now that he had awoken, so he got up and set about preparing himself for his day. A little later, he joined his wife in the kitchen where she was occupied with gently rocking a crib. He walked over and smiled to see the baby contentedly sleeping, oblivious to the turmoil that he had caused in the Hampton household. Anyone knowing the recent family history of the Trevarthen's would immediately recognise that this little child was one of Paul Trevarthen's progeny. He was born in the middle of April, as his mother had predicted, but he was weak and it appeared that he would not live through the night. The vicar was called to baptise him and he spent his first night in the kitchen of the Trevu household, where kettle and pans boiled and steamed through the night to help his breathing. Mrs Hampton, nursing a son of her own, offered herself as a wet nurse to the child and had spent many a sleepless night ensuring that the sickly baby survived. Her devotion had ensured that the innocent had improved and soon all worries about his beginnings were left behind, though he continued to make his demands paramount in the Hampton family as he craved the attention that he had received in his early days.

"That boy makes more noise than our two ever did, Emily," Jonas said with a smile, letting his fingers gently sweep the tuft of black hair on top of the baby's head.

"I know, dearest, but 'e's a fine fellow and a son fer Paul to be proud of, when he can bring himself to come and see 'im," sighed his wife.

"As soon as Chloe is better, he'll be down here, you know that, Emily, but until she gets back to good health he will not leave her side. Miss Daisy said they had a terrible job to get him to sleep at all in the first week. By her bed the whole time," said her husband.

"She's lucky to still be alive at all," said Emily, "but Mrs Gurney said she is beginning to get the colour back into her cheeks and has asked to see the little mite."

"Paul won't allow that until he is sure she is well recovered, so frightened was he at nearly losing her," Jonas informed her. Emily left the child sleeping contentedly and set about to prepare their breakfast. Later that morning, the estate manager was surprised in his office at the farm by Paul Trevarthen himself. Ever since the birth of the child, he had not set foot on the farm and had stayed the whole time in the house. He looked drawn and tired, but he managed a smile when he saw Jonas and asked after his son immediately. Paul looked relieved when he was told how well the boy was progressing and even had to laugh when Jonas told him how loudly such a small infant could cry.

"Mrs Trevarthen coming on now, Paul?" asked Jonas, although household gossip had already informed that Chloe was indeed recovering.

"Thank God, yes! She is much improved and has begun to fret for her son," he told his manager, then paused, wondering how to go on.

"Well, he will be sorely missed, but when the time comes for him to go back home, you have only to let us know," remarked Jonas.

"Thank you, Jonas. Thank you for all that you and your wife have done, for I do not believe we would have fared so well throughout this turmoil without your ability to run the farm and Emily's determination to nurture and look after my son," said Paul, clearly relieved. He advised Jonas that he would discuss the situation with Dr Dunstan and would not do anything that would affect his wife's health. Paul made to take his leave, then stopped at the doorway and turned back, a sad smile on his face. "Denzil says there will be no more children, so I owe you a considerable debt of gratitude, for there was a time when it looked as if I was to lose them both. Thank you again, Jonas," he said simply, before taking his leave and striding quickly back to the main house.

By the bedside of his sleeping wife, Paul Trevarthen sat and pondered the chain of events that had brought him to the brink of losing his wife and young child.

It was his eldest son's unexpected arrival in the household that had caused so much consternation. George had written to his father, announcing his attention of going to university. Paul had promptly written back, stating that his son was to dismiss the idea from his mind immediately. By virtue of the fact that he was the eldest son, his future would involve taking over the farm. Although his father did not object to him continuing to work on subjects that held an interest for him, the necessity of learning how to manage the estate would be his major preoccupation. George wrote again, pleading that he could afford the time to further his education before involving himself in the task of becoming a 'country yokel', as he worded it. As Paul said to Jonas at the time, he found that expression particularly cutting. Jonas, in a failed attempt to pacify an angry Paul, had pointed out that George's attitude could be put down to disappointment and the ignorance of youth. The letter that George next received left him in no doubt that he would not be allowed to entertain hopes of a university education. The letter even hinted that, should he attempt to proceed further with this matter, then the financial benefits of being a part of the Trevarthen family would be seriously curtailed. Paul's eldest son, normally such a quiet and malleable character, uncharacteristically lost his temper at this implied threat and at what he saw as his father's ignorant intransigence. Hiring a chase, he returned home to have it out with his father, face to face. On arrival, he sought out Paul and found him in his study.

At the beginning of their confrontation, George had tried to reason with his father. What was the point of such a good education if he could not use it for further study? he had queried. Paul implied that studying at home, as he himself had done, would be sufficient for his needs. George, annoyed at this rebuff, asked him to define precisely as to what needs his father was referring. In George's opinion, his father's lack of understanding was revealed by his subsequent stuttering explanation. In truth, Paul had not considered his son's future at all, other than to presume that he would do as his father had done and come home to the farm. George, in love with learning as his father had been before him, wanted more opportunities to expand his horizons. Unlike Paul, he wanted the chance to travel and thought his father's idea archaic, telling him that the world had changed since Paul' s youth. To have his son tell him that he considered him to be bordering on dotage inflamed Paul beyond reason. Their voices climbed in volume as the argument continued. Grace, concerned to hear such an unexpected outburst between father and son, sought out her mother for, of all the women in the house, Chloe would have the ability to calm the situation. When the two women arrived in the study, George was refusing to follow his father's shouted demands. Paul, becoming increasingly enraged by his son's uncharacteristic stubbornness, grabbed George by the shoulder to shake some sense into the boy, as he saw it. However, his son was infuriated beyond reason by his father's complete disregard for his feelings and lack of understanding. Unable to control his temper, he took exception to his father's physical treatment of him and furiously aimed a punch at him. In a boxing match, the blow he delivered would have received acclaim for its style and economy of effort. It caught his parent squarely on the chin and would have floored a lesser man. Paul staggered, but on regaining his balance lost his own temper completely. Chloe and Grace screamed simultaneously at what they were witnessing and George dropped his guard at the sound. His father attempted to pull back the fist that barrelled towards his son, but too late. The blow knocked George backwards and he tripped over a low stool, fell against his heavily pregnant mother and knocked her to the floor. There was a stunned silence in the room for a moment, during which time George hastily scrambled to his feet, but his mother remained where she lay, her face contorted with pain. Her whispered request for the doctor to be fetched at once left both males scrabbling, shamefacedly, in haste to accede to her request. Grace it was who quietly and serenely took control. She sent her father to the kitchen to instruct Mrs Gurney to have water put to the boil and George to take horse to Penzance, to fetch Dr Dunstan. Both men set off to complete their tasks and when her father returned, his daughter instructed him to carefully carry her mother to the bedchamber. Once there, he placed her gently in the bed and was then ordered from the room by Grace, who remained calm and in control throughout. He attempted to object, but his daughter merely opened the door and pushed him through it, instructing him to fetch Mrs Gurney and one other female, preferably one with experience of childbearing. Mrs Gurney and Mrs Pascoe, Davy's wife, soon found themselves attempting to make Mrs Trevarthen's situation more comfortable for her. It was obvious that Chloe's fall had started the onset of childbirth but, though the birth itself was over quickly, the child's cord was wrapped around its neck and only swift action by Mrs Gurney saved him from expiring on the spot. When Denzil Dunstan arrived, he was relieved to see the steps that Grace and her sensible companions had taken. From then on, Denzil was preoccupied in attempting to save Mrs Trevarthen's life and experiencing the greatest difficulty in so doing. At one point she appeared to be lying in a sea of blood, but he persevered throughout the day and by nightfall her situation seemed to have improved. Chloe was very weak and would need considerable rest to recover her strength, Denzil had told her.

Dragging himself back to the present, Chloe's husband silently vowed that he would never again jeopardise his family by losing his temper with any of his offspring. A sincere wish on his part but, unbeknownst to Paul, a forlorn hope for all of that.

CHAPTER 15

TWO months had passed since that dreadful day, but Paul was only now beginning to regain some control over his life. He had been shattered and shamed by what had occurred and could hardly believe how close to disaster the family had been. Many tears had been wept by his wife's bedside as he willed her well again. The father and son, subdued and ashamed, had spoken only briefly since that day and certainly no mention of George's future education had been discussed. George had sought the company of Jonas Hampton and had indeed shown an interest in the running of the estate. But despite his despairing attempt to both relieve and please his father, it had been borne in upon him that this was not the path that he wished his life to take. When it appeared that his mother was beginning to recover her health, he returned to school, preferring the company of his fellows to the stifling atmosphere of Trevu. His father had not apportioned any blame on George, indeed, he had attempted to heap all the responsibility at his own door. But this attitude did not lessen his son's own sense of guilt. Paul's second daughter, Daisy, as forthright as ever, called father and son to task and withered them both with her speech. She would have continued to harangue them if it had not been for Grace, who had undertaken the running of the household with ease. She swiftly decided that Daisy would best be put to work in assisting with the day to day care of her mother, thus curtailing her opportunities of speech with the others. Grace, with the confidence of a born housekeeper, oversaw the menus, made sure that any necessary shopping was completed, inspected the tradesmen's wares; even going so far as to reject any that she considered below standard, and taking her turn to nurse and care for her mother. What Paul would have done without her, he could not imagine and his pride in her abilities, in spite of the strain he was under, leapt to new heights.

Finally, the day came when Chloe Trevarthen left the confines of her bedchamber and was brought downstairs to the back parlour, where she was settled comfortably in front of a fire, which burned pleasantly in the grate. Her expressed desire was to see her latest son but when he was brought to her, she became saddened by the knowledge that, in her weakened state, she would be unable to care for him as she would wish. Emily Hampton held her hand, smiled brightly and said, "Why, don't 'e worry Mrs Trevarthen, the little mite can stay with we fer as long as you do want. I shall bring 'en to see 'e every day an' you can see how he's grown, an' when you be feeling back to your old self 'e shall come back to his home."

Chloe thanked her profusely, her eyes brimming with tears whilst her son slept on, unconcerned with the drama that had brought him into the world and that was still causing upheaval in Trevu. Slowly, friends and neighbours were allowed to call and Aunt Caroline took up residence for a week, ushering visitors on and off the premises rather in the manner of an aide-de-comp. These visitors went a long way to revive Chloe's spirits and when she heard of Joanna Penrose's widowhood, she penned a letter at once, expressing her sadness at the loss of her husband.

When a letter from London arrived, informing them all that Joseph Bolitho and family were to return to Cornwall at the beginning of the next month, his brother braced himself. Joey Bolitho adored and admired Chloe and with deep foreboding, Paul knew he would not respond sympathetically to the actions of either his brother or his nephew in almost bringing about the death of Joey's beloved sister-in-law.

"Chloe! Such a beautiful little fellow," breathed Sarah-Jane, enraptured to see her latest nephew. Reaching out her arms, she desperately inquired, "May I hold him?" Reluctantly, the baby was passed over to Sarah-Jane's waiting arms. It was not that Chloe Trevarthen wished to deny her sister-in-law the pleasure of having the babe in her arms, rather that she had the child to herself for such short periods during the day. She would never be able to thank Mrs Gurney enough for saving her child from dying almost at the moment of his birth and to Mrs Hampton, for ensuring his survival since that time. However, her weakness and the lack of time she could spend with him fretted her unbearably.

As Sarah-Jane contentedly rocked the infant, Chloe politely enquired as to the details of their recent travels. Mrs Bolitho enthused about the sights of London and Paris, of their visit to Joey's friends in Brittany and, on their return to England, of their sojourn with the Rickards. Almost every sentence contained references to Nicky, Mrs Trevarthen observed, but there was a wistfulness about her and Chloe concluded that the arrival of the little boy into their family did not seem to have made Sarah-Jane any less anxious to have a child of her own.

In Paul's study, an awkward interview was taking place. He described the argument between himself and his son and how this had brought about the recent catastrophe, whilst Joey listened, wearing an inscrutable expression. Paul squirmed inwardly, for he hated to be placed in such a position. Since the relationship between the two men had first been forged, Paul had often found himself in this situation. Joseph Bolitho had, to a marked degree, inherited Redvers Trevarthen's characteristic impassiveness and Paul, still struggling with guilt, found it difficult to explain what had happened as clearly and concisely as he would have preferred.

"I know I should not have lost my temper with George, but his attitude . . . his attitude . . . and if it were not for dear Grace I'm not sure that we would not have lost . . .lost her," Paul stumbled. Unable to continue, he turned away to hide his anguish. He then heard a soft footfall cross the room to his side and felt the pressure of a hand on his shoulder.

"There's many an action starts with 'asty words, Paul, that if we could 'ave our time over 'gain we would wish to change," Joey softly murmured. "I see Nicky's father in 'is face every single day. If I let the guilt of what I did come between me an' the boy, what sort of life would I give the child? Live with what you did, Paul, but don't let it ruin your life. Chloe need 'e now more than ever."

His brother nodded, took out his handkerchief and blew his nose. After a moment of quiet reflection, they began a conversation about the Bolitho's recent time abroad. Joey even brought a smile to Paul's face when he described Nicky's reaction to people talking to him in a foreign language. They then talked of the spate of fatalities that had occurred within the town and Paul remarked upon Joanna Penrose's coldness at the loss of her husband.

"Almost as if she seemed glad to be rid of him, Joey," said Paul, distastefully.

"Well, wouldn't my idea of a proper marriage," remarked his brother.

"True," responded Paul, nodding, "but then, if you look behind the doors of Penzance society, most of the couples wed for position and status and not for love. God, in my youth I must have had every eligible young girl thrown at me by their designing mothers! I can't remember if I was more afraid of the daughters than of the mothers, but I know I would be in a constant panic at those dances and balls that Aunt Caroline used to drag me to, and when I went to stay with Sardi in London, it was no better there."

Joey laughed and said, "You poor fellow!"

His brother blushed and then went quiet. "At least Joanna Penrose will not attempt that with Melior, poor child," Paul observed sadly, and when he saw Joey's raised eyebrow went on to inform him that, because of the severity of her fever, she had been left unable to speak or to hear.

"Poor little mite," responded Joey, and shook his head sadly. Paul agreed: it seemed so unfair that the most animated of Joanna Penrose's children should be afflicted in such a way.

Later that day, the Bolitho's called at the Penrose household to offer their sympathy. Mrs Penrose sat in the withdrawing room with her three daughters who were perched on the settle. Joanna, despite being attired correctly in her mourning dress, did not look the part of the grieving widow. She accepted their sympathetic pronouncements but seemed to care little that her husband had died. More, the impression given was of a woman annoyed to discover that her financial arrangements had been passed over to the control of the executors and that the trust set up by her late husband did not allow her to spend the fortune that he had accumulated through his business affairs, as she would have wished.

"Not that I would be able to hold a ball at this moment, or that I would wish to," she complained, remembering to whisk out her handkerchief and dab a dry eye, "but, really, it was so inconsiderate of Manville to die just at this precise time." She went on to explain that Jennifer's wedding would take place, but would now be an unusually quiet affair. "If poor Mr Tregenza had been in better health we would have waited, naturally, but he told me that he suffers so badly that, come the morning, it is a miracle that he can open his eyes at all," she pronounced.

Sarah-Jane lowered her gaze and said nothing, but could well remember her time spent in that particular family's house. Mr Tregenza was not in good health, it was true, but he had a will of iron and would probably live for many years to come. However, remembering his manipulative mother, old Mrs Tregenza, she could well believe that her son would play upon his illness to a marked degree.

"And what is poor Loveday to do?" proclaimed Joanna in frustration. Seeing the bemused look on Mrs Bolitho's face, she explained that Thomas Rutter had been on the point of declaring for Loveday. "The same illness that took Manville, took him! She cannot cast about for another man, with her father so recently deceased. One must observe a certain amount of decorum, naturally, but it is all so annoying. I have often asked myself why this catastrophe should have fallen so heavily on this particular family."

Mrs Bolitho pointed out that, from what she had been told, the rampant disease had affected many families, but Mrs Penrose would have none of it and considered her family the most devastated. "Loveday will have to wait another year, if we are to be correct in our observances. By that time, Grace Trevarthen will be of marriageable age and you cannot tell me that she is not the most beautiful young woman in the county, for I will refuse to believe it! It is truly so unfair I could weep with frustration!" she cried, once more having recourse to her handkerchief, but shedding real tears on this occasion. Her outburst had stunned the Bolitho's into silence, but Joanna Penrose had more to complain about. She went on to shock them further by announcing that it would have been better if Melior had died, for what man would want her now?

"I shall be left to care for her for the rest of my life," she moaned, "I ask you, Mrs Bolitho, what have I ever done that I should have to suffer such a penance?"

The Bolitho's turned to look at her daughters, sitting so quietly with their hands clasped in their laps. It was noted that the similarity of their posture was not mirrored in their expressions; Jennifer appeared almost to be smiling with self-satisfaction and Loveday bore a scowl. But Melior, thin and pale, seemed to be staring into the far distance, her eyes bathed in sadness.

When they took their leave, the Bolitho's walked to their home in silence. When they arrived, Joey commented upon what they had witnessed, saying that Melior deserved their sympathy, for she had suffered a double loss. But as for the others in that room, they seemed not to miss poor Manville at all.

"That Miss Melior's a dear little maid," he observed. His wife agreed with him, pointing out that her only blessing would be that she, above all others, would not have to listen to Joanna Penrose's complaints about her situation.

"Joanna had never a kind word to say of her husband whilst he lived and now he has died, I cannot imagine her to be any more charitable with his memory," said Sarah-Jane, sadly.

"True 'nuff," agreed her husband, then added with conviction, "but Miss Melior was the apple of Manville's eye, an' Joanna can neither fergive nor ferget that fact."

Just at that moment, the door flew open and in scampered young Nicky, shouting: "Bonjooer!" at the top of his voice. He rushed across the room with his arms outstretched and was lifted into Joey's arms.

"Can we go swimmin' day?" he asked, and his face lit up when he was answered in the affirmative. After a visit to the kitchen to ask Mrs Nancarrow if she could supply them with suitable provisions, they set off to spend a pleasant afternoon on the beach at Marazion. There were closer coves and beaches, but Joey had no intention of taking the excitable child to them. Marazion, with its long stretch of flat sand presented a safe prospect for the lesson. Joey had managed to teach Nicky the rudiments of swimming, but the child needed to develop his abilities, although the little boy was of the opinion that he could swim around the Mount and back without any problems. It was a fine day and Joey considered that, if they took advantage of the best of the summer weather, then by the end of the year the little lad could be an accomplished swimmer. He prided himself on curtailing his trips to Bristol, for now he had more time to spend with his beloved wife and little Nicky. Now that Sarah-Jane had set up her nephew as manager to her hotels and packet inns, they had even more time together. The child had grown since entering the Bolitho household and had filled out, so that he no longer resembled the emaciated boy that had been caught stealing turnips. At times, Joey had cause to worry about what the future would bring, as he could not imagine that the boy would never know of his true beginnings. But he convinced himself that when Nicky had attained a certain age, his father's disappearance could be explained in a manner that would be acceptable to all of them.

During that summer, Joey Bolitho discovered for the first time the joys of family life, spending hours in the company of his wife and the boy. The people of Penzance found much to gossip about with regard to the family, although their interest was particularly focused on Joey, as they found it almost unbelievable to see the man so often with a smile on his face. Joey's former smuggling friends shook their heads, considering that no good would come of Bolitho's actions and for his own sake, he should send the boy away.

Just such a discussion took place in the kitchen of the Mankee household. Seth sat in his favourite chair in front of the fire, calmly puffing his pipe whilst Esme Mankee, busily preparing a fish stew for the family's supper, gave vent to her opinion regarding the boy, who had taken up residence in the Bolitho household and had given rise to so much gossip and rumour.

"I dunno why Joey can't see whas' goin' 'appen," remarked Esme Mankee to her husband. "Once that boy knaw what 'appened, an' 'e will soon 'nuff, there'll be 'ell t' pay." Seth shrugged his shoulders and continued to puff on his clay pipe, staring reflectively into the distance.

"Might be the makin' of 'en, missus," he said, after a moment.

"Dussen be so daft!" returned Mrs Mankee, sharply. "Tidden too late fer 'en to send the boy away, an' it'll be fer the best fer both of 'em. Why did 'e take 'en into 'is 'ome, after all?"

Upon further reflection, Seth removed his pipe and said, "Ever since 'e found out Paul Trevarthen were 'is brother, Joey 'ave 'ad to change 'is ways. Findin' out 'e was Redvers boy an' Paul takin' 'en into 'is family, gettin' married, one thing after another 'ave come 'is way in the past few years an' none of it bin' anything like 'e 'ad deal with afore. Tidden easy fer a man to learn live in a new way. missus. Joey an' 'is missus, 'em got no children, so why shouldn' 'e take in another man's son?"

"Cos Joey killed 'is father!" Esme swiftly rejoined.

"Nobody can prove that, Esme, so you'd best not repeat it," he warned her swiftly, before adding, "Perhaps Nicky Glasson is still livin' somewheres."

For answer, Mrs Mankee brought her knife down on the last fish and took off its head with one clean cut. "I'll b'lieve that when this 'ere fish go swimmin' out in the bay 'gain," she snorted, waving the decapitated creature at her husband.

"Bleddy fool!" came Seth's terse reply. Then he got to his feet, informed his wife he was going for a drink at Josh's and left the house.

CHAPTER 16

"I am afraid I shall be at church, Harry, and will be unable to attend," replied Paul with a smile. The youth looked downcast but, undeterred, he enquired if Miss Daisy would be able to accompany him in any case.

"You see, sir, it will be such a spectacle. Apart from the Royal yacht, there will also be the Royal squadron in attendance and I do not doubt that a number of private yachts will be sailing with them. They will turn the headland at some point during the morning, depending on the force of the wind, of course, and I assumed that, it being such a rare sight, you would wish to attend," enthused Harry Pendray. He smiled reasonably, but inside he fumed to think that Mr Trevarthen would put an attendance at church above the opportunity to see the King on his way to Ireland for his holidays. He was certain that other people from Penzance would be there to watch them go around the Long Ships. Of course, George the fourth was not so well regarded amongst the populace as his wife had been, but he was still the ruling Monarch and a man of Mr Trevarthen's social class would attend out of duty, Harry had assumed. If he was to be honest, the boat building apprentice had no wish to see the King at all. It was the yachts that had provoked the desire in Harry's breast to see the event. It was also an opportunity to escort his oldest friend, Daisy Trevarthen. They had had few chances to be together since their schooldays and the King had inadvertently provided him with a reason to have a whole morning of her company. Why the dratted fellow could not have contrived to round the rocks at the Land's End today, he did not know, but he could not believe that his benefactor would deny his daughter such a treat; both to witness the regal event and to be in Harry's company.

Paul shook his head and was on the point of refusing his permission when he heard his brother address him from his chair by the table.

"I could attend in yer stead, Paul, fer Nicky would enjoy to see it, I've no doubt. I would be in me niece's debt if she would offer to look after the young scamp fer me," said Joey. He raised his eyes to his brother's face and smiled reasonably.

" 'Twill make no difference to me to go an' see it, fer I shall not be at church, as you well knaw," he added, with a twinkle in his eye. Only the previous day, Paul had suggested to him that, as a well-known member of society, it was only correct that he should accompany Mrs Bolitho to church. Sarah-Jane attended diligently and Paul knew that it grieved her that her husband, although well versed in the bible, repeatedly refused to attend. Joseph Bolitho had stoutly defended his stance. As a youngster, he had learnt to read from the bible, with the notable assistance of a vicar's wife. As payment for her services, he had become her lover until forced by his employer, Barney Rickard, to end the relationship. Whether it was through the memory of the lady's embraces or his own natural intelligence, he had always maintained the ability to quote from the bible at length. The local vicar had admitted to Paul that even he did not have Mr Bolitho's familiarity with the good book and had often found himself out of his depth during discussion with the ex-smuggler at various social gatherings. However, Joey Bolitho only entered a church in order to attend a baptism, wedding or funeral. To enter as a member of the congregation was not something that he had ever wished to do, he had once explained to his shocked brother, as he did not believe in the existence of God. Paul, though he knew full well of his brother's dislike of religion, was thunderstruck by this admission. He concluded that Joey had not been given the opportunities and experiences to which he himself had been subjected as a youth. Sally Bolitho's profession had not revolved around the life of the church, after all. He resolved that he would take care to discuss the matter with his brother at some future time. However, Paul now faced a quandary: whilst he desired for Daisy to attend the church with himself, as she always did, should she be denied the treat of witnessing this rare event with her uncle? Whilst he pondered, George and his younger brother entered the room. Harry lost no time in informing his old ally, George, of the excursion that was proposed for the morrow. Not only did both of Paul's sons express a desire to go, but they handsomely offered to squire their sisters as well. Paul now found himself in an impossible position: should he object, he would no doubt incur the wrath and disappointment of his elder children, but if he agreed that they could indeed attend he would compromise their attendance at church. The family had been brought up as devout Christians and missed going to Church only through sickness or some such other catastrophe. In Paul's mind, to stand on the cliffs at the Land's End, to witness the debauched King go sailing by on a jaunt to Ireland for his holidays, was not a valid excuse. He sighed and turned away to stare out of the window, distracted only when his wife entered the room. George had taken her by the arm and was solicitously leading her to the chair that had recently been vacated by Joey. When Chloe was informed of the topic under discussion she considered that, perhaps the visit would be of benefit to her family, as the opportunities of witnessing such an occasion were not so often to be experienced in this remote part of the country. Young Harry smiled broadly at her, for he was well aware that if Mrs Trevarthen would sanction such an event, then her husband would not go against her wishes. It was as the young lad surmised and Paul acquiesced to her wishes with hardly a caveat, although he was still troubled to think that, on the morrow, the Trevarthen pew at St. Martin's would be suspiciously empty.

Daisy clapped her hands together with glee when she was informed of the proposed treat, and as it was inconceivable that she should go without her sister, Grace was also to become a member of the party. As Nicky would wish to be accompanied by his friend, Samuel, it was considered that young Alice should also be allowed to attend. She declined, however, solemnly stating that she would prefer to stay with her Mama, having no wish to stand on the windy cliffs to look at a fleet of boats. The problem regarding the transportation of the enlarged group was solved, as the party would make use of both the Bolitho's and the Trevarthen's carrriages. Joey arranged that he would arrive at Trevu with Nicky to allow Samuel, Grace and Daisy to travel in his carriage, whilst George, Jack and Harry would travel in the Trevarthen's.

Early the next morning, when they arrived at their vantage point, Nicky was the first to alight from the carriage and had to be physically restrained by Joey, lest he ran over the cliff edge in his excitement. Grace managed to shepherd the two youngest members of the group into order without raising her voice, an achievement her uncle considered most commendable. Daisy, Harry and George wandered about together in a group, deep in conversation. Jack, however, had brought his painting equipment and was busily involved in finding the best position to set up his easel. Various other equipages began to arrive as the morning wore on, most notably that of Sir Reginald Bonython and his wife, accompanied by young Melior Penrose. The men in the two parties merely exchanged nods of acknowledgement, but Miss Trevarthen walked across to the carriage, with her two young charges in tow, to greet Lady Bonython and Miss Melior. Melior, equipped with a small book and pencil, wrote down that she would prefer to walk about with Miss Trevarthen, rather than sit in the carriage. Lady Bonython was immediately agreeable to this action, being of the opinion that Melior retained her right to a place in society and should not be shunned, as her mother was wont to do with her. Indeed, the reason given for her to attend at the event was her mother's insistence that, as she could neither hear nor speak, it was pointless for the child to attend with the rest of the family at church. Lady Bonython made a point of asking Melior if she would wish to be present, but her mother answered for her, stating that the child could have no opinion on the matter due to her disability. Melior took hold of Nicky's hand and Grace to Samuel's and with the young boys grouped between them, the small company walked about on the cliff top, waiting to catch sight of the reason for their visit.

Meanwhile, Joey Bolitho, finding himself free from responsibility of any of his young charges, stood alone, staring out to sea. After a short while, he became aware that someone was approaching, and he turned to see Sir Reginald, puffing a little from the exertion, walking towards him.

"Fine day, Bolitho," remarked Sir Reginald, curtly. In truth, he felt embarrassed to have to address the man at all, but his wife had despatched him to talk to Bolitho with the instruction to amend his silly feud. "I think 'tis best you admit yourself at fault, Reginald, and if you cannot bring yourself to do that, then attempt some conversation with him, at least," she had commanded. He had protested that, at one time he had stood in imminent danger of losing his life at the man's hands. But she disallowed this remark on the grounds that if he, with all his experience of the smuggler's past exploits, believed Bolitho fool enough to murder the head of the Preventatives, then he deserved to be thought an idiot and a candidate for the asylum. Rattled, he pointed out that Bolitho could be a dangerous adversary. "Then don't encourage him to be yours by prolonging this feud," she rejoined, before adding, "After that unfortunate incident at Mevagissy and the loss of those poor men, your standing cannot afford to be weakened further by being at odds with a reformed smuggler."

"He could return to it at any time!" protested her husband.

"Not he," Lady Bonython returned softly, and smiled. "That man is in love with his wife. He will break no law whilst she has him in her fetters."

On greeting the ex smuggler, Sir Reginald thought for one moment that the man would not even deign to reply, but then considered that this was churlish of him, for Bolitho was a remarkably well-mannered man when he wished to be. Sure enough, Bolitho turned to face him and, after a moment, remarked that indeed, it was a fine day. He also commented that he had not expected to see them attending the spectacle, and certainly not with Miss Melior in their party.

"Mrs Penrose has little time for the poor soul these days," remarked Sir Reginald, "but my wife and I have a great fondness for the child. She feels the loss of her father dreadfully, but Joanna will neither acknowledge or recognise that fact."

"It appears to me that Mrs Penrose be more aggrieved at losing control of Manville's fortune than she be at losing 'im," remarked Joey, acutely.

"Quite so, Bolitho," agreed Sir Reginald. They stood together quietly for a moment, surveying the horizon, until a loud, braying laugh broke the silence, causing both men to turn. Before them stood a gentleman, his head thrown back, obviously in the midst of enjoying a merry jest. This gentleman presented a rather peculiar appearance: his clothes were extremely dishevelled and of a rather old fashioned style, his greying brown hair was long and tied back at the neck and instead of the more common apparel of trousers, he was wearing knee breeches. Elaborate ornamental buckles adorned the tops of his shoes. He stood beside Jack, who, seated at his easel, was unselfconsciously laughing with him. Joey's eyebrows snapped together in anger and he opened his mouth to scold Jack for his lack of manners, but was stopped by Sir Reginald's voice at his side.

"Old Neddy is here, I see," he commented jovially.

"Neddy?" enquired Joey in puzzlement, although he understood that this strange gentleman was the one to whom this epithet belonged.

"More correctly, it should be Sir Endymion Peake," remarked Sir Reginald, "but because of his peculiar laugh, he has always been known as Neddy, at least for as long as I have known him. Famous artist, don't you know? Even sold a couple to the late king. Agricultural scenes, I believe. Strange thing, Joey, but he always dresses like that, though he is certainly rich enough to attire himself as well as the finest in the land. Rather an eccentric fellow though. Owns a large estate in Yorkshire but is rarely at home, as he prefers to drift about the countryside, drawing and painting whatever takes his fancy. Never fear, Joey. He looks a sight but he is completely harmless." Turning to Joey, he inclined his head towards the gentleman and suggested he follow him across to be introduced.

Sir Endymion was as jovial as he was strange of appearance. He praised Jack fulsomely for the depictions of seagulls, which the young artist had hastily drawn whilst waiting for the main spectacle to come into view.

"Though he should have lessons, man," he informed Joey, with a bright smile. "A lot of talent there, but wasted. "This..." and here he pointed at one of Jack's drawings, "...will never fly. Too short in the wing, lad. Observe, observe and then..." Jack waited with interest at what this exciting man was about to tell him, "observe again. That's the only way to get what you see depicted anatomically."

Abruptly, he turned to Joey and enquired of the lad's father, and on being furnished with the information, announced his intention of paying him a visit. Unsure as to how his brother would feel about Sir Endymion's proposed arrival at Trevu, Joey was about to advise the gentleman that perhaps a letter in the first instance would be the more correct procedure, when a cry went up from a group of people who had been busily scanning the horizon with their spyglasses: the fleet was coming into view. There ensued much excitement, although Sir Reginald and Mr Bolitho appeared the most unimpressed about the appearance of the convoy.

"Shouldn't say it, Joey, but the man's a damn coxcomb," muttered Sir Reginald in a hoarse whisper.

" 'Ess, sir. I got agree with 'e there. Still, 'tis a pretty 'nuff sight when all be said an' done," replied Joey.

"True, very true, Bolitho," nodded Bonython, not at all surprised to find himself in agreement with the ex smuggler.

Harry rushed across to Jack's side and asked him to draw as much and as quickly as he could, for he wanted as many pictures of these magnificent creations as he could lay his hands on. Jack obliged and even Sir Endymion, borrowing some paper and a brush from the young artist, began to dash off some quick sketches with ease. Young Jack could only observe with envy the man's ability to convey, with just a few lines, the splendour of the yachts. Harry, his eyes shining, turned to George and remarked that he thought it the finest thing he had ever seen, but George did not seem to be quite so impressed. His eyes were turned in the direction of his sister, who stood alone, abandoned by young Pendray in his haste to communicate his wishes to Jack. Unlike almost everyone else in the assorted group, she had no desire to witness the passage of the Monarch. Instead, her eyes had turned forlornly towards Harry.

A cry of "God save the King!" went up from several members of the crowd, but it was not taken up by many of the people present and Joey had to smile as he heard the bedraggled artist add the words, "Save him for what, I pray?" to the end of the acclamation. Obviously, Sir Endymion was not an admirer of this particular royal, in common with so many of the crowd there to bear witness. The sight did provide much to admire, however; every yacht in full sail and borne along by a good breeze. Those with spyglasses were able to view the sailors aloft, all turned out in their uniform of blue jackets and white trousers. The Royal Yacht led the way, followed by the Royal squadron and various private yachts. It was the sight of these splendid vessels that captured Harry's heart. Many a time he had dreamt of building such beautiful creations and was determined to return to Mr Vigus's boat yard with his head full of new ideas and designs. As the flotilla turned up St. George's Channel, the crowd that had gathered began to disperse. Sir Endymion, deep in conversation with young Jack, suddenly announced that he would accompany the Bolitho contingent back to Trevu to meet with the boy's father. Mr Bolitho, astounded by the man's lack of manners, advised against this action and even had recourse to Sir Reginald to point out that Mr Trevarthen would not wish the peace of his Sunday shattered by the arrival of a stranger.

"Nonsense!" rebuked the artist, and turned away from both men. To Jack, he asked, "Your father would be thrilled to meet me, would he not, young fellow?" Jack, proud to be asked, responded in the affirmative, convinced that, like him, his father would be just as excited to meet this inspiring man. Into this situation walked Grace and Melior, followed by their young charges. Grace smiled calmly as she was introduced to Sir Endymion. Noting the excited gleam in her young brother's eye and making use of her increased responsibility following her mother's illness, she invited the stranger to lunch with great politeness. As smoothly, she then turned to Sir Reginald and invited his party to return with them also.

"I shall go on ahead with Samuel and Nicky to arrange the matter. Cook is expecting quite a large number to return with us, so a few more will not make a significant difference," she said, smiling serenely. Lady Bonython pointed out that Miss Melior's mama would need to be informed of the reason for her daughter's late return. But Grace merely said that they could send a message to the Penrose's once they had arrived back at Trevu. She beckoned Melior to her and, taking her notebook, wrote a hurried explanation in it. Melior eyes lit up with delight as she realised that her time away from her Mama was to be lengthened. The girls, including a somewhat downhearted Daisy, set off in the Trevarthen carriage well before the main party had prepared to leave. Sir Endymion and his new protégé helped each other to pack away their various pictures and paintings into Joey's carriage. It was with a barely suppressed temper that, eventually, Mr Bolitho himself was allowed to sit in it, albeit rather squashed over to one side by numerous sheets of paper, some still wet and laid delicately across the seat. George, Harry and Sir Endymion sat on the opposite seat whilst Jack, his enthusiasm undimmed, sat beside the coachman and kept up a continuous chatter with his latest friend, through the hatch behind the coachman's seat. Sir Reginald and his wife followed on at a sedate pace, her ladyship's delicate condition making it impossible to travel at speed over the rough road that led back to the Trevarthen's house.

When the swollen entourage arrived, they were met by Paul Trevarthen on the steps of Trevu. No doubt he was somewhat daunted to find that he would be entertaining more guests than he had at first anticipated, but he was far too well-mannered to show any sign of annoyance. Grace charmed him with her account of the delight and praise that Jack had received from the recognised artist, and calmly pointed out that to fail to invite Sir Reginald and his wife, the only people present who actually knew Sir Endymion Peake, would have been foolish in the extreme. As for inviting Miss Melior, "Well, Papa ,how could I arrange to send her home alone when she was in the company of the Bonython's?" enquired Grace, with a sweet smile. Chloe pre-empted any dissent from her husband by announcing that Grace had handled the matter most sensibly. As his wife appeared not to object, Paul would not go against her approval by countermanding that which his daughter had arranged. As the adults and elder children would be lunching in the dining room, Grace left her parents to greet their guests, then withdrew to the dining room to supervise the seating arrangements. When the Bolitho's carriage arrived, the younger members quickly alighted and dispersed to various parts of Trevu. Daisy managed to claim Harry's undivided attention and led him off to the garden and Jack disappeared into the library with his collection of pictures, so George found himself left alone to amuse Melior Penrose. He was somewhat daunted to have to address a young female in any case, but the prospect of having to communicate with someone who could neither hear nor speak to him made him feel clumsy and awkward. However, his young guest had a most infectious smile, he observed, and so with a mixture of gestures and written notes he found communication with her far easier than he had at first assumed it would be. Truth to tell, George thought Melior's sense of humour to be most appealing and, although he had no idea why, to be the recipient of her beaming smile delighted him beyond measure.

However, his father was somewhat daunted when he had his hand shaken by the artist who insisted that he was to be known as 'Neddy' by his host. Turning to Paul's wife, Sir Endymion kissed Mrs Trevarthen's hand with great reverence and waxed poetical about her beauty, expressing a desire to paint her portrait and those of her delightful daughters. Upon the arrival of the Bonython's, arrangements were made to carry the invalid into the house and as the meal was ready to be served, her ladyship was taken immediately to the dining room. The rather comical figure that the artist presented was balanced by his entertaining manner. He seemed incapable of sitting silently for any length of time and kept up a flow of amusing conversation throughout the meal. It was difficult, Paul admitted, not to like the fellow, but he was rather worried that his dear Jack was completely under the man's spell.

Sitting at the head of his table, Paul politely enquired if any of the artist's family lived in the area.

"Not to my knowledge, dear chap," the artist happily responded, then continued in a jovial tone, "Was married once, y'know. Years ago. The lady in question ran off with the footman...or was it the butler?" He looked puzzled for a moment. "It was the butler. I remember now, because m'father kicked up a terrible fuss about it."

"I am so sorry," said Mrs Trevarthen, sincerely.

"Yes, dear lady, and so was my father. Said he was the only butler he ever had who never came drunk to the dining table," beamed Sir Endymion. Daisy hastily stifled a giggle and George valiantly bit his lip in an effort not to laugh out loud. Upon it being explained to the artist that Mrs Trevarthen was sympathising with him over the actions of his wife, he apologised for his mistake. He then shocked the company still further by stating that he quite understood why the lady had followed this course, as he had spent his wedding night painting a moonlit scene that he was quite desperate to catch.

"One of my best works, y'know. Or at least, the best of the early ones. The light was quite entrancing!" he mused, lifting his head and staring heavenward in contemplation of the remembered scene. Paul found himself dazed by the incessant chatter of his unusual guest, but also surprised to find that the gentleman managed to keep up a flow of varied conversation whilst consuming all the food that he had placed on his plate. Neither was he averse to quaffing his way through several of glasses of wine, but the alcohol seemed to have no effect on him and he continued to entertain the party. When the meal was finished, he took Paul by the arm and escorted him into his own library to show him the sketches that had been made both by himself and young Jack. Sir Reginald and Joey took a turn about the garden after their meal, silence being preferred to the superabundance of chatter to which they would have continued to be subjected in the presence of Sir Endymion.

In the library, Paul could only envy Sir Reginald and his brother, for once he stood before the several works that had been created during the morning, the talkative artist could not stop enthusing about them. He had high praise for Paul's son, but also admonished Jack's father most severely for having made no effort to find a teacher to encourage and improve the boy's undoubted talent.

140

"Wasted, y'know, Trevarthen. You have a talented boy here and he's going nowhere," remarked Peake, pointing to Jack, who stood by his father and gleamed with pride.

Paul blushed, but attempted to point out that the far west was not the ideal location for artists wishing to improve their skills, and he considered his son far too young to be sent away from his home to further his artistic education.

"Quite right, my dear fellow!" agreed Sir Endymion. "But allow me to solve this problem for you. I'm most impressed by the area and consequently have taken a cottage at St. Buryan, in order to dash off a few scenes of my own. No problem at all if you should send the boy to me whilst I am employed about my own work, and I can school him in the finer points as I go along. Had lessons with Reynolds myself, don't y'know. We all have to learn at someone's knee." At this point, he patted Jack on the head. Judging by the expression on his son's face, Paul would find it nigh on impossible to refuse permission for his son to be taught by this man, but he tried to raise some points of dissent. Peake overruled him with the utmost affability and advised Paul to set his mind at rest by sending the boy, along with a servant to carry his materials.

"Find one with an interesting face. Portraiture is such a challenging craft y'know," he exclaimed and considering that he had won the argument, he slapped Paul on the back and asked to be shown the garden. Here he found Joey and Bonython, sitting on the bench and talking quietly to each other. He strode towards them and then seated himself between them. Smiling at them both, he exclaimed in a booming voice, "Damned fine garden," Then, replete with good food and fine wine, he promptly fell asleep.

"Isn't he just wonderful, father?" enthused Jack breathlessly, staring at him in admiration.

"Yes, Jack," breathed Paul, his head still whirling, "Wonderful!"

CHAPTER 17

"NICKY!" Joey Bolitho's voice bellowed out across Trevu's yard, his breath becoming clouds of mist in the bitingly cold November air. The young ginger-haired boy, clasping his jacket tightly around his chest, stopped running immediately and turned towards the steps where his guardian stood, tall and resolute. The child tried to look innocent but at the sight of Joey's raised eyebrow, he reluctantly took a small puppy from underneath his jacket. "Give the puppy back to Samuel an' then make sure 'tis taken back to its mother," commanded Joey. He watched as young Samuel Trevarthen appeared from the small stable block with a guilty look on his face. Nicky, with dragging feet, turned back towards his friend and passed the little animal to Samuel. They stood talking quietly together for a moment and then disappeared into the building.

"Problems, Joey?" enquired his brother, as he walked from Jonas Hampton's office back to the house. He had heard his brother's shouted instructions to his young charge and could not wipe the smile from his face. Ever since Nicholas Nankivell had entered his brother's home, his one desire had been for a puppy of his own, but Joey Bolitho had refused to allow any animal in his house. At Trevu, there appeared to be an abundance of dogs with their progeny, but the young lad had never succeeded in getting one as far as the yard gate without being discovered and made to return the valued possession. Even Paul had argued that the boy would benefit from the companionship, but to no avail. It was not that his brother did not like dogs, but he considered that, with the layout of the house in Chapel Street, a small animal left to career about the house could lead to an accident and he did not believe that it should be left alone to fend for itself in the stables.

"Trying take away another of yer puppies. Young Sam is keen fer 'en to 'ave one of yer last litter. When the boy is older an' more able to take care of it, maybe I'll change me mind, but fer the time being I won't 'ave one in me 'ome," Joey explained to him. Paul laughed and shook his head, advising his brother to give in immediately, as the day would be upon him, soon enough, when Nicky would get his way. Joey grinned in return, but said he would continue the battle of wills as long as he was able.

"What time are 'e expecting Peter to arrive?" he asked, casting a glance in the direction of the farm entrance.

"Knowing Peter Fleetwood as I do, it could be anytime," his brother laughed, "for if he catches sight of some pretty damsel en route, he is more than likely to be waylaid." Joey guffawed with laughter and nodded his head in agreement.

"Do 'e knaw why 'e took it into 'is 'ead to come an' see 'e, yet? Seems a strange time to come. I thought 'e was coming down fer to spend the Christmas tide with 'e, anyhow."

"I have no idea, but he did mention that it had to do with George, though nothing to do with his studies or his life at university," admitted Paul, a puzzled look on his face.

" 'Ave 'e 'ad more news from George?" Joey asked, tentatively.

142

"Not mentioning anything out of the ordinary, Joey. He seems to have settled down well to university life. Chloe and I thought his youth would be a handicap to him. However, he is in the company of Sir Vyvyan Lose's boy, who has a most amenable disposition and as they have been firm friends for many years," Paul recounted, "it is as well that they continue to study together. For the life of me, I can see no reason for Peter's visit. But I am not altogether worried, as George has intimated to us in his letters that all is going well and he is enjoying his studies immensely."

They decided that there was no point in standing outside to await Peter's arrival and Paul suggested a brandy to help keep out the cold, so they entered the house and headed for the back parlour, always Paul's favourite room. He knew that there would be a good fire there and as their respective wives were closeted together in the withdrawing room, they would have the opportunity to imbue more brandy than if they were in their presence.

Thanking him for his drink, Joey took a chair by the fire and stared at his glass. Paul expected that he would remain silent until, quite suddenly and without prompt, Joey began to describe the continued problems he was having with his wife on the subject of children.

"I love 'er dearly, Paul, but when she do go on 'bout 'avin' children I dunno what to do stop 'er. 'Tis like she's crazed 'bout it. Don' matter 'ow many times I d' say I don't want them, Sarah-Jane say she don't believe me an' I'm only bein' kind to 'er fer the way she treated me all they years ago," said Joey in a despairing voice. "There's always someone 'avin' babies somewhere. The Tregenzas, the Roskillys, her brothers and now William John's goin' be a grandfather! Then, on top of all, Pascal had word from Jean-Pierre to tell me that it appears Matthew Calloway's wife is with child! If Sarah-Jane idden goin' on 'bout 'ow unfair it all is, she's pleading with me not to leave 'er fer another woman, like Redvers did to 'is wife. Bit difficult explain if 'e didden, I wouldn' 'ave bin born, or you either," he said, looking directly at his brother. Paul nodded sympathetically, but he found it difficult to say anything.

"I said to 'er, 'We got a good marriage, I'm 'appy, children or no children,' but she wouldn' 'ave it. Said I'm bound want a son like other men," he cried. "Then she d' go on 'bout me an' Nicky. She think I'm a good father to 'en, but then that make 'er think 'bout me not 'avin' any of me own. Bleddy 'ell, Paul, 'tis 'nuff drive a man insane!" He took a gulp of brandy, leaned back in his chair and closed his eyes, exhaling loudly as he did so.

Paul could find nothing to say, his house was full to the rafters with children and he could not imagine life without them. He believed his brother when he affirmed that he did not want to have children, but he knew Sarah-Jane from when they were children together and could imagine how doggedly she would stick to her quest. When they had played as youngsters on the farm, she had trailed behind him everywhere and no matter what dangerous pursuit he undertook, she would attempt to follow in his footsteps. That Sarah Jane's misery had reached such a desperate situation that Joey, so reticent about his feelings, had felt forced to voice them to him, proved how dire the situation in his household had become.

"The other day, I caught 'er drinkin' me best port!" announced his brother, in a voice heavy with disbelief, as if the recollection of the event still shocked him to his core.

"Drinking your port?" echoed Paul, equally amazed.

"Aunt Leah 'ad told 'er some tale 'bout 'avin' an egg beaten up with port. S'pose be good fer getting with child! I thought the servants was after it 'cos the level kept goin' down, an' then come find out 'tis me own missus! Then when I d' say she's to stop drinkin' it I'm told I don't want 'er 'ave children 'cos I must 'ave another woman somewhere! Don' matter what I say, she got an answer fer me," Joey said in an angry voice. "I don't mind admittin' it, Paul, but I'm at me wits end with it all," he said and took another gulp of his brandy. Paul walked over and refilled his glass, setting the bottle on the table.

There followed a short silence, until Joey broke it with another pronouncement: that his brother was not the only one to receive written correspondence from Aunt Leah. Trevarthen's eyebrows were raised in query and Joey continued, in an exasperated voice, "Aunt Leah 'ave written to ask for our permission for Janey - our serving maid, that was - to marry. She 'ave had her child, a girl, an' both be doin' very well. Settled in grand, so me aunt wrote me, and 'ave become very popular with all 'er staff. One in particular be most enamoured of 'er, me aunt said, an' as she 'ave no family, Janey thought it best if our permission should be sought fer 'er to get married. I wrote an' said 'twouldn' nawthin do with we but Aunt Leah said Janey wished fer it."

"Is her intended one of the household or a local fellow?" asked Paul.

"Oh, 'e be one of the 'ousehold all right. 'Tis Mr Nairn 'imself!"

"Good Lord!"

"I knaw! Could 'ardly believe it meself but 'e 'ave taken quite a shine to the maid. So if we two be agreeable, he wishes to marry 'er and take on the baby as well."

"But . . . I mean . . . surely, that would be awkward . . . for the little girl, I mean. She will hardly resemble Mr Nairn, after all?" queried Paul, as diplomatically as he could. Well he knew how unpleasant having a different colour skin could be and imagined the young girl would be placed in a similar situation as he was in his youth.

There was an embarrassed silence from his brother until, finally, Joey cleared his throat and explained just who it was who had fathered Janey's child. Paul's brows snapped together immediately.

"Am I to assume that Janey was removed from your household to save any gossip concerning myself?" he demanded.

Bolitho nodded solemnly and waited for the explosion of wrath that would come from his brother. However, none was forthcoming. It took only a little thought for Paul to realise that, at the time, his brother had followed the wisest course. It would only have brought even more shame and gossip to the poor child if society had insinuated that the baby was the result of a liaison between himself and the Bolitho's serving maid.

"What with 'e staying at the 'ouse some nights when we bin' drinkin', people was bound say the baby was yours, Paul," Joey explained.

Paul sighed heavily, admitting that Penzance society would have thought precisely that. He could imagine the distress that such gossip would have caused his dear wife and family.

"Aunt Leah knew the position and seein' as she 'ad Mr Nairn workin' fer 'er, I knawed she wouldn' goin' treat Janey badly cos' of the colour of 'er child," Joey remarked, his brother not failing to notice the pride in his voice as he spoke.

"Well, I for one cannot fault Mr Nairn, for he seems a most estimable gentleman and I would not quibble to give my consent to the union," advised Paul.

"I didden. Paul," announced his brother, "I wrote an' said I d' give me permission fer the marriage. So now me aunt 'ave wrote me to say she thought it only right, seein' 'as how Janey 'em got no family, that I should be the one to give she away. Sarah-Jane 'ave told me thas' what I should do, so I wrote to say I would do as Janey wished, but after the service I would come away again. Aunt just be trying get me in the place again. I know she!" Joey said, with feeling. He stared at the carpet for a while and then raised his eyes to his brother and said, "I met some crafty females in me time, Paul, but I believe that woman be craftier than most."

His brother had to laugh at his discomfort, and their conversation on the subject was brought to a close when they heard a familiar voice in the hallway. They left their seats and headed off to greet Peter Fleetwood. Peter, never at a loss in praising the female sex, was busy showering Beth with compliments and when the Mr Trevarthen appeared on the scene, she turned a face scarlet with embarrassment towards him.

"Thank you, Beth," Paul said, firmly. "You may go about your business now. I will escort Mr Fleetwood to the withdrawing room."

"Thankee sir," gasped Beth, and dropping a hurried curtsey she rushed from the hall.

"Peter, my old friend," said Paul, turning to his guest, "Still practising the art of flirtation, I see. I would prefer that you do not turn on the charm with my servants, as I believe I previously advised you."

"Frequently, my dear chap. In fact, I am amazed at what a moralist you have become over the years," Peter told him, jovially. To Paul, the man standing before him, with a wide grin across his face, had barely changed. He still resembled the young man he had met all those years ago at his mother's house in London. Time was beginning to etch some age upon his features, however, and he had become a little fuller in the figure, although he carried himself so erectly that it was not particularly noticeable.

He shook Paul warmly by the hand, before turning to Bolitho and greeting him in just as friendly a manner.

However, before the dinner hour, Peter asked for a private word with his host as he had something that he wished to discuss with him. Comfortably ensconced in the cosy back parlour, he eyed his friend over the top of his glass of glowing brandy and began a line of conversation that would enable Paul to discover what had brought Peter to his door at such an unlikely time.

"As a matter of interest, dear fellow, what would your reaction be if I was to tell you that I was to become ennobled?" Peter queried, a lazy smile on his lips.

Paul looked shocked for one brief moment and then went off into a peal of laughter. When he had recovered, he enquired as to when this event was likely to be taking place and asked if he would be required to bow to his old friend upon meeting him in future. Peter looked amused, and assured him that bowing would be obligatory, naturally. He then informed him that, at the beginning of the following year, he was to be made a lord following his services in the diplomatic core. "M'father is most pleased by it, naturally, but I can't say that I care too much for it. It is only a title after all and does not bring any lands or properties with it," remarked Mr Fleetwood, calmly.

"Well, I consider it to be a great honour for you, Peter, and well deserved. You have spent your life criss-crossing the world in the service of your country and 'tis only fair that they should honour you," remarked his host.

"Thank you, old chap. So you have no aversion to such an honour being placed upon me?" he asked.

"Good Lord, no!" returned Paul, and added, emphatically, "None whatsoever."

"Well, I am glad to hear that, for it makes what I now have to tell you so much the easier to impart," rejoined Peter, blandly.

Paul looked puzzled and his brows began to furrow when his old friend appeared to steer the conversation from his own ennoblement to a discussion of his wife's relations.

"To be honest, Peter, I can't tell you much about them. 'Tis Chloe you should be asking. I know that Lord Wrothford has three daughters and some grandchildren - a couple of girls, if I remember correctly. Truth to tell, we have little to do with them. Chloe has never been fond of her uncle, or he of her and when she married, I was made well aware that I was not particularly welcome in the family," he informed Peter, without a trace of bitterness.

"Lord Wrothford has been in touch with me, as he knew I was an old friend of the family. You see, he has a particularly awkward matter to contend with in the not too distant future. To put it bluntly, old boy, he has no heir and so his title will pass out of his immediate family to the next in line," Peter informed him, quietly. Observing his old friend's face, he could not help but smile at the blankness of expression that he saw there. He could well imagine that, had it been Paul's brother with whom he was having this conversation, then the dawning light of understanding would have been lit long ago.

"Surely, you are not to be the next Lord Wrothford?" cried Paul, in disbelief.

"Of course not, Paul" said Peter, with a twinge of exasperation. He sighed and then continued quietly with his explanation. "Wrothford has no heir through his own marriage; there are no male cousins. The only heir that is in line to become the next Lord Wrothford is his eldest great nephew." He waited for Paul to digest this before continuing. Unfortunately for Peter, his old friend was not following the same line of genealogy that the absent Lord and Mr Fleetwood had pursued a few weeks beforehand, in the comfort of his lordship's town house.

"Great nephew," Paul mused quietly to himself, and then cast his eyes upwards as he tried to pin down the identity of this gentleman. He had to admit that he had never concerned himself with his wife's relations and apart from her grandmother, knew very little about them. Naturally, they corresponded with Chloe but had never shown any inclination to be at all friendly towards himself, nor any members of his family. Since his marriage almost eighteen years ago, neither he nor his wife had ever visited them. Blushing, he remembered that, during their disastrous separation a few years before, his wife had not even informed her uncle that she was no longer resident at Trevu.

"Wrothford has a married niece," prompted Peter, patiently, waiting for some sign of understanding.

"Has he?" remarked Paul, and then laughed at himself for being such a fool. "Why of course he has, Peter! What an idiot you must think me? 'Tis Chloe! My wife is his niece and..." he stopped abruptly as realisation struck him like a thunderbolt. "And George is his eldest great nephew!"

"Precisely, dear chap," sighed his old friend. He watched in amusement at the emotions that rapidly crossed his companion's features. Peter had expected surprise, but not anger.

"It will not be," announced Paul, fiercely, "for I will not have it so! George is my heir, not his, and I will not have him become the next Lord Wrothford!"

"My dear fellow, I'm afraid there is nothing you can do. [1]Iacta alea est. Short of starting a revolution, the system will not alter to suit your needs. Think about it old chap, 'tis not such a bad thing for George. Damned fine estate, don't you know! Can marry into the best families in the land. If her uncle had been more accommodating years ago, Chloe herself could have had her pick of the gentry. 'Twas only that he did his best to beggar the poor girl that she was not so advantaged as she could have been. Her wealth was due entirely to the efforts of the Dowager, Lady Wrothford, who made it her business to see that the poor child should have had her chance in society," observed Peter.

"Are you implying that, by marrying me, she did not make an advantageous marriage?" snapped Paul, angrily.

"Not at all, old boy, but you must have been aware that Lord Wrothford made no attempt to see his niece well established, and that it was entirely through the efforts of her grandmother that Chloe had the opportunity to even be seen in society?" queried Peter.

Paul's brow furrowed and he cast his mind back to his first visit to London. If he had to be truthful, it had never occurred to him. Marriage was not uppermost in his mind in those days, as he had little thought for any other woman than Dorothea, Daisy's mother. It was only through the effort of Chloe's grandmother and his own mother that the young couple were forced together. Chloe had been willing to marry him and, as it appeared to him at that time, all hope of marriage to his beloved Dorothea was lost, thus Paul had consented to the union. It was not a love match; the adoration he now felt for his wife had not always been so, and had grown only after the first few years of their marriage. A blush darkened Paul's face at the realisation of it. Still, George to be the next in line to Lord Wrothford! It would be comical if it were not so serious.

"I have plans for George, Peter. His becoming heir to large parts of Berkshire do not play a part in them," avowed Paul.

Peter sighed again, and impressed upon his host that there was nothing he could do to alter the fact: the succession would have to pass to his eldest son.

"Wrothford is almost seventy, and he has had to accept the inevitable. He asked me to call to see him at the beginning of October, at his town house. He shares your frustration in this predicament," he said.

Anything further that Paul wished to add was interrupted by the sound of the bell for their dinner.

---

[1] The die is cast

"I will have to discuss this with Chloe," announced Paul bitterly, "before it is even mentioned to George. I would appreciate it if you do not mention the matter to her before I have had a chance to do so."

"Naturally, old fellow. Won't say a word, although it is only fair to tell you that, in all probability, your dear wife has more of an idea of the position than you realise," observed Peter, smiling lazily.

Grace and Daisy dined with them that evening, so no more mention was made of either George or Peter's future elevation to the peerage. Paul discussed the matter with Peter again over their glass of port. Upon rejoining Chloe, they found that the girls were still in her presence, so again, no reference was made to the matter. However, when he finally climbed into bed beside his wife, it was Chloe who asked Paul what it was that troubled him, for to her it was obvious that something had occurred to disturb her husband.

He explained the matter to her as briefly and precisely as he could. There followed a long silence, until finally, Chloe said softly into the dark, "I have been aware for some time of the likelihood of just such a thing happening, Paul, but when George and yourself had such a devastating altercation over his wish to attend university, I thought it best to bide my time before I mentioned the matter. I am sorry, Paul for I know it is not what you wished for George," she concluded.

"No," he replied, resignedly, "it is not the outcome I imagined when he was born. He was my son and heir and no other man's. Now I feel that he has been taken away from me. And what of Trevu? He will not wish to have the bother of this place once he is made aware of the lands that will become his from his great uncle's estate."

"Perhaps another son could become the recipient in his stead?" suggested Chloe, hopefully.

"Jack will have to take it on, for he will be the next in line," muttered Paul. Chloe closed her eyes at the thought. Her poor, artistic son, whose soul lit up at every opportunity to paint or draw, would now have to forfeit his own dreams of a career dominated by painting, to take up the reins of the farm. If any of her sons should have the task imposed upon him it should have been Samuel, as he had a love of the place that extended beyond the house and land. Young Sam was always to be found around the farm with the workers, studying them at their work or watching how the animals and crops grew and prospered. Only last week, she remembered, Paul had proudly announced that Sam had known, automatically, which of the cattle that had been sent to market would fetch the best price. Then there was the problem of Sardi's businesses. Who would take on that responsibility? Grace would be the obvious choice, though she knew full well that her husband would not agree to that idea, merely because Grace was a female and he did not consider that women were capable of such things. It had come as a shock to realise that her husband, in spite of his own mother's renowned abilities and business acumen, did not believe that women were capable of running their own business. Long into the night, they lay in each other's arms and discussed the dilemma that had appeared so suddenly in their midst, Chloe despairing less at George's elevation than his father. For Paul, the prospect was an appalling one, and even when his dear wife had finally closed her eyes and drifted off into sleep, he lay staring at the ceiling until the misty light of dawn broke into the chamber.

The next day, Paul advised Peter that it would be correct to inform his brother of all that was to happen. Joey was delighted at the news, considering that it would not be a problem as, in relation to the large estates in England, Trevu would be a small matter to have to worry over.

"One of yer boys would do a grand job of seein' to this place, Paul. With the mine gone, it will be less of a worry fer them an' they can concentrate on the farming side of things," he enthused.

His brother shot him a frosty glance. " 'Tis not just the farm, Joey, there is the matter of my mother's establishments. I had thought to let George take over all as I did myself, but I am not so sure that Jack will wish to learn the running of them," announced Paul, crisply.

"Shouldn't think so," laughed his brother, in reply. "Truth to tell, I can't see 'en runnin' this place either; Jack's into the paintin' life."

This admission did nothing to improve Paul's demeanour, and it was a rather disgruntled father who took on the responsibility of informing his progeny that their eldest brother's status would eventually have to change. The youngest children stared blankly at him, having no idea what their father was communicating to them, but Jack and the girls knew full well what such a change would mean. Grace and Daisy were excited to think that their brother would now be a lord.

"I would hope that none of my family would consider themselves to be better than they are, merely because a member of it has been elevated above the common," he told them, moodily.

Intuitively, Grace realised how hurt her father felt at the change in her brother's circumstances. Jack, intently studying his father's face, asked the question that Paul had been dreading.

"Will George still inherit Trevu along with his other estate, Papa?" he enquired, fixing his father with a worried look.

"It would be most unfair if he should do so, an' I think he would find it difficult. Consequently, I will make arrangements that you will become heir to the property in his stead," Paul advised him. Jack's look of despair pulled at Paul's heart, but he could not bring himself to discuss the matter further. Turning on his heel, he left the room.

When he rejoined the adults in the withdrawing room, he noticed the different reactions that the strange news had produced amongst them. His dear wife looked saddened at the turn of events, his brother grinned and pointed out that they had never had a lord in the family before, Sarah-Jane had been most impressed with the news and Peter merely smiled serenely. Paul decided it would be for the best not to inform George by letter, as the lad was returning at the beginning of the following week for the Christmas holidays and he preferred to tell him face to face.

However, later that morning, his temper knew no bounds when two letters arrived for him in the post. One came from his son and the other from Lord Wrothford. With deep foreboding, he had opened his lordship's letter first and had discovered that the fellow had already communicated to George the change in his circumstances that would be brought about as the heir of the Wrothford estate. Paul ripped open the second letter from his son, finding to his chagrin that George seemed not to be at all worried by the news, which would irrevocably change his future. His son's complacency, in the face of the novel situation that he now found himself in, shook his father to the core, and Paul moaned bitterly to his wife that he seemed to be the only member of the family not to be delighted with the news that Peter had brought them.

"I think that unfair, Paul, for I do not wish for this. And as for dearest Jack, how will be that poor child take to becoming your heir? It is not what he wishes at all, the poor dear," she remarked with heartfelt sadness.

"Well," retorted Paul, angrily, "if, as you have all pointed out, George is to have no choice in the matter, then why should Jack?"

"But, Paul," pleaded his wife, "Jack should not be forced to take on the responsibility if he does not wish to do so!"

"Why not?" snapped her husband, his temper getting the better of him. "I have been forced to accept that which I cannot control. Perhaps Jack should discover, as have I, how cruel life can be!" Feeling that his small world was collapsing around him, he stormed from the room, slamming the door behind him.

When George returned to his home at the beginning of the following week, it seemed to him that nothing about the place had altered in the slightest. Even old Davy shuffled across the yard to greet him as usual. He moved with still greater effort than he had when the young man had left at the end of summer, but as always, George pretended not to notice.

"Do I call 'e yer lordship, sir?" he asked, a twinkle in his eye.

"I'm afraid that would be a bit premature, old friend," laughed George in reply, passing his bag to one of the stable lads who was smiling up at him. He braced himself for the reception he was to receive upon his entrance into his home, knowing that, of all the people that waited within, it would be his father that would find the meeting the most trying. Before he reached the door, it was thrown opened by Jack, who, on catching sight of his brother, ran down the steps and angrily informed him that he thought George had served him a 'damned underhand trick'. Shouldering the bag that contained his drawing materials, he brushed past him without further comment and made his way to the stables. Jack was to go for his lessons with Sir Endymion and even the arrival of his brother, during this momentous time for the family, would not alter his plans by as much as a few minutes.

Beth stood at the top of the steps to greet him, her eyes wide open in awe. She fumbled a curtsey and, taking his coat and hat, informed him that the family had gathered in the withdrawing room to meet him.

"Yer uncle an' aunt be there too, sir," she gasped, breathless with excitement. "An' that Mr Fleetwood what 'ave come down from Lunnon." At the mention of this gentleman's name, her cheeks flushed a deep crimson. George, failing to notice, politely thanked her and made his way to the large room, which was set to one side of the dark hallway.

The hubbub of conversation stopped immediately as he entered the room. He smiled back at the sea of faces before him but noted at once that his father's face held no welcoming smile on it. He greeted his mother with a kiss and then turned to shake his father's hand, but the acknowledgement he received from him was perfunctory in the extreme. However, because the others were excited by the news that had so recently come to him, he made no comment, imagining that they would discuss the matter at a more private time. Daisy hugged him excitedly and Grace smiled warmly at him. His uncle clapped him on the back and congratulated him on his good fortune. Peter Fleetwood greeted him in the same manner, whilst his aunt clasped his hand in hers and told him how delighted they all were at the change that was to occur in his life. Upon hearing his father cough, rather too loudly, he thanked them all for their good wishes and proceeded to talk about his time at university and at how well he had been progressing with his studies. He pointedly made no further reference to anything else.

When, later that day, he did get to discuss his position with his father, he found the meeting a most difficult affair. Paul could not, in charity, blame his son for that which the future now held for him, as it was beyond George's control, after all. What irked him was his son's calm acceptance of his fate. His father had expected that his first born would view with horror the prospect of changing his station in life, but George did not consider that his life had been blighted in any way whatsoever. He pointed out to his father that it would prove to be far more enjoyable to spend his life in close proximity to centres of learning, than to be bereft of the academic establishments that he so loved to frequent.

"Of course, I can appreciate that this is not what you would wish for me, Father. But for myself, I will be well satisfied, for in all honesty I am not the one for the running of this place. I have tried to show an interest, Papa, but it is not in my heart to do so. I am convinced that Sam will make a much better fist of it than I could ever do," he advised his father.

"Sam is not to take over the farm. If you are not to inherit it, it will go to Jack, as he is the next in line," Paul said, sharply.

"But father, that would be most unfair, for nobody believes that he would want to have anything to do with the place!" protested George.

"Then perhaps you will understand how I feel, that the property I have loved and cherished for you has now become so despised," his father snapped, angrily.

"I do not despise Trevu, father," George pleaded in a subdued voice.

"Do you not, my son? Well, that is the impression I have been given to understand from you," retorted his father. Turning his back on him, he advised George to leave, lest he should say more that he might well regret.

Meekly, George let himself out of the room and headed off to find his mother. Of his parents, it was always she who had the more understanding temperament, and she would recognise that his future position would provide for his needs to a far greater extent. Whilst Trevu, in all its remoteness, might never be satisfactory. Unlike his father, he did not have the desire to shut himself away in a small room translating mouldy Latin texts. He wished to follow a path of scientific study and he had no desire to live out his days concentrating on the running of what he now believed to be a rather small estate. Lord Wrothford had assured him that, apart from signing a few documents, he employed a great many agents to deal with such tedious matters, as had most of his ancestors before him.

"And if Father had more understanding, then he would not even think to appoint Jack in my place," he told his mother, sadly. "But then, 'tis his lack of understanding that causes so much ill feeling."

"I know, dearest," she sighed, as she gently stroked his arm, "but your Father has had much to contend with over the years. The position he inherited from his father was only one part. The position he built for himself and his family, he founded with his own strength of character. Imagine how he feels now? What he sees as his hard-won achievements are to be taken away from him, merely because some barely known relative has failed to produce a male heir. If my uncle had fathered a son, he would have continued to ignore this side of the family for the rest of his life. He had never made any overtures of friendship to your father, neither before nor since our marriage. I have never told Papa of this, but I know that my uncle despised him because of his colour and his low standing." She raised sad eyes to her son's face. "It is not what your father would have wished, I know. But a part of me does rejoice, George, if it only be because that hateful man has to accept that it will be your father's son, and not his own, that will eventually take his place."

He hugged his mother gently and remarked that perhaps, like Davy, they were all being premature. Her uncle was still alive and in good health, so perhaps it would be many years before any such change in his life would have to occur.

"I hope in all the excitement you have not forgotten my birthday, Mama," he joked, hoping to put a smile on her face with his humour. "I have travelled all this way in great expectation, you know," he avowed.

His mother did smile, boxing him gently and calling him a mad fool. It greatly pleased George that he had removed the sad look from her face. His task now was to do the same for his father, but he was wise enough to know that it would not be an easy feat to accomplish.

CHAPTER 18

JOEY BOLITHO and his sister-in-law, Chloe, sat opposite each other on the settles in the drawing room. The woman looked sympathetic, but the man appeared puzzled and his brow was furrowed, as if deep in thought.

"I dunno, Chloe. Sarah-Jane do go see Aunt Leah most weeks. Maybe 'twas something Aunt Leah said to 'er, but she's behaving strange, there's no doubt about it," Joey said. Slowly, a blush formed on his cheeks as he added, "Keeps kissin' me and 'uggin' me. I mean, not that we didden afore, but 'tis every waking minute! Sit down to a meal an' she's staring away at me with a great smile on 'er face, an' then all of a sudden she's on her feet an' next minute got 'er arms roun' me neck an' she's kissin' me 'gain!" He gave an awkward laugh and added, cheekily, " 'Tis lovely, mind."

Chloe laughed with him but remarked sagely that, if his wife was displaying such happiness, then he should have no worry for her. Instead, he should be glad to know that his wife was content. "For it is obvious to me that your marriage was meant to be, and Sarah-Jane is only showing her love and admiration for you, Joey," she advised him.

Joey Bolitho smiled proudly at her words. He went on to detail the wedding that he and his wife had attended at the chapel, in the little village next to Trevanoc. When asked, he did admit that he had adamantly refused to return with the happy couple and his aunt, to partake of the wedding breakfast at her house. He did not inform his sister-in-law that his aunt and wife appeared to be extremely fond of each other, a fact that had troubled him greatly. However, he detailed how well Janey had looked and how proud her husband, Mr Nairn, appeared and he told his sister-in-law that the couple looked set to enjoy a happy marriage.

Paul, once he had been acqainted by his brother of the real reason for Janey having been spirited away, had told his wife. Chloe would be forever grateful to her brother in law for his thoughtfulness in the matter, and she knew the pain it had caused him to swallow his pride and ask for his aunt's assistance. She could imagine the strain it had imposed on him to meet with his aunt again, and knew from what Sarah-Jane had often told her that the two women schemed and planned on many occasions to have him return to Trevanoc. But they had always had their plans thwarted by his complete refusal to contemplate such a visit.

Undoubtedly, Joey's actions in taking his servant away from Penzance had saved the Trevarthens from great distress, for she was well aware that, even after all these years, her husband was still looked at askance. The inward-looking social circle of Penzance loved a scandal more than anything else and the arrival of another coloured child in the vicinity would be levelled at her husband's door, even if he had spent the last year closeted away in his London house. With George's news still the main topic of conversation, perhaps even that poor youth would have had to contend with the implication of fatherhood, although, unlike his father and grandfather, George had not yet shown any inclination to be at all interested in members of the weaker sex. However, knowing the clique that surrounded the waspish Mrs Penrose, that state of affairs would be no bar to their overactive imaginations. Of course, the news that George was to become the future Lord Wrothford had galvanised the majority of the matrons in the locality to come a-calling at Trevu, more often than not with their respective daughters dragging along behind them. Her husband had even threatened to remove the bell from the door and to padlock the farm gate, so wearying were the constant callers to their house.

"I 'ave tried to talk to Paul about the way 'e be treating Jack, Chloe, but sorry I am to 'ave to admit it, 'tis bin to no avail," commented Joey, breaking in on her thoughts. She smiled sadly and thanked him, saying that perhaps time would solve all. Her uncle was still in good health, she told Joey. And if her husband could be made to appreciate that fact, then perhaps he could be made to realise that Sam might prove worthy of taking over the running of Trevu, when the time came. The door opened and her husband entered the room. His normally happy countenance appeared more clouded these days, but he still looked pleased to see his brother.

Paul had mellowed little over the matter of his son's ennoblement and barely any time was given to the matter during conversation amongst the family. George subtly brought any discussion with his father around to the subject of farming - whereupon his father would bombard him with information - or else they discussed literature, where the son had more opportunity to become a partner in the dialogue with his father. For young Jack, life was not so pleasant, as his father had insisted that he spend part of every day either in the farm office with Jonas, or out and about on the farm. The results of this were not quite as Paul had intended, as the young artist spent his time recording the men at work. On one occasion, he produced a very fine study of the farm agent, which so impressed Jonas that he asked if it might be within his means to buy the portrait. Jack promptly passed it over to him and when he took it home to his wife that night, she was so pleased that she enquired if it would be possible for young Mr Jack to paint a family group for them. Jack cheerfully obliged and produced another fine painting for their front parlour. When his father questioned him as to what he had learnt over the previous two weeks, he was disappointed to discover that his son could only tell him that to paint children, one had to be quick of hand and eye in order to catch their expressive little faces. His father advised him that, in future, it would be better if he spent his time taking more notice of what was happening at various locations around the farm, and not to idle away his time painting.

"After all," Paul announced, authoritatively, "you can always dash off the odd picture in your spare time."

Jack did not deign to reply to this comment, but looked at his father as if he was an inmate of the lunatic asylum. Increasingly, Mr Trevarthen was finding that Jack was not the malleable young creature that he had been in his younger years. He had, in fact, become quite manipulative, for it was not long before Sir Endymion Peake bearded Paul in his library, advising him to alter his plans for his artistic son, lest his painting abilities were to be wasted. His derogatory comments concerning rural farmers annoyed Paul and he advised Neddy that, as he was only a 'jobbing artist', as Paul rather rudely called him, it was none of his business as to what was to happen to his son. Later that evening, Paul had narrated the tale of his argument with Sir Endymion to his wife, but forbore to mention that Neddy had called him a 'blithering nodcock' as his pride was still smarting that he should be so addressed in his own house. At the back of his mind, even Paul understood that he was being unfair to his son, but barely controlled anger simmered within him. Those around him could only hope that time would soften his mood and that he would finally see sense, allowing his son the freedom of expression that the poor lad so desired.

As Paul crossed the room to sit beside his wife he looked towards Bolitho. "All is well with you I hope, brother?" he asked, with a slight smile lifting the corners of his mouth.

"All be very well, Paul," Joey replied, with an answering smile, but his was the wider and the more complete.

At his dinner table that evening, Joey was amazed to see his wife so distracted that, when he complained that the soup was cold, she told him that it did not matter. He blinked in surprise, for he rarely made a negative comment regarding the food, it being her pride and joy to set a good table. Joey appreciated that it was not easy for the servants to ensure hot food at all times, but to sup his way through a bowl of cooled soup was more than he was prepared to do. He pushed the bowl to one side and watched for his wife's reaction, but she did not notice as she was busily eating a rather large – for Sarah-Jane, at least - portion of spiced beef and vegetables. Her husband sat and watched her with a puzzled look on his face. Catching sight of his expression, she immediately left her seat, walked over to him and kissed him. Not a rare occurrence for, of late, she seemed compelled to want to show her love for him and although he relished her attention of him, he could not deduce the reason why she should suddenly wish to treat him in such a way.

When they finished their meal, she smiled at him in a coquettish way and retired to the withdrawing room, leaving him to his drink. Intrigued, Joey decided that he would forego his nightly quota of port and was soon seated beside her on the settle. Immediately, Sarah-Jane reached out, caught hold of his face in her hands and looked into his eyes. He noted how her own eyes shone. Not with desire, he realised with a pang, but with a gleam that he had never seen before.

"Dearest, I have waited to be sure, but I can save this news no longer," she told him, her voice breathless with excitement. "It is the best of news, dearest. The moment we have waited so long to celebrate. A baby, Joey, at long last there is to be a child for us!" As she said these words she let go of his face, buried her own against his chest and began to sob with happiness. The effect on her husband was not so dramatic; at first, he stared at the glowing fire, seemingly unable to comprehend what his beloved was telling him. In the early days of their marriage he would have accepted the news of a child with a mixture of pride and love, but time had altered his perspective. The continual haranguing from his wife on her lack of fecundity had dimmed his appreciation of fatherhood. He adored his wife and when he told her he wished for no other it had, in his mind, applied as equally to any offspring as it had to other women. Even young Nicky had become part of his family more by default than by desire. He loved the little chap, it was true, and he cared for and protected him and would not give him up now. However, he knew that if circumstances had been different and Lucy Nankivell had lived, he could have given up the boy without a qualm. Now he was being forced to accept a stranger into his household and he did not share the happiness that was so evidently being displayed by his beloved wife.

"Are . . . are 'e sure, dearest?" he asked, awkwardly.

"At first I did wonder if it could be my age," she sniffed, but then she recounted, excitedly, how Dr Dunstan had assured her that she was indeed with child, but had advised her to wait a while before broadcasting the fact. That very day he had confirmed that, in his opinion, it would be in order for her to break the news, as her symptoms and continued good health had indicated that all was progressing as it should.

"I have told Aunt Leah our news," she gabbled on, not noticing that his body had stiffened at her words, "and like Dr Dunstan, she advised caution but also said that, if it were indeed true, then she wished us every happiness."

"I bet she did!" rasped her husband, cut by a sudden stab of jealousy that his aunt, of all his family, should be informed of his wife's condition before he had been made aware of the change in their circumstances.

His wife, in her happiness, failed to notice the anger in his voice. Instead, her excitement undimmed, she continued. At first she had lost hope, she said, and imagined that her childbearing days had come to an end. With a nervous laugh, she apologised that she had treated him badly for so long. But now that the news was so wonderful, surely he could not fail but to be as thrilled as she was herself? Sarah-Jane failed to recognise that her husband was not responding to the news in the way that she had imagined he would. Blinded by her condition, she happily told him that the child would be a member of their family in June. Perhaps even on Joey's birthday, she enthused, joyfully. Eventually, she lifted her head and looked up into his face, smiling brightly at his puzzled frown.

"I can see you are shocked, my dearest, but it is the best of circumstances for us. Never again will I have to suffer the disappointments that have so plagued our marriage with my lack of children. I can give you the son you so richly deserve," she dramatically assured him.

"It...might be a maid," he answered, nervously, trying to summon a delight to match that being displayed by his wife.

"Certainly not! I am determined it is a boy," she firmly pronounced, "and I do not think I would countenance for it to be a girl after all the trials I have had to endure to bring me to this happy outcome." For one brief moment, she noted a certain reticence about her husband, but her happiness dispelled his look and when she asked him if he was not as thrilled as she was herself, he had smiled and agreed with her, that it was indeed the best of news.

They spent the evening with their arms about each other, his wife scarcely seeming to pause for breath as she talked on about the excitement of her situation. Her husband, staring into a future he had not foreseen, kept his own counsel. But if his dearly beloved was so pleased then he would not show, in any way, how her news had disquieted him. Locking away his negative feelings, he assured her that he was as happy as she. Sarah-Jane, thrilled with delight, would not have noticed if he had displayed emotions of despair on being informed of his approaching parental status.

That night, in their bed, he held her close and told her of his love for her, assuring her that she had made him the happiest of men and that the child would be the best of all children. She sighed with contentment at his words and he strove to believe them himself. But, in some strange way, a part of him felt a sense of loss, that what he had always treasured, a bond between their two souls, would never be recaptured once the unknown infant made its entrance into their marriage.

The following morning, Sarah-Jane expressed a wish to inform the household of her condition but her husband, feeling suddenly awkward and shy, balked at being present for the announcement and offered instead to inform young Nicky of the advent of the new arrival. Thinking it best that the boy be informed at once, he entered his bedroom as the child was on the point of clambering out of bed. If Mr Bolitho, in his naiveté, had assumed that this was to be the easier of the two tasks: informing the young boy that Sarah-Jane was to present him with a playfellow, he was soon to learn otherwise.

Nicky Nankivell stared at him with his large eyes as the information was relayed to him. He then asked if the child would be arriving within the next week. Joey explained that it would not appear in the household until sometime in June. Nicky balked at the prospect of having to wait a lifetime until the baby put in its appearance. When he realised that it was to be of diminutive stature and unable to play with him, immediately his little face showed great consternation, as he had assumed that someone of Samuel Trevarthen's size and proportions would arrive promptly and without fuss. Further, he looked revolted when it was pointed out to him that there was a possibility of the child being a female. He eyed Joey suspiciously for a while and the prospective parent enquired as to what was worrying the child.

"If 'tis all right for you to 'ave a baby, how come I idden allowed 'ave a puppy?" he queried, his lips forming a pronounced pout.

Joey sighed loudly, looking heavenwards for assistance, then reiterated that when Nicky was older, perhaps he would be allowed to have such an animal, but for the present, they could not accommodate one in the household.

"You'll 'ave be'ave yerself, Nicky, fer Mrs Bolitho's goin' need rest afore she do 'ave the baby," Joey informed him, authoritatively. He then wished the words unsaid as Nicky immediately asked, "Why?"

"Well...cos...cos...they just do, thas all!" retorted Joey, knowing the explanation inadequate but unable to divulge any more. Nicky noticed that his guardian appeared to be getting rather hot, as his face had turned a very red colour. Although he was annoyed to think that he would have to be a good boy for such a long time, he shrugged his shoulders indifferently, told Joey that he was hungry and asked if he could go to get his breakfast. His guardian, feeling in need of sustenance himself after his baptism of fire, told him that it was an excellent idea. Feeling a trifle light-headed with the events of the last twenty-four hours, he helped the youngster wash and dress himself before leading him off to the dining room for his breakfast.

At the bottom of the stairs, Minnie, her face beaming, congratulated Joey, as did every member of his household that crossed his path that day. In the wider environs of Penzance, the news spread like the wind and the knocker seemed not to stop. Even his brother and his wife visited from Trevu, as the information had been relayed to them by a line of servants and tradesmen. Chloe hugged him to her with delight and fell to tears of joy with Sarah-Jane as they discussed the happy event. His brother shook his hand warmly and told him it could not have happened to a more deserving fellow. Thinking it appropriate, they decamped to Josh's inn, where Mr Bolitho found it necessary to refuse a vast amount of alcohol, such was the delight of the incumbents of the hostelry at his good fortune. Joey, his head a whirl, tried desperately to take stock of his altered circumstances, though at the back of his mind, a small voice pleaded that his life remain unaltered. He knew that the revelation he harboured would have to stay hidden from his beloved. The news that she was with child was, to her, the best she could have ever hoped for, and there was nothing Joseph Bolitho would ever wish to do that would in any way give rise to the slightest despair in the woman he had adored for most of his life.

An oath suddenly erupted from Paul Trevarthen, shattering the peace of the breakfast table, at the head of which he was sitting. His wife looked shocked, whilst her daughters stared at their plates, saying not a word. Jack, busily consuming a hearty meal, stopped eating for a moment and glanced at his father in surprise, but he was a growing lad and returned to his plate after a slight pause.

"I will not have it! Damn the man!" continued Paul, so angered by the content of the paper in his hand that he was oblivious to the effect he was having on the female members sitting around his table. A stifled giggle broke the tension in the air, and he looked up to see Daisy with her hand over her mouth and a decided twinkle in her eyes.

"Well might you laugh, Daisy!" he stormed, "but I can assure you that what is being proposed in this," and he held up the letter and shook it angrily, "will not come to pass whilst I remain head of this household!"

Reading his mail at the breakfast table was not Paul's usual preference, but the circumstances of that morning had led to this abnormal situation: Jonas Hampton had gone to Penzance at an early hour as, on checking the Trevarthen carriage, he had found a broken carriage lamp. Upon locating the spare lamp, he found that it, too, had been damaged. Annoyed, and knowing that the ladies were to visit with Mrs Crebo that day and would possibly not be returning from Truro until late in the evening, he wished to replace both of the glass front panels in good time. He had picked up the mail whilst he was in Penzance and it had been delivered to Mr Trevarthen on his return. As the Master of Trevu was heading towards the dining room, he had taken the letters with him. His wife and daughters were talking of their plans for their outing and his son had nothing to say to him, as was usual of late, so he had flipped through the post and had opened one whose script he could not recognise. From his angry expletives, it was apparent to the household that he was not best pleased with what he had read.

"Whatever is the matter, dearest?" asked his wife, in a soft voice, hoping to calm his obvious chagrin.

"That blasted Poulson!"

"Who?" Chloe asked, bewildered.

"Poulson, you know the fellow I mean!" he shouted in frustration. Chloe stared at him, trying to comprehend what he was talking about.

"Do you mean my mother's husband, Papa?" asked Daisy, innocently.

She watched as her father's mouth set in a hard line and for a moment she thought he would not reply. But finally, he spoke, confirming that the person he was talking about was indeed Professor Poulson of Oxford, the husband of the former Miss Dorothea Petherick.

"Apparently," he snapped, "the man has developed a conscience and has decided that, having no family of his own, his remaining assets will be bestowed upon his late wife's only child when he dies. I had presumed that due to his gambling habits he would have nothing left, but that is not the case, judging by the amount of money he informs me he has had placed in a trust fund. He is not in the best of health and thought it best to inform me of his intentions, lest he should die before I had news of it. Well, he should have saved his ink, for that damned filthy money will not come into this family!"

An embarrassed silence followed his remarks until Jack, finally full, wiped his mouth with his napkin, smiled brightly at his father's angry face and announced, "I think you'll have a problem with that decision, sir."

All eyes turned towards him as, unruffled, he continued to regard his father with a warm smile, though hidden within it, his mother thought she could detect a glint of steel. It was almost as if her son was pleased to see his father so discomforted.

"And what do you mean by that statement, my boy?" thundered his father, rattled by Jack's pleased expression.

"Well, I'm no scholar like yourself, father, as you well know, but from what I understand however...er...filthy this money is, it will not become part of your estate at all! It will belong to Daisy and as such, she can do as she likes with it!" Jack concluded, triumphantly.

Another silence filled the room as the truth of Jack's observations sank in. Paul appeared lost for words; he stared at his son in disbelief as a cold fury slowly filled his body.

"What I have stated will apply, have no fear of that, any of you." he intoned, enunciating his words slowly and carefully, though his anger was still apparent in his voice. "I will not have this money left to my daughter, for the bulk of it derives from the disgusting practice of slavery that Daisy's grandfather involved himself in. If any one of you thinks that I would allow so much as a farthing of it to come into contact with my family, then you are very much mistaken!"

Unwisely, Daisy bravely pointed out that it was as Jack had said; that the money would come to her and not her father and therefore, he had no right to deny her the right to receive it.

"Whilst you live under my roof, my girl, do not fill your head with the thoughts of such largesse coming into your possession," he hissed at her, his hands clenched hard together in an attempt to control himself.

Dorothea's daughter lifted her chin in defiance of him. This bequest was, albeit indirectly, from her own mother and it was being denied to her by the man who had taken her into his family only after seeing the wretched conditions she had been forced to endure in an orphanage. True, she could not remember what her life had been like at the horrible institution that she had

159

been placed in and could only remember her full and happy life as a member of the Trevarthen family. However, she had been told that her father had not wished for her to be a part of the family at all, and it was at her stepmother's insistence that she be brought into the household. Now he was trying to usurp her right to a bequest which, despite its mired origins, had been put into trust for her. If her father could have loved her mother so much that he was prepared to overlook the fact that she was a slave trader's daughter then surely she should be allowed to inherit through her mother's husband that which this unknown gentleman considered to be rightfully hers?

Speaking slowly and quietly, yet with scarcely contained fury, Daisy replied, "It will, when the time comes, be my inheritance, Papa and if I should wish to lay claim to it, then I will."

"If you touch a penny of it, my girl, you will not do so as a member of this family!" vowed Paul, shaking with temper.

"Please! Please, everyone, please try to be calm. Surely we can talk this through reasonably and calmly," pleaded Chloe, trying desperately to diffuse the situation. She looked around the table, hopelessly trying to catch the main protagonists' eyes, but to no avail. Daisy was staring unflinchingly at her father and he in his turn glared belligerently back at her.

Into this tense atmosphere, Jack was heard to excuse himself from the table. "I have to go to the estate office, you see," he remarked sarcastically, and his eyes swept the table and came to rest on his father's face. He smiled, but without affection, and then turned to his sister and said, "If I were you, Daisy, I should, at the first opportunity that presents itself to you, take your money and run. I would myself, if I thought I could," he ended, almost as an afterthought.

His father, shocked to hear such a pronouncement, ordered him to keep his place, but Jack was already at the door. He opened it with a swagger and walked through without so much as a backward glance.

In a moment, Paul was on his feet to follow the boy, but as he passed his wife's chair she reached out, caught hold of his arm and soundlessly shook her head. Breathing deeply, he hung his head, retraced his steps to his chair and sat down heavily. Chloe cleared her throat and advised the girls that, if they had finished their breakfasts, then she preferred that they leave the table and prepare themselves for their journey to Truro. Silently, the girls left their places and the room, knowing full well that their Mama would have plenty to say to their father once she had the opportunity to be alone with him.

Daisy wished to stay near the door in order to overhear their discussion but Grace, the elder, would not allow it and frowned at her. Reluctantly, Daisy made her way up the stairs in her sister's wake. Grace might have respected her parents' privacy, but once they were in the confines of their bedroom, she was quite willing to enter into a discussion with Daisy about the events that had so enraged their father.

Meanwhile, in the dining room, Paul hung his head in shame as his wife chastised him for his language and for losing his temper.

"I respect your feelings, Paul, of course I do, and I quite understand that you consider this money to be of such a vile descent that it should not come into this household. But Jack was in the right of it when he told you that this is a matter for Daisy to decide, not you. Now you have antagonised your daughter. How can you expect Daisy, of all people, to listen to you with any degree of sense when she sees her own father ranting..." but here, her husband broke in on her speech.

"I did not rant!" he snapped at her.

His wife sighed and then resumed her speech, "...ranting on about the evils of this bequest. I do not understand what has happened to you of late," she said, sadly. "You seem not at all to be the man I married. First George is in the wrong for being your first born, then Jack is to be turned into a farmer when any fool can see that he lacks the aptitude for it and certainly has no love for it. And now poor Daisy is harangued because she is to receive a bequest. It is not her fault if this money has been left to her and it is not your right to attempt to deny it to her. The money comes from her mother and goodness knows that poor woman had precious chance to allow her child anything. The money exists, regardless of its source and perhaps if Daisy would wish to use it for good and not evil, then it would be more acceptable to you."

Moodily, her husband studied the carpet and would not lift his face to look at her. She was immediately reminded of Jack who, as a child, would refuse to see or admit to the fact that he had been at fault when caught out in some misdeed. With this in her mind and in spite of the unhappy atmosphere in the room, she found herself smiling at him. When, eventually, he raised his face and caught sight of her smile, it should have warmed his heart, but he felt that even the most beloved of his family no longer understood him. Wearily, he picked up the rest of the discarded post and excused himself. Without even dropping a kiss on her curls, which was always a part of their morning ritual, he left the room and sadly made his way to his office.

Later that morning, Paul was still sitting in his office, trying to come to terms with what appeared to him to be serious insurrections taking place within his family, when a knock came and his brother peered around the door.

"Can I come in, brother?" he asked with a smile. Paul nodded, and Joey entered. He could not fail to notice that the man was in a despairing mood, and it was not long before Paul had recounted to his brother the news that he had received and the subsequent argument at the breakfast table. Joey pursed his lips as he studied the offending letter that his brother had passed to him. When he had finished his perusal, he told Paul that, whilst he sympathised with his position, in all honesty, there was little he could do. Upon the death of Professor Poulson, and when Daisy had reached her majority, the money would be rightfully given into her possession. The writer had indicated that his medical man had been honest with him and had warned him to put his affairs in order. Poulson had stated that his illness had forced him to change his lifestyle many years ago, so he had made arrangements for his money to be invested in various stocks and shares more than a dozen years before. Wise investments on his part had ensured that the money that would come to Dorothea Petherick's daughter had increased twenty-fold from what had already been a considerable amount.

"It is tainted money, Joey," said his brother, "and I wish for Daisy to have nothing to do with it!"

"All money be tainted in some way or other, Paul," Joey quietly advised him. Paul looked at him in surprise as his brother continued, urbanely, "That money you picked up in Mrs Glasson's cottage...every penny of it came from

161

me, payment to 'er to cover the loss of 'er boy. Now 'tis put in trust fer when Nicky is older an' I 'ave added more to it since. Do 'e think, if I 'ad let the boy's father live, I would still be 'ere to add to the account? I'd be dead an' gone long since, me body chopped up fer science, probably!" and he had to laugh at Paul's horrified expression in response to his words.

"My money back then, Paul, the money that I gave so freely to widders an' orfans, came from my lawbreaking ways. Thas' tainted money, but it 'ave 'elped a lot of people live lives better than they could afore. Twas wrong, I know, to come by it through me smugglin' ways, but I did try to do some good with it also," he concluded humbly.

Paul nodded, but explained that the revulsion he felt for Daisy's inheritance stemmed from the fact that, originally, the money was accrued due to Petherick's profits in the slave trade. "My mother used - and I still use - some of her wealth to help the less well off in society, but her money did not start its life as the profit from the sale of one poor soul to another and it is that fact that cuts into my heart," he announced, sadly.

Joey raised an eyebrow at him. "You goin' 'ave give a lot of thought to yer attitude, Paul," he cautioned. "Yer children be growing up an' they idden goin' look at the world through their father's eyes. Tidden right fer you to expect them to see life the same way as you d' do."

His brother sighed. He knew Joey to be right, he told him, but he had found all the recent changes in his life so hard to deal with and to comprehend. "Life had seemed so normal, following a set pattern and now, through no fault of my own, changes are being imposed upon it by outside influences that I cannot control," Paul said in a quiet voice, and then, loudly and angrily, added, "And it's so damned unfair!"

"You be right there, brother!" affirmed Bolitho. "I 'ave often thought my life to be unfair, but there are times when all be well an' when that 'appens, I be damn grateful."

His brother's face broke into a gentle smile. "And is life fair for you at the moment, Joey?" he asked, quietly.

"Bleddy right it is, brother!" swore Joey, and a happy smile broke out on his face. Upon seeing it, Paul himself laughed for the first time that day.

"My marriage, Paul, well, 'tis a wonderful thing. If you'd a' told me six months ago that I could 'ave bin this 'appy...well, I wouldn' 'ave believed 'e, an' thas the truth!" he expounded with a satisfied grin. "My Sarah-Jane be so thrilled with everythin' that 'tis a pleasure to see 'er so. I got tell 'e I wouldn' sure whether be pleased or no when she told me, but now . . ." He paused, gazing at his brother with a mixture of satisfaction and disbelief on his face, then continued, "Well, now 'tis such a joyous time I can't remember what it felt like afore, when it looked like we was never goin' 'ave children." Paul smiled back at him, pleased with his delight at his approaching parenthood and humbled to think that his own parental life was causing him so much heartache at this present time.

"Chloe and I are so pleased for you both. I consider that it is no more than you deserve, Joey, for I know my children think you the best of uncles," said Paul, and he noted the blush that filled his brother's face as he spoke.

He leant forward and picked up the ill-fated letter from his desk, then opened a drawer and deposited it on top of a pile of papers that already resided within. Turning to his brother, he told him that perhaps, with some quiet reflection, he might find a way of handling what was, to him, a shameful situation to be placed in. He then inquired if Joey would wish to partake of lunch with him.

"I was 'oping you was goin' ask me," replied Joey. With a mischievous grin he offered up the explanation that, as various members of Sarah-Jane's family were coming to call that evening, he had ordered her to rest and presumed that lunch would be a dismal affair without her company. "I brought Nicky along with me an' I spec'late 'e an' Sam be enjoyin' a meal right now, if I know yer Miss Claverin'," he said, raising an eyebrow at Paul.

"You devious fellow, you!" laughed Paul, seeing the humour in the situation, and it was a far happier man who sat down to his meal in the dining room, than had been there earlier that day.

CHAPTER 19

IT WAS raining and young Nicky Nankivell was not best pleased. Now he would have to stay indoors and not go to the bay to swim. He could sit and read the new book that Mr Trevarthen had bought for him but it would not be as pleasurable as swimming in the blue waters of the bay with his guardian which was, he thought, the best fun he could have. But that morning, when he had rushed to the window to look outside, there were grey clouds hanging over the castle on the mount and he knew he would not go unless the sun came out. He wondered, hopefully, if perhaps Sammy Trevarthen would come to play with him, instead? The house was always busy now with people coming to see Mrs Bolitho, or 'Mama Bolitho' as Nicky had christened her. She loved for him to call her by this new name and would always hug and kiss him when he used it. Besides, she liked to cuddle him anyway and he enjoyed the attention that she unfailingly gave him. For some strange reason he had always called her husband 'Mr Bolitho' although, if the truth were told, the man was his favourite amongst the adults and it would have been more fitting for him not to be so formal when addressing him. But somehow, because it was frowned upon to call him 'Joey', as did most of his friends, he had continued to use this title. His guardian, on the other hand, used various names to address him and not all of them were polite. Mama Bolitho had told his guardian, on many occasions, not to use some of them but Mr Bolitho seemed to forget, especially if Nicky had done something to annoy him. The young lad did not mind at all that Mr Bolitho used these words when talking to him, because they were the best of friends. Young Nicky thought it perfectly correct to use nasty words to your friends, especially if you did not mean them. And he knew his guardian liked him, because he would tousle his curls or gently tweak his ears, and frequently catch him up in his arms and hug Nicky to him.

The youngster had finished fastening most of the buttons on his coat and set off downstairs to the dining room for his breakfast. When he got there, he was most surprised to find not a scrap of food laid out on the sideboard. He looked at the clock by the wall. Nicky was only just learning to tell the time but he thought that the hands were in the right place for the breakfast hour so, puzzled, he left the room and crossed the hallway to take the stairs to the kitchen. The noise of excited chatter drifted up to him and the warm air and smell of food hit him as he began his descent. The kitchen, thought Nicky, was the best of all the rooms in the house because his other friend, Mrs Nancarrow, always found special treats for him. When he arrived there, Minnie and Mrs Nancarrow were so busily employed with setting pans of water to boil that he went unnoticed until he spoke, whereupon they jumped and both turned in surprise to see him standing behind them.

"I'm 'ungry!" he announced, with a slight pout of disappointment on his lips.

"Oh, my dear!" exclaimed a distracted Mrs Nancarrow, brushing the back of her hand across her forehead, "I forgot all about 'e!" Quickly, she cut and buttered some bread, which she liberally spread with some honey, then filled a large cup with milk and placed everything on a tray for him. This was not at all what Nicky was accustomed to and he was about to complain that he would also like some cold ham. But Minnie was ordered to take both the tray and Nicky to the dining room and to return to her duties in the kitchen as fast as her legs would carry her. The young boy found himself seated at the table in the dining room in a trice and, because he was always ravenous, commenced his meal before Minnie had reached the dining room door. There came the sound of rapping at the front door and the serving girl had to make a detour to attend upon the caller. Nicky, straining his ears, caught the sound of a man's voice and easily recognised it as that of Mr Trevarthen. Perhaps Sammy was to come and play with him after all, thought Nicky with glee. But Mr Trevarthen's voice sounded strange, as if he had a great deal to worry about, so the young boy reasoned that perhaps he was not to have the hoped-for company. With a piece of bread in his hand, he climbed down from his seat and cautiously opened the door that led into the hallway. Peering out through the small crack, he could see that Mr Trevarthen and his wife had called, but they did not look at all happy. He wondered if he should run across to them so that they would know he was there, but something about their worried expressions stopped him.

"A fine boy!" he heard Minnie say, and for a moment wondered if she was talking about him, though he did not think so, as she more often than not called him a pest and a nuisance. Intrigued, Nicky listened intently to what she was telling the couple, as she hurriedly took Mr Trevarthen's hat and gloves.

"Master sent fer Dr Dunstan in the early hours an' twas some easy birth! Easy as anything! But the poor doctor 'em bin able to stop 'er bleedin'," blurted the serving girl, worriedly, then burst into a bout of tears. Immediately, Mrs Trevarthen moved forward to console her, but Minnie sobbed that she had to get back to the kitchen and excused herself, running down the steps and leaving the Trevarthens alone in the hallway.

Thinking themselves unheard, Paul Trevarthen turned to his wife and stated, worriedly, "I hope that Joey will not suffer as I had to do when you were brought to bed the last time, dearest, for I almost went mad with worry for you." He caught up her hand and squeezed it, "Still, Denzil is a fine practitioner and I am sure that all will be well," he said with reassurance. However, the face that looked back at him was creased with worry.

"Yes, yes of course, Paul," answered his wife, "and we must not forget that she has been so healthy whilst she has been carrying, and to have such an easy birth, yet..." Nicky, however, heard no more, as Mrs Nancarrow appeared from the kitchen and took them off to the withdrawing room, their voices becoming an indistinct murmur as the door closed behind them. Resuming his meal of bread and honey, Nicky made his way back to the lonely dining room table.

In the withdrawing room, Mrs Nancarrow was hastily acquainting the couple with the events that had transpired that night. Mrs Bolitho had produced a fine boy with no trouble at all, she told them, her voice brimming with disbelief, but from that moment on there had been severe complications. Mrs Trevarthen watched the cook's anguished face as she went on to explain that, no matter what Dr Dunstan did, he could not stem the haemorrhage.

Suddenly and uncharacteristically, she burst into tears and lifting up her apron, she buried her face in it.

"Why that sainted soul got be taken from we, I dunno!" she sobbed, "an wha's poor Mr Bolitho goin' do? 'E do live fer she!"

Paul Trevarthen swallowed hard to keep back the tears that threatened to overwhelm him, whilst his wife sat, stunned, at his side, twisting her gloves in her hands.

"My brother?" he asked, tentatively.

"With 'er, sir," gulped Mrs Nancarrow, desperately trying to master her tears. "Dr Dunstan brought Maddie fer midwife to 'elp 'im, but once 'e knew what things was like, 'e 'ad yer brother in to be with 'er. I got the stable boy to go fer 'e, sir, knawin' the fondness you 'ave fer each other an' I thought be best 'ave a man 'ere fer when...fer when..." but she could not continue and hung her head, mute with despair. After a moment, she gathered her strength and looked up again, saying, "Master goin' need 'e afore the day is out, sir." At her words, Paul caught his breath, for he could not bear to think of what the cook was implying. 'Why?' he thought, 'had not my own dear wife suffered as badly? My family survived that terrible ordeal.' Then he realised that at no stage had Denzil Dunstan called him to be at his wife's bedside. Only if Denzil believed he was not winning the fight to save Mrs Trevarthen, would Paul have been called to be with his wife, as now his brother had been summoned to be with Sarah-Jane.

They turned as they heard footsteps running down the stairs and Mrs Nancarrow excused herself, hurrying into the hallway. They heard Maddie Olds, Dr Dunstan's servant, explain that she was off to the Wherry to fetch back a recently widowed woman, who had delivered not two days before, to act as wet nurse.

"Her own didden last the night, a poor weight an' sickly," she told the cook, hurriedly, "an' the poor soul be grieving something fierce. If 'tis all right, I'll bring she 'ere, 'cos I don't want fer the baby to be away from Mrs Bolitho until she do pass away."

"Oh!" cried Mrs Nancarrow, crushed by Maddie's statement, "there's no 'ope then?"

Maddie shook her head, authoritatively. "Seen it scores of times, Mrs Nancarrow. A shame, a shame 'cos she was a lovely woman, but the Lord 'ave called 'er an' she'll be in 'is arms by nightfall." With this bald affirmation of the state of affairs, she picked up her cloak, which lay across a hall table and placed it around herself to help keep off the rain. She then left the house in order to collect the poor bereaved woman that she had spoken of, who would come to feed the babe, sleeping so soundly in his crib in his mother's bedchamber.

Returning to the Trevarthen's, the cook said that she had pans of hot water to be taken up the stairs and that as soon as she had further knowledge of the situation, she would come back to tell them. Left alone, Paul Trevarthen slowly put his arm around his wife's waist who turned to him, hid her face in his shoulder and began to cry, softly. Paul's own tears trickled down his cheeks and fell onto the straw of her bonnet.

Within a short time, Mrs Nancarrow had returned and told them that Mrs Bolitho wished to see them both. "She's is so proud of that poor little babe that she wishes fer you to see 'en," she explained, with a heavy sigh.

"And Joey?" asked his brother, worriedly, "How is he bearing up?"

"Why, he is all bright with smiles for her, Mr Trevarthen, sir, but 'e seems not to notice anybody else an' do speak only to 'is missus," she said. The sad little procession was then led up the stairs to the bedchamber.

Denzil Dunstan, worn and haggard following his fruitless attempts during the night, opened the door to them and brought them into the spacious room. Two chairs had been placed beside the bed. Close by, a crib took pride of place. In the bed lay Sarah-Jane, pale and weak, yet her eyes burned with a fire that neither Trevarthen had ever seen before. Lying on the bed beside her was her husband, his arms around his wife's body, holding her as tenderly as if she had been thistledown. He did not turn his head to look at them but stared steadfastly as his beloved wife, his hair uncombed and his face unshaven. Every time his wife turned to look at him, his face lit up with a smile, which hid from her sight his all-consuming despair. Joey did not look to speak to them, but he knew them there, and when his brother reached across the bed and gently grasped his hand, Paul felt the desperate squeeze that he received in return. He could imagine his brother's torment, but there was nothing that could be said, and so the little company sat in silence by the bed. Sarah-Jane lay at peace, so full of pride and love that she did not seem aware of the sadness that pervaded the space around her.

"Oh, Chloe! My dearest Chloe! You have come. Look at him," she said, waving a weak arm in the direction of the crib. "Is he not the most perfect child?" Chloe nodded, a brave smile on her face, and when invited to do so, gently removed the sleeping babe from its bed and cradled the infant in her arms. Paul, when asked, agreed with his wife that the child was beautiful.

"You are pleased, are you not, Joey?" asked Sarah-Jane, who was worriedly examining her husbands expression.

"Sweet'eart you 'ave made me the 'appiest of men. Such a 'ansome son an' a fine, strong child," he affirmed, with a wide smile. His wife's face lit up at his words and she reached out and gently stroked his cheek, seeming not to notice his unshaven features. She gave a contented sigh and closed her eyes, a gentle smile on her lips. They thought she would have no more to say, but suddenly, she looked again upon her husband and smiled brightly at him.

"Dearest," she said, softly, "You must make sure he is loved and treasured, for well I know that this gift has cost me dear." Joey's eyes opened wide with surprise and he tried to protest, but she silenced him by placing her hand over his lips. "I know, dearest, I know," she whispered and it was then that she saw his eyes fill with tears for her.

"My dear, sweet love," she murmured, raising her hand to gently wipe away the tears which were now streaming down his face. He caught up her hand and dropped a kiss into her palm, whispering her name in despair.

"Such a love we had, Joey," she said, gently, all the while a soft smile playing on her lips, "A bond that ties us forever." He could only nod his head, but he raised it again to look into her face when she said, "But time will heal your hurt, beloved, and when the time comes, never fear that I shall not wish for you to take a good wife for yourself, and a loving mother for our son. I would not have him denied the love he deserves, Joey, when I am no longer here to be with him," and then she added, so softly that he almost did not catch her words, "or you!"

The fear of losing her made him desperate, and he shook his head and vowed to follow her, but she told him she would not have him throw away his life and deny his son a father. "Hear me, Joey, I will not have you do that for me, do you hear?" she cried, her voice growing strong again.

He nodded and it seemed to satisfy her, for she closed her eyes and began to doze gently. Denzil crossed quietly to her side and felt for a pulse. Having found it, weak though it was, he walked away to his chair at the side of the room and sat down, impotently. So, the little company sat and waited for the inevitable moment, the only sound an occasional murmur from the sleeping baby, to interrupt the doom-laden silence.

After an hour, Sarah-Jane awoke again, but saw only her husband's face gazing lovingly at her. "Oh, Joey, my dear, dear, sweet Joey," she breathed, weakly, "Such...a...love...we had...my dearest..." and with her final breath, he heard her whisper his name for the last time. Her head slumped against his arm and he knew that the dream had ended and his nightmare begun. Joey, to whom death was not a stranger, did not need the doctor to tell him that she had gone. He knew it by the feel of her lifeless body, but he could not let her go and only pulled her the more desperately towards him. He held her fast, as if the warmth of his own body and the strength of his grip would bring her back to life. He cried out that she should not leave him and rocked her like a mother would keen a lost child. Chloe turned a face full of tears and despair towards her husband. Hastily, he wiped his own face and then motioned her to take the baby from the room. Dr Dunstan tried to say a few words, but Paul nodded towards the door, silently directing him to leave the room. And so only the two brothers remained, as guardians to Paul Trevarthen's oldest friend and Joseph Bolitho's dearest love.

Paul bided his time, letting his distressed brother caress his wife until he knew that he should take him away from the overpowering sadness of the room. Respectfully, Paul walked around the bed until he was by his brother's side. Then he placed his arm around him and said, quietly, "Come, brother, come. The women will be here soon, Joey, to arrange her laying out. You can come back to see her then, but you must leave her now." Joey moaned and shook his head, ran his fingers through her tumbled curls and kissed her dear lips, which cooled rapidly in the heat of the summer day. His brother pulled him slowly away and took him towards the door. With one last despairing look at the woman who had been his life's desire, lying so serenely in her bed, Joey Bolitho, blinded by tears, allowed his brother to lead him, stumbling, from the room.

Nicky Nankivell sat in his bedroom, with his chair pulled up to the window so that the light would fall on the pages of his book, the better for him to read it He was still feeling hungry and felt justifiably annoyed to have been both ignored and partially starved. When he had finished his breakfast, he climbed down from his chair and went off in search of his guardian. Minnie, rushing down the stairs and looking worried and flustered, told him to go to his room until he was sent for. He stuck out his lips at that and would have argued with her, but the serving girl looked different today, as had the Trevarthen's, so he mumbled under his breath about it not being fair and, with dragging feet, headed slowly towards his room. Once there, he slumped into his chair for a while, then decided to read his new book. Opening it at the first page, he ran his finger underneath the words and began to read aloud in the silence of his room. When he had almost reached the end of the story, he came across a word he did not recognise and began to kick his booted foot against the wall underneath the window in frustration. So, when the door to his room opened and Mr Trevarthen strode in, Nicky was delighted to see him. He did not return Nicky's beaming smile, but the boy was not perturbed, as Mr Trevarthen could read and he would know the word that the young boy could not recognise.

"What's that, sir?" asked the young lad, half turning in his chair and pointing to the offending word. Softly, the tall man crossed to his chair and looking down, caught his breath when he saw where Nicky's finger pointed.

"Angel," Paul said, quietly, staring incredulously at what Nicky had indicated. The young boy did not quite catch what he had said. "Engine?" he queried, uncertain, as it made a nonsense of his story.

"No, not engine," said Paul, and slowly repeated the word. Nicky nodded his head as if he had known it all along and then asked what it meant.

"That's a name given to people who have...who have died and gone to heaven," he explained, biting down hard on his lip. He pulled a chair towards the window and sat down beside the young boy. Nicky, looking puzzled, asked hopefully if Mr Trevarthen would like to read to him.

"Not at the moment, Nicky, but I promise I will do so in the future," he told him quietly. Bracing himself, Paul coughed, cleared his throat and told the young boy that he had some very sad news to tell him. Young Master Nankivell stared at Mr Trevarthen with large, enquiring eyes.

"Mrs Bolitho was having her baby and she became very ill. Dr Dunstan came and he tried his very best but..." Paul began, tortuously. He was interrupted by the young lad, who told him that Dr Dunstan had wanted to cut his foot off. Mr Bolitho would not let him and that was why he still had it, and he lifted his leg to show Mr Trevarthen. But the man reached across and caught hold of the boy's little hand to stop the flow of reminiscences, then he continued with his painful explanation.

"You see, when the baby had been born, Mrs Bolitho was so poorly that she was not well enough to stay alive, and very sadly she has gone to sleep for good. She has gone to be an angel in heaven, like the little girl did in your book," he told him, slowly and carefully. Nicky's eyes began to fill with tears and his lip began to tremble. He knew what Mr Trevarthen had meant. The kind lady would never hug and kiss him again, tell him stories and do all the lovely things she did for him. His granny went to sleep, too, and she never came back to be with him.

"What about the baby she wanted? What happened to that?" Nicky sniffled, his little voice breaking up with sobs. "The baby is well and he is a little boy," Mr Trevarthen told him, trying to sound pleased. "Perhaps they could send the baby to heaven to be an angel an' we can have Mama Bolitho back with we?" Nicky suggested. But he knew it was hopeless, and unable to control himself he let out a great howl for the loss of such a lovely person from his young life. He was greatly eased to find himself comforted in Mr Trevarthen's arms, and he knew that he was very sad, too, because the man was crying just as much as the young boy. When they had stopped sobbing, they dried their eyes on Mr Trevarthen's very damp handkerchief and with a loud sniff, Nicky asked after Mr Bolitho. Touched at his concern, Paul swallowed hard and told him that Mr Bolitho was very upset about it, and that he must be a good boy and not to bother him for a long time, because he was very sad.

"It's not fair," Nicky bawled once more, "I bin good a long time because the baby was going to come and now I got be good again." Paul could not help but smile at his reasoning, but he impressed upon the young boy the need for him to be very good indeed, because Mr Bolitho was going to be especially sad to have to say goodbye to Mrs Bolitho. Paul then explained that he had to go in order to talk with someone. Noticing the little ark placed high on a shelf, he asked Nicky if he should get it down for him to play with. The little lad creased his brow for a moment and then nodded. After all, Nicky reasoned, if Sammy was not to come and play with him today, he might as well amuse himself with the toy on his own. Paul left him sitting on the floor under the window, explaining to a rather battered elephant that he had to be quiet, because there was a great sadness in their house today.

Minnie came for Nicky at lunchtime and took him down to the kitchen with her. Nobody said very much and he noticed that people kept sniffing and wiping their eyes. The serving girl was the worst of all and would occasionally burst into sudden tears and bawl loudly, whilst Mrs Nancarrow told her to stop, lest the Master should hear. When they had finished eating, Mrs Nancarrow picked up the young boy, took her seat by the fire and rocked him in her arms.

Mr Trevarthen had been so busy he had barely the time to eat a luncheon. His brother had refused all food but had taken the glass of brandy, which had been placed in his hand whilst Paul had been with him. Paul had arranged for the news to be carried to Sarah-Jane's family and then, sitting at his brother's desk, he had written three notes in haste; the first to his eldest son, the second to the Rickards and the last for Richard Nairn at Trevanoc, all detailing the disaster that had befallen Mr Bolitho. To write so baldly to Leah Bolitho with the news was more than he could bear so, considering the fondness that he knew Mr Nairn to have for the old lady, he thought him the best person to break the sad news to her. A lad was sent down into the town to catch the mail and another despatched to Trevanoc on Joey Bolitho's swiftest horse. He had arranged for a cabinet-maker to supply the coffin, shortened the dining room table, on which it could be placed, and saw to it that all the curtains were drawn that faced on to the street. Then he had the spare bedchamber made up for his brother and had overseen the setting up of chairs in the dining room and the placing of some discreet candles. When her body was brought down, his heart welled up at the sight of her, lying calm and peaceful in her coffin. He returned to the small upstairs room where his brother sat, staring sightlessly out of the window at the magnificent sweep of the bay that was laid out so gloriously before him. Paul sent for hot water and shaved his brother, as Joey did not seem to care to do it himself, he then went through the linen press and coaxed him into dressing himself in his best clothes.

"You would be fine for her, brother," crooned Paul, "You know how she would wish for that, for truly she so admired you when you looked of your best." His brother nodded, dumbly. Paul's heart fell when they entered the dining room and Joey caught sight of her again: Gabriel Hendra, the cabinet-maker, had provided a splendid coffin and had lined it with the finest white satin. A pale pink velvet cushion supported Mrs Bolitho's head over which her glossy brown tresses trailed. Her pale face appeared to glow with translucent light that peacefully shone out from her resting place. When Joey's eyes fell upon that cherished countenance, he moaned softly, and almost lost his footing as he rushed across the room to caress her sweet face once again. After a while, his brother spoke softly into his ear, persuading him to move away and sit on the top chair, which was set to one side of the table. Joey sat down heavily, but his eyes, pools of despair, continued to gaze upon his beloved with a longing that ripped at Paul's heart. However, at the sound of a knock at the front door, a change came over him. Although he stared as resolutely as before, Joey's features slowly turned to stone and his expression set as rigidly as that which lay across the face of his beloved, who lay in her casket, looking for all the world like a beautiful marbled statue.

They came in their droves, all through that long afternoon, to cry for her and to share his burden of grief. Each in turn offered their condolences and shook hands with Joey, who responded as if he were an automaton, sitting stock-still in his chair and seemingly unaware of his surroundings. Amongst the mourners, many of whom were from the town, were Sarah-Jane's brothers, who came with their wives. Also present were Mrs Penrose and Mrs Roskilly, who sobbed loudly and bitterly. Finally, Sir Reginald Bonython approached. He held on to Bolitho's hand for a long time, but could not find any words to say that could ease the poor man's grief. His wife, unable to attend, had written a note of condolence and Mr Trevarthen took it from him on his brother's behalf, promising that he would ensure Joey had knowledge of it. When, finally, the two brothers had been left alone in the room, the door slowly opened and a head full of ginger curls appeared around it. Catching sight of Joey, Nicky Nankivell let out a whoop of delight and bounded across the room, throwing himself into his guardian's arms before Paul could stop him. Shocked by Joey's lack of response, and noting that the man was not looking at him but at the wooden box on the table, he turned his own gaze towards it. Wide eyed, he took his fill of the sight of his dear Mama Bolitho, lying asleep on her bed of shiny cloth, and thought she looked truly beautiful. It was difficult for him to imagine that she could never wake again, but he understood that it could never be. He settled on his guardian's lap, reached down and caught up the almost lifeless hand that rested on the man's knee, squeezing it with all his might. Slowly, his guardian pulled his gaze away and rested his eyes on the young boy's earnest face.

Nicky beamed happily back at him. Remembering that he had to be good, he said, in a soft voice, "Please don't be sad. Mama Bolitho has gone to be a beautiful angel with my Mama and Nana and...and my Dada!"

If Nicky had hoped to make his guardian smile, he was to be disappointed, but Mr Bolitho pulled the boy to him and held the young child tight against his chest. Young Master Nankivell felt hot tears on his face and knew they were not his. He had tried not to cry again, as he wanted to be good, but he knew he had to be very kind to his best friend because he was so sad. Consequently, he struggled to free his pinioned arm and, when he had done so, he reached up and softly stroked the man's wet cheek with his little hand.

CHAPTER 20

SLOWLY, the carriage made its way up the road that led to the front of the fine house. The sun shone upon the scene and the house seemed to shine back as it basked in the glory of the beautiful day. Beside the carriage, keeping pace with it, a man sat astride his horse. He appeared not to appreciate the setting, in fact, he scarcely seemed to notice the scenery at all. When the group had arrived at the front of the house, the carriage halted at the steps leading up to the front door. The rider dismounted and passed his reins to a respectful stable boy, who had come running to hold the man's mount for him. He raised his face to look towards the house, but his expression did not divulge his thoughts and the blankness upon it seemed to be almost in opposition to the radiance that shone all around him. From the house, another man descended the steps rapidly and headed towards the visitors, a look of sadness and concern on his features. Richard Nairn, the estate manager for Trevanoc, had not expected a visit from Miss Bolitho's nephew. Joey Bolitho had always steadfastly refused to call upon his aunt, if at all possible, and the recent bereavement that the man had suffered, Nairn reasoned, would have rendered a visit even more unlikely.

"I 'ave come to see Miss Bolitho," her nephew announced in an expressionless voice, lifting his blank eyes towards Mr Nairn.

"Of...of course, Mr Bolitho, sir," replied Mr Nairn, unsure of what else he should say to the poor fellow. He had attended the funeral of Joey's wife not three days before. As estate manager, he had gone to represent his employer, Leah Bolitho, but he had a great admiration for Joey and the dear lady that had been his wife and would have attended out of respect for the couple in any case. Now, Richard Nairn firmly clasped Bolitho's hand, hoping to pass some strength from himself into the body of the hollowed man, but in his heart, he knew it to be hopeless. The face that stared back at him offered up no response and, after a moment, Joey Bolitho turned away and moved to open the carriage door. He reached up to give his hand to a diminutive lady, who clambered awkwardly out of the vehicle, this being the first time that the woman had ever used such a form of transportation in her life. Then, Bolitho reached into the carriage and lifted out a small crib, in the midst of which a newborn baby slept, contentedly. Holding the crib, Joey turned back towards his aunt's estate manager, who stared back at him, clearly bewildered.

Silently, Mr Nairn turned and retraced his steps to the house, with the small procession following in his wake. Once inside, he led the way to the withdrawing room where, as always, Miss Leah Bolitho sat in her high-backed chair. When they had gained admittance, Nairn stood back to allow Mr Bolitho to speak with his aunt.

Joey walked forward and placed the tiny crib at her feet, ignoring the hand that reached out towards him. In a voice from which all emotion had been drained, he flatly announced, " I brought 'e what 'e wanted so much, Aunt Leah - an heir fer this place!"

Her eyes filled with tears at his words, but he had more to say. Indicating the small woman at his side, he said, "This be Mrs Polglaze, who 'ave come fer to wet nurse the baby. I 'ave seen that she be well paid fer 'er services..." and reaching into his pocket, he produced a large roll of bills and passed them into his aunt's outstretched hand, before continuing, " ...and this be payment for its keep."

Leah's shock at the boldness of the statement caused her to catch her breath. Her sad eyes tried hard to find some expression in his face, but all trace of feeling had left him; he merely stood, resolute and emotionless, before her.

"My poor boy," she said, her voice shaking with feeling, "you knaw you and your family be welcome here. 'Tis yer home and I would wish that you come to be with me at Trevanoc, you do knaw that." Yet Joey was shaking his head before even she had finished speaking, breaking her heart still further.

"I want no part of this family, aunt. My..." and here he paused, summoning the words to continue, "My Sarah-Jane told me I was to see the baby treasured an' loved, so I 'ave brought 'im to you, fer I knaw you will do that."

"Joseph!" the old lady pleaded, "it is for you, also, to love the poor innocent. You knaw she wanted so much to give 'e a son!"

He stared at her, his expression unfathomable, but when he spoke again, his chilling words filled her with despair. "We bin an' paid too 'igh a price fer this gift, Aunt," and he pointed at the occupant of the crib, "fer we 'ave lost both our lives in the attempt. I want no part of 'im! The child be yours, to do with as 'e will."

Two tears ran down her cheeks, but her nephew showed no response to her distress and merely announced, "I be goin' on now!" Abruptly, he turned on his heel and headed for the door. She called his name and half rose from her chair, her body shaking with the strain of it. "Joseph, my dear Joseph! Don't go!" she called out to him, desperately. "You can't leave the poor innocent like this. Unloved an' unwanted!"

"Love 'im if you will, keep 'im if you want an' call 'im anythin' you've a mind to!" he threw at her as he reached the door. Then, without a backward glance, he left the room. The stunned occupants of the room heard the front door slam, then the sound of galloping hooves, heading away down the gravelled road. It was followed, a moment later, by the noise of the coach, slowly lumbering away in the wake of the disappearing rider.

At Trevu, the Trevarthens sat together, their hands entwined and their faces showing the strain of the last few days. Paul could hardly believe that the events of late had taken place at all, whilst Chloe's sad face reflected the pain she felt, at both the loss of a dear friend and the distress that her passing had caused both to her husband and his brother. Since the funeral, they had seen little of Joey for, once his wife had been buried, he had seemed galvanised into action. Reports came back to them that he had made visits to his lawyers and that he had seemed to be meticulously putting his affairs in order. Paul was sick with worry that Joey was to do some harm to himself, but Chloe reminded him that they were present when Sarah-Jane had made him promise not to do such a thing. "Well you know how he would not go against her wishes in life, Paul. He will obey her," she told him, adding, with a sob, "even from the grave."

Of course, the practicalities of the situation had occurred to them, as it appeared to have done for Joey. And so they resolved that it would probably be for the best if Paul's brother came to live at Trevu for a while, with his son and young Nicky. Later, when Joey's grief was not so raw, he could return to live in Penzance if he wished, but they felt that they should not press him on this matter. "After all," reasoned Mrs Trevarthen, "he has a household of his own and if he wishes to remain in his own home, then it is only right that he should do so. We cannot tell what he would wish to do for his future."

A knock at the door brought their thoughts back to the present and Jonas Hampton entered the room, to request that the Master should come down to the stables sometime that morning, as he thought that one of the mares looked unwell and he wanted Paul's opinion. He thanked Jonas and told him he would follow on shortly. Mr Hampton politely smiled and left the room.

"I might as well go now, if you have no objection, my dear?"

Chloe shook her head. She would go part of the way with him, she said, as she thought that a turn around the front of the house would be beneficial. The front side of Trevu was more likely to have a fine breeze there, for the weather had turned hot and sultry and she felt a walk outside would help revive her spirits.

Consequently, the couple were at the bottom of the steps, when Jack, returning from his studies with Neddy Peake, came across them. The whole family had been devastated by the loss of Joey's wife, but Jack felt it particularly as he had such a fondness for the man. As a young lad, he had worshipped him as a hero and that sense of admiration, although tempered with age, had never been lost. He caught sight of his young brother, Sam, who was talking with a group of workers who were sharpening their scythes by the lower barn. He called out to him and the little lad came running, beaming at the sight of him. They walked back to the house together and began to talk amongst themselves as they approached their parents

However, at the sound of a horseman coming up the drive, all turned as one to see who was approaching. Recognising his brother, Paul called out to him, but there was no answered greeting, only a raised hand in reply. The rider was not alone, sitting proudly before him was young Nicky Nankivell, the widest of smiles on his young face and his arm wrapped around his chest in a protective manner. The Master of Trevu noted, with a shadow of concern, the two bags strapped across the beast's rump and as his brother's horse ambled up to them, he waited patiently for them to dismount. Young Nicky, clearly bursting with excitement, was the first to speak.

"Look Sam!" he shouted, his little face aglow with delight, "Look what I got!" Opening up his coat, he lifted out a tiny puppy, which gave an unconcerned yawn as it found itself in the bright daylight. Almost completely white with only a small, dark patch on its side, it was not the most handsome of creatures, but it more than satisfied the youngster. Paul raised his eyes from the young lad's delighted features to his brother's blank expression and thought that, perhaps, Joey had been wise to invest in the young animal, as it had undoubtedly brought so much pleasure into his protégé's young life at a moment of great sadness. "I called 'im Spot," gabbled Nicky, "and 'e keep licking me!" he concluded with a delighted giggle.

"Hold tight!" Joey suddenly commanded and, catching hold of the young boy, lifted him towards his brother, who immediately held up his hands and took hold of him. Gently, he placed Nicky on the ground and at once the excited youngster ran towards Sam, the better to show him the little creature that had obviously enchanted him so much.

Mr Trevarthen brought his gaze back to his brother, frowning as he noted that Joey had not dismounted and was, instead, busily untying the smaller of the two bags. Successfully releasing it, he lifted the bag down and dropped it close to his brother's feet.

"Tha's some of his clothes," he stated, unemotionally, "an' when 'e need more they be at the 'ouse. Send fer 'is toys an' books when you've a mind to, 'cos Mrs Nancarrow 'ave the runnin' of the place an' can see to anythin' for 'e. There be a fund set up to cover the cost of 'avin' him with yer family and me solicitor will be in touch to explain it to 'e."

"But, Joey, I...I don't understand?" queried Paul, perplexed, "surely you will be staying here as well? Chloe and I would wish for it most particularly. Of course, I realise that you may have business to see to at this precise time but after you return you will be most..." but his brother held up his hand and stopped him.

Looking coldly into his brother's eyes, Joey stated, "I be goin' away, Paul. I wen't be back, so I thought it best to leave the boy 'ere, 'cos I can 'ardly drag 'en round with me. I knaw you an' Chloe will take good care of 'en." At his words, the two young boys stopped their excited chatter and young Nicky turned a worried face towards his guardian. Bolitho went on to explain that he had made arrangements for the boy's wardship to be passed over to Paul.

"If you cannot take Nicky with you, then what of your son? Surely, if you cannot travel with the lad, you would not think to drag a babe in arms around with you?"

"I put 'e with Aunt Leah," replied Joey, swiftly and without a trace of feeling. "She was always wanting an heir for her place, so now she bin an' got one."

Shocked, Paul's mouth fell open and he stared at his brother, stunned into silence.

"Dear Joey," pleaded Chloe. "This cannot be. I know that you are hurt and grieving still, but the time will come when you would wish for your loved ones to be around you."

He turned his head and studied her face for a while, but her pleading expression could not penetrate the cold ice that blocked the way to his heart. He knew himself alive, although he felt as dead as his beloved, but he had successfully contained the pain that had wrenched him these last days, keeping it locked away from his fellow man and in so doing, had barred those close to him from gaining access to his feelings.

"My loved one, Chloe," he said, coldly and precisely, "be gone." Then he turned his gaze towards the little boy, who was gently caressing his puppy, and told him that he had to be a good, because the Trevarthen's were going to look after him.

"I be leavin' you 'ere, Nicky," he told him, "an' I 'spect you be'ave yerself."

Nicky raised an appalled face towards him, whilst the puppy let out a little yelp, to remind the person holding him to smooth down his coat again, because he liked it so. The young lad did not notice, his eyes beginning to well with tears.

"Why?" he asked, with a sob, and then added, tearfully, "I bin good!" But his guardian only looked at him with a face of stone and did not respond to his question. Instead, Bolitho turned back towards his brother and his family, still grouped together in front of the house.

"I'll say my goodbyes, brother. I 'ave much to thank 'e fer, but I can't bring meself to say more now," he stated, baldly. Then he abruptly turned his horse and began to set off back the way he had come. Paul called out to him, but there was no response.

Jack, standing beside the young Nankivell, heard him sobbing and looked down at the now distraught child, appreciating immediately the devastated sadness that the young boy felt. Young Nicky, understanding his own predicament, thought quickly, fondly kissed his dearest puppy and then placed him tenderly in Sam's hands, telling him in a broken voice to keep him safe for him. Jack, knowing what was required, already had hold of his little bag and placed it in the boy's small hand.

"Run, Nicky, run!" the young man urged, "before he should get away from you." Nicky needed no extra endorsement and, holding tight to the bag, began to chase determinedly after the departing horseman. He called out his name, but to no avail, for the man would not stop.

Paul started forward, but his son had him by the arm. "No, father," he ordered. Casting his mind back, Jack remembered a time, many years ago, when he had chased down that same track after a departing loved one, only to be stopped by his father. Softly, he said, "Let the boy go, for well can I remember the sadness of such a loss." Bemused, Paul turned towards his son, feeling a stab of pain in his heart as he saw again the scene that Jack could still recall so vividly. Shaken, he looked to his wife, but she was staring at the running boy who tried so desperately to attract the man's attention with his calls.

"We should stop him, Chloe, for it is not right that he should go after him," he told her. But when she turned to look at him, he was surprised to see that her expression was a mixture of resignation and hope.

"Jack is right," she said, "Let Nicky go, for if you wish to see a dead man live once more, then you must allow the living to be with him." He stared at her as the meaning of her cryptic remark became clear to him. Eventually, he joined his wife in watching as the youngster determinedly continued to run, whilst the man rode on, equally determined to sever the knots that tied them all together.

Nicky, panting with exertion and hampered by the bag, kept calling in a shrill voice, but Mr Bolitho would not respond to him. Behind him, Nicky heard young Jack Trevarthen shouting at him, clearly instructing him to drop the bag and to run as fast as he could. The little chap released his burden immediately. It fell away and sprang open behind him, the contents spreading across the lane, dancing and fluttering in the breeze. One of his treasured boots bounced along the ground and plopped into a large puddle by the side of the road. The loss of the bag, however, had enabled Nicky to increase his speed and he believed he could catch his guardian, until he noted that the man had set his horse to a gentle canter. Terrified at what he realised he could be about to lose, he shouted as loudly as he could, "Mr Bolitho!" but again, to no avail, as the man was almost at the corner and would soon be lost to his sight.

Nicky, tears pouring down his face, could not bear it and screamed out the first words that came into his mouth, "Dada! Dada! Don't leave me."

From their vantage point, the Trevarthens heard the anguished cry. Then, with a mixture of satisfaction and dismay, they saw the rider pull his horse to a stop and turn it around, in order to meet the running boy. They watched as Joey leant down and pulled up the young boy, holding him tight in his arms. The horse stood quietly as the pair embraced each other for a long while, the boy clasping his arms tightly around the man's neck. Then the rider gently wiped the tears from the boy's face and his own. Settling the child to rest against his body, he picked up his reins, before turning his horse again and setting off once more to Penzance. At the corner, he raised his hand in farewell and in the next instant, they had disappeared from the Trevarthen's sight.

CHAPTER 21

THE tall man gave a sigh of relief when, finally, he pulled up his horses outside of a large house. He was unused to having to journey in a foreign country, and having to travel to such a remote location had necessitated several stops at various inns along his route. In some, the standard of cleanliness left much to be desired, whilst in others, the accommodation had been excellent, but an appreciation of the hostelries had not been his principle concern. It was with a sense of disbelief that he had come to this place at all; he was here only because of a fortunate meeting with an old acquaintance, who had brought him from his home; certain that, at last, he had found the quarry that Paul had searched for so diligently during the past five years.

Almost from the time his brother had left him - standing in disbelief and full of despair - at Trevu, Paul Trevarthen had tried to find him. He had made enquiries locally but, finding no help there, he travelled to Bristol, again with no success. Joey had been there, but had stayed for only a day and a half to sort out his business interests, before setting off again - with a small boy in tow, he had been told. Doggedly, Paul followed him across the country to London, but there lost track of them both, so he thought to carry on to Dover, where he had bought his brother a house as a wedding gift. Upon calling at the house, he discovered that the property was occupied by a family who had taken a long lease on it. His enquiries proved to be fruitless, as the current occupants could only give him the name of the agent with whom they had dealt. In this gentleman's office, Paul discovered that the trail led him all the way back to Penzance, where the fees accrued from the rental of the property were to be deposited in his brother's account. Deciding to return to London, he called in on his old friend, Lord Stroudley, the former Peter Fleetwood, and asked him whether he could use his contacts in the government to find the whereabouts of his brother.

"Of course, dear boy," said Peter, though he smiled resignedly, pointing out that, as Joey Bolitho had spent the greater part of his life avoiding detection, it would not be an easy matter if the man had it in mind not to be found.

Upon arriving, once again, in Cornwall, Paul began a fresh search, convincing himself that, before the end of the year, he would have run his brother to earth. He had tried to glean as much information as he could regarding his brother's former smuggling contacts, but all the men in the Seagull, that he knew had dabbled in the trade in former years, could not help him.

"See, 'tis like this, Paul," explained a sympathetic Seth Mankee, "Joey was the one who knew everybody. 'Twas only 'e an' Licky that 'ad the runnin' of the smuggling trade. Now, if Licky bin' abroad fer years an' nobody 'aven't seen sight nor sound of 'en, 'tis goin' be jes' as easy fer Joey do the same. Truth to tell, I spec'late they two old pals 'ave met up 'gain," he concluded. Paul, knowing, as Mankee did not, that Skewes had been killed, sincerely hoped that this was not the case, but he kept his own counsel in the matter.

Bolitho's solicitor and bank manager were even less forthcoming, although they were equally as sympathetic. They could not tell him where his brother resided and could not divulge the information if they did, they remarked, pointedly, as Bolitho's business was confidential. However, Mr Teague, the bank manager, advised him that Joey was keeping up the house in Chapel Street. His reason for doing so, Teague speculated, would be that he meant to return to his home at some stage. Mr Trevarthen was much struck by this observation and had set much store by it, but as the years rolled on, he began to lose heart that he would ever see his brother again.

Paul despatched letter after letter to anyone that had been in any way connected to Bolitho but even Joey's oldest friends, the Rickards, had had no contact with him. And so it was with great surprise that he chanced upon an old acquaintance, whilst visiting Truro to see his aunt, who was well aware of the location of his brother.

A short while after Paul's brother had been widowed, Sir Reginald Bonython had given up his position with the Custom's service and taken his wife to live at Bath. Her illness was becoming progressively worse and he considered that, as he had heard many glowing reports on the healing powers of the waters, then perhaps his dear wife's illness would improve if she could take them. At the beginning of her treatment there was a marked easing of her pain, but gradually her tribulations returned and, slowly and painfully, she lost her battle to survive. Bonython buried his beloved Elizabeth and quietly mourned for her in his house in Bath for over a year. Then, unexpectedly, he was asked to once again take up his old post, due to an increase in smuggling in the county. At first, he felt he should refuse. But, after some consideration, he surmised that, perhaps, by re-attempting to curb the waywardness of the Cornish, he might once again be able to fill his empty life with some meaning, at least in part. And so he sold his property and returned once more to the place he knew best and the land he loved most.

When the two men chanced upon each other in the street, they expressed their delight at meeting again after such a long time and began a discussion on what had happened over the intervening years. It was only at the end, as they were shaking hands to part, that Sir Reginald asked Paul to convey his best wishes to his brother. With a crestfallen expression, Trevarthen explained that such a thing would not be possible, and recounted why it should be so. Sir Reginald smiled to himself, then announced, "Your brother's in Brittany, Paul, and has been for the past four and a half years." He then proceeded to divulge the name and address of the person with whom the boy, Nankivell, and his guardian resided. Poor Mr Trevarthen could barely speak for the shock that this news gave him. As soon as he could command himself, he vigorously shook Sir Reginald's hand, words of thanks tumbling from his lips. Only then did he think to ask Bonython how he had access to such information.

"When your brother's activities were brought to my attention in years past, I tried, to the best of my abilities, to keep track of the crafty fellow. In Cornwall, this presented me with no small difficulty because, try as the service might, we could not establish anything against him for lack of evidence, but I did not have the same problem across the Channel in France. Over there he was not committing a crime, merely purchasing goods, and Joey always knew that, as long as he could get them into this country without being apprehended, he could survive for, as you know, he never once fell prey to any agent or informer. Consequently, I always had a fair knowledge of what he

F J Warren

was upon when abroad, as I had a concentration of informants in the areas that supplied the smugglers with their contraband," explained Sir Reginald.

"He has not gone back to the smuggling, surely?" exclaimed Paul in alarm.

"No, dear fellow, don't be alarmed," Bonython kindly informed him. "Your brother would appear to be assisting an old friend, a wine merchant and, from the reports I have received, he is making quite an enterprise of it. There is no escaping the fact: that brother of yours is a considerable businessman."

"Yes, yes he is," said Paul, delighted, and asked once more for confirmation of the name and address of his brother's landlord. On arrival at his Aunt Caroline's, the good news tumbled from him like water from a pitcher and the poor lady burst into tears upon hearing that her eldest nephew had been found at last. Jubilantly, Paul arrived back at Trevu. He rushed into the parlour, lifted Chloe off the settle and gave her a crushing embrace, narrowly avoiding being stabbed by his wife's sewing needle. Delighted as she was by the news, Chloe realised that Paul would need some assistance just to get to France, quite aside from finding his brother, for her husband only travelled out of necessity and had never been abroad in his life.

Here, their old friend, Peter, proved invaluable, providing letters of introduction to various members of the British Embassy in Paris as well as arranging the route and transportation needs. When he set out at the beginning of August, Mr Trevarthen had been fired with enthusiasm for the journey and this had helped him to weather the many inconveniences that he had experienced along the way. A seasoned traveller would have revelled in such adversity but Paul, always a lover of his home comforts, did not derive the same pleasure from such. Upon reaching Paris, he contacted a Mr Carruthers at the Embassy and was delighted to find that this gentleman had organised his trip from Paris to Brittany down to the last detail.

At the house, Paul, still sitting in his hired curricle, looked around for somewhere to tie his beasts when the main door of the house burst open and a short, rotund gentleman, with an extremely fat, yet cheery countenance rushed towards him. For a moment, Paul thought he was calling: 'M'sieur very go away' to him in French, but he then realised that the man was attempting to call him by his surname and could not pronounce it correctly. Relief flooded through him as he at once understood. For the man to know of him at all meant that he had to be a close confidante of his brother. The man turned and shouted across to a building at the side of the house. Immediately, a young boy appeared and took hold of Paul's horses. Now, standing at the carriage, the man, whom Paul took to be Jean-Pierre Duchamps, began to speak to him in poor English.

"Welcome, M'sieur Trevatten, welcome. I am most 'appy you are to be .... er .... ici .... er...chez moi," he said and indicated, with a broad sweep of his arm, the house behind him. His happy face beamed with delight when Mr Trevarthen thanked him in good French.

"My God! You speak French! That's wonderful! I do not speak very good the English, you understand, and it is very difficult for me," he admitted, relief written into every delighted wrinkle on his face. He invited Paul to come into his home and soon, Mr Trevarthen found himself seated in Madame Duchamps' best room and plied with wine and food. Mr Trevarthen took a glass of wine but politely declined the food, explaining that he had recently

180

lunched at the inn by the bridge in the last village. Madame Duchamps tutted in disgust, raised her eyes heavenward and shook her head. This brought a smile to Paul's face that won her heart, so she assured him that tonight, when he sat down to dine with them, he would learn what a well cooked meal should taste like. He smiled and thanked her and she left him with her husband. Jean-Pierre leaned across and studied Paul's face closely, remarking that, as Paul's brother had told him, there was not, indeed, much resemblance between the two men. Mr Trevarthen acknowledged the truth of this, and then asked after his brother and young Nankivell.

"Nicky will be here soon and I expect your brother to be back sometime this afternoon. He has been away, visiting vineyards for me, but I know that he intended to be here today. I expect that he had to stop in Lannion for a little while," and as he mentioned this fact, his face coloured dramatically as if he had said something he should not have. Mr Trevarthen looked enquiring, so Duchamps raised both hands and shrugged dramatically, announcing, "We are men of the world, M'sieur Trevatton, and he has a mistress there." Paul's look of surprise at this bold statement confused Jean-Pierre a little and, so as not to worry his guest, he pointed out that the lady was of no importance, as his brother liked to visit lots of women. If poor Duchamps thought he had calmed his guest with these words, he was disappointed, as Paul's eyes widened with disbelief at what he was hearing.

"Do not worry, my friend. It is perfectly natural! Joseph does not love them, they are a..." and he thought carefully before saying, with confidence, "...they are a diversion, you understand! No female can have his heart again. He lost that a long time ago." In spite of himself, Paul found himself nodding in agreement. Of course, he should not have expected his brother to behave like a monk in the intervening years, but he was extremely surprised to learn that he seemed to have returned to his libertine ways.

"I expect, like me, you enjoy the comforts of a mistress, do you not, M'sieur Trevatten? I mean, a wife can provide only so much. It is true, is it not?" enthused Jean-Pierre, companionably, but his guest's expression gave him much room for doubt about the wisdom of his remarks.

"I do not have a mistress, M'sieur, but I do not object to others enjoying one if they so wish. If I should be surprised, it is only because I did not expect my brother to have returned to his former ways so soon after the loss of his dear wife," he stated in a disappointed tone.

"If it is only his timing that worries you, M'sieur Trevatten, Joseph took a long while to learn to live without his love. When first he arrived with Nicky, it was most noticeable that he had a desire to drink his sadness away, but that boy was a wonder. Each time Joseph raises the glass to his lips, Nicky is watching him. At first, your brother says nothing and continues to drink but then, one day, he explodes with temper and asks angrily why Nicky should stare at him so. 'Because you are a drunk!' says the little boy. You understand my wife and I have known your brother for a very long time and it is not a good idea to tell him such things. For a moment, I thought that poor Nicky was going to be in very serious trouble with his guardian but from that moment on, Joseph did not drink so much." Smiling kindly at Mr Trevarthen, he reached out and patted Paul's hand. "They are very close, those two, and I do not hesitate to tell you that, without that little boy, I think you would have lost your brother for good. So, if Joseph should like to chase a few women, it is not so very bad, is it not?" he enquired, his round cheeks dimpling as he spoke.

Paul shook his head and gave a short laugh, as much at himself as at his host's explanation. M'sieur Duchamps smiled back, delighted to see his guest's response. As he went on to tell him about a very good brandy he had, that he was sure Paul would be pleased to try, a horse was heard to canter up and around to the back of the house, where the stables were kept.

"Mon Dieu!" cried Jean-Pierre, a smile lighting up his face, "it is your brother, M'sieur Trevatten! He is back!" He sprang to his feet and ran to the door, then suddenly ran back into the room, caught hold of Paul by the arm and proceeded to drag him along through his house. Mr Trevarthen stumbled in his wake as Jean-Pierre rushed through the large, airy kitchen, which led out to the courtyard at the back of the house. Bursting out of the open doorway, Paul's host was about to shout to the man who had just dismounted when a loud voice was heard to shriek, "Papa!" From the road at the back of the courtyard, a ginger haired lad ran flat out towards the latest arrival at Jean-Pierre's home. The youngster threw himself into the arms of a tall, well-dressed man who stood with his back to the doorway, out of which Jean-Pierre and his guest had tumbled. Paul recognised his brother's familiar posture in an instant, but his size seemed to have reduced dramatically over the intervening years. To Paul, he appeared much thinner than when he had last seen him, but he quickly surmised that this could be due entirely to the cut of his clothes. Young Nicky looked more like a youth than the angelic toddler that Paul had last seen, but he still had the appearance of a cherub about him and probably would have until his dying day. His expression of delight certainly added particular charm to his features. He was gazing in adoration at his guardian, talking incessantly in fluent French, when, suddenly, his gaze shifted and he caught sight of the stranger in the courtyard. His eyes opened wide with surprise and he ran across the yard in the direction of Mr Trevarthen, shouting "Uncle Paul!" at the top of his voice. Joey Bolitho whirled around and looked his brother full in the face for the first time in five years. The delight that shone from Nicky's young face was not mirrored in Bolitho's expression, Paul noted, shocked at the thinness of his brother's face and the cold, enigmatic gaze that fell upon him. It hurt Paul to see such an expression, but he had little time to reflect upon it, as young Nicky was upon him and had cast himself into his arms. His tongue did not seem to stop wagging and in a short space of time he had asked after everyone, especially Sam and the young puppy, Spot.

"They are all fine, Nicky. Give me some time and I will tell you all about them, I promise, especially that scamp of a dog of yours!" and Paul gently tweaked the young boy's nose in affection. Nicky grinned back and turned towards his guardian, his wide smile fading as he looked at Joey. There was no smile of greeting for Paul Trevarthen. The face that, so recently, had looked with love upon Nicky, had now become set in its familiar stone mask. The youngster frowned, then turned towards Paul and said, confidentially, "He has moments of blackness, you see, Uncle Paul, but usually they do not last so very long." Taking account of the disappointment in Mr Trevarthen's face, he added, "I expect he is tired after his journey. He travels a lot for M'sieur Duchamps, you see."

"Yes! Yes, of course, Nicky. I quite understand," acknowledged Paul, but the brother he had spent so long looking for seemed, in that moment, to be as lost to him as ever. Joey Bolitho, the aloof smuggler that he had acknowledged all those years ago at their first introduction in the Seagull Inn, had reclaimed the body and soul of his brother and Trevarthen felt chilled at this recognition. What a fool he had been, he reasoned, if he thought his brother, who had laid so many careful plans to cover his trail, should now welcome him with open arms, as Nicky Nankivell and Duchamps had so recently done.

Paul greeted his brother, nervously. "Hello, Joey." "Brother," came Bolitho's curt and unfeeling response, coupled with a brief nod of the head. Then, catching up his horse's reins, he silently led the animal past Paul's hired curricle and towards the stable.

Paul's host stared in astonishment at the back of his old friend as he disappeared from sight, then he turned to Mr Trevarthen.

"I...I will talk to him," Duchamps spluttered, but Paul held up his hand and remarked that he thought it best to return to his wine. "No doubt, when my brother wishes to converse with me, he will do so," said Paul, and with a despairing smile, he turned and headed back the way he had come.

Some time later, the door to the front room was opened and Joey Bolitho appeared, holding an empty glass. After carefully closing the door behind himself, he made his way to the table and picked up a bottle. Following a quick glance at the label, he filled his wineglass and then took a seat directly opposite to his brother. Joey took a small sip of wine and then raised his blank eyes to look directly at his brother.

"Well done, Paul," he announced, coldly, "I would not 'ave thought you capable of such a feat after I 'ad worked so 'ard to remain undiscovered."

"I had help," replied Paul, quietly. "As you can imagine, this is not the sort of enterprise that I would consider myself capable of undertaking, much less completing."

"Quite!" acknowledged Bolitho, tersely. Trevarthen recounted his long search and how a chance meeting with Sir Reginald had brought forth a result.

"With the help of Peter and his friends at the Embassy, it did not take so very long to run you to earth, once I knew where you had hidden yourself," he told Joey. But Bolitho's expression did not alter and he continued to stare at Paul, inscrutably.

Try as he might, Paul could not see a trace of emotion behind the mask that his brother wore but he blundered on, sure that he would awaken some part of him to a response, even if it be only of anger.

"Of course, I have much news of...of home..." he said, awkwardly, but Joey's expression gave not so much as a flicker, so he continued, bluntly, "...and of your aunt and son."

For a brief moment, a muscle twitched on Bolitho's cheek, but it was the only sign that Paul could catch that his words had registered with his brother.

"Is George ennobled yet?" Joey enquired, blankly, and took another sip of his wine.

"Not yet, no, but Wrothford is ailing and it will not be long before that mantle falls upon his shoulders. He has had five years, as have I, to get used to the alteration in his station. Strange to tell, Wrothford took quite a liking to him in the end. Circumstance forced them together and so they forged a relationship, if not of respect, at least of tolerance. The biggest problem facing my son is Wrothford's determination that he should marry his granddaughter, thus ensuring that his Lordship's own bloodline will continue. But George, as defiant as ever, is equally determined not to affiance himself to the young lady, as he has his eye on another damsel," Paul informed him.

"Anyone you know?" enquired Joey, coldly. Paul shook his head, bemoaning that his eldest was as tight-lipped about his personal life as ever.

"Grace and Daisy must be married by now, I imagine," said Bolitho, but in an offhand way. Again, his brother shook his head.

"Grace, so she tells me, is far too busy to contemplate matrimony. She has taken over the running of my mother's enterprises and is doing an excellent job. She spends most of her time traversing the country and has even travelled to Manchester, to oversee the setting up of another establishment there. Under my direction, the business did not expand, but Grace had the foresight and ability to see that this situation needed to be rectified, in order to take advantage of what she calls the 'new money'. It is no longer necessary to fund your business on patronage, as Sardi had to do. The prosperity of the ordinary person is rising, dramatically, and it is this market that my enterprising daughter is bent on catching. You will no doubt be pleased to hear that your beloved Jack is no longer to be the Master of Trevu when I come to the end of my days. Responsibility is to pass to Samuel, who seems to have the makings of a farmer, more so than either his grandfather or myself." Paul noted that his brother had raised his brows in enquiry and continued with his narrative. "The last I heard of Jack was that he had arrived in Venice with Sir Endymion in tow. So far I think they have travelled halfway around Europe, but with Jack's artistic temperament and spirit of adventure, I do not think that this will be his last port of call."

"You did not mention Daisy," said Joey, acutely, and a shadow fell across Paul's face at the mention of her name.

"She is in Oxford," he replied, abruptly, "with her stepfather." Joey's brows rose higher still, so Paul plunged on.

"I could not reconcile myself to Daisy's wish that her mother's legacy should be used by her and so, as soon as she reached her majority, she left to be with Poulson. Apparently, so George tells me, the fellow dotes on her, and nothing I said or did altered her perception that the money with which she had been endowed was anything other than hers by right and did not come to her through the detritus of the slave trade. She believes that, if she should use this gift well, then she will be doing no wrong, but I cannot and never will hold to that opinion and I am sorry for it, but it has created a division within the family." After a moment's sad reflection, he raised his eyes to his brother's face and announced, bluntly. "I cannot abide a division within my family, Joey."

"I, on the other 'and, dear brother, am quite prepared to abide by one," replied Joey, swiftly and with a hint of anger in his voice.

"Are you, Joey?" countered Paul. "Your aunt grows weaker by the month. We thought she would not last till Easter but she rallied again, seeming to draw strength once more. She lives for your son, of course, but grieves the loss of the boy's father so keenly." He watched as Joey's face slowly began to show signs of annoyance, but Paul continued, smoothly, "Chloe and I visit as often as we can, at least once a month, but we are no substitute for that which those two poor souls are lacking."

"Enough!" snapped Joey, in a sudden flash of temper, "I wish to 'ear no more of them!" He drew breath deeply for a moment, regaining control of himself. Then, pointedly, he said, "I would thank you, brother fer your concern and your efforts to find me again and now you 'ave, you may return to Cornwall, secure in the knowledge that I am well and 'ave no need of anythin'."

"I have come to bring you home, Joey," his brother told him, simply.

"This 'ave become my 'ome, Paul, and as to goin' back, well, that can never be, for there is nawthin' there for me and I 'ave no wish to return to the place of my birth. So, after you 'ave rested, you may return and inform all that would be interested to knaw that fact," was the cold reply.

Paul bit his lip and swallowed hard. He had known for a long time that his brother would, if he so wished, sever all connections with his family and that Paul could have no chance of imploring him to return. A chance remark to Peter had created a chain of events that, in turn, had slightly tipped the balance in Trevarthen's favour and he now felt emboldened to make his stand.

"So be it, Joey! If I cannot force your return, others might be able to do so," he said, cryptically.

A look of puzzlement crossed his brother's stern features, swiftly followed by an expression of dawning realisation.

"See to it that Nicky be got ready to leave with me, brother," Paul said and got to his feet to indicate the conversation at an end.

Joey Bolitho abruptly rose, caught hold of his brother's arm and turned him back to face him. "What the 'ell do 'e mean? Wha's Nicky got do with it all?" demanded Joey, wrathfully.

"Why, don't you remember, brother? Before you left Cornwall, you made Nicholas Nankivell my ward! To my certain knowledge, it has never been revoked. I am Nicky's guardian, Joey, not yourself, so you have no choice but to give him over to my wardship as you originally proposed!" announced Paul, who, despite feeling his heart hammering against his ribcage in his fear, outwardly kept his composure. He had made his move and, feeling more empowered than he had expected, plucked Joey's vice-like grip from his arm, marched to the door and left his thunderstruck brother alone in the room.

CHAPTER 22

IT HAD taken a whole month for the arrangements to be made but eventually, Paul Trevarthen and Nicholas Nankivell were ready to set sail for Cornwall. When the moment was upon him, the young Nankivell solemnly thanked the Duchamps for their many kindnesses to him. In a philosophical frame of mind, he shouldered his bag, marched up the gangplank and stepped onto the deck of the ship. Paul Trevarthen then took his turn to offer his gratitude to the couple, for all they had done whilst he had stayed with them. He allowed them to kiss him, although he felt awkward to be the recipient of such effusiveness. Bowing once more in thanks, he turned and headed onto the gently rocking ship that was tied up at the quayside.

Grasping young Nicky by the hand, Paul exchanged a smile with him, then they both turned to face the quay and waited patiently. Joey Bolitho smiled at Madame Duchamps and said a few words that the watchers on the deck could not catch. Whatever was said, it made the lady smile and giggle and when she was taken into Bolitho's arms, she let out a shriek of delight. Joey was equally boisterous when he turned to Jean-Pierre and hugged him tightly. This gentleman regarded his old friend for a long time, delivering a long speech with a kind smile. Finally, Bolitho was released and with a wave of his hand, he turned towards the ship and was soon on board, standing with his arm around Nicky's shoulders. The group on the shore waved again as the ship cast off and within a short space of time, it had left the safety of the harbour and had begun breasting the waves, on its way across the short stretch of sea towards Cornwall.

"Coming to your cabin, Nicky?" asked Joey, abruptly. The young lad nodded and followed in his wake as Bolitho strode across the deck and headed down towards their berth. Paul Trevarthen watched them go without a uttering a word, concluding that some silence would be beneficial at this time, enough having been said for now. Casting his mind back, he thought of how he had Peter to thank for his brother's decision to agree to return to his homeland. Not only had Lord Stroudly used his various contacts to ensure that Paul's visit took place without event, he had also foreseen that Paul would find it no easier to encourage his brother to return with him, when finally they met after such a long time apart.

"Damn it, Paul!" he exclaimed, "the fellow is just across the channel! He has had ample opportunity to return, or to contact you, at least. It would appear to me that Joey is determined never to return. The only way to persuade him is to use some, er, I hesitate to use the word coercion, perhaps 'diplomacy' would be more appropriate." Paul, remembering his bemusement, had not believed that his brother would not fall into his arms upon seeing him again. Luckily for him, he had taken Peter's advice and made his arrangements, taking into account his brother's reaction to his arrival in Brittany. Naturally, the letter from Joey's solicitors, appointing him Nicky's guardian, was crucial but on its own would not be enough to make his brother give up his life in Brittany. Of course, such a document carried no jurisdiction there, but Peter, with the help of various government officials, arranged for other documents to be produced and these had proved effective in making Bolitho set foot on the ship.

When Trevarthen had pointed out that he was Nicky's lawful guardian, it had taken Joey only a moment to realise that such a document mattered not a jot in another country. He had followed his brother into the garden and did not hesitate to point this out to him.

"I know," said Paul, calmly, "but in this case the French Government have been persuaded that I should be the one to take care of Nicky and not yourself. Therefore, they will recognise my right to take him into my guardianship."

"What the 'ell 'ave they got to say to anything?" demanded Joey, his temper rising.

"Quite a lot, actually," replied his brother. "You see, prominent French officials often visit England to stay at a certain establishment in Berkshire - an ancestral home of a member of the nobility, you understand. Here, they enjoy the pleasure of the rural pursuits that the English so like to indulge in such as hunting, shooting and fishing, not to mention drinking and feasting. Of course, whilst our French friends are in residence, a lot of politics are discussed with the various members of the English government, who happen to be staying at the same establishment during their sojourn. When they all decide to go to the capitol, this noble gentleman allows the use of his town house for..." and here, Paul shrugged his shoulders and smiled urbanely, "Well, you know."

"'Tis bleddy Wrothford's places you be talkin' 'bout, I s'pose," snapped Joey, and his frustration deepened as his brother nodded his head in affirmation.

"Well, what with my son being Wrothford's heir, the two governments would wish to see that my business in France should go as smoothly as possible, for neither country can forget that we were at war with each other not so many years ago," Paul advised. He reached inside his coat, produced an official-looking document from his pocket and passed it to his brother. "The French government very kindly made sure that, although you are welcome to visit their fair country as often as you wish, you cannot continue to live as a resident. And, as it has come to their attention that you have already lived here for over four years, they feel that, perhaps, some time spent in your own country would be preferable to being locked up in a French prison."

"They can't do that, I 'ave done nawthin' wrong," argued Joey, reaching out and snatching the paper from Paul.

"I know that, Joey, as well as you, but we are but mere pawns in this game. If they do not wish to upset their cosy 'across the channel' politics by affronting the next Lord Wrothford, then it is for the best that they comply with the wishes of that gentleman's father in this delicate matter," Paul announced, feeling quite triumphant.

Joey Bolitho twice read the document, but knew he had no redress in the matter. As his brother had stated, he could continue to visit as and when he wished, but he would not be allowed to take up permanent residence in the country. As it had been pointed out to the officials in Paris that this was precisely what he was doing at the moment, if he failed to leave France within sixty days, an order would be issued to eject him from the country until such time as they saw fit to allow his return. It stated, however, that if he went of his own volition, he would be allowed to return without let or hindrance.

"You damn scoundrel, Paul! You 'ave boxed me up right an' tight!" thundered Joey, in a blazing temper.

"Yes, brother," replied Paul, quietly, "I rather think I have," and then allowed a grin of satisfaction to cross his face.

Not to be outdone, Joey took the document to the local priest for his perusal, but upon reading it, the man came to the same conclusion as Joey, advising him to have his legal representative study the paperwork. This, Joey did, but there was no help for him, for this gentleman advised him that the document was perfectly legal and nothing could be done to alter it. That was not good enough for Bolitho, so, like a fish on a hook, he squirmed and writhed in an attempt to free himself. He even went so far as to attend upon various government officials in Paris to plead his case, but without success, as they advised him that it was a fait accompli and that he should give in with good grace. At the embassy, Mr Carruthers informed him that the British Government would not back his claim that he had been a law-abiding citizen of his adopted country. And as the French Government did not wish him to remain within their borders at this present time, his only option was to return with his brother. Fuming, Joey contemplated a flight across Europe. Upon speaking to Nicky, the lad had agreed to go with him, though his youthful face lost some of its sparkle at the thought. It came as a shock to Joey to realise that, although the child would follow him to the ends of the earth, in his heart, Nicky wished to return to Cornwall.

Paul Trevarthen watched with quiet amusement as his brother slowly came to terms with the action that had been taken against him. Very rarely had Bolitho been in a situation where he found himself without control. In this game, however, he had been outplayed and he knew it. That realisation had hit him, hard, and his coldness towards Paul became more apparent with every passing day. However, Joey Bolitho was nothing if not determined and he decided that, as soon as he had arrived back in Cornwall, he would reclaim his wardship of Nicholas Nankivell and so loose the hold that his brother now held over his life.

Their journey to Cornwall was uneventful, neither man having much to say to each other, but when the boat nosed into the harbour to dock, Joey could not fail to feel a shiver of excitement course through his body at the sight of his birthplace. Penzance seemed bigger than before and Paul explained that it appeared to expand with every passing year.

"When we were children, Joey, it seemed little more than a village, but now it has become a sizeable town," Paul told him as they surveyed Penzance, which shined like a jewel at the side of the bay. Joey nodded, but then refused Paul's offer of a bed at Trevu, flatly stating that he had his own property and he would make use of it.

"Mrs Nancarrow was told to expect you, so it will not be an inconvenience for her," Paul advised him, diplomatically. His brother shot him a swift, irritable glance, thinking that Paul should have been so confident of his return that he could make such arrangements on his behalf. Joey kept his own counsel and all the while he schemed as to how to break free from his brother's controlling influence. When he and the boy were finally on the quay side, he refused to shake his brothers hand and taking young Nankivell by the arm, he turned his back on Paul, heading in the direction of his old home.

Various people stopped in surprise to see him back in their midst, much altered but still recognisably Joey Bolitho, and raised their hands and voices in greeting. He acknowledged them all, but did not stop to converse with any of them. When he got to his own front door, it was thrown open before ever he had the chance to touch it and Mrs Nancarrow, her eyes brimming with tears, grabbed hold of Nicky and covered him in kisses. If he had let her, she would have probably greeted Joey in the same fashion, but the house was a world of bittersweet memories to him and, in order to control his feelings, he covered himself with a sheet of the hardest ice. His priority was to reclaim his adopted son, so, after a sleepless night, he presented himself at his solicitor's office the following morning, confident that it would be a small matter to revoke his permission for Paul to continue to have wardship of Nicholas Nankivell. His solicitor agreed that a document could be drawn up to that effect, but his next statement cut short the smile that had begun to lift the corners of Joey's mouth.

"Once your brother puts his signature on the document, Mr Bolitho, everything will be as before and the young fellow will again be in your care," said Mr Treloar. He then asked if he should arrange for his clerk to begin the wording. Joey nodded dumbly, the consequences of his hasty flight, five years before, now beginning to crowd in upon him. Now he would have to go, cap in hand, to his brother in order to rescind the original document, and he had the feeling that Paul would have yet more from him in order to pay for his signature.

That afternoon, he hired a horse and a pony and headed to Trevu, with an excited Nicky at his side. In the yard, a young lad rushed across to take their beasts. When Bolitho enquired after Davy, he was told that he had passed away three years before, but that his wife and youngest daughter still lived in their cottage if he wished to call upon them. Joey shook his head, dismounted and began to walk towards the front door of Trevu. Their arrival had been spotted, however, and a tall young lad, the image of his father when he was of the same age, came rushing out of the house with a large white dog bounding along at his feet.

"Sam! Spot!" shrieked Nicky in delight and rushed towards the pair. The panting dog barked in excitement and in a moment, all three were bundled together in a cheerful reunion of excited youth and ecstatic canine frolicking. Even Bolitho had to smile at the sight of it, as it was difficult to watch without laughing at the dog's comical attempts to get attention from the boys.

"Welcome back, Joey," said Paul from the top of the steps, and a beaming smile spread across his face like the dawn of a new day. Joey frowned, but knew that he had to tread carefully, so he greeted his brother with civility, if not amiability and climbed the steps to the doorway. Once inside, Paul led him to the withdrawing room, whereupon Chloe rushed from her seat and clasped her arms about her brother in law with unashamed delight. This greeting shook him and Joey felt his heart melt a little because of it. As he looked down into her dear, sweet face he thought her features just as perfect as before. Her hazel eyes, brimming now with tears, were as bright as ever and her happy smile could not fail to warm any man's heart, even one as broken and battered as his. She pulled him across the room to the settle and with the sheer force of her personality, Chloe made him talk to her of his and Nicky's time away from them. Trevarthen leaned against the mantle, saying nothing and watching with interest. He noted with satisfaction that, although Joey might be treating him frostily, his wife was receiving a far warmer reception. Chaos ensued as the two boys rushed in to the room. At one point, it seemed as if Mrs Trevarthen was to disappear from sight as Nicky tried to hug her, whilst Spot seemed equally determined to receive a reception as rapturous as that which Chloe gave the youngster. When, eventually, a semblance of order was restored, the youngsters, along with Spot, left the room and headed for the stables to admire Sam's new pony. Joey politely took tea with his sister in law and bided his time until he could talk to his brother alone. He had the impression that his brother was aware of his intent, for it seemed to him that Paul was determined to keep Joey talking to his wife for as long as possible.

"Now you are back with us again, I suppose it will not be long before you should wish to visit your son," said Chloe, and before Joey had a chance to reply she continued, "He is such a handsome little fellow, Joey, and so tall for his age. Very bright and always smiling. He never fails to ask for you each time that we visit, so desperate is he to meet his father." Her brother-in-law's expression dramatically hardened and he announced, angrily, "I 'ave no plans to visit with my aunt, Chloe, so I do not imagine that I will be seein'...seein' 'im."

Embarrassed at Chloe's shocked expression, he lowered his eyes, so as to avoid her look of anger. But he could not dismiss her words and she harangued him for his coldness towards the poor innocent. "That you should despise him so, Joey! He talks only of you, what cruelty on your part! At our every visit, he asks always if we have news of you and if we think you will be coming to see him. Can you imagine how hard it has been for Paul and myself? Each time, we tell him that we have heard nothing of you, but can only hope, as do the rest of the family, that soon his father will be coming back into his life. Do not attempt to tell me that you did not feel the lack of a father yourself, for Old Davy was forever telling me that you liked nothing better than to sit and listen to tales of Redvers exploits!" she finished with a snap.

"I 'ad the 'appiest of marriages, Chloe, you knaw that an' with 'is birth, my life ended! I 'ave no wish to see 'im an' I 'ave no need to see 'im," rejoined her brother-in-law, coldly.

Mrs Trevarthen rounded on him, "You foolish man! Sarah-Jane gave her life for you because she wished for you to have a son. I can remember how proud she was on the day of his birth and how she asked you to love and cherish him. A fine example of a caring father you have proved to be, Joey!"

"I 'ave suffered..." began Joey but by this time, Chloe, enraged by his attitude would not listen to any excuses and angrily interrupted him.

"You have suffered! What about that poor child? Then there is Paul! He has spent five years searching for you, trying everywhere to find you and never giving up hope, although none knew if you were alive or dead! When Sarah-Jane died, I lost my dearest friend and had not even the consolation of helping her poor husband grieve and come to terms with his loss. There is nothing Paul and I would not have done for you, Joey and now to find that you...that you..." but Mrs Trevarthen could go no further as, overcome by her emotions, she burst into tears. Paul started forward immediately and his brother, shamefaced, made a mumbling excuse and left the room.

Outside in the fresh air, Bolitho took a deep breath, but it did little to revive him. He had not expected to enjoy his visit to Trevu and had not looked forward to it. He understood that part of his brother's plan to bring him back to Cornwall would involve his becoming acquainted with his son, but had determined from the outset that it would never be. He imagined that, had his wife lived, then perhaps through her influence and that of his aunt, together with the presence of the child, he would have mellowed and the family would have been brought back together. With her death, however, he could see no possibility of this taking place. When all he was left with from the most idyllic time of his life was an innocent, helpless babe, he had felt consumed with a cold anger that this stranger had ruined his happiness. His promise to his dying wife had to be kept, so his aunt could have his unwanted child and he could hide himself away in a quiet corner of his desolated world and drink himself to death. He knew that this was precisely what he would have done, had it not been for Nicky. But the boy had found a place in his cold, shuttered heart and try as he would, Joey could not dislodge the hold the youngster had over him. He had even returned to Cornwall instead of going elsewhere, as he could see that it was here that Nicky wished to be. From the stables, he could hear Sam and Nicky's laughter and he felt a pang of remorse that he should have denied the boy so much over the past few years. Catching sight of the old wooden bench, on which Davy would sit and sun himself on bright days, he strolled over to it and sat down. Almost as soon as he had done so, the image of the old man returned to him. He smiled as the memories of Davy's many tales of his father came flooding back. Joey felt again the excitement of hearing about Redvers. The recollection of a father he never knew, recounted to him by an old man who knew almost as much about Captain Trevarthen's life as the man himself.

It was here that Paul found him when he left the house to go in search of his brother. They did not say a word to each other, but Paul took the space on the bench beside his brother and sat down, waiting patiently for whatever Joey wished to say. Awkwardly, Joey offered an apology for upsetting Chloe but Paul merely nodded and remained silent.

"I am 'avin' a legal document made up for the return of Nicky as my ward. 'It'll be ready fer Friday. I 'ave need of you to sign it," said Joey, flashing a glance at his brother's impassive face, "Would you do that fer me?" he asked, quietly.

There was a long silence until, finally, Trevarthen cleared his throat and said, with quiet authority. "Will you attend your aunt when I visit with her on Thursday?" As Paul spoke, he continued to stare at the house and did not look at Joey at all.

Joey studied his boots and said nothing, but his mind raced with the implications of his brother's remark. If he wished to have the charge of his chosen son - for he understood that it was in that light that Nicky stood in relation to himself - then he would have to comply and identify himself to the other, unwanted child. It was a high price for Joey to pay and he could not bring himself to do it. Slowly, he shook his head and announced in a subdued voice that he would not go with Paul to Trevanoc. Paul sighed and solemnly told Joey that he thought they had nothing further to discuss. With these words, he stood up and began to make his way back to the house. Joey watched him go, moodily, until Nicky came bounding up from the stables and caught sight of him. "Dada!" he shouted and rushed across to speak to him.

Joey tousled his hair and smiled at his beaming face, warmed to see the happiness displayed there. "You seem be enjoyin' yerself, Nicky," he said.

"Oh yes!" gushed the boy in reply, "Sam's new pony is beautiful and he says I'm allowed to ride it any time I want and do you know that since the day I left, Spot has always slept on his bed? Sam says Spot is my dog and not his, so if I would be allowed to take him home with me, I can do so, but I have told him that I think it would be most unfair because Spot loves Sam so. Perhaps one day I will have another dog to call my own, but it is not so important." Impulsively he put his arms around Joey and hugged him tightly. "I would rather have you about me than a dog," he said shyly, in little more than a whisper. The man felt a lump rising in his throat and he swallowed hard. Gently squeezing the boy's shoulder, he asked him if he would wish to spend the night at Trevu, provided it could be arranged, so that he could continue to renew his friendship with Sam after their time apart. Slowly, the boy lifted his face and stared suspiciously at Joey. "No, no thank you," he said, quietly.

"Why ever not?" asked Joey, surprised by the change that had come over the lad.

"Because I would not wish for you to go away and leave me here," said Nicky, with a look of disquiet on his face.

"I wouldn' do that!" exclaimed Joey, but then remembered with a jolt that this was precisely what he had tried to do five years before and it was understandable that the young lad should worry, in case the same thing was to happen again. He pulled the boy to him and hugged him, whispering into his ear, "You be my Nicky an' I shan't ever leave 'e again, you understand me?" He saw the head of ginger curls nod vigorously and felt the small arms tighten around him. He was suddenly enveloped by fear, as it dawned upon him that Paul could so easily break the promise that Joey had just made to the lad. Then he reasoned that his brother was not a man to do such a thing and he relaxed. Worry came over him again as he wondered if Paul, so wishful for him to go to Trevanoc, would not use the law to countermand the contract that he had made with Nicky. Surely, he would not be so vengeful, Joey imagined, but a nagging fear prompted him to call out to Paul, now almost at the top of the steps.

At the sound of his brother's voice, Trevarthen turned and looked back towards the bench where the couple sat.

"I'll go with 'e," called his brother, a note of exasperation in his voice.

"Coach or horses?" asked Paul, desperately trying to hide his satisfied smile.

"We'll ride!" replied Joey. Paul nodded and advised him that he would call for him at nine on Thursday. Then, without another word, he turned and let himself back into Trevu.

Word buzzed around Penzance as news of the surprise return of Joey Bolitho spread throughout the town and old friends and acquaintances were not slow to call. Amongst the first was Mrs Penrose with her daughter, Melior, in tow. If he did not relish having to receive a visit from the lady, Joey was well aware that to refuse her admittance to his home would be the greatest insult. It mattered not to him, but he had the lad to think of and he was aware that a goodly portion of the local gentry looked upon the youngster with disdain, for his background was not considered to be of the most advantaged. If he did not treat society with respect now, then when Nicky was older and looking to wed it would be of no use for Bolitho to attempt to cast about him for a suitable family. A fair number of them would not look kindly upon the lad at such a time and no matter what financial advantages Joey should give the boy, he could so easily be shunned. Joey smiled at the irony of the situation, to think that he was taking his responsibilities as regards the young lad so strictly, but he loved Nicky. He recognised in him the one person who had seen Joey through his darkest days and. although it had taken him a long time to appreciate it, he was aware of the debt that he owed to the boy.

Joanna Penrose was pleasantly surprised by Mr Bolitho's appearance as he seemed to her to look no older. In fact, he reminded her quite forcibly of the arrogant, young smuggler of bygone days. His thinness, she fondly imagined, could so easily be rectified with the help of a new wife and some good food. With such thoughts prominent in her mind, the widow determined to place herself in a position to help him. She had taken much care with her appearance that morning and had fussed her maid for not arranging her curls more advantageously. Adorned in her most elaborate of bonnets, her recently purchased expensive jacket and her favourite fashionable dress, she made the short walk to the Bolitho's house and gained admittance to the property, where Mr Bolitho and his ward politely greeted both herself and her daughter. Joey could not fail to notice that, although everything about Mrs Penrose was most elegant, her daughter looked quite dowdy by comparison. Time and circumstances had not dealt kindly with the youngest Penrose child. Her cloak, Joey noted, had been patched at some time and as she was a thin, lanky young girl, a dress designed for a larger woman had been adjusted to fit her shape and not much care had been taken to ensure that the resulting garment in any way flattered the young damsel. In fact, her mother had considered it good money wasted upon the child for, her disability aside, Melior's expression scarcely varied from one of bored indifference. If Joanna had not been quite so busily employed in attempting to deliver several artful gazes in Mr Bolitho's direction, she might have noticed that, today, Melior's expression showed no sign of boredom whatsoever. Like her mother, Melior was also surprised by Mr Bolitho's appearance, but also recognised in it the loneliness at the core of the man's being and understood it well. Since the loss of her beloved father, she too had learned to live without his constant love, as Mr Bolitho had endeavoured to do without his own dear wife by his side. For one brief moment, their eyes met and Mr Bolitho was surprised to see the light of understanding in the young girl's gaze. Then, almost as quickly, she assumed a blank expression, leaving him daunted.

"Yer daughter has grown to a good height, Mrs Penrose," remarked Mr Bolitho, courteously, and for want of something better to say, added, "Take after 'er father's side of the family, I s'pose." With a sigh, Mrs Penrose noted that it was probably correct to assume so. Joey's brow furrowed a little as he noted that the moment her mother had begun to speak, Melior Penrose shifted position somewhat to enable her to look at Mrs Penrose's face. Yet, when he had spoken, she had seemed to be staring at him. He thought her behaviour strange. Joanna chastised her more than once for being such a fidget and rapped her soundly and repeatedly across the back of the hand with the shaft of her parasol, a habit that she had clearly picked up since the girl's illness and subsequent loss of hearing. Joey felt most sympathetic towards the poor child.

Mrs Penrose had, by now, launched into a long speech about the effects of being widowed and how she had felt so desolated by Joey's loss, having had a similar experience herself.

"You don't need to tell me how you have suffered, dear Mr Bolitho, for when I lost my own dear Manville I was inconsolable," she moaned, and sniffed loudly before hiding her face for a brief moment behind her handkerchief.

"I assume you will be making arrangements for the boy?" she enquired, suddenly changing the subject.

"I beg pardon, Mrs Penrose?" enquired Joey, bemused.

"Young Mr Nankivell here, and we mustn't forget your own dear child, must we?" she said and smiled ruthlessly at Mr Bolitho, who had no opportunity to reply, for she answered her own question. She assumed, she said, that he would be making suitable arrangements for the young lad's education and, no doubt, Leah Bolitho would have everything well in hand with regard to his own dear son.

"I have always thought Miss Bolitho a most capable and honourable lady and I am sure that her care of your son is perfectly adequate. Now that Nicky is back in Cornwall, no doubt you could arrange for him to go to Helston as young George Trevarthen did. I am sure that the young fellow would not wish to be around you all the time, and his spending the greater part of the year at school would no doubt be the best for both of you." As she spoke, the couple on the settle unconsciously drew closer together and Joey placed a reassuring hand on Nicky's arm. Mrs Penrose failed to notice this small action, however, and continued in the same vein, explaining to Mr Bolitho that, as a single gentleman of some consequence, Penzance had much to offer him.

"Have you not noticed how the town has expanded whilst you have been away, dear Mr Bolitho? We have a theatre and a thriving music society, as well as so many other attractions. I would attend far more than I do if only I could find a suitable escort to squire me," she forcibly concluded, fastening him with her most brazen smile.

Mr Bolitho struggled to remain impassive in the face of this unlooked-for approach. Thankfully, at that moment, Mrs Nancarrow - who was standing in lieu of a serving maid until a new one could be appointed - knocked at the door to announce the arrival of Mr and Mrs Roskilly. Joanna Penrose's infamous glacial expression settled on her features and she rose to her feet, announcing her intention to leave, realising, she said, that so many of his friends would wish to visit with him, now that he had returned to his home. She held out her hand and Joey politely shook it, but she ignored Nicky Nankivell completely, though he had politely stood up and held out his own hand towards her. However, Miss Melior did take the trouble to smile upon him, and to shake his hand, causing Nicky to break into a warm, beaming smile. She shook Mr Bolitho's hand as well and when he looked down into her face, he was intrigued to see the amused smile that was resting on her lips.

194

What she thought so funny, he could not imagine, for he was well aware that Miss Melior could not have heard any of her mother's conversation.

The Roskilly's had barely sat down when the Dennis family arrived, and as they were soon followed by the Tregenza's and their young family, Joey began to feel his temper growing. Nicky charmingly excused himself for a moment and left the room to seek out the cook, advising her that the Master was getting rather annoyed and that he thought it best if Mrs Nancarrow could advise any more callers that Mr Bolitho was otherwise engaged. She smiled and nodded in agreement, then turned to descend the stairs to the kitchen, thinking all the while that Nicky Nankivell was becoming a fine young gentleman.

Joey Bolitho was relieved when the last of their guests had finally left the premises, but only until Mrs Nancarrow presented him with a tray of calling cards, left by the numerous people who had not been fortunate enough to gain admittance during the afternoon.

" 'Aven't they got nawthin' better do with their time than go a callin' on one another?" he ranted in annoyance. However, Nicky soon put him back into a good humour by laughing at Mrs Penrose and her strange manner.

"That woman was always funny 'eaded," announced Joey, laughing, but Nicky successfully wiped the smiled from his face when he mentioned that the lady in question seemed quite enamoured with him.

"Well," said Nicky, "I would not worry that you will only have Mrs Penrose to admire you, if I were you, Dada. Now that you are a single gentleman, I expect all manner of unattached ladies will come to call on you." And with a sunny smile, he left the room before he had a chance to notice the look of blank amazement that had settled across Joey Bolitho's normally enigmatic countenance.

CHAPTER 23

AT THE farm gate, Joey Bolitho pulled up his horse and bluntly told his brother that he could not go on. He had tried hard not to give in to the growing fear within him but at the last, panic overpowered him and his nerve failed. When he had cause to visit in the past, there was one person only that he feared to see. But now, in addition to his aunt, he would have to face his son. He advised his travelling companion that he wished to return, but Paul seemed unperturbed, calmly advising him that to get so far, only to be afraid to continue, showed great cowardice on his brother's part. Furious, as Paul knew he would be, Bolitho rounded on him for branding him so, but to his annoyance, Trevarthen merely smiled.

"I speak only the truth, Joey, and you know it. Meet with them this once, then I will do as you have asked and Nicky will once more come under your wardship. It is not my intention to hold out against you after this first meeting and, if in the future, you decide that no further meetings are to take place, I would not have the right to demand otherwise." Paul spoke solemnly, yet smiled ruefully to himself as he considered that he would probably use all his powers of persuasion to encourage his brother to attend upon his family in the future. Paul was pinning all his hopes on the fact that, once the despised son had become known to his brother, then Joey would not have the heart to disown the lad further. It was a risk, he knew, but after a long discussion with his wife they had both come to the conclusion; that to hold out against a personality as strong as Joey Bolitho's would be neither practicable or possible.

Joey regarded his brother angrily, but the prize was there for the taking and he had only to suffer the one meeting, then both members of his family could be abandoned as before. And he could do that; if he wished to close his heart to someone than he was capable of accomplishing this quite easily. Defiantly, he told his brother he would continue.

"I 'ave no interest 'ere, brother," he coldly stated, "for they are both nawthin' to me. "Why, I 'ave never even asked fer 'is name, fer 'e be no more to me than any unknown child would be!"

"Zachariah John," his brother promptly replied, and went on to explain: "Your aunt called him firstly after her brother and then after Sarah-Jane's father, John Williams. The little fellow developed a determined personality as he grew and proclaimed himself to be known as Zacky, and that is the name he has answered to ever since. I am sure that, as he grows older, he will decide for himself which name he prefers, but you will find your aunt completely besotted with him. I am convinced that, if the boy proposed to be known as Satan, she would oblige him accordingly and possibly without a qualm," he added with an amused smile.

As they were expected, two men took their horses immediately upon their arrival at the house and Richard Nairn rushed forward to greet them. It was only natural that he should take Bolitho's hand first and when he did so, he held on to it for an inordinately long time, shaking it vigorously in his excitement. With growing trepidation, Joey found himself taken into Trevanoc

196

and escorted briskly through the house to meet with Leah Bolitho. Face to face again after their time apart, Joey could not fail to notice how frail she had become, but it was also apparent that, in spite of her infirmities, her steely personality had not diminished in the slightest. Leah Bolitho had need of a bath chair, having lost the use of her legs, but she held out her hand towards him and motioned him to come to her. She was shocked, as were many others, to see how thin her nephew had become in the intervening years, but her eyes brimmed with tears to have sight of him again. When he finally placed his hand in hers, he was surprised to feel the strength of her clasp and she would not or could not let him go. He mumbled an awkward greeting but she seemed not to notice. She motioned him to sit in the chair drawn up in front of her, all the while keeping a tenacious grip on his hand.

"My dear boy," she smiled, "Such a joy to 'ave you here again. We 'ave missed you so dreadfully and my beloved Zacky talks only of you." Then she surprised him by saying that the boy had not been told of his arrival, in case Mr Trevarthen's plans had not come to pass. "He knows you are alive, my dear Joseph, and that gave 'im great comfort, as it did to me. When you feel the time is right, I will send to fetch him to you, but I understand the pain you are feeling." All the while she talked, she kept patting the back of Joey's hand, that still she clasped so tightly, and consequently was unable to wipe away the tears that were running down her cheeks. At her obvious delight, Joey felt some of his anger dissipate, yet the fear that gripped his heart still remained.

" 'E 'as a look of you about him, but he 'ave her green eyes and not blue, as are yours. And when he do look at you, 'tis just like she be there with you. Remember how she would stare in that marked way she 'ad? It do my heart good to see it, Joseph, and I 'ope, my dear, truly I do, that it will give you comfort to know your dear love do live on in 'im," she told him, but her words of comfort only added to his trepidation. Paul, regarding his brother from his seat on the settle, could see the strain the old lady's words were placing on him, but he knew that this first meeting would prove the most difficult for Joey and allowed that Miss Bolitho revelations were causing him great pain. There was no doubt that she would have continued, but suddenly the door was heard to burst open and a young voice shouted, excitedly, "Is he here?" closely followed by the sound of scampering footsteps.

"Nanalee! Dicky said my Dada had come. Is it true?" came the voice again, drawing ever nearer. Then, before Joey there appeared a sturdy young child, his head covered in a mass of black curls. He rushed past the side of his chair and threw himself towards the old lady. He was well dressed in what appeared to have been his best clothes, but they had been severely muddied in several places and a trail of dirt from his boots were left behind him as he ran. Leah Bolitho released her hold on her nephew at once and turned her enraptured face towards the young boy.

"Look at you!" she scolded, happily, "You naughty angel, you! What will your father say to see you in such a state?" But the boy was too excited to listen and began to clap his hands together. Oblivious to the man in the chair sitting directly behind him, he noticed that Mr Trevarthen was in the room. "Uncle Paul!" he squealed delightedly and ran to him. Paul hugged him tightly and then lifted his eyes to his brother's blank face. Slowly, he turned the boy around so that he faced the stranger in the chair and quietly said, "This is your father, Zacky. Go and say hello to him, for he has not seen you for a long time," and he gently pushed the boy in his brother's direction.

Wide eyed, Zacky stared at the stranger before him and then, before anyone could stop him, he threw himself at the man and clambered on to his lap, covering him in mud as he did so. Then he wrapped his arms tightly around Joey's neck and kissed his cheek. Joey was dazed by the shock of his sudden arrival and Zacky's actions on seeing his father, and he did not return the boy's affections. Zacky pulled back his head and beamed into his father's face, then loudly shouted, "Nafan! Nafan, come and look! I told you I had a Dada!" Shyly, a young coloured boy appeared around the side of Joey's chair and solemnly stared at him.

"This is my friend. He's called Nafan," he told his father, then he reached down and caught up Joey's hand, holding tightly to it. He squirmed around so that he now sat on his father's lap and proudly announced, "See! I told you Nafan! I told you I had a Dada of my very own!" and he laughed in delight, a laugh very much like that of his mother. Both the sound of it and the appearance of the child awakened such a pain in Bolitho that he closed his eyes and turned his head away. When the laughing boy turned to look at him, he saw the man's actions and fear gripped him.

"Don't..." he began, and swallowed hard, before asking, "Don't you like me?" The man did not reply, because he could not control his voice. Uneasily, Zacky shifted his position on the man's knee, reached into his breeches' pocket and, after a little fumbling, produced a partly eaten red apple.

"We bin picking apples, would you like one?" he asked, worriedly, afraid that the man was disappointed in him and would not want him for a son. Joey looked again into the youngster's face and saw his beloved's green eyes, which stared at him so directly that his heart ached to see it, but there was something about the warmth of the child that he found he had to respond to, so he shook his head.

"Thank 'e, but I 'ave eaten," he replied, his voice a little strained. Immediately, a smile broke out on the child's face and Joey unconsciously smiled back. Leah Bolitho had been anxiously watching her nephew's face, and upon seeing Joey's reaction, she motioned to Paul that she wished to leave the room. Richard Nairn held out his hand to his own son and Nathan ran across the room to him, throwing himself into his father's arms, just as his friend had done. Quietly and without a word, the little company left the room, leaving the father and son together. Once in Trevanoc's large hallway, Leah enquired if Paul would push her for a turn around the garden. She had not had time to get outside the house at all that morning, she said, and it being such a fine day, she thought it a shame not to feel the sun on her face. Paul took the route through the back parlour of the house that opened out onto a flat, paved area where the wheels of the bath chair would run more easily.

Once in the garden, Miss Bolitho said that she hoped Paul did not mind, but she thought it best that the pair should spend some time alone. "That way, Joseph can acquaint 'imself better with my little angel, don't you think?" she enquired of Paul, who smiled and agreed that he thought it an excellent idea. She hunted for her handkerchief and wiped away the tears that were still clinging to her cheeks.

"Now!" she announced with determination, "How shall we go about to find a wife for 'im?" and she turned an enquiring face towards Mr Trevarthen.

Paul's brows rose in shock at her words, whilst she explained that his brother would have to make suitable arrangements to look after the boy and the best way he could do that would be to marry again.

"He can 'ardly look after himself by the look of him. See how thin he 'ave become, the poor dear! Obviously, he can hardly be expected to take my dear angel home with him, for he has only just set foot in the country himself. I knew that, if only he would meet with the child, he would fall under his spell, as he did with Zacky's mother. Now, he will wish for him to become part of his family," she stated, flatly and with confidence. She then surprised Paul still further by asking him if he knew of any suitable ladies that could be considered of marriageable quality for her nephew.

"I have given the matter no thought, Miss Bolitho, I must confess," replied Paul. All of Paul's time had been taken up with convincing his brother to return and then to meet with his son. As did everybody who came into contact with the boy, Paul was convinced that Joey could not fail to like and then learn to love the child. But as to the future prospects of the newly united family, he had not devised any plans at all.

"Well, my time is growing short, Paul, and I must leave that dear child in safe hands when I 'ave gone. His father will grow to love him, but for the moment I am content that he has responded to the boy at all, for I must admit I was most afeared that Joseph would not stay in the same room with him when first he saw Zacky," she remarked.

"Zacky is a most appealing little fellow and it would take the hardest of hearts not to like him," commented Mr Trevarthen.

"True, but the dear child got such a look of his mother about him that it must cut poor Joseph to the heart," she replied, sadly. They continued to converse for a long while about Joey's present situation and what changes would need to be affected to enable him to have his son return to his own home.

"Of course," remarked Miss Bolitho, with a hint of regret, "I should prefer that Joseph would come and reside here but I fear that, whilst I live, he will never do that. Yet Zacky knows no other home and he is most sincerely attached to Trevanoc."

"And to his Nanalee," Paul interspersed, a gentle smile on his lips.

Miss Bolitho beamed back at him, adding that they had much to think upon regarding Joey's son.

"His constant companion is Nathan Nairn, as you know, and both Richard and Janey have such a love for my little angel. He is as often at their house as he is here and dear Richard has often assured me that, should I have passed over before ever Joseph returned, then they would not stint in their love and attention to dearest Zacky," she announced with pride and affection. "I am relieved that the father and son have met, but well you knaw what an obstinate fellow your brother is. So like his grandmother in temperament, but I knaw he has a more forgiving heart and now that he has met the sweet child, I should think he would find it almost impossible to give him up again."

Just then, Richard Nairn came out of the house and strode towards them.

"I would hope you will not be offended, but Zacky has invited his father to dine with us for luncheon," he said. "Mr Bolitho seems to be as much under his son's spell as the rest of us, dear lady, for it was not long before Zacky had taken him to see his pony and when I last saw them, they were about to disappear towards the orchard, along with my boy. Zacky has informed his father that he was the right height to pick the larger apples that the two lads had been unable to reach earlier," he told them, chuckling heartily.

Miss Bolitho did not appear to be at all put out by this change of plan. She informed Paul and Mr Nairn that it might be far more agreeable for her nephew to be in the company of his son and his former servant, Janey, than to have to sit and dine with her. "After all," she added with a mischievous smile, "he has not shown, in the past, that he enjoys my company so very much."

Consequently, Paul did not catch sight of his brother again until the middle of the afternoon, when he saw Joey mounted on a fine grey mare from his aunt's stable, walking slowly up the lane towards an open gate. Close beside him came two small ponies with Nathan and Zacky astride them. Both boys were fiercely protesting that they did not need to have leading reins attached to their mounts, but the adult in charge of them appeared deaf to their entreaties and so the little group made their way sedately, if not quietly, towards a large, grassed field just off the lane.

Trevarthen spotted Richard Nairn, who stood in the yard and surveyed the departing group with amusement. Catching sight of Paul, he raised his hand and made his way towards him.

"Joseph seems to be taking his responsibilities very correctly, Paul," he laughed and then fell into step beside him as they made their way back towards the house. "I think he was pleased to meet with my Janey again, after all these years, and he said to me that he was delighted to see her so happy with her children about her. What with Zacky and my Nathan being such firm friends, it will be a shame that they will have to be parted," he concluded, and Paul could not fail to note the regret in his voice.

"Well, it will not be for a while yet, Richard, for my brother is not in a position to take on the responsibility for such a young child. Miss Bolitho is determined to find Joey a wife, for she believes it would hardly be fair if the child should not have the comfort of a mother about him. I know that your dear wife, along with his aunt, have lavished much love and attention upon him, but I arranged this event only so that my brother should meet with his son after all this time. As to what is to happen in the future, that will be for Joey to decide, but I do not believe that, at this present time, he will feel able to have the boy in his home. There are only three servants at Penzance at present and if he sets up his home there, as I believe he will, then he will have to look about him for some more. Then there is the question of Nicky, who stands as a son towards him. My brother would not wish to destroy the love the two have for each other, and he would first ensure that Nicky is not to feel slighted by having another brought into his home. Young Nicky is a most sensible and intelligent lad, and well I know that it is he I have to thank for keeping my brother in this world after the tragic loss of his beloved Sarah-Jane. The lad told me himself that Joey should have his son about him. He also believes it for the best if Joey would marry again, if for no other reason than he would find it so much the easier for a woman to run his household for him. Quite a sensible attitude for such a young man to have, don't you think, Richard?" The estate manager nodded in agreement and Paul felt relieved to have assuaged the man's worry that his son, Nathan, was to be deprived of his dearest friend so soon.

Towards the end of the afternoon, Paul took tea with Miss Bolitho and it was there that young Zacky and his father found them. Paul glanced surreptitiously at his brother, noticing the rather strained expression on his face. He considered that this was only to be expected after the tumultuous events of the day. However, the cause of his discomfort became apparent as young Zacky, still holding firmly to his father's hand, began to make representations to Miss Bolitho. It was not fair that his father should go away again, he said and questioned why it was not possible for his father to stay with him.

"We got plenty of rooms, Nanalee," pleaded Zacky, earnestly. Leah Bolitho stared steadfastly at her nephew, but whatever thoughts he had on the matter were not represented in his features and she assumed, correctly, that under no circumstances would Joseph Bolitho wish to spend the night under Travanoc's roof. However, she concluded that the child had indeed found a place in her nephew's heart and that this visit would become the first of many.

"Now, Zacky! What a naughty boy yer father will think you. He takes such trouble to come to see you and now you should pester him so!" She gently scolded him. "He knows he is welcome here as often as he would like to visit, but he have only just returned from abroad and he has a lot of business to arrange, now that he has returned."

Zacky hung his head, but his lips set in a determined pout and he was heard to mutter that it was not fair, because Nathan's father stayed with him all the time. Disappointed, but determined to get his own way, the little boy began to sob, the sound increasing in volume so as to place more pressure on the adults in the room. However, the little boy was not to get his way, for his father could not and would not stay with him. His aunt had been right, Joey reasoned. It would be the first of many visits, as his heart had indeed warmed to the child, but he could not bring himself to stay in this place. There was enough anger left in him to deny him that privilege and he understood. as had his aunt and Paul, that he was not in a position to take the child away with him to his own home. He had taken Nicky in when he had been younger than his own son now was, but despite having had a wife and a good sized household then, that event had nonetheless caused a tremendous upheaval in his life. He would have to consider carefully how to proceed, for Zacky was so very young and there were friendships and bonds in this place that he had no wish to sever. He sighed, bent down and lifted the crying child into his arms.

"I shall come an' see 'e again, Zacky," he began in a soft voice, but to no avail. Zacky, furious and afraid, rounded on him.

"No, you won't," he shouted angrily. "You won't come again 'cos you don't like me an' that's why you didn't come an' see me an'..." but he got no further.

"Stop that at once!" commanded Joey, firmly but without raising his voice. The little boy gulped and then blinked at him. Joey stared into his all-too-familiar green eyes and felt his heart contract at the sight of the child. She, of all people, would have wished for her son's happiness, thought Joey. Taking out his handkerchief, he wiped the tears from the boy's cheeks with a gentle touch and smiled at him.

"Now, my boy!" he began, "I would be some pleased if you could look after something fer me until I come see 'e again. Do 'e think 'e could do that?"

The small child, staring worriedly at his father, nodded solemnly, so Joey took out his treasured pocket watch - the first gift that his beloved had ever given to him - and placed it gently into the boy's small hands.

"Now!" he informed Zacky, "This 'ere watch be very special to me, 'cos a very beautiful lady gave it me an'..." but he was interrupted by his son at this point.

"Was the lady my mama?" asked Zacky, hopefully. There was a slight pause and then his father nodded. At once the boy began to smile, proudly. That he should be asked to look after something that his mother had given to his father! He imagined that Nathan had never been asked to do something as grown up as that.

"Now you must ask Nathan's father to wind it up for you to make it go, 'cos when I come back I shall want to see that it is workin' perfectly. You are not to take it out on the farm, but keep it somewhere safe fer me 'til I do come again. Is that understood?" Zacky nodded his head vigorously and, although tears still sparkled in his eyes, there was no denying that he wore a far happier expression on his face.

"Next time I come, I might bring another boy to see 'e. My other boy, Nicky. Would 'e like that?" asked Joey, a slight note of concern in his voice. He need not have worried, because Zacky nodded his head again, delighted to think that he would meet the famous Nicky that his Uncle Paul used to tell him tales about.

"Will you take a cup of tea, nephew?" asked his aunt.

For a moment it looked as if Joey would refuse, but he bent and placed the child gently on the ground and said, with a slight smile, that he would be pleased to do so. Leah Bolitho, suppressing the surprise that she felt at his response - for her nephew had shown her precious little regard in the past - asked Paul if he would kindly pour another cup for his brother and motioned him to a seat at the side of her chair. Her nephew need not have worried that he would have to enter into conversation with his aunt, because his son clambered onto his lap and demanded to be shown the face of the watch hidden under the case. His father obliged and was proud to discover that his son could tell the time.

"He is very bright for his age," his aunt informed him. "Next time you do come, perhaps my little angel could read to you an' you will see what a clever little fellow he is," she suggested, not without some pride.

Her nephew quietly responded, "I am proud an'...an' humbled to find him so, aunt, an' I am...am grateful to 'e for it."

For answer, Leah leaned across and gently patted the back of his hand. She then turned back to converse with Paul Trevarthen concerning the best winter fodder for the over-wintering stock on her home farm. She was wise enough to know that her nephew would find it hard to thank her for anything, let alone the love and affection that she had showered upon his son, but his speech had warmed her soul and she treasured his gift, deeply.

When, finally, the two brothers sent for their horses to be saddled, young Zacky tried bravely to hold back his tears. His excitement at meeting with his estranged father had not tempered as the day had worn on and his disappointment that he should be leaving him tried him sorely. However, his father instructed him again on the care that he was to take with the precious watch, which was to Zacky a doubly prized object, because it came through his mother to his father, and Sarah-Jane's serious expression settled on his face as he listened intently to Joey's instructions. This time, the pain that Joey experienced at the sight of the youngster's expression was balanced by the warmth and affection he felt towards the child. He could not call it love as yet, but neither could he live his life without sight again of this small part of himself and his most cherished wife. To catch a living glimpse of his dear wife was painful to him and throughout that day he had suffered much with his undying love for her, but there was also peace of a sort. He had regained something, some small part of his desperate loss was alive and slowly, almost unknowingly, it became a part of him again.

On the journey back to Trevu, the two men exchanged barely a word. Though Paul was desperate to have knowledge of his brother's opinion of Zacky, he was wise enough to know that Joey's undemonstrative expression was in place to hide his feelings and that it would be for the best if he allowed the silence to continue.

However, when they arrived at his home, Joey invited Paul to come and dine with him that evening, instead of returning immediately to his home. Paul felt no qualms about staying to eat with his brother instead of continuing on to Trevu, as he had already advised Chloe that morning that she should not wait dinner for him. They were met at the door by Mrs Nancarrow, who informed Joey that young Master Nicky was in his room and would be sent for immediately. She had kept their meal hot in anticipation of his arrival and assured him that it was no trouble at all to lay an extra place for his guest. She smiled delightedly at Paul, relieved to note that there was less of an atmosphere between the two men, and then informed Joey that there was a stack of calling cards on the tray in the hallway.

"That Mrs Penrose come a-calling again," she divulged, attempting to keep a straight face as she spoke. Joey's raised eyebrow elicited the information that this lady was, in Mrs Nancarrow's humble opinion, 'done up like [2]Lady Fan Todd' for some reason or other, but as to why that should be, she had no idea. Mrs Nancarrow's expression, however, belied her statement.

Joey swore under his breath and asked what excuse Mrs Penrose had given for her visit this time, for since his return she had called at his establishment every day, giving a variety of reasons for visiting.

"Something about needing to be squired to some readin', or some such like. Said she would not 'ave asked, only that Miss Penrose would be of no use to 'er on account that she wouldn' be able 'ear what was being read," she said, her lip curled derisively. Almost immediately, she turned and hurried away to her kitchen. As she trotted down the stairs, she quietly hoped to herself that the additional staff that was needed to run the expanded establishment would be in place before long, as fulfilling all the jobs required of her at that precise moment was becoming quite a strain.

Paul, studiously avoiding his brother's eye, looked up as a door banged at the top of the stairs and Nicky came running down towards them. He greeted Paul warmly, then turned to Joey and asked, with some trepidation, if the day had gone well.

"Yes, it went well, Nicky," advised his guardian, but he did not offer any more information and Nicky, well used to Joey's way, merely nodded and preceded them into the dining room. The youngster thoughtfully busied

---

[2]Lady Fan Todd: an overdressed woman

himself with laying another place for Mr Trevarthen at the table and then announced his intention of helping Mrs Nancarrow to bring up the dishes, on account that the household was understaffed at that the moment. When he had left the room, Paul complimented his brother on the young lad's consideration.

"Would that my brood had as much regard for the feelings of others," he remarked.

"You do 'em a disservice, Paul," rejoined Joey, "for they all of 'em be fair-minded to their fellows, as well you knaw."

"True," admitted his brother, "but I am full of admiration for the way you have moulded that young man and for the credit that he has become to you."

Joey, pouring two glasses of wine, had his back turned to his brother so Paul could not see his reaction to his words. His brother remained silent for a long while, then turned to Paul and passed him a full glass. "Truth to tell, brother, I think 'tis more like Nicky 'ave moulded me than the other way round," he noted with a wry smile.

Paul chuckled, but became serious again when they took their places at the table. "I never asked 'e why you changed yer stance to the children," Joey remarked. "I mean, you 'ave accepted that George is not to take over at Trevu, Grace 'ave left 'er 'ome to follow yer mother's occupation and Jack bin allowed to be the artist that 'e was always meant t' be. When I...I left there was no way you 'ad altered yer mind to any of those possibilities, I find it strange that 'tis the case."

Paul pursed his lips and then informed his brother that two circumstances had occurred to make him change his attitude. The first was, as he had now come to recognise, that his dear wife had worked tirelessly on his children's behalf to ensure that their talents and capabilities should not be wasted through the fault of his intransigent position towards them.

"An' the second?" queried Joey, intrigued.

"Why, 'twas the day you brought Nicky to Trevu. He was so proud to have a puppy at last that, in spite of that sad time, he could not contain his glee. Almost from the day he came into your home, he pestered you for a dog of his own and it was obvious to all that his joy knew no bounds with the arrival of Spot. However, he put all that aside to be with you. He was so young, and to give up that cherished possession so readily and without a thought for himself gave me much to think upon. What would my own children give up for me if I had not earned their love as you had with Nicky? I assumed that I wanted only the best for them and it was lowering to discover that, in reality, it was myself I was thinking more about and not my children at all," Paul told him, sombrely.

"And Daisy?" his brother gently enquired.

He saw Paul grimace but he answered him truthfully, "That hurts more than any other because of the issue of slavery. I cannot bring myself to recognise, in spite of her protestations that her money should be used only for good, that its value has, in my mind, been debased by its provenance. Perhaps I shall be reconciled with my daughter, but until that time comes I will have to accept her decision, as she has had to accept mine."

"Do the rest of the family keep in touch with 'er?" asked Joey. Paul nodded, then smiled wryly and said, " 'Tis only your bull-headed brother that does not,

Joey." They had no chance for further conversation as the door was opened by Nicky, who carried a large soup tureen, closely followed by Mrs Nancarrow, who brought a tray loaded with various dishes.

At the end of the meal, the boy retired to his bedroom while the men partook of their port.

Paul, well feasted, was not desirous of starting any conversation that could lead to any discomfort between the two men, so he kept his own counsel and waited to see if his brother would wish to initiate a discussion on the events of the day. After a prolonged a silence, during which time his brother stared steadfastly at the fire blazing in the grate, Joey suddenly announced that he had best look around him for a wife.

Paul stared in amazement at his companion.

"Beg pardon, brother?"

"You 'eard me, Paul," Joey flashed at him.

"I...I did not think that...I mean..." stuttered Paul, floundering about for the words to cover his surprise.

"Aunt Leah be infirm. Thas' obvious fer all t' see. That child will need a proper 'ome to go to when the time comes, but this idden the place. 'Twould be an injustice to take him from all he knows and loves and to bring him here with only Nicky and meself to look after 'im. Mrs Nancarrow would do her best and I could get 'im a governess, but much as I 'ate to say it, 'tis a mother for the boy thas' needed," stated Joey, resignedly.

Paul kept silent, not wishing to interrupt his brother's train of thought. "I bin selfish, I d' knaw, but when...when she died I couldn' think of nawthin' but me own loss. But 'e's my responsibility and I 'ave to face that fact, so I must cast about fer a mother fer 'en to suit 'is needs," Joey grimly concluded.

"And...and your own needs, Joey," Paul quietly added.

"My needs!" cried Joey, angrily. "My needs are dead an' gone, Paul! 'Tis a mother fer the boy I be wantin', thas' all."

"Yes, I realise that but..." began Paul, but his brother turned his cold blue eyes upon him and under that icy gaze, Paul lapsed into silence. After a moment, he glanced at the clock and suggested that he had better make his way home, so Joey got up and saw him from the premises.

As he rode home, Paul's mind was full of thoughts of his brother and his future. Although pleased to think that Joey had at last been reunited with - and reconciled to - his son, the problems that Joey had identified concerning Zacky's future had given him much to think upon. But Paul, knowing his brother's reticence to have others interfere in his life, resolved not to offer advice unless requested to do so.

CHAPTER 24

"I was only saying to dear Mrs Roskilly last Tuesday, how sad it is to see two such fine men without the comfort of a wife to support them, did I not, dear Sophia?" pronounced Joanna Penrose with authority, barely glancing at her friend for a brief nod of affirmation, before returning her polite smile to Sir Reginald Bonython.

This gentleman, well aware that it was not only himself but also Joey Bolitho to whom Mrs Penrose was referring, felt a moment's discomfort to find himself allied with such company. Of course, he realised his situation as regards his matrimonial state was entirely different from Mr Bolitho's. Bonython wished for a companion in life and had a love for the company of others, whilst Bolitho was attempting to find a suitable female to take on the role of mother to his son. Mrs Penrose was making it obvious to all who knew her that she saw herself as the most prominent candidate to fill the post of spouse to Joey Bolitho, and Bonython was only too aware of this. What that gentleman's thoughts were on that matter, Sir Reginald could well imagine.

Sir Reginald had purchased a rather fine establishment in Penzance, as he had a great fondness for the town and the beauty of its surrounding countryside. As head of the Customs Service, he had taken it upon himself to delegate, as much as possible, the responsibility of running the duties of this establishment. With the relevant posts filled by a quantity of determined individuals, all hoping to have the opportunity of stepping into his shoes when the time came, he found himself in a happy position. He was now able to while away his time without having to earn his salary with as much participation as he had previously been required to do. Felix Philpotts had been sent to Falmouth to give him more experience and a young Scottish officer had taken up his post in Penzance. This young man was delighted to find himself appointed to a position in this part of the country, as his uncle had previously occupied the post many years before, apparently without great success, and his nephew determined that he would prove more capable in fulfilling his obligations to the service. Sir Reginald smiled when he thought of the antics of the two young men as they determined to prove themselves more than adequate to their respective commands. With such diligence on their part, Sir Reginald gratefully found that he did not have to spend his days locked away in his office. This was not to say that Bonython was not well aware of the state of affairs as regards the smuggling and wrecking, which still occurred on a regular basis throughout the county. Over the years, he had come to the conclusion that the Cornish would have smuggled whether or not there were duties to pay on imported goods. So to assume, as he had liked to do in his younger years, that he was capable of putting a stop to their activities was, he now realised, foolish in the extreme. However, his network of officials was managing to contain the situation and as they now believed, as Bonython once did, that they could solve the problem once and for all, he was quite content to sit back and allow them to expend their energies on the matter. His thoughts were interrupted as Mrs Roskilly enquired if the new officer appointed to the Penzance post had expressed an opinion on the town.

"My husband had the pleasure of meeting him at the Library and thought him a very correct young gentleman. They had quite a discussion on his uncle, Mr Duncan Ross, for Mr Roskilly could remember when that gentleman occupied the post that his nephew now holds, you know," she informed him. "Dear Mr Roskilly was most pleased to hear that he is so determined to curb the activities of those horrible creatures." Her speech was cut short by Mrs Penrose, who remarked that Sir Reginald would not wish to discuss the matter whilst he was making a social call. This pronouncement had a double effect; Mrs Roskilly, rattled to be put in her place yet again by the redoubtable Joanna Penrose lapsed into silence in an attempt to think of a suitable retort and Sir Reginald took the opportunity offered to enquire about Mrs Penrose's youngest child.

Joanna, not best pleased that the conversation had taken such a turn, merely rolled her eyes in disgust and informed him that she believed her to be in her room.

"Possibly reading, for I cannot get her to set a stitch in her sampler. She is the most wilful child and will rarely obey my commands," she moaned with feeling. "Communication is so tortuous, and when I have written a list of the things I require that she should occupy herself with during the day, she frequently fails to do any of them!"

"Perhaps a turn about the town would be beneficial for her, dear Mrs Penrose. Although I am sure dear Melior would wish for younger company than mine, I would hope that she would find it pleasant to walk along at my side. I shall take great care of her, you can be assured," said Sir Reginald, and smiled upon the matron. Mrs Penrose was well aware of the fondness the gentleman had for her daughter. Indeed, the late Lady Bonython had often remarked to her that the 'sweet child' was so helpful and kind to her whenever their paths had crossed, that she had become quite a favourite with her. Sir Reginald, for his part, saw himself in the role of uncle to the girl and had always taken the time to write a little note in her book whenever he found himself in her company. Mrs. Penrose, realizing that it would be no bad thing for her daughter to be seen walking abroad with such a distinguished gentleman, sent for a serving maid and delivered instructions that her daughter was to attend upon her at once, attired to go out, as Sir Reginald Bonython wished to take her for a walk about the town. She was not of the opinion that a young man would wish to lay court to Melior, but her daughter came from a good family and she could not deny the fact that, should circumstances arise wherein a gentleman needed a spouse to add consequence to his household, then the girl was available to fill such a position. However, Joanna surmised, if such a gentleman existed, his situation would need to be desperate indeed to encumber himself with her daughter.

When, at last, Sir Reginald found himself about the town with the young lady on his arm, he noted with dismay that the garments that clothed the sweet girl were no more than adequate. Although well laundered, they were not at all what a young woman would wish to be seen abroad in. Her pelisse was particularly dowdy and had even been patched with a material of a completely different colour. Although he knew that Joanna had to rely on the trusts that her husband had set up for her, he was also aware that Manville had arranged a more than adequate jointure for the household. Mrs Penrose herself always appeared in the finest clothes, even if she did not always give the impression of an elegantly dressed matron.

Smiling at his companion, Sir Reginald gestured for her book and Melior passed it to him with a grin.

When he had written in it, he passed it back and saw her face light up with surprise upon reading his script. Taking her wide-eyed stare as her agreement, he walked her the short distance to the Martin establishment and proceeded to buy several yards of material. He then made enquiries as to the name and address of any local seamstress who could be relied upon to turn his purchases into suitable garments for the young lady. Instructions were then left with the manager to ensure that his parcels were to be delivered to this lady immediately. They then visited the local milliner, where Sir Reginald purchased three bonnets. It delighted him to see Melior clap her hands with pleasure as she tried on each one in turn in front of the mirror. He assumed, correctly, that her mother had never bothered to buy her daughter anything of such quality and had merely dressed the child in the cast-off clothing no longer required by her elder sisters. As to what Mrs Penrose would think about his attempt to clothe her daughter, he had not the slightest concern; that lady might see herself at the head of the social circle in the town, but his standing was by far the greater. Admittedly, his actions might irk the lady but he knew Joanna would keep her lip tightly buttoned, for she would not wish to acknowledge to her many acquaintances that it was Sir Reginald's money, that had enabled her daughter to appear more advantageously apparelled than had become usual. It was only a short walk to the house of Mrs Penstraze, the seamstress, and with a smiling explanation to the lady, Bonython passed Melior over into her capable hands and sat himself in her best parlour, whilst the lady showed Melior various patterns and took her measurements. After a short while they returned and the seamstress was informed that further quantities of materials would be delivered in the near future, to enable the lady to furnish Miss Penrose with additional garments. Upon hearing this, Mrs Penstraze, whose smile had widened considerably at this news, divulged that she had a number of garments that she had already prepared for a young lady of very similar proportions to Miss Penrose, that were no longer required. Mrs Penstraze had not received payment and had been in dispute with the lady's family when they had sold up their property and left the county, due to the fact that the father's business commitments had suffered a severe financial loss and he wished to put as great a distance between himself and his creditors as quickly as could be arranged. Seeing an opportunity to unload a financial loss of her own into this indulgent gentleman's hands, she gained his permission to lead Melior back into her dressing room and transformed the gawky child into a far more presentable young lady. When Melior returned to present herself to Sir Reginald, he blinked in astonishment at the change that had been worked upon her. True, it had not turned her into the most beautiful young girl in Penzance, but she certainly looked far better than she did when she had left her mother's home earlier that morning. The seamstress beamed at the gentleman's expression and proceeded to bring in the other garments that she had so carefully packed away.

"I did not buy the material, Sir Reginald, so if you were wishing to purchase them on the young lady's behalf, 'twould be far less than you would have had to pay for such a profusion of garments in the normal way," she advised him, cleverly but truthfully. Bonython, delighted to see his dear little Melior finally attired as was her due, would quite happily have paid double the price that the seamstress had quoted for the wardrobe of unwanted clothes. However, Melior's expression had altered to one of concern and she hastily took out her book, scribbled in it and passed it to Sir Reginald.

"Of course, my dear, but if I wish to spend my money on you, I will," beamed the gentleman, still smiling at the bargain he had just had the opportunity to purchase. Melior shook her head at his words before he had even the opportunity to write them in her book.

Sir Reginald Bonython had not been made head of the Customs Service because he lacked perspicacity. His eyebrows snapped together and he placed his hand under the young woman's chin and looked her full in the face.

"You little minx, Melior," he breathed, "I think you can understand every word, I say, can't you?"

Melior could not hide the look of guilt that swept across her features. She nodded dumbly and lowered her head in shame at her deception, but Sir Reginald lifted her head to look at her again and enquired how it could be that a deaf girl could follow his speech.

Melior bit her lip, then took a deep breath and said, "Because I interpret the words you say as your lips move, Sir Buttons. It took a long while for me to learn. I had no wish for Mama to realise that I could perform such an action, for if she had knowledge of it then I would not have been able to follow her speech, as she had fallen into the habit of talking to me as if I did not exist."

"Nor does she realise that you have regained your speech, I presume, you naughty child," he admonished with a smile.

"It is only my hearing I am deficient in, dear Sir Reginald, for I never lost the ability to speak. When I learned that dearest Papa had died, it suited my purpose not to have to communicate with anyone. If people went on to assume that I could neither hear nor speak, then I did not wish to do anything to correct their mistaken presumption," she admitted, as a blush stole into her cheeks.

"Knowing your Mama as I do, I can understand your motives, my dear," advised Sir Reginald, sympathetically.

"I do not wish for this knowledge to come to my mother's ears, however, dear Sir Reginald, for she can hear and I cannot. Please, dear Sir Buttons, please not to tell Mama. If she were to find out, then I would be banished from her sight and so lose my ability to follow her speech, for there is much she would not say in my presence if she knew I had knowledge of it," pleaded the young girl.

Bonython smiled down into the earnest young face, regarding him so worriedly, and grinned mischievously back at her. "I doubt you will ever realise how delighted I am to discover you so accomplished, dear Melior. It has given me great hope that in your future you will be cherished far more than your family regards you at present." For answer, Melior threw her arms up and about his neck and hugged him in relief. Mrs Penstraze, a witness to these strange events, was sworn to secrecy, for although Mrs Penrose did not use her establishment, various members of her coterie did, and it would not do for Melior's hidden abilities to be discovered. A suggestion by the gentleman that he should have offered more largesse for the garments he had already agreed to buy, ensured that her silence could be guaranteed. A good businesswoman, Mrs Penstraze would not wish to give out a piece of gossip for free that could, in the end, cost her very dear indeed.

When Joanna Penrose was informed that Sir Reginald had been on a shopping expedition with her daughter, her jaw dropped. She swallowed his good-natured explanation - that he was feeling in a particularly generous mood - with a large pinch of salt, but she would not wish to offend a gentleman of such high standing.

"Oh, dear Sir Reginald, if only you knew how difficult it has been for me to attire the child properly!" she cried, sighing dramatically, whilst Melior stared blankly at her, in her usual manner. Mrs Penrose then began a rendition on the difficulties of explaining to a person of her daughter's damaged abilities just what it was that was required of her.

"I don't know how many times I have got that girl to the draper's, only to have her unable to indicate what it is that she requires," she sighed elaborately. Smiling warmly at Sir Reginald, she then indicated, with a toss of her head, that her daughter's company was no longer required. Melior turned to face her benefactor and gave him a large hug, then, as she pulled away, delivered a very unladylike wink that caused his smile to widen. He did not stay for much longer in Mrs Penrose's company, but he did impress upon her how much pleasure it had given him to buy some gifts for the sweet-natured child. However, he stated that he would prefer his generosity not to be acknowledged to the wider society.

"I would not have it voiced abroad that I have advanced to my dotage, my dear Mrs Penrose, and I know that I can rely upon your good self to keep this small matter between ourselves. I was delighted that Melior understood precisely what it was that I wished to do on her behalf, as a sign of my dear regard for your late husband and my friendship with this family over many years, but I can also appreciate how difficult it must have been for you both since dear Manville was so abruptly taken from us," he artfully stated.

Mrs Penrose, delighted to discover that her friends would automatically assume that she had clothed her own daughter, could find no fault with his wishes and smiled graciously upon him, thanking him generously for his kindness. So they parted company, each in complete understanding with one another.

Understanding was not the word that could explain the look on Paul Trevarthen's face, however, when his brother informed him that he had made great strides in finding himself a wife. At first, surprise and then curiosity were displayed across his features, but he gathered himself and enquired of Joey if he indeed had a candidate to fill the post of wife, and what that lady's feeling on the matter should be.

"I 'aven't found anybody, but I 'ave made a list," Joey briskly informed him.

"A list!" gasped Paul, taken aback by his statement.

" 'Ess, a list. 'Ere," said Joey, fumbling in his pocket, "I 'ave it 'ere somewhere. Run yer eyes over it an' tell me what you do think." Paul found himself presented with a rather crumpled sheet of paper, on which appeared a list of approximately a dozen names, some of which had already been crossed out. As his gaze took in the personages before him, his eyes widened further with shock.

"But, Joey," he expostulated, "you cannot possibly be thinking of marrying any of these women!"

"Why not?" queried his brother, a puzzled look on his face.

"Well," began Paul awkwardly, "they are all perfectly respectable, I am sure, but they are not...they are not the right sort of women for such a position!" he finished in a rush.

"What 'e mean? What sort of position? I just want a good mother for Zacky. I 'ent looking fer no great beauty an' they 'aven't got 'ave money, fer I got plenty of that!" Seeing the uncertain expression on his brother's face, Joey then asked him to point out what it was that these woman lacked.

"In spite of all your protestations, Joey, you are to inherit Trevanoc and it would not be right for your wife to be someone whose previous occupation appears to be that of..." and he scanned the list again, "well, for instance, a fishwife from St. Ives," explained his brother, not without some discomfort.

"You mean Meg Treneer, I 'spose. Well, admittedly she do smell a bit, but that would soon wear off once she didden 'ave to do that work no more an' she's a good hearted woman," Joey vouchsafed, unabashed.

"I wonder if you are deliberately misunderstanding me," returned Paul in annoyance. He took a deep breath and went on to explain to his brother that the woman of his choice would have to have a higher social standing than any of the females on his list.

"How come?" asked Joey, warily.

"Because it would not do for you to marry beneath yourself. You could not go about the town with a woman such as one of these upon your arm and have her recognised as your wife. You know the society we live in, for goodness sake! The poor soul would be shunned in a moment, and no matter what love she should show your son, it would be of no avail. I, for one, am well aware of how painful it can be to be regarded with such disdain by your fellow man and it would not be right of you to inflict such punishment on these . . . these dear ladies," he advised him, as diplomatically as he could.

For a moment, Joey looked dangerously annoyed, but then he sighed heavily and taking the paper from his brother's hand, he despatched it to the fire in disgust.

"I 'spose yer right, Paul, but I'll find it 'ard goin', searchin' out a good one from amongst that crowd of silly'eaded souls that do think they be the cream of society," he muttered with disdain.

On entering the room, Mrs Trevarthen could not fail to notice the anger on her brother in law's face. However, on learning of Joey's predicament, she suggested that the Trevarthen's held a party, on account of the fact that George would be visiting them within the next two weeks. It would, she said, be quite appropriate to assemble some of the local society for a dinner, to be followed by a small dance to celebrate his visit.

"Well, I wen't be dancin'," announced her brother in law.

"I know that, Joey, but you would have a chance to meet with some of the local families and to observe any suitable ladies at your leisure. It has been brought to my attention that you never return the visits of the many callers to your home," she gently chided.

Joey blushed and admitted that it was indeed so, but that he felt awkward to appear on the doorstep alone. She nodded sympathetically and patted his hand, then asked if he would like to see the list of invitations before she sent them out. He shook his head and informed her that there were few members of local society that he liked to converse with. "I only went all their places when Sarah-Jane were alive to please she, 'cos she did like it so," he admitted, his gaze drifting as he looked back into some distant time and place. Softly, he added, "an' to see 'er dressed so fine, fer it did me 'eart good to see her so."

"Dearest Joey," whispered Chloe and took hold his hand and gently squeezed it. After a moment, he gave a resolute smile and brought himself back to the present.

"Don't 'spose you could leave that dratted Penrose woman off yer list? She's the bane of me life! Ferever callin' to see if I wish to escort 'er to some fancy do or other," he asked, though he knew the answer before he had even spoken.

"Hardly, Joey. She would feel so slighted, and it will give me the opportunity to invite her daughter as well, for I think the poor soul is treated abominably by Joanna and it will do her good to be in the company of the younger members of society," advised Chloe. After a moment's thought, she added, "It never fails to amaze me that she seems so able to communicate with my younger children. If she spends time with them, it is not long before you can hear her laughing with them. I know they love her company and she does all of that without exchanging a word with them. She is truly a wonder," she said with an appreciative smile.

It was not until he was making his way home that Bolitho paid any attention to his sister-in-law's statement concerning Joanna Penrose's youngest daughter. He had just entered the town itself when it struck him as odd that the Penrose child could laugh and yet could not speak. However, he had little time to ponder the matter as he noticed a young man, heading up the street towards him and dressed in the uniform of a customs officer. Although Joey had been a law-abiding member of society for many years, it took only the sight of a preventative to send a shiver of excitement down his spine.

Young Angus Ross regarded Mr Joseph Bolitho with a slight curl of derision on his lip. His uncle had often told him that the man was a scoundrel who, by rights, should have been gibbeted years ago. The knowledge that the much-discussed villain of the Ross household was now a prominent member of society and even on speaking terms with the head of the service himself had astounded the young officer. He could not believe, knowing some of the exploits that his uncle had recounted to him, that this fellow would not be involved in some illicit activities still, and he had decided to mark the gentleman's movements most carefully. He had not relayed this information to his superior, naturally, for if and when he managed to unmask the man, he wished for the glory to be all his own and not shared out amongst his fellow officers. His irritation knew no bounds when he discovered that Bolitho had left for his brother's house earlier that afternoon, but he determined to follow after him at once. Now, here was the damned man coming towards him, as cool as anything and with that self same arrogant look upon his face, that his uncle had so frequently described to him.

"Mr Ross, sir," said Joey, an amused smile on his lips.

Mr Ross fumed but could not, in all honour, ignore the man and so he acknowledged him formerly and proceeded on his way, his expression a picture of disgusted self-righteousness. Joey, aware that he had become an object of interest to the young preventative officer, turned in his saddle and kindly offered up the information that he would be residing at his home for the rest of the day. And would he wish for him to send out a jug of ale with the stable boy at about nine of the clock, in order that the young gentleman might slake his thirst? Mr Ross's shoulders stiffened at once and he turned his horse, informing Mr Bolitho that he had no knowledge of what he was talking about and that he was on his way to visit friends at Relubbas. Joey Bolitho felt himself back in his youth for a moment and felt a twinge of excitement run through him.

"Thas' very pleasant fer 'e, sir," he remarked and then added, with a mocking grin, that Mr Ross had best not to follow the road he was on, for it would take him in the opposite direction. Mr Ross, his face scarlet, muttered his thanks through gritted teeth and then had the problem of having to confront the devil as he made his way back down the street. As he made to pass by, Mr Bolitho politely tipped his hat again, then fell into step beside him and made polite enquiries after his uncle. Mr Ross could do no other than to answer his questions, although he felt as if he would like to knock the criminal from his horse, rather than to have to converse with him upon the public highway.

"A fine man, as I remember," recounted Joey, a merry twinkle in his eye. " 'E used to like to ride all over the place too, now I come to think of it. Seemed always to be chasing after somethin', but I never did 'ear that 'e found it. Me old pal, Barney, an' meself often used to see 'im go ridin' by all of a fluster. Very thorough 'tho. Come a-calling to our 'ome one night when the rain was '³enting down. Took apart the place we was stayin' in, I dunno why. 'Tis a strange thing to do and I often wondered if he wouldn' a bit addle 'eaded."

"I beg your pardon?" snapped Mr Ross.

For answer, Joey merely tapped the side of his head. Mr Ross took a deep breath, annoyed to have his relative so maligned, but announced that he had wasted enough time with idle chatter and that he had to be on his way. He slapped his horse on and made his way down the road.

When he heard Bolitho call out to him, that he would set aside some ale that evening, just in case, he swore under his breath and vowed to do what his uncle could not and bring the man down. With the optimism of youth, he believed himself perfectly capable to accomplish a task that no man in the service had ever been able to achieve. There had to be some way of bringing the smuggler to justice and he was determined to find a way of doing it.

---

³ henting or 'enting – pouring - as in raining heavily.

CHAPTER 25

IF MR ROSS thought his exploits had gone unnoticed, he was to be disappointed. The following morning, he received a visit from the head of the Customs Service. Bonython seemed to be in a jovial mood and congratulated him on the disciplined way he had organised his paperwork. He then went on to compliment him on his method of recording the information that they had gathered, regarding various supposed smuggling activities that were taking place around the district. He agreed that Porthgwarra Cove was, in all probability, worth a search for it was a favourite place for the freetraders to land and hide their stores, on account of its locality and the rock formations, that leant themselves so naturally to anyone wishing to hide their goods from sight. The young man, brimming with confidence, smiled proudly at his commander, but a look of chagrin crossed his face when Sir Reginald suggested that his attempts to track the activities of a certain Joseph Bolitho would be doomed to disappointment.

"Mr Bolitho is a respectable member of the community these days, Mr Ross and it would not do if he should find himself plagued by you," he informed the young man, kindly. The officer bristled, announcing his belief that a man with a history like Bolitho's could not possibly be as respectable as he liked to portray.

"I know," agreed Sir Reginald with a sigh, "I did not think it possible myself that he should remain so with a past such as his, but it is the case. He has lost all inclination to smuggle. He has not, however, lost his rough temperament, and I should not wish that you find yourself on the receiving end of it." A blush flushed through his cheeks as he added, " 'Tis a most unpleasant occurrence, I can assure you, to find yourself in his power."

"Do not worry on my part, Sir Reginald," the young man stoutly pronounced, "for I would not fear to go against him. Why, even if I had to lay down my life for the service, I would be proud to do so, in order that he could be taken with my blood on his hands."

"Well said, young man, well said," his superior announced in a congratulatory tone, "but I am afraid we would find it very difficult to discover any blood on Bolitho with which to accuse him and, in all probability, we would not have sight of your body at all. As I have pointed out, he breaks no laws these days. However, anger him enough and to all intents and purposes you would vanish without a trace." Mr Ross's eyes widened at his words, but Bonython continued in a calm manner. "To my certain knowledge, only two bodies were ever found that might be connected in any way to Joey Bolitho. The first was prior to when the gentleman in question took up the smuggling trade. It was presumed that, as a young lad, he had killed the man believed to have murdered his mother. However, he had an alibi, so no case was ever brought against him. The second murder that was widely believed to have been committed by him was of a local informer. I suppose Joey would have been about thirteen or fourteen years of age at the time. Quite young, in any case, but the execution was a masterly affair. A corpse with a cleanly cut throat was propped against the harbour wall with a quantity of empty kegs neatly piled around it. On his belt was a small leather purse, which contained only the one coin, a guinea. Any member of the community would not fail to be aware of the implications of such a display. The service had to wait almost a year before anyone was prepared to divulge further information to us. Even then, the poor wretches who did come forward disappeared with alarming regularity, as it was a precarious occupation for them to follow. I doubt not that they all carried their respective guineas to their grave, for it was always said of Bolitho that he would not accept the preventatives' coin."

"You believe them dead, sir?" asked Mr Ross, with as brave a voice as he could muster.

"I presume that they were killed and their bodies disposed of by throwing them down any number of shafts that are situated in the area. Possibly, they were taken out to sea and thrown overboard, probably with weights tied to them, for to my knowledge no body ever washed up on any of the local beaches, apart from the poor souls who lost their lives at sea in shipwrecks and the like," observed Bonython, prosaically.

"If you are aware of all this, sir, then surely some case could have been brought against the fellow. It is not fair that he should go unpunished," stated the indignant young man.

"Unpunished? Bolitho received a punishment, I believe, Mr Ross, but it was not administered by the state," observed Sir Reginald. Mr Ross looked enquiring, so he went on to furnish him with the details of Bolitho's wife's death.

"He loved her most dearly, you see, young man and her loss brought him great despair," he said softly, seeming to enter a reverie as if remembering the events of that time with much sadness. However, it was not, as Mr Ross supposed, the face of Mrs Bolitho that Bonython could see in his mind's eye, but of his own dear Elizabeth.

"I will take account of your words, sir, naturally, but if any circumstance should occur that implicates that...that gentleman in any deviant activity, then I shall feel it my duty to expose him," stated the young man with conviction.

"Admirable sentiments, Mr Ross, but as I have stated, please to take care. If he should tire of your following him about the district, he could well lose his patience, and his head, and see you despatched in a moment. I should hate for such a fate to befall you, for you show great promise and dedication in your chosen career," advised the head of the service. His officer, in spite of the words of warning, could not help but visibly swell with pride at the compliment bestowed upon him.

However, Mr Ross did take account of what he had been told and decided that it would be for the best if he discontinued his attempts to track Bolitho's movements. After all, they had not been particularly successful, for Bolitho seemed to be more aware of his own activities than young Angus had been of the infuriating fellow's movements. At first, he had supposed that it was Bolitho himself who had informed against him to his superior, but when the groom, where he stabled his horse, vouchsafed the information that he was as well not to try to implicate their Mr Bolitho in any intrigue, then he began to make some tentative enquiries into the man's character, rather than any activities that he might be engaged in. Amongst the higher levels of society in which Mr Bolitho moved, he was considered to be rather an outsider, but, conversely, also an integral part of their circle because of his relationship to the Trevarthen family. As it was pointed out to him on many an occasion, Bolitho was heir to the great land-owning family of the Crowan Parish and was due to inherit a greater acreage of land than his half brother at Trevu possessed. However, Mr Ross discovered that it was amongst the common people that the former smuggler was revered and loved. He considered this a most strange occurrence, for surely it was these same people who had suffered the most at his hands, as it was from their ranks that informers were usually chosen? Further enquiries on his part elicited the information that, although various fathers, uncles, brothers and sons had disappeared over the years, in all cases their disappearance had led to an improvement in the standard of living of the bereft families. It was obvious, he concluded, that whatever their personal thoughts regarding the actions of Bolitho towards their loved ones, his own deeds, albeit unpublished, had brought changes for the better to their situation in all cases. Most of the people who had knowledge of these long-lost informers did not regard them with a high degree of respect, for their behaviour in divulging the details of their fellows' smuggling activities had dishonoured them. For someone of such an upright disposition as Mr Ross, it came as a shock to discover that it was Joey Bolitho's supposed criminal activities that they admired and respected and not his inherited wealth and position. It gave him much food for thought and, although he detested the fellow, he spent many a long evening pouring over the dusty records books that lay discarded on his office shelves, noting the instances where it was believed the Rickard gang and, later, Bolitho's men themselves, had taken part in defrauding the country of certain taxes. One name in particular intrigued him, for it was of a young informer known as Nicholas Glasson who, like the others had disappeared without trace. The officer in charge at that time had sought to lay the case at Bolitho's door and had even thought to prove that Paul Trevarthen himself was implicated in the case. Young Angus was well aware that the relationship between the two men had not been established until some time after Glasson's disappearance and considered, from what he knew of the man, that Paul Trevarthen would be a most unlikely member of any smuggling gang. Mr Trevarthen, a staunch advocate of the league against slavery, had come across Mr Ross at a meeting given by a Methodist minister, which gave details of the situation that many discarded former slaves had found themselves in as regards their welfare and financial well-being. Angus was well aware that Trevarthen felt particularly strongly about the subject, and why this was so. At one point, he noted Mr Trevarthen seeming to brush away a tear when the Minister described the living conditions of one particular family that he had come across in the city of Liverpool. At the end of the talk, the Minister asked for donations to the cause and Trevu's owner was the first to descend upon the reverend gentleman, passing into his hands what appeared to the young customs officer to be a rather large roll of bills. The minister, somewhat overcome, had need of a chair to sit down upon, but whether that was due to the largesse with which he had just been presented or to the tiring effects of the speech he had spent the last hour delivering, Angus could not be sure. From that moment on, young Mr Ross had warmed to Paul Trevarthen and so could not understand how it was that the officer at that time, a Mr Hudson, should have been so convinced that this same warm-hearted gentleman was involved with Bolitho's supposed murder of young Glasson. When, a few days later, he chanced upon a piece of gossip, which informed him that the youngster, Nankivell, was not only the son of the missing man but also the ward of Joey Bolitho, he became even more confused. There was no doubt that Bolitho was of a charitable disposition; many he had spoken to would not hear a word against him and had attested to his generosity. However, even Mr Ross would have thought him a most extraordinary fellow indeed, to have stretched his humanitarian qualities so far as to murder a fellow, only then to adopt his son. Mr Ross concluded that Mr Hudson, in his zeal to entrap the smuggler, had incorrectly assumed that Nicholas Glasson had been murdered, when in all probability the young man, destined to be married to the young girl known to be carrying his child, had taken fright at the thought and departed with all possible speed.

George Trevarthen smiled indulgently at his mother and hugged her gently to him. He assured her that he was delighted at the thought of a ball being held in his honour, the more so when he heard that it would appear that Grace would be returning from her business commitments and might also be able to attend. He knew what joy it would give to both his parents to have their dear daughter back with them again, for once she had been given the opportunity to take over the reins from her father, with regard to their grandmother's establishments, his sister had been determined to prove her capabilities. That she had succeeded, and in the short time in which she had been in sole charge had almost doubled the profits from her business activities, had made her father especially proud.

"Well, to be honest, George, we are throwing the ball not so much in honour of your visit, but to enable your uncle to look about him for a wife. He is finding it particularly difficult to settle upon the right person," his mother advised him.

"So, dear Mama, I am merely a useful figurehead am I? How mean of you to see me in such a light and how lowering for me to be so considered," mocked George, a lazy smile on his lips.

Chloe, hitting him gently with her fan, laughed with him and scolded him for being such a tease.

"It seems strange to me that Uncle Joey would be experiencing any difficulty at all in attracting the attention of the female sex," he surmised.

"In truth, it is not the lack of it that is proving a problem, rather a surfeit, for the poor man is besieged by various widows and spinsters, all intent at throwing their caps at him. Mrs Penrose, in particular, has been most persistent and he has asked me most pointedly not to invite her," said Chloe.

Her son looked shocked and cried, "But Mama, it would not be correct for you to do such a thing! Why, if you did that it would be unforgivable, for I would not see Mel...er..." and he stumbled over his words, but quickly continued, "...Mrs Penrose being at all pleased to be so shunned."

"Oh! Do not worry yourself, George, for I made him see that he would have to suffer her attention, but he finds it impossible to return the various calls that certain families make upon him. He is quite adept at charming any female that comes within his range, if he wishes to, but when they present themselves before him, almost on a platter, as it were, he is quite taken aback and finds it most awkward to proceed in the matter. Also, your father informs me that the lady in question must fulfil the role of a mother to Zacky, for that is his prime object in looking for a wife. In fact I am worried that whoever he decides upon is not likely to be the recipient of any...er..." and now it was his mother's turn to stumble over her words, "...ah...affection at all, for he loved dear Sarah-Jane so, and you well know that he has no room in his heart for another."

"Well, if that be the case I pity the poor woman he decides upon," sighed George.

"Do not concern yourself on their part, George, for whoever he shall choose, they will have a highly respectable position in society through this marriage and I believe that your uncle will ensure that they want for nothing financially. There are spouses a-plenty in this locality who would wish their husbands to be so obliging, I can assure you," she concluded sagely.

Smiling at her son, she observed with pride what a handsome young man he had become. Unlike his father, George had grown his hair longer so that his black, shining curls were more pronounced and he had a pair of very fetching - or so his mother thought - side burns that had been allowed to grow upon his cheeks. Not as tall as his father and built upon more slender lines, he was, nonetheless, a well built young man and had attained the height of just over six feet. Chloe found it intriguing that this handsome son of hers had not arrived at Trevu with some dashing female on his arm, but as he was at his happiest when lost with his head in a book, she concluded that there would be plenty of time for him to settle down. Her maternal instincts took over and she could not resist asking him if he had met with any interesting young females since last they had met, although she knew the answer before she had even finished her question.

"Good Lord no, Mama! You know there is only one interesting female in my life," he announced, and she giggled girlishly as he pulled her towards him and delivered a large kiss on her cheek.

"You fool, George," she gasped, and at that moment, his father entered the room, clearly elated to see him home again.

"Father!" cried George and sprang to his feet, his hand outstretched in greeting and a warm smile of delight on his face. The two men briefly hugged each other and then fell to talking about what they had been doing since they had last been together. A serving girl arrived with the tea tray and the family took a light repast, assembled around the small table and still talking companionably together. Whilst there was a lull in the conversation, during which time his father took the opportunity to help himself to yet another slice of cake, George, seemingly occupied in brushing a crumb from the sleeve of his coat, enquired if his mother had passed on his good wishes to Miss Melior Penrose as he had requested.

"One cannot help but realise that her mother ignores her, abominably, and makes no effort on her behalf. I know you have such a fondness for her, Mama, for you always mention how the children adore her when she comes to call," he remarked, with studied casualness.

"Well, I do believe that if she could, Joanna would not let the poor child leave the house. Such behaviour as that would give rise to so much talk that even she would not dare. I always show dear Melior your letters so that she can read for herself that you have enquired after her, for I think her bereft of so much companionship and her mother will make no attempt to make her situation better in any way whatsoever. Although lately," she observed, thoughtfully: "it has to be admitted the sweet child has been clothed to a far higher standard than ever her mother cared to attain for her before, so perhaps she has her eye on a young gentleman for the girl. It would be pleasant indeed to think that some young man should offer for her, for she has such a loving temperament, and it would be so much the better for her to be in a husband's care and not her mother's." Chloe sighed and busied herself with filling her son's empty cup. It was as well for George that she should be so occupied, for his expressive face registered a fervent blush and a look of dismay at the same time. No matter what his parents thought of his marriageable qualities, he would have to proceed slowly if he was to bring them to realise, that the girl that their eldest son had set his heart upon was no other than the much maligned Melior Penrose. They had met infrequently over the years but on each occasion, George had been subjected to Melior's friendly and open smile and he was intrigued to find that she seemed to understand him so intuitively. George, not looking for a wife, nor even to fall in love, had discovered that, when away from Cornwall, his thoughts dwelt on her; at night he lay in his bed and saw again her smile and laughing eyes. It had come as a shock to think that he was so attracted to her and for the life of him could not believe he had fallen under her spell. She had not set out to entrap him in any way and had always treated him in a friendly manner, as if he had been an elder brother. Perhaps it had been caused by his lordship's determined efforts to have him offer for his granddaughter, he reasoned, and his feelings now were a reaction to the pressure he had been placed under. Whatever had been the cause of his attraction to her, it would appear that the object of his desire had found herself a young gentleman or, more probably, some fellow had been found for her, but in either case it pulled at his heart.

His mother, failing to notice that he had made no reply, passed him his cup and then offered him a plate of biscuits, which had so far escaped his father's attention.

"No thank you, Mama," he said, waving them away, "I would not dream of depriving poor Papa of nourishment," and he smiled at her, a little sadly, thought his mother. Why he should suddenly look dispirited, she could not imagine. Perhaps his determination to stay on good terms with his father had put such a strain on the dear boy and George, with his inability to hide his emotions, could not help but to show it.

"You cheeky young rascal!" responded his father, with a laugh. George flashed his mother a smile and Chloe grinned back in return, all her worries were despatched in an instant and she enquired as to whether he had any acquaintances that he would wish to invite on his own behalf. He shook his head, but agreed to look over the list of invitations that had been sent out, just in case his mother had not invited someone that he wished to attend. Once George had established that Mrs Penrose and her daughter had accepted their invitation, he lost interest in the other names on the list but gave the impression of being most attentive for the sake of his dear mother.

On the morning of the ball, an elegant equipage pulled up before Trevu's doorway. The steps were let down and an exceptionally well-dressed and extremely beautiful young woman descended on to the yard. She was a picture of elegance from the tips of her toes to the top of her head and she looked most out of place in such a rustic setting. However, the way she appeared and the way she behaved were entirely different as she thanked her servant and then turned to greet the men that had come running from Trevu's stables. She responded to them all in turn as if they had been long lost friends; such was the warmth of her demeanour that gawky young stable lads and wizened grooms fell under her spell yet again. Her father came bounding down the steps to greet her and one could not doubt the affection the two felt towards each other.

"Oh, Papa! It is so good to be home, but what is this?" Grace asked, as they entered the hallway: "So many flowers and decorations! Not all for me, surely?"

"I should say that they are, of course. However, you are commanded to attend a ball we are throwing for George this evening," he informed her, feeling light-headed at the sight of her again. There was something about the way she carried herself and the set of her features that reminded him of his mother and it delighted his heart to see it. "Come in to your Mama, and she will explain all to you." She kissed his cheek again and allowed herself to be led off to meet with her dear mother. When her mother informed her of the real reason for the ball, she could not help but laugh, it amused her to think that her dearest uncle should have need of their help to find himself a wife. But, she politely mentioned, she had so very little time to attend social occasions herself and she would enjoy the event immensely. She informed her mother, however, that she was so very tired from her travelling that she thought that she might rest a while, after first greeting her younger brothers and sisters. She partook of a light lunch, but then confessed that she was having great difficulty in keeping her eyes open and would retire to her room to rest, for she knew that it was to be a long evening. The Trevarthen's balls were infrequent but well attended, and their guests rarely left earlier than midnight to return to their respective homes. Consequently, Grace fully expected not to have the opportunity to return to her slumbers until well into the early hours of the morning.

At the Customs House in Penzance, Sir Reginald and Angus Ross beamed at each other, unable to conceal their delight. That morning, Mr Ross had been in charge of a party of men who had succeeded in confiscating a large quantity of brandy kegs from Porthgwarra. It was, as Mr Ross had surmised, an ideal place to conceal such items. Naturally, he would have preferred to capture the smugglers themselves and with this intention had lain in wait for seven nights, hoping to catch them when they returned to avail themselves of their illicit goods. Caution prevailed, for he could not bear to think that the kegs should be lost. He could not keep a continuous watch, as he had not the manpower at his disposal, so he had given orders for the goods to be seized. The consignment was transported back to Penzance upon an open cart. The scowling faces of the various locals that they met upon their way did not give him the impression that their actions were well regarded by the local populace. The contraband would half-fill the cellar of the customs house and both his superior and himself had good cause to smile, for such success was rare.

Both men were deep in conversation and did not notice that the horse that stood in the shafts of the cart had taken offence to a man's hat, bowling down the street alongside it and had shifted its position in alarm. This resulted in the cart being violently jerked and one of the kegs, jolted from its place, fell to the ground. Unfortunately, the slight slope of the ground upon which it lay caused it to roll and bounce towards the two men. A warning cry went up and both men stepped smartly to one side, so as to avoid being caught by the rolling keg. It missed Mr Ross completely but, almost as if it was bent on some sort of revenge on being wrested from its hidden lair, the keg pitched upon a stone and was propelled into the air, only to land with a loud thud on Sir Reginald Bonython's foot. The unfortunate gentleman issued a loud yell, closely followed by a choice selection of expletives.

"Damn and blast it, man!" he yelled at Mr Ross, "I believe that damn keg has broke my foot!" Groaning with pain, he had to be assisted from the yard by two of the men. Immediately, Dr Dunstan was sent for, while Mr Ross took it upon himself to cut away Sir Reginald's boot, for his foot was beginning to swell alarmingly and he knew he would only cause the poor man more discomfort if he attempted to pull off the footwear. Dr Dunstan concluded that, fortunately, no bones were broken, but the bruising and swelling would give rise to great discomfort. He produced a lotion from his bag with which to bathe the damage and this produced a cooling relief. Then the doctor firmly bandaged the foot. It was now impossible for any boot to fit over Denzil's handiwork, so he suggested to his old friend that the local shoemaker be sent for. When this venerable artisan arrived, he scratched his head for a moment before going back to his shop and returning, a short while later, with a wooden patten. With two leather thongs, he succeeded in strapping the appliance to the base of the heavily bandaged foot. When he had completed his labours, Sir Reginald found that he could stand upon his feet again, although he was still in great pain.

"I am expected to attend the Trevarthen's ball tonight, but if I shall need assistance for every step I am to take, I suppose I shall have to cry off," moaned Sir Reginald with a grimace.

"See how you feel when the time comes, Reggie, for if you do not walk about too much you should be able to pass the evening, if not in comfort, at least without too much pain," advised Denzil, helpfully. "With a bit of assistance, I expect you will be able to manage exceedingly well," he added.

Sir Reginald stared morosely at him. But after giving the matter some thought, and noting that his foot was no longer throbbing quite so much, he decided he would attend after all. He then advised Mr Ross that, as his invitation had stated that he could bring a guest, then Mr Ross could fill that capacity, for, he deduced, young Angus could serve as his assistant for the evening. Taken aback, the young officer expostulated that he was not sure that the Trevarthens would approve to have him in their house.

"Why ever not?" thundered Sir Reginald, "They will take no exception to you, for the Trevarthens are not at all stand-offish - not as are some of the families around here. Anyway when they see the predicament that I am in,

221

they will be most sympathetic, I can assure you." Mr Ross attempted once more to voice his opinion, but Bonython advised him to make himself useful and to get him a large glass of port from the local hostelry, for he felt in great need of a drink.

So, later that evening, Mr Ross found himself assisting his employer to a seat in the large withdrawing room of Trevu. In his capacity as a lowly customs officer, it was not the habit of Mr Ross to attend upon such large gatherings, but, as a considerable number of the people at the dance were known to him, he did not feel as awkward as he at first presumed he would. His hosts were most sympathetic to Sir Reginald and his predicament, and arranged seating for him immediately, so that he would not have to spend the evening putting any weight upon his damaged foot. As there was also a delicious punch available, he was soon comfortably ensconced with a glass of this excellent beverage in his hand. Various of his acquaintances came to converse with him and were soon regaled with the tale of the runaway keg. In this way, he was able to pass an enjoyable evening and did not need to have Angus Ross permanently at his side, so the young man was able to move about and chat to various people in the room. A frown descended upon the brow of Mr Ross when he caught sight of Joey Bolitho standing in the midst of a veritable throng of women, but he began to smile, unconsciously, as he realised that the man did not appear to be enjoying the experience. However, ever watchful for his charge, his eye was caught by Sir Reginald's stick being waved in the air. He immediately crossed the room to see why his attention had been sought, and found that Sir Reginald wished to introduce him to the young man for whom the ball was being held. Mr Ross found himself looking at the face of a handsome young man, of a similar height and age to himself. Whatever his opinion about the young man's uncle, he found himself deep in conversation with this personable gentleman and immediately thought him an excellent fellow. However, George was soon taken off by his father to meet with a local landowner and Mr Ross, finding himself stood idly by his employer, sipped his glass of punch and surveyed the crowd before him. He found himself bristling when he noted that Joey Bolitho appeared to be walking directly toward them, but there was nothing he could do, for at that moment, Sir Reginald raised his stick in greeting.

"Sir Reginald, Mr Ross," greeted Bolitho, and smiled at them both. On making enquiries concerning Bonython's injury, he was most sympathetic.

"Damn 'eavy thing, a keg of brandy," Bolitho advised. Before Sir Reginald could reply, Mr Ross could not help but to interpose in an irritated tone, "Well, you of all people would know that, Bolitho!"

The smile on the ex smuggler's lips widened and he turned his attention to Mr Ross, his cold blue eyes warmed with the twinkle of amusement that danced in them. "Sure 'nuff, sir," he agreed, in a reasonable tone," but I never 'ad the misfortune to drop one on me foot."

"That's enough, Ross," snapped Sir Reginald, testily, determined not to have his helper create any ill feeling. It would not do if the young fool should annoy the host's brother at such a grand occasion, although he noted with relief that Bolitho appeared to be laughing at the silly fellow and had not taken offence.

Rebuffed, Mr Ross bit his lip and turned his face away to survey the crowd, in order not to have to speak to the fellow at all. He seethed with frustration. He would so much like to have accosted the man with questions about the smugglers loot, for he believed that of all the people in the room, this was the man who would be able to furnish him with the most information about the contraband. As his eye wandered over a group of guests at the entrance to the room, a young lady seemed to glide into the mass of people that milled around. As she did so, a quantity of young gentlemen surged towards her and she laughed and smiled at all around her equally as she exchanged greetings with them. Angus had already noted that there were some very fine looking young ladies amongst the gathering, but this particular female was an Aphrodite by comparison.

"Oh, I say!" he announced in wonderment, and stared, enchanted, at the newest arrival, "What a beauty!" Sir Reginald and Bolitho turned to see who it was that had attracted his attention. To the surprise of Mr Ross, Joey Bolitho raised a hand across the room in greeting to the damsel. Immediately, she waved back, left the group gathered around her and made her way across the room towards them. Mr Ross, open mouthed to think that this gorgeous apparition was heading in their direction, almost forgot to breathe, such was his trepidation at meeting this woman. To him, she appeared the most wondrous being it had ever been his privilege to set eyes upon. He noted with some chagrin that, upon reaching their group, she threw her arms around Bolitho's neck and kissed him on his cheek. She turned to Sir Reginald, who beamed at her - rather in the fashion of a silly schoolboy, thought his assistant - and upon enquiry, he related again the reason for his unfortunate accident. Mr Ross, who had heard the tale at least ten times that evening, should have looked bored. But when presented with such beauty, standing less than three feet away, he could not possibly be so. All he could do was stare at her, an expression of wonder on his face.

CHAPTER 26

JOEY BOLITHO, his hand held tightly by this wondrous damsel thought it his duty to introduce her to the young man and so he said, "Grace, my dear, allow me to introduce 'e to Sir Reginald's 'elpmate." When he had effected the introductions, he released his niece and stood back to watch the young couple conversing. In all honesty, it was Grace who seemed to be doing the talking for the poor chap appeared tongue-tied. Joey and Bonython exchanged grins as they watched. Mr Ross, however, finally took his courage in his hands and enquired if it would be possible for Miss Trevarthen to allow him a dance later in the evening.

"Why certainly, Mr Ross," replied Grace and smiled at the young man who grinned so idiotically at her. "Do you waltz, perchance?"

"Wa...waltz?" he replied, "Oh yes, yes! I mean, yes I do!"

"Well, I shall put your name down for the second waltz. Papa does not really approve of couples dancing in such close proximity to each other but men of his age are such old fogies, don't you think, sir?" she enquired, tapping her uncle playfully on the arm with her fan. Joey tipped up her chin with his finger and joked with her that she was not to cast aspersions about his age.

Mr Ross, now thinking the gods had bestowed the greatest gift imaginable upon him, attempted a reply, "Just so, Miss Trevarthen." He gasped, realising that he should not have maligned his host and attempted to extricate himself from his mistake. Grace heard her name being called by a group of damsels, and so his mumbling explanation was foreshortened as she excused herself politely and made her way to group of giggling girls.

So transfixed was he by what had just happened to him that it was fully five minutes before it dawned upon Mr Ross, that the beautiful lady that he was soon to have in his arms was none other than the niece of the hated individual standing before him. It was a disconcerting thought, but the anticipation of the forthcoming dance meant that he had little time to ponder it and he instead concentrated on trying to stop his hands from shaking and his heart from beating quite so rapidly. Sir Reginald, hearing his named called rather loudly, looked up and discovered Mrs Penrose, with her daughter in tow, heading purposefully towards them. Bolitho, on recognising the voice, rapidly excused himself. He bowed to an annoyed Mrs Penrose, just as she had reached the little group, made his way across the room and was soon deep in conversation with his sister in law.

With the hidden reason for the evening's entertainment uppermost in her mind, Mrs Trevarthen had given much thought to the various females disporting themselves around the room.

"I thought the widow Harvey, from Sennen, was looking particularly fine this evening, Joey," prompted Chloe, raising her eyes to his inscrutable face.

"Fair," mused Joey, "but she got a mouthful of Waterloo teeth and a laugh like a donkey!" Undaunted, she pointed out various other females, but as these were mostly singular ladies who, because of a variety of deficiencies, had given up all hope of ever attracting the attention of the opposite sex, she knew her efforts were doomed to disappointment.

"There is always Joanna Penrose," she said, playfully, then laughed at his astonished expression. It was a serious matter, however, for her brother-in-law's situation was becoming more desperate with the passage of time. Leah Bolitho could succumb at any time, for her health had deteriorated markedly over the past year and indeed, considered Chloe, it was only that lady's indomitable spirit that had sustained her for so long. That Joey was aware of the fact only heightened the urgency of the situation. His determination in finding a suitable mother meant that many of the females would be dismissed, on the grounds of not having the personality to pay attention to any other person apart from themselves. Although he had stressed that he was not particularly concerned regarding their appearance, Joey had to find a female whose other qualities were acceptable to him.

Glancing around the room, Chloe noted that her son was deep in conversation with Miss Melior Penrose. Considering that this conversation required a certain amount of hand waving and a great deal of time spent writing in Miss Penrose's little notebook, it was commendable that he should take such time with her and she smiled with maternal pride. 'Trust George, to take such care of another,' she thought, smiling fondly at the pair.

The musicians struck up and couples soon filled the room as the dancing began. Miss Grace Trevarthen had reserved the first dance for her father and so Mr Ross, not hampered with a partner, stood with his back against the wall and watched as the couple performed the steps with great elegance. It was almost impossible for him to drag his eyes away from them both, yet his attention was finally drawn to the Bolitho fellow, who appeared to be surveying the proceedings with a jaundiced eye. It gave him a youthful pleasure to realise that the man was not enjoying the proceedings and when, at the end of the dance, he saw Bolitho's expression harden still further as he was accosted by Mrs Penrose, he could not help but to smile at the fellow's predicament. However, when it was his turn to stand up with Miss Trevarthen for the promised waltz, he could scarcely stop himself from shaking, such was his excitement. If she noticed, she did not refer to it and when the music stopped, he was given the added pleasure of leading her to a seat at the wall. He offered to fetch her a glass of lemonade, but she shook her head, instead enquiring as to how he was finding Cornwall and whether he liked his chosen profession? At first, he stumbled over his words but Grace, of all Paul's children, had a delightful way of appearing to be entranced by whatever another had to say to her and he soon felt completely at his ease, chatting happily away.

George Trevarthen escorted his partner back to her beaming mother and politely complimented the young lady on her dancing abilities. Smiling gracefully, he then withdrew. This damsel sighed at his departure, but was pleased that she had danced with the young man. He was soon to be ennobled and for that reason alone, her mother appeared to be bursting with pride. George's eyes sought the room for Melior Penrose, but she was sitting with Sir Reginald and he did not like to interrupt them, for Melior was furiously scribbling in her book. Later in the evening, he would take the opportunity to talk with her again and make known his intention towards her. Her mother, he knew, would not be disappointed in the match, for it would add greatly to that lady's consequence. But as to his parents' opinion, he was less sure.

Noticing that Mrs Penrose was busily engaged in talking to his uncle, he thought he would take the opportunity to save him from her clutches and to engage her in conversation himself, and it was with this intention that he made his way towards them. George could not fail to notice the look of relief that crossed his uncle's face as he greeted them both.

"Oh! Dear George," beamed the redoubtable lady, "I was only telling your uncle how proud he must be to see what a fine young man you have become. Such grace in the ballroom, as well! You must make your parents so proud of you, for you have such charm and elegance for your age. You must come to a select musical soiree that I shall be holding on Thursday next. Little more than twenty people will be there and drawn only from Penzance's finest, I can assure you. You will be so kind as to oblige me, will you not?" Without waiting for a reply, she turned to his uncle and offered him a similar invitation, couched in equally forthright terms.

Although the youngest gentleman had no intention of refusing her invitation, the elder sought desperately for an excuse to refuse. Joey cried off on the grounds of a previous engagement but politely thanked her for her invitation. Mrs Penrose frowned darkly at him but then, not wishing to annoy the man, smiled as warmly as she could and announced that she was sure there would be other occasions. Mr Bolitho smiled back and admitted, rather coldly, George noted, that he was convinced that there would be. Joanna took a sweeping look around the room, hoping to see how many of her acquaintances would be taking note of the fact that Joey Bolitho was in conversation with her, when her eye alighted on her daughter, sitting beside Sir Reginald Bonython. The child was, for once, adequately turned out, a pale yellow dress setting off her auburn curls admirably. But as she could not dance and could barely communicate with her fellow man, she thought it a complete waste of time that the girl should even have been invited and assumed that the Trevarthens had done so purely out politeness.

Melior stared boldly back at her across the room and Joanna, with her back to Mr Bolitho, sighed with exasperation.

"Look at my daughter, gentlemen," she said elaborately, "have you ever seen such a drab of a girl before? I sometimes wonder if she was merely put in this world to annoy me, for there can be no other reason for her existence. Such a shame she did not pass away when her father died, for there is no doubt in my mind that it would have been for the best. She cannot speak or hear and, judging by the expression on her face, she is incapable of putting two thoughts together accurately," she bemoaned. The child continued to stare, her expression remaining unaltered.

"I blame her father, you know," continued Joanna, now in full flow, for she liked nothing better than to inform people of the dreadful life she had to lead with such a burden as her daughter, "for he would spoil her so, as she was always his favourite. Such a relief to me to think that he should have succumbed as quickly as he did, for I have no idea how I would have managed, should he have lived and have been similarly damaged. Yes," she concluded, "I awake most mornings relieved to think him gone." She turned around to face Mr Bolitho, but young Mr Trevarthen garnered her attention. George was shocked to hear such sentiments and attempted to convince Mrs Penrose that her daughter had a delightful personality, but his uncle was staring at the

226

young girl with a puzzled look on his face. Slowly, he watched as Melior reached into her reticule, took out her handkerchief and discreetly wiped away a tear. Melior Penrose had lost her hearing a number of years ago and yet across a crowded room, where, even had she not been deaf, she would not have been able to ascertain what had just been said by her mother, somehow the girl had divined what had been recounted about her and her beloved father. Intrigued, he excused himself, on the grounds that Sir Reginald was attempting to attract his attention and leaving George to extol Melior's many virtues to her infuriated mother, he crossed the room.

"Shall I procure 'e a glass of lemonade, Miss Penrose?" he enquired. Melior, taken off-guard to be addressed by the man, nodded and then, in an almost comic realisation of what she had done, she picked up her book, offering it and her pencil towards him.

Sir Reginald, realising the poor girl's mistake, turned Melior's face towards him and announced to her that if she was going to give away her secret, there would be no better man in the room to keep it than Joey Bolitho. She nodded, looking ashamed to have been so easily caught out. Sir Reginald, still looking at Melior in order that she could see the words he addressed to Mr Bolitho, explained to him that Miss Penrose would prefer that her mother not be informed of her daughter's ability to fathom people's words as they uttered them.

Large brown eyes, full of pleading, were directed towards Joey. He smiled reassuringly, before announcing that he enjoyed keeping secrets and that he would be back in a moment with her glass of lemonade. When he returned, he presented her with her glass, bowed politely, made his excuses and moved away. Even then, he could feel, but could not see, that her eyes were following his every step. It gave him a thrill of delight to think that Joanna Penrose, of all people, was being hoodwinked so cleverly by her own much-maligned daughter and he wrested the smile from his lips with great difficulty.

The dinner itself was a splendid event and the guests were treated to a prodigious array of dishes and much fine wine. When they returned to the ballroom to continue the dance, those gentleman that wished to do so were allowed to disperse to the library, where several card tables had been set up for their pleasure. Although Mr Trevarthen did not like to gamble, he would not deny the pleasure to others. Sir Reginald, a little bored to think of spending the rest of the evening watching the dancing, was delighted to take advantage, not just of the company of many of his male friends but also Paul's thoughtfulness in leaving several decanters of fine spirits in the room. In spite of the persistent throb in his foot, Sir Reginald was having a most entertaining evening and could not remember when he had enjoyed himself quite so much since his dear wife had passed away.

Joey, who was by now bored of the whole evening, wished himself at home, but Chloe and Paul had gone to considerable trouble on his behalf and he did not want to appear in any way ungrateful to them. Dutifully, he took up a position by the door, which led to the corridor to the back stairs. Usually, only the servants would wish to take that route to the upper rooms, for it was quite dark. The children, however, all made use of it, for it led directly to the passage where the side door to the garden was situated. So it was that Joey alone heard the young child's cry of dismay. When he looked out into the darkness, he could make out young Treve Trevarthen, clutching a plate to his chest. He noted that several of the little cakes he had accrued to himself now appeared to have fallen to the floor. Smiling, he was about to go forward to help his nephew out of his predicament, when he heard a noise and stepped back into the shadows. Melior Penrose came rushing out of the dining room, holding before her a larger plate on which several delicacies resided. Not seeing Mr Bolitho, she carried the plate to young Treve and put her fingers to her lips. Treve wiped an eye and pointed to the cakes on the floor. Hastily, Melior dropped her platter on a table and bent down to gather up the damaged cakes. They were inedible, but in order that no one should inadvertently step in them, she opened up her reticule and dropped them inside. Picking up her plate, she then joined the young child on the steps and sat down beside him. Carefully, she wiped the face of the tearstained child and began to dab away the remnants of the creams and custards that had spoilt the front of his clothing. As the little fellow was in his night-shirt and had begun to shiver, she removed the lace shawl from about her arms and wrapped it around him. He beamed to see the array of food that she had managed to procure for him and they sat for a while in companionable silence, whilst he munched his way through the many delights, which Melior had retrieved for him from the now depopulated dining room. When this had been accomplished, he allowed his mouth to be wiped and then leaned, sleepily, against his accomplice. Melior placed the platter to one side and, getting the tired boy to his feet, she slowly led him back up the stairs to his room. Intrigued, Joey stayed where he was, and when the girl returned, he watched as she picked up the empty platter and discreetly returned it to the dining room. Melior was crossing the hallway when she noticed a shadow, which lay across the floor. She turned immediately and caught sight of Mr Bolitho, watching her antics. She giggled, staring boldly at him. Lifting her finger to her lips once more and with a merry twinkle in her eye, she returned to the dance. What he had just witnessed gave the man much food for thought for, in Melior Penrose, he had seen the very qualities that he wished to discover in a woman that he would want for a wife. What a shame that the young woman in question should be little more than a child herself, for he was old enough to be her father and had no wish to cause yet more scandal in his family by taking such a young innocent for a wife. He laughed at himself as the thought suddenly struck him, that Miss Penrose would have to be in desperate straits indeed to even think of marrying one so far above her in years. With this lowering thought, he returned to his contemplation of the available females in the ballroom.

George Trevarthen studied the whirling, dancing people before him and wondered, idly, if he should wait another day before asking Melior Penrose for her hand. He wanted to establish that the sweet girl would wish to marry him, although in his heart he could not but believe that she would jump at the chance of matrimony, if only to get herself away from her tortuous life with her mother. He was a quiet, sensible young man and cautious in the extreme, but he had fallen deeply in love and he found the whole experience quite unsettling. He wished, therefore, to resolve the problems that he faced as quickly as he possibly could. His parents would accept his choice, for he had chosen from a good family. Her mother would jump at the chance to marry her daughter off, especially to someone of his standing. The Wrothford's would be appalled, though he cared not a jot for that. It was Melior's reaction that caused him the most concern, for she gave the impression of being enamoured of no one and he would have liked her to show him some mark of interest, if only for his pride's sake.

Young Miss Penrose was completely unaware that there were two gentlemen at the dance that had even thought of her in terms of marriage, the former because he admired her skills with children and the latter because he had lost his heart to her. She had come to terms with her inability to hear soon after it had happened, it was the loss of her beloved father that had caused her much more heartache. Life in the Penrose household had never been happy from that time on, for she missed her father dreadfully, but she was a determined individual and refused to have her spirit crushed, even by one so domineering as her mother. Although she would not wish to acknowledge it, she had inherited her mother's ruthless streak and it was that ability that had helped her endure the continuous abuse from her parent that would have crushed a lesser individual. In spite of her mother's cutting remarks, she was enjoying the evening, for no other reason than it had allowed her some freedom. The majority of the young people at the dance had a duty to find themselves a partner and because of her disability, she had no reason to presume that her circumstances would make her suitable to be placed on any man's list of desirable young woman. Having no delusions about her looks, she knew that her lot was to remain at her mother's side and she had resigned herself to that fact many years ago. There would, however, be occasions, like tonight, when she could experience a sort of freedom and she would take that opportunity and grab it with both hands. She was standing and watching the band playing, a wistful expression on her face, for she could not hear them, when she became aware of someone at her side. Turning, she looked into the earnest young face of George Trevarthen and smiled happily up at him. He held out his hand for her book and writing quickly, asked if she was enjoying herself. She nodded and wrote in reply that it was the best of all evenings. And so they continued to converse in this manner, as they had done earlier in the evening. George wanted to enquire as to what Melior's sentiments might be towards himself, but to boldly write such a thing in her book was more than his natural reserve would allow him to do. However, he knew that he would have to steel himself to do it and picked up her book, determined to write of his love for her, but at that moment, her mother appeared before them.

Joanna was not in the best of moods, for she had been infuriated by Mr Bolitho's actions in avoiding her at every available opportunity. Dressed in her finest, she had believed it a simple matter to garner the man's attention, yet had been thwarted by him at almost every turn. Now, she had broken her fan, having snapped it shut in temper, and knowing that her daughter possessed one, she sought to borrow hers. The silly child had no idea how to use one artfully in any case and, more often than not, she pushed it into her reticule to keep it out of the way. Aware that the kind-hearted Trevarthen boy was doing his best to entertain the annoying child, she smiled briskly at him before catching hold of her daughter's arm and removing her reticule, without even attempting to write an explanation. She pulled open the neck, but upon reaching her hand inside, an expression of shock and disbelief crossed her face. Melior's hand shot up to her face in dismay as her mother produced a crushed cake from the inside of the bag. Shaking with temper and oblivious to her surroundings, she screamed at the shocked girl.

"What have you done, you useless child? Have you not enough at home that you must steal when out and about?" and so furious was she that Joanna shook the remnants of cake from her hand and slapped her daughter across the face. At once, George put his arm protectively around Melior and ordered Mrs Penrose not to strike her daughter again. Joanna, shaking with temper, that the young man should address her in such a fashion, was unaware that the commotion had now made her the centre of attention of a group of interested onlookers. Shouting at her daughter, she accused her of being neither more nor less than a common thief.

Tears welled up in Melior's eyes and she shook her head, whilst George, aware of her distress, turned to comfort her. He was to be shocked still further as Melior took a deep breath and shouted back at her mother.

"I am not a thief!" she cried angrily, "How dare you say such a thing!"

Melior's speech surprised the assembled group, but at the revelation that her daughter could speak, her mother was shocked to the core. Joanna swooned and fell back into the arms of the gentleman standing behind her. Looking up into this gentleman's face, she noted his ice-blue eyes regarding her with hostility. Hastily, she regained her footing and made great play with her handkerchief, dabbing at her eyes.

"Oh! Oh, Mr Bolitho! What am I to do? In spite of all my care for her, I have nurtured a deceiver and a thief! If only you knew, dear Mr Bolitho, the suffering I have had to endure and now to be so dishonoured!" she whimpered, intent on gaining the man's sympathy.

"Well," announced Joey in a soft voice, "tidden all bad, Mrs Penrose, fer now you knaw Miss Penrose can communicate, you won't 'ave no problems in finding a 'usband fer she." As he looked into her face, she noted with anger that he appeared to be laughing at her. Joanna, throwing all caution to the wind, turned and looked at her distressed daughter.

"A husband!" she announced with disgust. "Who in their right mind would wish for a thief and deceiver for a wife, that's what I would like to know?" By now, she was almost screaming, unable to control her emotions.

George, his protective arm still around Melior, heard her sob and his heart contracted to see her so distressed. It was not how he would have wanted to make his announcement, but he determined to wrest his dear love away from that wicked woman and an opportunity had presented itself that he would be a fool not to take. He drew breath, but before he had a chance to speak, he heard a soft voice say, "I would, Madam. If she'll 'ave me, I'll marry Melior Penrose."

If there had been consternation before this announcement, now there was uproar, for Joey Bolitho's words shocked all assembled around them. The orchestra had stopped playing when they became aware of the commotion and loud whispers were passed back through the thronging guests. Soon, all were aware that Joseph Bolitho, the ex smuggler, had offered for the hand of the deaf-mute Melior Penrose, a child of half his age. Joanna gave vent to a loud shriek and swooned away completely, unable to bear the consequences of what she had just heard. George looked aghast, but Melior had not said a word and merely stood, shaking within his grasp. That he was still coming to terms with the fact that his beloved could speak, let alone that his uncle should have asked for her hand, had left him reeling, but he was resilient. Noting that Mrs Roskilly was attending to Mrs Penrose, he took Melior by the hand and as they moved away, the crowd stood back and allowed them to pass, staring at them as they did so. Guiding Melior to a settle at the side of the room, he sat beside her, took up her hand and gently squeezed it. She smiled at him through her tears, but she had stopped shaking and was no longer looking so distressed.

Meanwhile, Paul Trevarthen was involved in a heated discussion with his brother in the back parlour. Once he had become aware of what had transpired, he had left his poor wife to deal with the consequences and had grabbed hold of his brother, propelling him from the room. Once in the safe and secluded atmosphere of the parlour, he rounded on him and began by questioning his sanity.

"What on earth possessed you to say such a thing, you fool?" he demanded.

Joey shrugged his shoulders. "Seemed fair enough to me, Paul, fer 'tis obvious Joanna 'ave made the poor maid's life 'ell. She can be Zacky's governess, an' you knaw I'm lookin' more fer a mother fer 'e than a wife fer meself. I realise I got marry 'er, but thas' no matter, fer she wen't be no trouble. Anyway she 'aven't said she'd marry me, so what are 'e in such a fuss about?" he reasoned.

Paul raised his eyes heavenwards and said, slowly and through gritted teeth, "After that public display, Joey, she can hardly do any other!"

"Well I didden start it. It was that blasted woman's fault!" said Joey, beginning to feel annoyed with Paul.

His brother sighed heavily and announced, "That blasted women, should Melior accept you, will become your mother-in-law! Have you thought of that? In fact, have you thought of the consequences of anything?" but it was obvious that Joey had not, for an expression of shock crossed his face and he slowly shook his head.

Paul, seething with frustration, crossed to the side table and poured two large brandies. He passed one to his brother and threw the contents of his own glass down his throat in a single gulp.

"Our attempt tonight was to assist you to procure a suitable wife, not to have you set the whole of Penzance about its ears, Joey! God knows what can be done now to unpick this tangle?" He sighed in frustration and poured himself another drink.

"I doubt very much that Miss Penrose will accept me. I'm 'ardly well thought of in 'er family, after all!" Joey announced, forthrightly.

His brother shook his head in resignation. Then, remembering that he had left his dearest Chloe to mend all, determined to get back to the ballroom at once. Their return caused a rise in the hubbub of conversation in the room, but Paul gave the onlookers what he hoped was a calm and reassuring smile and set about to look for his wife. He discovered her seated in a little alcove at the back of the room. Beside her sat Mrs Penrose, who was lying back on the settle with her eyes closed. Mrs Roskilly, who was busily waving smelling salts under her friend's nose, could scarcely wipe the gleeful smile off her face at Joanna's predicament. Paul's wife was just as busily engaged in patting the lady's hand. When the gentlemen presented themselves before them, she flashed a look of fury at her brother-in-law, who had the grace to lower his head in shame.

"George and Grace have questioned Melior," advised Chloe. "They have discovered that Treve woke up and came down to the dining room to help himself to some food, and Melior assisted him. The cakes in her reticule were those that Treve had dropped and she picked them up from the floor so that no one should step on them and possibly slip over. She had not stolen them at all and so, in spite of Joanna's protestations, she is not a thief."

"But she is a deceiver," moaned Joanna from the settle, "for, even if she cannot hear, she can speak perfectly adequately!" and with these words she sat up and opened her eyes. It was, perhaps, unfortunate that the first person she should see would be none other than Mr Bolitho. She shuddered dramatically and announced with loathing, "My mother was quite right! You are nothing more than a product of the gutter, Joseph Bolitho and it is my sincere wish that you return to where you would be most at home!"

For answer, Joey bowed and thanked her politely, but the amused smile on his face was there for all to see. "I be lookin' fer a governess fer my boy, Zacky, Mrs Penrose. I reckon as 'ow yer maid will do nicely, but to make it respectable, I'm prepared to marry 'er," Joey advised his shocked audience. "But if she 'aven't a wish to marry me, I won't be offended. If you do object then I'll quite understand, but sounds to me like you'll be glad get rid of her!"

Paul once again lifted his eyes to heaven and began a stumbling speech, in an attempt to rephrase his brother's explicit words.

"I know precisely what your brother said, Mr Trevarthen, for his statement was quite plain! I would inform you that I could not care less, for if the silly child would wish to throw herself away on that...that..." She sought for a word that would adequately encapsulate her feelings of disgust and dismay, but she could think of none suitable for use in polite company. Dramatically waving her hand in a circle, she instead returned to bemoaning the fact that she had been so badly treated.

The men withdrew with alacrity and Paul beckoned to Grace, standing and talking with Mr Ross. The couple came across the room towards them and he asked his daughter to instruct the band to begin to play again. Mr Ross, amazed at what he had witnessed, glanced at Mr Bolitho, who seemed completely unabashed by the furore that had erupted around him. The customs officer was quite envious to see the man so cool and collected. Paul and his brother continued on their way across the room and as the music struck up a waltz, various couples began to dance once more. When they reached the place where Melior and George were still sitting, they noted that the two had been joined by Sir Reginald Bonython, and the man did not look best pleased at what had occurred.

"What do you think you're playing at, Bolitho?" he demanded, angrily.

"Miss Penrose can always refuse me, Sir, fer 'tis 'er right. An' to be fair, 'tis only proper she d'knaw I 'ave no love fer 'er, but I didden like see the way 'er mother was abusin' the poor maid, an' thas' why I did it," explained Joey, moderately.

Sir Reginald sighed, for he had felt protective towards the girl in his own way. He turned to Melior and smiled before beginning his speech. He explained that it was perfectly in order for her to refuse Mr Bolitho's proposal, for as the man had pointed out, he had only done it in order to save her from further harassment from her mother. Also, he added kindly, she was not to be afraid of having to return to her mother's home, for arrangements would be made to enable her to live under another's roof in perfect propriety. He did not say that he referred to his own residence, but all who heard him knew what his speech had implied. George breathed a sigh of relief, for now, Melior would not have to dread living with her mother and would finally be free, after all.

Melior thanked them all for their kindness to her and smiled, gratefully. But when she looked at the ex-smuggler, standing so tall before her, the amused sparkle returned to her eyes. On seeing it, Joey smiled back and was even on the point of laughing when Melior said, sweetly, "Thank you for your kind offer, and I would be honoured to marry you, Mr Bolitho!"

CHAPTER 27

IN HIS office and standing in front of his desk, Angus Ross looked justifiably worried. Sir Reginald, firmly ensconced in the customs officer's own chair, was not looking best pleased. Angus had worked so hard to win the man's favour and he had no wish to annoy him.

"You did what?" thundered Bonython.

"Sent for Bolitho, sir, for I assumed he would have more knowledge of it than anyone," explained Mr Ross, "for it was by the merest chance the body was discovered. If it had not been for the wishes of the adventurers at Wheel Dameris, then the mine would not have been subjected to the survey. The surveyor is in quite a state, sir, as you can well imagine, for the shaft proved difficult to descend. To find himself face to face with a man's skeleton when he was sixty feet down and alone in a kibble, well, it terrified the poor fellow." Sir Reginald did not reply, and appeared to be chewing on some imaginary food, so Mr Ross took a deep breath and continued with his tale, "I have made arrangements that Mr Kelynack, the surveyor, should rest and recover his sanity in the nearest hostelry, I have also paid for his board. Some local men recovered the remains for me, sir, and I had it transported to Dr Dunstan's, in the hope that he would be able to confirm the cause of death. I then sent a note to the coroner. It was only when I observed the malformation of the hand, that I brought to mind the description of the missing informer known as Nicholas Glasson and Bolitho's supposed involvement in his disappearance," he concluded in haste.

"Damn it, man!" fumed Sir Reginald, "Could you not leave well alone? What right had you to assume that these bones were those of Glasson anyway? Any number of men might have had deformed hands and...and not been able to save themselves from falling down the shaft!"

"Why, sir, because of this," he said, and as he fumbled in his pocket he continued to relate his information, "The skeleton still had the remnants of clothing about its person, and a leather belt was still in place, from which was suspended this..." and he held out his hand, displaying a badly perished leather purse. Carefully upending the fragile object, a golden guinea fell onto the table, rolled in a circle and finally came to rest directly between the two men. Presented with the gleaming coin, Sir Reginald Bonython at once knew of its significance, and what the implication of its discovery and that of the skeletal remains would mean to the man who was, even now, making his way to the Custom's Office.

Not six months before, he had given away his sweet Melior Penrose in marriage to that same man. He had plenty of misgivings, it was true, but somehow the oddly matched couple was seen to be making a success of the strange arrangement. Melior was undoubtedly far happier as Mrs Bolitho than she had been as Miss Penrose, and Bolitho's son was enraptured with his father's new wife and his new mother. Whilst the child still resided with his aunt, the Bolitho's visited frequently and Melior often stayed at Trevanoc, though, for reasons of his own, Joey Bolitho himself would not. Furthermore, Paul Trevarthen had informed Bonython only a week ago that when he and his wife had visited last, Leah Bolitho had been full of praise for her nephew's wife and her love for young Zacky. Now, when his beloved Melior seemed at last to have created a haven for herself, it was to be cruelly taken from her by this disastrous discovery. Why that young fool Ross could not have assumed that it was no more than some passing miner, probably in some drunken state who had mistaken his way and fallen to his death, he did not know.

A knock at the door made both men jump and when Sir Reginald called out, Sergeant Tiddy showed Joey Bolitho into the room. Taller than Mr Ross, he inclined his head towards them and said, "Afternoon, Sir Reginald, Mr Ross," in a friendly manner. However, when his eye alighted on the solitary coin lying in the middle of the table, the smile on his lips froze, though he said not a word.

"Ah!" began Bonython awkwardly, "Mr Ross, get a chair for Mr Bolitho," but Joey shook his head and said that he preferred to stand.

"As you will," sighed Sir Reginald. He then launched into the tale of the discovery, watching all the while for some sign from the ex-smuggler, but not by so much as a twitch of a muscle did Bolitho's features alter.

"Of course, we cannot confirm that the body belongs to Nicholas Glasson but...but we have reason to believe that...um...because of..." and he moistened his lips, nervously, "because of this guinea and its significance...it might possibly be the case that...um...er..." and here the head of the service floundered to a halt.

Mr Ross, brimming with the excitement of the moment, could not contain himself. Turning to the man who had become his personal Nemesis, he cried out, "We believe him to have been murdered and that you have knowledge of it, and possibly had a hand in it as well!"

The blank expression on Bolitho's face dimmed the light of enthusiasm in his own eyes, but, still brimming with confidence, he announced that he had also sent for the boy.

"Your ward, Mr Bolitho, your ward will know of this!" he announced, defiantly. It was his intention to say more, but Bolitho advised him to leave young Nankivell out of it, for he was born after the father's disappearance and could know nothing of the matter.

"True, sir, true, but I cannot imagine that the boy, living as he does in such a small town as this, has not heard various rumours that abound concerning yourself and your past. It is my belief that if he does not already know some of the details of his father's disappearance, then it would be something approaching a miracle. If the body that has been recovered should be his father, than he should know of it, for it is his right," ascertained Mr Ross, triumphantly.

"You do not appear to 'ave 'eard me, Mr Ross," rejoined the ex smuggler, coldly, "I said you was to leave him out of it."

"For what reason, if not that you are attempting to hide your guilt, Bolitho? I say the boy shall know of it and when he arrives, I shall question him about the matter, to see if there is perhaps more information that can be garnered concerning this affair," the customs officer informed him, almost dancing with delight.

"Once more, Mr Ross, and for the last time. You are to leave Nicky out of this business!" said Joey, an edge of anger to his voice.

Foolhardy in the extreme and possibly through ignorance of the consequences, Mr Ross drew himself up to his full height and announced defiantly, "I will not!" Sir Reginald had time to utter one groan of despair before Bolitho was across the room, his hands around the young man's neck. Whether or not murder was in Joey's mind at that moment, perhaps not even Joey himself knew, but he would have the man silenced to protect his beloved Nicky. Bonython, horrified at the proceedings and knowing he had not the ability to stop Bolitho on his own, called for the guards. Together, with the assistance of the three men who came running in from the outer office, they succeeded in pulling Joey off the young officer and held him back against the wall - with some trepidation, for the fellow looked capable of murder. Mr Ross, his eyes streaming, clutched at his throat, gulping down deep breaths of air. Even now, he would not give up and attempted to speak out against the man, but was capable of no more than pointing a finger at him.

Sir Reginald, not wishing for the situation to escalate further, positioned himself between the two men. Placing the tip of his cane against Bolitho's chest, he ordered the guards from the room. They turned worried faces towards their superior, for no person would wish to abandon another to Joey Bolitho when he was in this sort of temper.

"Get out!" he barked at them, authoritatively, "Leave the office and go about some business in the town or what have you. I can handle this matter now. 'Tis merely a slight disagreement between these gentleman!"

Sergeant Tiddy regarded him with a look of disbelief, considering that perhaps Sir Reginald had run mad, to label the sight of Joey Bolitho attempting to strangle another nothing more than a 'slight disagreement'. He opened his mouth and began to protest, but Bonython would have none of it.

"Get out!" he repeated. Releasing their hold on Bolitho, the men left the room, one or two of them muttering under their breath that the world had run mad.

"Stay your ground, Joey!" ordered Sir Reginald. He fumbled in his pocket and when he had found his flask, held it out behind him to his assistant, not for once taking his eyes off the man who stood before him. Joey, his eyes blazing, put up his hand and grabbed hold of the cane, but Bonython said, softly, "Don't, Joey, for you have more to lose than to gain if you do." and the calm in his voice diffused Bolitho's anger somewhat. Finally, Mr Ross, his throat burning with bruising and brandy, spoke in a rasping voice.

"Assault, sir! You are my witness, sir! The fellow assaulted me," he gasped, barely able to form the words, such was his discomfort.

Sir Reginald had indeed seen what Bolitho had done to his assistant and knew full well that they had a strong case against him, for that reason alone. However, when he spoke, his words rocked the ground Mr Ross stood upon.

"I did not see anything, Mr Ross, I'm afraid," he calmly informed him.

"What?" cried Mr Ross, his voice made stronger with disbelief. If Bonython thought to cover for the man, for whatever reason, he for one would have no part of it. "The men know of it, sir, for they had to assist me," he affirmed.

"The men, Mr Ross, will know only what I tell them to know," Bonython advised him with authority. The young man opened his mouth to speak again when a knock at the door caused all heads to turn. Slowly, Sir Reginald lowered his cane and ascertained that Bolitho's composure had returned before he called, "Enter!" in a firm voice.

He could not fail to notice Joey's head turned towards the door and the look of desperation in his eyes, but he turned away and looked down into the young, worried face of Nicholas Nankivell.

"You wished to see me, Sir?" said Nicky, respectfully, but he appeared nervous and ill at ease.

"Ah, yes, young man, yes!" began Bonython, although he was not exactly sure what to say to the lad. Mr Ross, still seething with indignation, angrily blurted out, "A body had been found and is believed to be that of your father. It would appear that he either fell or was thrown down a mine shaft, and about his person was this!" Reaching over, he picked up the coin, holding it between his finger and thumb, and held it out in front of the boy's face. Joey saw the head of ginger curls and the coin as it sparkled and shone in the light and felt his heart contract within him, as the past and present merged into one point in time.

"Do you know the significance of such a coin, my lad?" Nicky nodded, his large, worried eyes fixed firmly on Mr Ross's angry countenance.

"Informers for the preventatives received such payments, sir," he said, his voice little more than a whisper.

"That's right, my boy, that's right," enthused Mr Ross, "and are you aware of what a certain gentleman would do, in times past, if he came across anyone prepared to inform against him and his activities?"

All eyes were now fastened on the youngster, who stood stock still in front of his questioner. Slowly, the head nodded again, but not a word was uttered. Turning his back on Mr Ross, he stood and faced his beloved guardian. Slowly, his eyes began to fill with tears and Joey started forward at the sight of it, but his beloved boy cried out "No! Don't touch me! Tell me first! Tell me it isn't true, Papa!" he pleaded, desperately. Joey could not lie to the lad and hung his head. Nicky sniffled, and wiped his nose on his sleeve.

"Charlie Mankee told me you had killed him, but I would not believe it then and I don't want to believe it now," he whimpered, tears streaming down his cheeks. "Tell me the truth, Papa. Tell me," he pleaded, his sentence ending with a sob.

In front of the head of the Customs Service for Cornwall, and the local area officer, Joey Bolitho raised his head and looked his dear child full in the face. Any admission in front of the assembled company signalled his death knell and he knew it. Slowly and distinctly, so that all could hear him, he said, "I'm sorry, Nicky, but I did. I'm the man that killed yer father."

Sir Reginald Bonython, with a witnessed confession in his grasp, hung his head in despair, but his assistant almost crowed with delight.

"We have him, sir! We have him!" he shouted, joyfully.

The young boy, still sobbing, could barely speak. But finally, he bravely tilted his head, looked at his guardian and said, angrily, "I hate you! You've lied and deceived me all these years. He was only young and a cripple. Why? Why, Papa, why?"

Joey hung his head and shook it slowly from side to side, unable to answer him. In anger and frustration, Nicky threw himself at him and began to beat on his chest with his fists, shouting his hatred for him all the while.

"I could kill you," screamed Nicky, and Joey reached down and pulled out his knife from its sheath. Holding the blade in his hand, he presented it to the young boy.

"Do it then, Nicky," he quietly advised him, "fer I killed the man who murdered my own mother, an' you 'ave the right to do the same. No one 'ere would deny it to 'e," he humbly concluded.

Nicky, enraged, took hold of the handle and pulled it from Joey's hand. Holding it above his head, he determined to plunge the knife into his guardian's deceitful heart, but his arm wavered and he could not do it. Dropping the weapon from his grasp, he threw his arms about Joey, sobbing loudly. Joey Bolitho pulled him protectively into the crook of his arm and laid his cheek against the boy's head. "Fergive me, Nicky. Fergive me," whispered Joey, his voice wavering.

Sir Reginald sighed deeply and leaned back against the table in front of which he had just stood, transfixed by the admission he had heard, and watched the reunited couple with a thoughtful expression on his face. Mr Ross, his face shining with barely suppressed excitement, announced his intention of arresting the fellow there and then.

"Oh! Damn and blast it man! Be quiet!" remarked his superior, testily.

"But, sir..." began the young officer, and again, he was silenced. He turned his attention to the scene before him, and something about the sight of it slowly ate away at the fervour he felt for the success of his work. There was no doubting the love the man had for the boy, or the boy for him. Feeling humbled by the scene before him, he lowered his gaze to the floor. What he saw there made his eyes open wide with disbelief and he began to speak again.

"I say, sir," he began, but was once more ordered to remain silent. This time, however, he would not be deterred. "Bolitho, sir, he's bleeding. Look!" and he pointed to the floor where a pool of blood had formed underneath the man's right hand. Nicky, hearing his words, looked at the fast growing stain and then caught up his guardian's hand to see it dripping with blood. His long forgotten nightmare exploded in his mind at the sight of it and with all the distress and turmoil of his experiences of the afternoon, he let out a loud, bloodcurdling scream.

"Shhh!" crooned Joey, " 'Tis all right boy. 'Tis only a cut." Obviously, when Nicky had wrenched the knife from his guardian's hand, he had succeeded in cutting him. Bonython caught hold of Joey's arm and lifted the palm to the light, the better to study the wound.

"Mr Ross!" he commanded, "Go for Denzil at once and bring him here."

The young officer wavered for a moment, and then set off at a run. On his return, he found Bolitho ensconced in his own chair with the young Nankivell sitting by his side on another. The boy was not sobbing so dramatically, but it was obvious that he was still very distressed.

"See to the boy first, Denzil," advised Joey, quietly, and Dr Dunstan quickly dispensed an obnoxious tasting liquid that he insisted Nicky should drink.

"A mild sedative, that's all, my lad," the doctor told him, then he turned his attention to Bolitho's laceration. It was a long cut, which lay diagonally across the palm of the man's hand, and it was bleeding profusely. He cleaned the wound and then expertly sewed it up, before placing a dressing on it and securing it with a bandage.

Sir Reginald Bonython, as head of the customs service, coughed discreetly and enquired of his old friend if he had noticed anything untoward about the remains, upon which he had recently performed a post mortem. Denzil looked towards the man and boy seated opposite to him, noting how the youngster reached out and caught hold of his guardian's hand, holding tightly to it. He had found evidence that a bone in the neck had the mark of a cut across it. From this, he deduced that the deceased had probably had his neck cut and that the assailant's blade had sliced through to the vertebra at the back of the throat. He could state that quite correctly, he reasoned, and there would not be a medical practitioner in the land who would countermand him. He stared at the former smuggler, whose face was a blank mask, but the young boy could not hide his emotions and regarded him, a pleading look in his eyes. Denzil smiled, then remarked that he had been unable to say how the deceased had died. Dr Dunstan made it known that it was unlikely to be any other body than that of the Glasson fellow, for he knew of only one person with that particular malformation of the hand. He had deduced that, as the remains were of the same age and height as the missing young man, he felt safe to make that conclusion. His reason for the young man's death was simple. As it was known that Nicholas Glasson had been drinking that afternoon - for there were witnesses to that effect - then, possibly, he had fallen down the shaft in a state of intoxication.

"Who's to say?" he concluded and shrugged his shoulders.

Sir Reginald smiled gratefully and thanked him for his services. So, Dr Dunstan picked up his bag, made his farewells and left.

Mr Ross, feeling somewhat deflated, sullenly announced, "But we heard him admit it, Sir. He confessed. The law of the land..." Sir Reginald held up his hand to silence his virtuous babbling.

"You may have heard him, Mr Ross, but, due to age and infirmity, I have to admit that my hearing is not what it was. I appear to be suffering from a form of deafness," he informed the young officer.

Mr Ross, flabbergasted, rudely inquired, "Would that be the condition known as convenient deafness, sir?"

Bonython beamed and replied with a nod, "It would indeed, Mr Ross." He smiled sympathetically at the young man, and Angus found himself smiling back. "Let the knowledge that you were the one who finally trapped your man be enough for you. I do not think we need to display the catch, do we?" asked Sir Reginald, artfully.

Mr Ross, the smile still quivering on his lips, looked his superior in the eye and then admitted, "I believe that this condition that you suffer from sir, appears to be catching, for I seem to have fallen victim to it myself."

Nicky, his eyes drooping with the effects of the sedative, let out a loud yawn, so Bonython advised Bolitho to take themselves off to their home. "I'll call in later to see how you are going on," he advised him. Joey, now standing, bent down and scooped the exhausted lad up with his good arm. He struggled to hold him, for he was well built for his age and Bolitho was incapacitated. At once, Mr Ross stood forward and, taking the boy into his own arms, advised Joey that he would carry him home if Mr Bolitho would be so good as to lead the way. Bolitho calmly regarded the young man and Mr Ross noticed the look of respect he gave him. 'Well,' the preventative officer consoled himself, 'it was no small thing to earn the fellow's respect, at least.' He passed through the door that Bolitho held open for him and then followed in his wake as Bolitho returned to his home.

Mrs Melior Bolitho regarded the group in the hallway with wide eyes, but immediately took charge of the situation and arranged for Nicky to be put to bed. After making sure that all was well with the boy, she came downstairs and discovered her husband, a glass of wine in his left hand, sitting nonchalantly in front of the fire.

"A nasty cut, so Mr Ross said, and to your right hand," she remarked. "I would assume you will need my assistance to write for you until it is mended."

"I'll manage," replied her husband, determined not to have to make more use of her than was necessary. It was a strange marriage indeed, for Joey Bolitho had not attempted to utilise the help of Melior in any other capacity than that of a mother to his son. What her thoughts were on the matter, he did not know, but he had a great respect for her dealings with young Zacky and his aunt and he would be the first to admit that Nicky adored her. All in all, he thought to himself, he had solved his marital arrangements quite satisfactorily.

Although it was difficult to manage one handed, he adapted to the situation very well, but it was when he sat down to dine that he realised he was placed at a distinct disadvantage. A pair of merry brown eyes twinkled at him from the other end of the dining table as he attempted to cut his meat using only his good hand. It was more difficult than he had imagined and when a piece of ham shot off his plate and landed on the floor, he swore, profusely. His wife, smiling to herself, got up from her seat, walked to his place at the end of the table and, without a word, proceeded to cut up his meat and vegetables as if he had been a child. When she had completed her task, she returned to her own seat and resumed her consumption of her meal. Her husband, seething with indignation, glared at her from the other end of the table and demanded her attention. Melior, wilfully not regarding him, carried on with her meal, her face a picture of innocence, although she had frequently to bite her lip in order not to laugh out loud. When their meal was completed she got up and walked past him in order to leave the room. Joey, still simmering with his treatment at her hands, swiftly caught hold of her arm and pulled her around to face him.

"Don't think to play yer tricks on me, Mel, fer I will not 'ave it, you understand?" he angrily demanded. Any other person would have quaked in their shoes to be so addressed, particularly by Joey Bolitho in a temper. But his young wife looked him directly in the eye and laughed, then pulled her arm free from his hold and boldly left the room.

"Damn the maid!" he swore out loud, then sat and consumed his port in a blazing temper. Joey rejoined his wife in the withdrawing room, but she had her head in a book and did not look up, even when the fire puffed out a cloud of smoke as the door was banged shut behind him. Short of making the girl look at him, he could not communicate with her, so, after pacing up and down the room for a few minutes to ease his frustration, he selected a book from the shelf, sat in his chair by the fire and began to read.

When Sir Reginald called as he had promised to do, Melior was delighted to see him and immediately engaged him in conversation. She did not attempt to question him regarding her husband's injury, for well she knew that it was unlikely that either gentleman would explain the matter. She also knew, however, that on the morrow, young Nicky would be a lot more forthcoming. Melior had learned patience long ago and was quite content to wait in order to be made aware of what had taken place that afternoon. After a while, Bonython politely asked if he could speak with her husband alone. She stood up and left the room at once, declaring that, as it had been a busy day, it was her intention to retire for the night. The gentleman stood up as she left the room and, flashing a saucy look at her husband as he held open the door for her, she walked into the hallway and turned towards the stairs.

Bonython, smiling indulgently, watched her go and commented that she was a sweet child. "She has a will of iron!" muttered Joey, indignantly and proceeded to relate her actions at the dinner table. His companion laughed out loud and his amusement made Bolitho recognise the humour in the situation, he soon found he had to join him in laughter.

Sir Reginald, enjoying a large brandy, asked after Nicky and was informed that he was fast asleep. Bonython watched Joey's eyes glittering in the light from the fire, he knew himself on safe ground at last and advised his former quarry, that he would see that young Ross would not destroy his peace of mind in future.

"I advised him that...er...should he wish to advance his way through the service, he had better learn some diplomacy. After all, it would not do to cause any altercations within the family," he said and shot a quick glance at Joey's face. Always perceptive, Joey's brows snapped together. "Family, sir?" he queried.

"Yes, Joey...um...family. You see, man, I'm not cut out to be a widower and you have graciously allowed Melior's mother into your home, almost from your wedding day. So, I considered that, if you can be so open-hearted, perhaps I could be the same," he said, colour beginning to flood his face.

"She's my wife's mother, an' when the women 'ad settled their differences, I saw no reason fer keeping 'er from this 'ouse. Mrs Penrose is aware of the advantages that 'ave accrued to 'er daughter through 'er marriage, an' treats Melior with far more respect than ever she did afore." Joey spoke diplomatically, choosing to forget the names that his mother in law had hurled at him when it became known that he was to marry her daughter. However, since his marriage they had formed a truce of sorts. Mrs Penrose was not oblivious to the fact that she had only to mention that her finances were not particularly healthy at any time, and her new son-in-law would write out a draft on his bank, at once and without question.

"Quite so, Joey, and delighted I am to see it, for it has considerably improved Mrs Penrose's temperament. I don't think anyone who was at the Trevarthen's party that night would ever think that such would be the case. When Melior accepted your proposal, all hell broke loose, as you well know," he recounted, then added with a chuckle, "and the little minx wiped the smile off your face as well, an' I remember correctly."

Joey grinned at the memory and admitted that he had not expected such a thing to happen. However, he informed his guest that he thought the arrangement had turned out well; he knew that the boys adored her and because of that he could not wish for a better outcome, for he thought Melior was quite content to act as a mother to them. Sir Reginald regarded him quizzically for a moment, but kept his own counsel.

"You mentioned something about family," remarked Joey, never one to lose the thread of a discussion, "Am I to knaw more?"

"Ah, yes!" continued Bonython and for a moment, looked rather sheepish. "Well, as you may have noted, Mrs Penrose likes to be seen at various social gatherings, as I do myself, but the singular state is not the most satisfactory one and I...that is to say...It has become apparent to me that...um..." but Joey interrupted him.

"An' 'ave Mrs Penrose accepted 'e, Sir Reginald?" he queried, a smile hovering on his lips.

"Almost before I had finished asking her, Joey," laughed Sir Reginald, and then added, "A not unsuitable alliance, Joey, for we do not wish always to be in each other's company, but this marriage will enable us to visit with our friends without having to be regarded as social pariahs for our lack of a companion. Possibly, the thought that she would become Lady Bonython might have had something to do with it, of course, but I may be making an uncharitable assumption in mentioning that fact!"

Bolitho, still grinning, threw back his head and laughed aloud. "If I would 'ave been told, a few months ago, that I was to become not only Joanna's son-in-law but now yer own, I would 'ave thought it impossible" he said, merrily, then he stood up and generously refilled his companion's glass. The two men sat and talked companionably until the clock struck twelve, when Sir Reginald glanced guiltily at the timepiece and apologised for keeping Joey from his slumbers. He left the house a short time later and smiled to himself all the way home, considering that, all in all, having Bolitho for a son-in-law and his dearest Melior for a daughter would be an entertaining experience. His future wife, not being a fool, would do nothing to antagonise her husband-to-be, for Sir Reginald would brook no nonsense on her part. As he knew, she could hardly wait to be called Lady Bonython and she was busily giving him the impression that she intended to be a most compliant companion in their future life together.

Joey, feeling in an extremely good mood in spite of the pain from his hand, retired to his bed and with some small difficulty began to disrobe, prior to climbing into his solitary bed. It was only when it dawned on him that he would be unable to remove his boots with one hand that a frown appeared upon his face. The servants had retired an hour ago and he had no wish to disturb them, for only Mrs Nancarrow and the serving girl slept in the house. He could hardly summon the servant, a fourteen-year-old girl, to help him undress, he realised and with his cook's rheumatic joints, he did not think she would be capable of pulling off his boots in any case. Knowing Nicky to be fast asleep, he had concluded that he had two choices: to spend the night with his boots on or to go to his wife's room and awaken her. Thinking the latter the best option, he picked up his candle and headed for her bedchamber. After successfully opening the door, whilst holding his light in the same hand, he strode over to Melior's bed and, placing the candle on the table, gently shook her awake. Drowsily, she opened her eyes, but when she saw who was in her room, she sat bolt upright in the bed and smiled delightedly to see him there. Her smile disappeared, however, when he explained that he had only come to her as he had need of her to take his boots off. She frowned, but put back her covers and climbed out of the bed. Successfully removing them, she threw them to the floor in temper and climbed back into the bed.

"I thought you had come to me for another reason," she angrily muttered and turned her back on him in disgust. Joey sighed, for he had often explained to the young girl that their marriage was for the purpose of his being able to provide a mother figure for his young son, and for no other reason. However, gently turning her to face him, he held the light to one side to enable her to see him speak and told her again of what he expected of her in his household. To his horror, tears welled up in her eyes.

"When I visit with my sisters, they laugh at me, Joey!" she sobbed, "for they know that I am a wife in name only and wear a ring on my finger for propriety's sake. I watch them talk about me to their friends and I know what an object of fun I have become!"

"Melior, dear child, I 'ave told 'e what great regard I 'ave fer 'e..." mumbled her husband, then he hung his head, unable to finish.

Pulling out a handkerchief from under her pillow, she blew her nose and then wiped the tears from her cheeks. "Best to wish you goodnight, husband, and best to take your boots with you, for it would not do to give rise to more gossip, should you leave them in my chamber!" she flashed at him, then she turned her face into her pillow and started to sob again.

He could not bear to see her so distressed and carefully placing the candle on the table by her bed, he placed his left arm around her, raised her up and held her in his arms, rocking her gently for the child she was. After a while, she became quiet. Then, suddenly she lifted her face towards him and impulsively reached up her hands. Placing them on either side of his face, she placed her lips on his and kissed him. In that kiss, he recognised the love and the longing, but he had entered into an honourable contract with the girl in his arms and could not break it. He drew away, allowed the light to shine in his face and told her again that it could not be. She raised her chin defiantly at him when he told her to look at him, for he had more that he wished to say. He was somewhat disconcerted by the knowing smile which had appeared, rather abruptly, on her countenance, and before he had time to realise her intentions, she turned to the candle and blew it out. Plunged into darkness and with no means of communicating with her, he swore loudly, but again her lips found his and denied him further speech, useless as it now was in the blackness. He knew it should not be, but the darkness and desire played their part in awakening him to her. Lifting the covers, he climbed in beside her, hearing her call his name and feeling her arms caress him. The voice in his head, calling out to him that he had married a child, faded as the woman in his arms passionately caressed him. Deafened by desire and blind to consequences, his lips found hers and he returned her passion.

CHAPTER 28

DAISY TREVARTHEN had written to her father, advising him that Poulson had died at the beginning of the month. As she had no longer to care for him, she had arranged for a trust to be established, to enable her to set up a charitable hospital, in order to fulfil her desire that the despised inheritance and the cause of so much friction between them should be put only to good use. Paul considered replying, but his pride had been wounded by his daughter's actions and he would not commit pen to paper. Conversely, her mother had written that she considered such action to be a fine and magnanimous gesture on Daisy's part, and had even suggested that Grace's help would be invaluable, for her business acumen was substantial. When informed of the proposal, George insisted on becoming a patron, for he had been made well aware that his name carried weight in Oxford, not only due to his academic past, but also because he was the future Lord Wrothford. Daisy, rebuffed by her beloved father, wholeheartedly threw herself into the venture, determined to prove to him that, in spite of her actions, she was worth his love.

A previous institution, that had closed due to lack of funding, was purchased and brought up to standard with the very best equipment available. As money poured into the old hospital, it came to life again and in a short space of time, it had opened its doors to the poor and disadvantaged. Daisy, full of pride with her efforts, wrote to her father, asking him to come and see to what good the despised money had been put. But again, there was to be no reply from Paul. Her mother's letter contained the comments that she considered her husband 'a recalcitrant old fool' and although the words made her smile, her heart ached to see him again. Daisy even tried to enlist the help of her old friend, Harry Pendray, but in his letter of reply, he wrote that he considered it unlikely, that any words of his would help to mend the shattered relationship. He penned details of the boat he was employed in building, informed her as to how the work was progressing and what a fine sight she would be when completed. But, as was usual, there were no loving words for her. His apprenticeship over, he had secured the post of head foreman in the Vigus boatyard and loved every minute of his working day, enthusing with owners and workmen alike on the qualities of the various boats that were being built at the yard. Harry could converse with anyone on the subject, even to the point of boring his listeners with his enthusiastic descriptions, but to write the words that Daisy had longed for, for so many years, was more than he was capable of doing.

Within six months, Daisy had invested the whole of her mother's inheritance in a trust to enable the hospital to flourish. Taking what had been left to her by Professor Poulson, she bought herself a small house on the outskirts of Oxford and settled down to a solitary existence. Lonely and bored, she did not know what to do to pass the time. Having no desire to sit and read or to sew samplers, she decided that, as she had been responsible for establishing the hospital, then perhaps she would be able to offer assistance in the day to day running of the place. So, every day, she presented herself at the door and took on a variety of tasks in helping to tend the sick. The staff looked at her askance, for those with the money to be charitable were, more often than not, hardly desirous of involving themselves in such menial work as Miss Trevarthen was prepared to do. For Miss Trevarthen, however, it helped to assuage the guilt she felt at disappointing her father and to dull the ache she had always felt when she thought of her dearest Harry. It was the greatest irony of all that, when she picked up an infection from a patient, it was to be in her own hospital that she received treatment.

Trevu appeared to be a hive of activity when Joey Bolitho and his ward cantered into the yard. He saw Jonas Hampton calling out to the men as they led out a pair of carriage horses and, acquiring his attention, asked what the reason for all the commotion was.

"Word have come through that Miss Daisy be taken bad, Joey. Paul is going to her and I have sent Tom on ahead to make all ready on the way," he replied, but could not stop to say more, for he had to rush back into the stables.

"Best not stay too long, Nicky," advised Joey to his ward, "for they be in some state over this news."

Inside the house, servants rushed around, assembling bags. Paul, looking harassed, came running down the stairs, shouting instructions as he ran. Joey hailed him and asked if there was anything he could do, but Paul shook his head, distractedly, and rushed to his office. Joey sent Nicky off to find Sam and followed in his brother's footsteps. His calm good sense was put to good use and he managed to assist his brother in arranging his affairs, so that the farm could operate smoothly whilst he was away.

"It was such a shock you see, Joey, for she had written only the week before that all was progressing well," muttered Paul, castigating himself for his stupidity in not writing to the dear girl. "If I had," he said, "she would have returned to see us and would never have involved herself in this stupid business."

"You gave 'er no choice, Paul, an' she be as determined in 'er own way as you be pig 'eaded in yours," Joey said, frankly. His brother cast him a withering look, but somewhere in his tortured soul he knew Joey had spoken the truth. Bolitho, watching Paul's frantic attempts to organise himself, offered to accompany his brother.

Gaping in astonishment, Paul advised him that he had no time to wait for him to return to Penzance and pick up a bag. Joey calmly stated that he could buy all he would need on the way and could send word to his wife that he would be away from home for a while.

"She wen't worry," acknowledged Joey, with a smile, adding, "she's a good maid an' will understand that you would need the company along the way." He was convinced that his wife would also appreciate Joey's calm nature and good sense, which would greatly assist Paul on the journey. A year of marriage had opened his eyes to many sides of his wife's personality and taught him to appreciate the fact that, although he considered that he had married a child, in reality, she had far more maturity and accomplishments than he had been prepared to recognise at the beginning of their marriage.

Paul, grateful to have someone to share the burden, agreed, so Joey went off to find Chloe and assure her that he would take good care of both her husband and daughter. Chloe, normally so calm and controlled, burst into tears of relief, but quickly dried her eyes. Joey's next task was to find Nicky, but this was soon accomplished by standing in the hallway and bellowing his name. The youngster hurried along the landing, with Sam in hot pursuit. Quickly, Joey explained what was to happen and told him that it would be all right for him to stay at Trevu with Sam, as he was sure that Chloe would not mind. It was now his turn to be surprised as Nicky announced, with dignity, that he would return to Chapel Street to be with Melior, for he would not have her left alone without a man in the house. Joey controlled the smile that wanted to appear on his lips, but his eyes danced with amusement and pride at the boy's words.

"Thank you, Nicky," he said, "I appreciate yer kindness on my...on our behalf," he added, hastily correcting himself.

In the early hours of the third day since they had left Trevu, a distraught gentleman and his assured companion alighted from their carriage at the entrance to the imposing hospital. A light beckoned at the door and Paul hastened towards it. An official, forewarned that they would be arriving, was on hand to conduct them to Miss Trevarthen's room and when they were taken in to see her, Paul burst into tears at the sight of his fever-ravished daughter. Her uncle sent for the doctor in charge and demanded details of the young woman's condition. This gentleman assured him that he had done all he could, but he explained that the fever would decide the outcome, for there were not the medicines available to do more for her. Paul, wracked with fear and exhaustion, nodded dumbly, but Joey would have none of it. He demanded details of other medical luminaries in the area and made the doctor write out a description of Miss Trevarthen's illness. Thus armed, he set off to find them and glean their respective opinions. Never before having set foot in Oxford, he accomplished his aim in contacting each name on the list by asking for directions from anyone that crossed his path, from humble urchins to well dressed gentry. He went to the university itself and, making use of Professor Poulson's respected name, explained that the late gentleman's stepdaughter had succumbed to a serious, possibly fatal, ailment and he was seeking to find assistance from the scientific establishment within their walls. Joey, using all his charm and not inconsiderable intelligence, procured the name of a well-known doctor, who had a practice in London. Of all the medical men in England, he had been assured that this gentleman's abilities and his efficacious remedies were the most highly thought of amongst his peers. On his return to the hospital, he found that there was no change in his niece's condition. Her poor father sat by her bedside, unable to do more than pat her hand and call softly to his unhearing and unknowing daughter. Joey arranged for more nursing care for his niece, dismissing one lady on the spot when he caught a whiff of the gin on her breath, and then set off himself to bring Mr Sedgemore from his post. At first, the learned Doctor refused to go with him, even when Joey produced a roll of bills and held it under his nose. Bolitho, rarely one for not getting his own way considered that, if all else failed, he would kidnap the man and wrest him from his home by force. However, he decided on another ploy and so, with a derisive look on his face, he stated, "I would 'ave thought you would wish fer the distinguished gentlemen in Oxford to 'ave the chance to be impressed by yer abilities, but I see that be not the case. 'Tis obvious to me that you 'ave less faith in your talents than they do, an' I 'spose 'tis only right fer 'e to 'ide away in this grand 'ouse an' let they believe you be a cleverer fellow than you are."

"How dare you, sir!" exclaimed Mr Sedgemore, much put out by these remarks. He considered himself the finest medical practitioner in the land, for that was the epithet normally attributed to his name. "I am perfectly capable of curing these conditions and do not need to travel all the way to Oxford for my reputation!"

"If you say so, sir," responded Bolitho, but the look on his face gave the impression that he did not believe him. Exasperated, Mr Sedgemore rang for his servant and demanded that a bag be packed for him. He then went to his consulting room and busied himself amassing various medicines, which he did not believe would be available to him outside of the metropolis.

On arrival in Oxford, Mr Sedgemore took charge of the sickroom. After a brief examination, he quickly established that Daisy was suffering nothing more than a particularly severe form of marsh fever. He proceeded to make a series of changes in the sickroom and in the method of nursing care that she was receiving. Her father was grateful, impressed by his knowledge and professionalism. Her uncle, less so, for he concluded that much of the work performed by the medical practicioner was little more than common sense. However, he had to admit that his niece had soon begun to respond to the treatment and by the third day, she was able to respond to her father. When she smiled at Paul and weakly said, "Oh! Dada!" Paul promptly burst into tears and begged her forgiveness for his hardness towards her. Daisy sought for his hand and squeezed it gently, but soon lapsed back into a deep sleep.

"Best thing she could do," advised Joey, who took his brother from the room and bullied him into partaking of some food. Paul, so worried by his daughter's condition, had been scarcely able to face eating since he had arrived. The second time Daisy Trevarthen opened her eyes that day, it was to see her dear brother George and her beloved Harry Pendray, sitting on either side of her bed. Colour flooded into her face at the sight of them and, in spite of her wasted looks, she appeared so much improved that Paul took to his bed, in order to rest from his almost continuous duty of watching at her bedside. It had been his idea to write to Harry and his employer, stressing the seriousness of his daughter's condition and requesting that his workman be allowed the time to come to be with his old friend. Harry, almost paralysed with fear that he should lose his oldest and dearest friend, put all thoughts of boats from his mind and took the next available mail coach. George, on the other hand, travelled in comfort from Berkshire in his own travelling chaise. Like Daisy's father before them, they were dismayed to see her so ill, but heartened to hear that she had awoken and had recognised Paul earlier in the day. The brothers, gratified to see the improvement in Daisy, wrote to their respective wives that all was progressing well and that as soon as she had recovered her strength, they would be returning to Cornwall with her.

In the evening of the following day, however, their hearts fell again, for Daisy appeared to suffer a relapse. Mr Sedgemore, annoyed that his patient had not been able to sustain her improvement - because he felt it reflected badly on his abilities - again tried to ameliorate her condition. The patient appeared to be suffering difficulty breathing and he noted a rash upon her skin. This gave him cause for great concern as, in the past, when he had noted such symptoms, he had invariably found it difficult to improve the condition and the patient frequently died.

He explained as best he could to her father that, given her weak state of health, it was unlikely that Miss Trevarthen would be able to pull through. Paul, lifted from despair to the heights of delight, only to be plunged back down again, could scarce comprehend what the learned gentleman was telling him.

"But...but she was so much improved, surely it is within your power to see her through this setback?" he cried, fear clutching at his heart. Mr Sedgemore shook his head, informing him that the two complaints that his daughter had suffered were entirely different conditions.

"The one, with good practice and scientific medication, was quite easy to remedy, but at the moment she appears to be suffering from a tracheal disorder and for that, there is nothing that I, or anyone I know of, can do. Sometimes the patient recovers, it is true, but in your daughter's case I do not hold out much hope. She is too weakened by her previous illness to survive this second assault upon her person." He shook his head, then shook Mr Trevarthen's hand and informed him, bluntly, that as he held out no hope, he would be returning to London.

"I cannot perform miracles, Mr Trevarthen, sir," he announced, " and there are no medications that I can offer to resolve the situation. Believe me, dear sir, were they at my disposal, I would not hesitate to use them. Medical science progresses, Mr Trevarthen, but at no more than a snail's pace and it is therefore likely that there will be many casualties along the way. I am afraid that, in my considered opinion, the poor young lady for whom we have all wished so much and for whom I, in particular, have fought so hard, will not survive this additional tribulation. I am sorry, sir, but I can do no more."

Paul tried to urge him to stay but Mr Sedgemore would have none of it. Convinced that defeat was staring him in the face, he wished to put as many miles between the patient and his reputation as he could. He did explain to Paul that the trachea was severely infected and that, in all probability, his daughter would die of suffocation, because there were no medicines available that could counteract the ravages of the infection.

Joey, returning from the mail office with two letters from Cornwall, was just in time to see a post chaise and four thunder past him as he entered the driveway. With disgust, he noted Mr Sedgemore sitting bolt upright inside, looking neither to left or right. Hurriedly, he returned to the sickroom and came across his brother, in a state of collapse at what had happened. Paul had managed to inform the two young men of what the departed practitioner had said, but when he mentioned that his dearest child could not recover, he gave way to his emotions.

"The trachea is infected, you see, Uncle Joey," explained a shocked George, in a voice from which all emotion appeared to have been drained, "and she will not be able to breathe as the disease progresses. Slowly, her own body will choke her to...to death!"

"No," whispered young Harry, reaching for her hand and grasping it tightly, "it can't be. She was getting better, Mr Bolitho, I will not have it!"

Joey Bolitho stared at the poor girl, rasping for breath upon her bed. Like his brother, he had felt elated at her recovery but, unlike Paul, he felt compelled to do something in the face of the disaster that faced them. Joey Bolitho, as great a reader as his brother, had read every published work that had ever come his way, on whatever subject. Something, a name, began to repeat itself in his mind. Informing the others that he was off once more to the university, he hurriedly left the sickroom and obtained entrance yet again to that establishment, requesting any medical references to a French physician called Pierre Fédèle Brétonneau. After some searching amongst the dusty shelves, they produced a small pamphlet that had been written by a gentleman of that name.

They smiled apologetically at the strange Cornish man, and pointed out that it would be of very little use to him, for it had been written in French. They could make arrangements for it to be translated and if he would be so good as to return in the morning, it would be ready for him.

"No matter!" advised Joey, abruptly, "I 'ave the French!" and taking hold of the pamphlet, he ran all the way back to the sickroom.

Paul barely noticed his entrance, but Joey sat himself down in a corner and hurriedly began to read through the work that he held in his hand. He blinked when he read the physician's remedy for the particular illness that he was describing, but undeterred, Joey took out his knife and advanced upon the tortured body in the bed.

"I need a tube," he advised his nephew, considering him the only one capable of rational action, "'bout that long and this wide," and he indicated the dimensions with his finger and thumb.

"A what?" cried George, perplexed at his uncle's request.

"Quick, man," shouted Joey, "unless you wish to see yer sister die before yer very eyes!"

George, stung into action, rushed from the room, to return a few moments later with a collection of clay pipes in his hand. "They were all I could find, Uncle!" he explained, guiltily, but Joey grabbed them at once and proceeded to break one of them to the size he required.

Hearing the crack of the fired clay, Paul raised his head, and looked at his brother through his tears.

"What are you doing, Joey?" he demanded, his voice breaking on a sob, "and at a time like this?"

"In France a few years back, I read about this fellow who 'ad discovered that if you put a tube in the windpipe of a patient who be choking from what seem to be this disease, they do be able breathe through the tube. The patient he worked upon survived, Paul. 'Tis the only chance yer maid got, brother!" he said, earnestly. Paul, seeing his brother's knife in his hand, cried aghast, "No! You cannot, Joey! No! I will not let you!" Getting to his feet, he attempted to bar his brother from his beloved daughter's bed.

"Bleddy 'ell!" fumed Joey, commanding his nephew to hold his father back so that he could assist Daisy. George assumed a composure that he was far from feeling and roughly took hold of his father, holding him back against the wall. In the meantime, Joey demanded Harry's assistance. The poor young man, his hands shaking, removed the pillows from behind Daisy's head so that her body lay straight upon the bed, more like a corpse than ever before. The poor girl, so enfeebled, had no strength to resist, but continued to gasp desperately for air.

Feeling beads of perspiration on his brow, Joey Bolitho grasped his knife tightly in his hand and with his fingers, found the appropriate spot in her windpipe and proceeded to make a small incision. Blood spurted out and ran over his hands. Hastily, he took the proffered tube from Harry's shaking hand and with great care and dexterity, inserted the apparatus into the aperture in his niece's throat. Immediately, her distress was alleviated and air was sucked through the tube and into her lungs. Paul, screaming at his brother that he would not have him cut her throat, summoned up his remaining strength and threw his son from him, so that he fell to the floor. In a stride, he had his brother by the throat and pulled him from his precious child's bed, aghast at what he had seen Joey do and fully expecting to find a bloodied body stretched before his eyes.

"She's breathing, sir!" whispered Harry, in amazement, "Oh my good lord, sir!" but he could say no more and laid his head against her body, letting his tears flow. Paul Trevarthen, seeing the miracle of the breathing figure before him, sank to his knees at the bedside, unable to speak. In the meantime, George and Joey helped each other to a standing position again. Gently, Joey moved his brother to one side and arranged a dressing around the tube, he then asked for assistance to bind the pipe in place around Daisy's neck. Three pairs of hands were immediately held out towards him and it was not long before the operation was accomplished to his satisfaction.

Standing back from his handiwork, he allowed himself a slight smile. The irony of the situation did not escape him, however, for it was not the first time that Joey Bolitho had used a knife upon a person's throat, but this was the only time he had used it to give life and not to take it. Quietly, he left the occupants of the room to be with their beloved and went to his room to wash the blood from his hands. Slowly, he walked to the chair by the window and, remembering that he had a letter to read, he reached into his coat and broke it open.

On a single sheet of paper, Melior had written that all was well. Then Nicky had written that he was to rest assured and that he had everything in hand with regard to the welfare of the inhabitants of Chapel Street. Young Zacky had even scrawled a greeting to him before Melior's script filled the last half of the letter. She informed him that she had received notification from the manager of his wine merchants in Bristol, that the plot next to his business was for sale. He had asked if Mr Bolitho still had an interest in buying it. Melior advised him, that she had instructed that the manager was to make an offer for the property, for one hundred pounds less than the asking price, and that she would write to her husband to sanction her decision. If he wished to communicate with his manager, he could do so directly from Oxford, but that she did not wish for the sale to flounder for want of time. She added that they were relieved to hear that Miss Trevarthen was recovering, and that she had more news to impart to him, but would do so on his return.

He smiled at her style of writing, what other woman would have taken it upon herself to undertake such a business arrangement in her husband's absence? Her confidence in the matter astounded him but, he had to agree, she had made the right choice and although he was prepared to pay the asking price and more to obtain the site, he admired that she had sought to offer less, for he would have done the same. He was reading the letter for a second time, still smiling to himself, when there came a knock at the door. When his nephew entered, he smiled at him and asked how his niece was faring.

"Resting peacefully, Uncle," replied George, "with no distress in her breathing whatsoever."

"Glad to 'ear that, George!" announced Joey, adding that he hoped she would continue to prosper and that, from what he had read, he believed that she would soon start to recover from the coils of sickness that had enmeshed her.

George nodded and pulled up a chair, placed it beside his uncle's and sat beside him.

Joey waved the letter at him. "'Tis from Mel," he said, "and that minx bin' about doing some business on my behalf! She's a rare madam an' no mistake!" and he chuckled to himself. George felt the elation of the last half an hour slowly ebb away and the familiar pain that he carried in his heart returned at the mention of her name.

"She...I mean, Aunt Melior, is well, I hope?" he asked quietly, feeling the title awkward to use in reference to her.

"Seems be," admitted Joey, nonchalantly. He lapsed into silence and then chuckled aloud. "'Tis a strange thing, nephew, but I do get on some well with she. When 'e do think she be younger than Daisy, 'tis a marvel an' no mistake!"

George managed a smile and then asked nervously, "You marvel at her age, Uncle, but you must love her, surely?"

"Love 'er?!" exclaimed Joey, in astonishment. He threw back his head and laughed, "Dussen talk so daft!" However, in a moment, he became serious and turned to look at his nephew. George appeared to be regarding him with much sadness shadowing his face. Puzzled, his uncle's brows drew together, but he assumed that it was a reaction to all that had befallen them recently.

"When you do find yerself a maid, George, you'll understand what I do mean. We do all fall in love once in life. Fall in love with the one person an' no matter what 'appens, they be the ones we can never ferget. Yer father thought 'imself in love with Daisy's mother, but 'twas your mother he do love more than anybody. I fell in love with my Sarah-Jane. Tidden a woman born thas' goin' take 'er place, I tell 'e. But there's a special bond people do form with each other an' some people do call that love. I wouldn' want to 'urt or 'arm my Mel in any way, an' I got a great respect fer 'er, in spite of how young she do be. I've grown used to 'avin' 'er about me, an' I should sorely miss what she 'ave added to my life an' 'ow she 'ave worked to bring my boys closer to me. I 'ad much that needed to be fergiven, nephew, by both they boys." Here, Joey paused and bowed his head, before adding, "Particularly my Nicky." George noted the shame apparent on his uncle's face and waited as he gathered himself. Eventually, Joey continued, "She it was made me confess to Nicky of my crimes and why I 'ad committed them. An' then she sat both they boys down and told them that I 'ad been a bad man in the past, but that I 'ad changed my ways and was strivin' to earn their fergiveness." Joey sat in silence for a while. Finally, he lifted his head, his eyes shining. "Tidden a woman alive got my respect the way that young maid 'ave," he avowed, "an' I got be 'onest with 'e, George; there'd be some 'ole in my 'eart if she wouldn' there to fill it. Do 'e understand' what I bin tryin' say, nephew?"

251

George nodded his head, sombrely. He could appreciate the heartache her loss would cause his uncle, for that same heartache had desolated his own life.

"I am...am relieved to think you happy, Uncle," he said, simply. Joey suddenly remembered that he had a letter for his brother and passed it to his nephew, asking for it to be delivered.

"I'll do it at once, Uncle," remarked George, with a sad smile. As he rose and went to put his chair back against the wall, Joey caught hold of his arm.

"Don't look so downhearted, George. If you bin thwarted in love, don't let it ruin yer life. Without my Sarah-Jane, I 'ad no life, but now I bin given a new one by Melior an' I 'spect when the time do come, the same will 'appen to you. An' if you marry a maid you do like but don't love, well, who knaws what will become of it?" In a strange way, it gave George consolation to think that the woman he loved had made another happy, in spite of the differences between them. Perhaps it was not the case, as he had often imagined, that if he had asked before his uncle on that fateful night of the party, than she would have accepted him. If she could be happy with his uncle, then it might be as she had wished all along. He could never know, for he would not ask such a question of her, but there was a relief from the anguish of imagining his dearest trapped in a loveless marriage. His uncle might not think to call it love, but whatever it was that Joey Bolitho felt for his wife, it came as near to that emotion as any other George had yet come across.

Daisy's condition continued to improve with every passing day and after a week, Joey advised his brother that he had business to conduct in Bristol and wished to travel there to facilitate some arrangements that he wished to make. Paul, still contrite at his actions towards his brother, thanked him humbly for all he had done, not only for himself, but for his dearest child. But Joey waved aside his thanks and left for Bristol the next morning. When he arrived, he discovered that Melior's instructions had been carried out and that to secure the property, all that was needed was his signature. He felt a twinge of pride when Mr Tate, who had managed his business for so many years, unreservedly praised his wife for her practical abilities and undoubted business acumen.

"Mrs Bolitho stated, quite categorically, that when one wishes to sell to advantage, then one must accommodate your merchandise and display them well, in order to interest your prospective clients. Now that, Mr Bolitho, is a business brain much suited to your own philosophy, if you don't mind my boldness in saying so, Sir," he praised. Joey nodded in agreement, a smile forming on his lips as he did so.

Paul wrote to him, informing him that they would be setting off by easy stages to take Daisy home on the following Monday, so Joey replied that he would travel on to Cornwall without returning to Oxford, as it did not appear that he would be needed. Harry would accompany them on their return journey, Paul advised him, as George had been called away to Berkshire, his Lordship having taken a turn for the worse and hopes were fading for his recovery. They would meet again in Cornwall before the month was out and, Paul added, in a much happier state than when they had left. So, Joey travelled on alone, hiring horses as he went, not wishing to bother with a chaise to transport him for, when travelling, he was at his happiest to be able to do so as lightly as possible.

Upon arriving in Penzance, he reached his home to be greeted by his serving girl, who gave him a coy smile. Mrs Nankervis herself seemed to have a knowing grin on her face. He assumed that his household was gratified to know that Mr Trevarthen's daughter had survived her brush with death and thought no more of it. When Nicky threw himself into his arms and hugged him tightly, he also appeared to be grinning uncontrollably. It was when he saw his wife that something began to nag at him All was not as he had left things, for she appeared more confident and mature. He praised her for her conduct over the purchase of the plot of land in Bristol and stated that her actions had been invaluable to him. She glowed with pride at his words and he smiled in a friendly manner towards her.

The serving girl brought in the tea tray, still grinning from ear to ear, and Joey noted how respectfully his staff treated his wife. He considered himself a fortunate man indeed to have the dear girl for his helpmate. It was only when he had started on his second cup of tea that he remembered; that she had mentioned in her letter that she had even more to tell him.

"You 'ave more news, Mel? What 'e bin on upon now? Bin an' bought the Mount 'ave 'e, now 'e got the knally of doin' business?" he asked, a twinkle in his icy blue eyes.

Melior beamed back at him, and then informed him, in a casual, offhand fashion, that she was to have a baby.

The cup fell from Joey's hands and bounced across the carpet. "A what?" he bellowed at her, his eyes wide open with astonishment. Still amazed at what he had heard, he demanded to know how such a thing could have happened. Melior attempted to look demure, but failing miserably, she merrily informed him, " I presume the 'thing', as you would call it, husband, happened in the normal manner!" and unable to contain herself, she went off in a peal of laughter at the thunderstruck look on his face. Struck by the stupidity of his own remark, he began to laugh with her, then stood up and went to sit beside her on the settle, gently placing his arms around her.

"I have been violently sick every morning for two weeks, husband," she complained with a laugh, "and although I wanted you to be the first to know, I am convinced the whole of Penzance has been informed of my condition."

"Poor Mel," he whispered. Though she could not see his lips, the light kiss on her curls confirmed that he was not at all angered by the news. Strange that a man of his reputation should have mellowed to such a degree, she thought, but then a light touch and a will of iron had much to recommend them. She snuggled into his arms, feeling his hot breath on her cheek as he whispered endearments to her that she could not hear, but could feel transmitted to her through his gentle touch.

That night, they lay in each other's arms, content to lie together after their separation and delighted to think that their small family was to be made even more complete. Their harmony was to be disrupted, however, for in the early hours, a rap came at the door and the household was awoken, to discover that Joey Bolitho must make for Trevanoc with all possible speed, for his aunt lay dangerously ill.

A tall man lay asleep in the chair, a blanket over his knees to warm him, whilst the dying embers of the fire glowed like tired jewels in a grey cloud. On the other side of the large bedchamber, the old lady stirred in her bed and opened her eyes. The single candle lit the room with a warm glow, softening the man's features, and Leah Bolitho smiled with delight to see him there.

That he should have come to her, after all the troubles he had endured so recently, filled her with pride. The shyness that she had seen come upon him when he had sat with her all through the day, and talked to her during her waking moments of the baby that was to be born to him and his new young wife. There was much she had regretted about her nephew, his life and her own treatment of him, or more correctly her lack of it, but she thought them reconciled at last. In his unemotional way he had shown her glimpses of himself that he had tried so hard to hide from her on their previous encounters. She had welcomed the sight of them and her heart had soared with a peace that she had never found in his company before. He had even read to her from her bible, choosing the passages himself, and his thoughtfulness and kindness had given her much joy. She saw him stir, then suddenly he was awake, blinking at her in surprise, for a moment finding himself where he had never expected to be.

"See, nephew," she said, in a soft voice that he had to strain his ears to catch, "you have spent a night under Travanoc's roof at last!"

He grinned back at her, with her beloved Zacky's smile on his lips and something of Miriam's wickedness too, she noted.

"Can I get you anything, Aunt?" he asked quietly, and before she could reply, he picked up the kindling and encouraged the fire to flame again.

"No, I don't have any needs, my dear boy," she told him, softly, as he took the chair by her bedside and sat himself in it. She smiled happily at him and seemed to doze again, but only for a little while, for soon her eyes were upon him again.

"This was your grandfather's room, you know," she announced, softly. "He loved it, for the rays of the rising sun flood in at dawn. 'It fills the room and my heart with light,' he used to say." Suddenly, her smile grew even wider and she confided in him, "I shall be pleased to meet with them all again, dear Joseph and to tell them of you. I have no sadness to leave behind me, for I have run my course and have only joy to take on my final journey. I leave you my dearest love, nephew, and in God's care, for he will not let so good a man as you have become, fall again." She saw him lower his head at her words, "A little faith, my dear, even in an unbeliever, is never wasted, you know," and she giggled, rather in the manner of a mischievous girl, he thought. He grinned back at her, but self-consciously reached out and caught up her frail hand in his. Leah looked at him and sighed, then began to speak again, her voice frail and laboured now, so that he had to lean forward to catch her words.

"Let the sun in, Joseph, my dear, for I would see my blessing in God's light," she announced. Puzzled as to her meaning, he went to the window and pulled back the curtain. At once the light flooded in, filling the room, and he turned back and saw her drink her fill of what she could see. With the smile still on her face and the image before her that she had treasured for so long, Leah Bolitho, alone but comforted, stepped boldly out on her last journey.

Softly, Joey returned to her side, bent down and kissed her cheek respectfully, hoping, but not supposing, that the image would be conveyed to her. Gently, he closed her eyes and after a few moments alone with his thoughts, he wished her farewell fondly, before quietly letting himself out of the room.

CHAPTER 29

IN THE garden at Trevu, in the middle of the lawn, three young boys played at ball with each other. The elder, Treve Trevarthen, instructing his younger playmates, a black haired boy and a dark skinned boy, as to how to play the game he had devised. A young girl watched them, but she kept making surreptitious glances towards the house and was not part of the game at all. On the bench facing the house sat Melior Bolitho and Chloe Trevarthen, deep in conversation. It was noticeable that Melior would often turn away as she spoke, to survey the faces of the others that were gathered there as they conversed with each other. She laughed, shyly, when Chloe asked a question of her, and placed her hand on her stomach and nodded her head. On the other side of the garden, her husband and his brother sat, bathed in the sunshine that shone on them from a cloudless sky.

Paul Trevarthen, seeing his sister-in-law's action, enquired politely of his brother if he was to be a father again. His brother, holding an infant of about eight months on his lap, smiled to himself and said, quietly, "I believe so, brother, but I 'aven't bin told. Melior bin stayin' a-bed late these last few days an' that idden like she. I know she'd like another, an' 'as promised it to be a boy the next time." The baby on his lap gurgled with delight, reached up to catch hold of the bright chain attached to his watch and began to pull on it. Gently, he disengaged it from her fingers. "Thas' enough of that, Miss Leah," he said, with a broad grin. Catching hold of her hand, he kissed her fingers and then dropped another kiss into her tiny palm. The child laughed and chuckled with delight at the sensation. Her deep auburn curls - a deeper hue than her mother's - and her shining blue eyes - a match for her father's - made the child a beautiful sight to behold and her proud father shook his head in wonder at her.

"I don't mind another girl," he said, smiling at his daughter and blowing gently on her face. The child laughed again and began to bounce up and down with delight. Paul watched him and thought it a wondrous sight, for the man's face had softened so completely that he was almost unrecognisable. The hard, uncaring smuggler, suspicious and cold, seemed a world away from the doting father who revelled in the joy he shared with his youngest child.

After a while, Joey realised that he was ignoring his brother and sought to remedy it. "I bin thinkin' whas' best to do 'bout Trevanoc. We bin livin' there quite well this last month, an' what with the children keepin' us busy an Melior seem 'appy wherever she do be, I bin wonderin' if we don't move up there. Keep me 'ome in Penzance, of course, but Trevanoc is a fine new 'ouse an' we got good neighbours. Tidden so far away that I shan't be callin' on 'e Paul, you knaw that, an' 'twould be a fine thing if yer family come to stay fer I would like that. Aunt Caroline 'ave bin wishful to visit, so I 'ave arranged to send the coach fer 'er next Wednesday an' said she may stay as long as she do wish." He chuckled to himself as a thought occurred to him, "I 'spect she wen't like the décor, but then you knaw what our Aunt be like! That woman idden 'appy less she got somethin' to 'ave a moan about!" Paul threw back his head and laughed at his brother's acute observation. However, he understood that, with his young son's love of the farm and a fine house like Trevanoc, his brother would be a fool to continue to live in Penzance. Young Zacky and Nathan had grown up together and were almost inseparable. Paul considered it would be a crime to part them by having the young boy live away from all he loved and knew. Watching the two friends playing together, so happily, he felt a pang of jealousy that he did not have such companionship in his own youth. Fate had been cruel, he sadly considered, to deny when they were younger the shared affection that the two men now felt for each other. His brother's soft voice broke in on his thoughts and brought him back to the present.

"Daisy an' 'Arry be goin' on all right, I 'ope?" enquired Joey, conversationally.

Paul chuckled and nodded his head, before announcing that they had arrived back in Falmouth from their honeymoon on the Friday of the previous week. "Daisy wrote to me to say that all is well, although she found it difficult to credit that there were so many boatyards to be found along the Severn. She believes she has visited them all, but cannot be sure. Harry is now fired with enthusiasm, he is determined to buy his own and to set himself up in business, although Mr Vigus still wishes to make him a full partner. Bert would have been so proud of him, to see how well he has progressed," he finished in contemplation.

"Tidden only 'is son 'e'd be proud of. You bin' like a second father to they boys, Dick as well, fer I knaw damn well 'twas you that got 'im taken on by Rodda when 'e 'ad finished 'is schooling, an' I believe 'e be a better lawyer than old Rodda ever was," stated Joey, noting that Paul's face had darkened with embarrassment at his words.

"Bert's boys made their own achievements," said Paul, "it had precious little to do with me."

"If you d' say so," said his brother, and smiled at little Leah again. "Any more news from the family? Seeing I bin up Trevanoc, putting things in order for the last month, I 'aven't 'eard anymore from 'e."

"Forgive me, Joey, I should have written, I know, but Grace arrived unexpectedly to visit and then Aunt Caroline came to stay, and I have been so busy about the farm it seems there were not enough hours in the day. I heard from Jack on Monday, but I cannot imagine that he will be returning to these shores before next year at the earliest. George is in good health and writes that he has been well entertained by his houseguests recently. Various writers and academics have spent the last month on the estate and he has been to London and acquired several more volumes for his library, so he seems quite content," he announced.

"None of they be thinking of matrimony, by the sound of it," stated his brother.

"Possibly Grace," Paul replied after a moment's contemplation.

His brother smiled, knowingly, "Mr Ross still in attendance, I presume?"

Paul grinned and nodded. "Of course, he is determined to do well in his post here in Penzance but when Grace comes to stay, he is forever calling at the house. The poor fellow may not be aware of it, but if she has him, it will be on her terms. He might wish to prove himself in his chosen career, but I know Grace is very appreciative of his organisational skills and I imagine she thinks he would make an exceptional business partner."

"Do she love 'en?"

"Difficult to say but she is much like Sardi and knows her own mind. She certainly shows him a decided partiality that none of the other young men in this vicinity seem to merit from her. Goodness knows, there are plenty for her to choose from, for as soon as it is known that Grace is at Trevu, all manner of suitors arrive on our doorstep. However, as I said, she is much like her grandmother and she will have him if, and when, she decides on the matter. Poor Angus will have to give up his profession, though, for my daughter will not wish to be a dear little wife, waiting at home for his return from chasing about the countryside after smug...um...the less law-abiding amongst us," and he shot a quick look at his brother, noting that he smiled at his words. He was delighted to see the change that had been wrought in him and continued with praise for his daughter. "I cannot believe how well the business has developed since she has been placed in charge of it and, as I mentioned before, it provided an excellent income when I had the running of it. A part of me should be embarrassed to see how well Grace has done, but I am far too proud of her to let it bother me." He sighed and admitted, "Age has made me serene, brother. For instance, Jack's every letter contains references to various females. At the moment, it appears that he is residing at the home of a widowed Italian contessa. What the situation is, precisely, I cannot be sure, but he informed me that he had almost completed his portrait of her and as his description of her contained the words 'voluptuous' and 'intoxicatingly beautiful' I think it best to leave it to your imagination as to what his living arrangements are!" he finished with a laugh.

"I thought she was French?" remarked his brother, with a chuckle.

"That was the last lady he was painting, the one with the wicked eyes and excellent proportions," advised his brother, "I doubt the fellow will ever settle down and if he does, well, I pity his poor wife, for he will lead her a merry dance!"

Joey threw back his head and laughed and his daughter, delighted by the sound, gurgled with glee.

"George is still following the singular path, I presume?" Joey enquired, after a moment. Paul nodded, "I suppose he will be attracted to a woman at some time in the future, but he shows no inclination to marry at present. He has plenty of females throwing themselves at him, of course, but he seems not to wish to become involved with any of them. I did think at one stage that he was contemplating the married state, but it must have come to nothing, for he has mentioned no word to me. He was always a serious and reserved fellow and if he has been disappointed in love, he will not be in a hurry to seek solace in matrimony. You know George, he loses himself in books at a moment's notice, so perhaps he is not so lonely as I imagine him to be," he concluded with a sigh.

"Time will tell, Paul, 'e's young yet," advised Joey, who then looked up and smiled as a tall, ginger-haired youth came out from the house towards him, closely followed by a taller, dark complexioned boy with a panting dog following closely at their heels. They were laughing and joking together and it was not long before they had joined the men at the bench. Nicky Nankivell put out his hands for the child and when her father released her to his care, he lovingly kissed her little nose and lifted her high into the air, so that she squealed with delight.

"Papa, shall I take Leah in? For I would not want her to get overheated in this sun, it is quite strong, you know!" he admonished.

"Ask yer mother," Joey told him. He watched the youths turn and stride across the garden, stopping briefly to talk with the youngsters enjoying their game on the grass.

"He's a fine boy, Joey. You must be very proud of him," said Paul, watching them talking with his wife and sister-in-law.

"Damn right!" announced his brother, "Wants to learn the wine business. Well, tidden such a bad idea, fer Zacky be all fer the farm, like yer Samuel is fer Trevu, an' Nicky understand the business an' got my contacts in France, so 'e be well set up for learning the trade. An' it wen't be many years afore 'e'll be thinking of settling down and settin' up 'is own 'ousehold." At that moment, Alice wandered over to young Nankivell's side and began to engage him in conversation. She looked up at him, coyly, with a smile trembling on her lips, and it was obvious for all to see that she regarded the youth with obvious admiration.

At this spectacle, Paul and Joey exchanged glances with each other, then burst out into loud laughter at the thought that had occurred to each of them.

The sound of a carriage pulling up the drive made Joey turn his head, although he had not a view of it from the sheltered garden.

"Sounds like you got visitors, Paul," he said. His brother nodded and informed him that the Bonython's had intended to call, if time allowed them.

"Bleddy 'ell!" muttered Joey, "We 'ad they up Trevanoc with we yesterday. I b'lieve Joanna be followin' me around."

"Lady Bonython is just so full of the visit to France that she has just made with her husband, that she must needs tell everyone about it," Paul said. It was not long before they heard voices coming through the withdrawing room and Joey appeared to murmur under his breath, but he was perfectly polite when her ladyship came into view. She waved airily at her daughter and then advanced upon the two men, leaving her husband to follow in her wake.

Paul and Joey, now standing to greet her, behaved most politely, but breathed a sigh of relief when she espied young Nankivell, still holding her granddaughter in his arms, and headed determinedly in his direction.

"Melior! What are you thinking of? That poor child will be covered in freckles! Chloe, dearest!" she exclaimed, exchanging a perfunctory kiss with her daughter and Mrs Trevarthen. Sitting herself beside them, she began to regale them with her time in France, but she took the precaution of passing her parasol to Alice so that she could hold it over the infant's head and shade her from the light.

No one in the garden could fail to hear her remarks about the beauties of Paris, and how she considered it most strange that neither of the two women seated on each side of her had ever been to see the wonderful city.

"I was only saying to my dear husband, on the way here, what poor spouses you have that they should not think to take you," she exclaimed, giving each a pitying look in turn. Neither lady seemed much abashed by her attitude, and when Lady Bonython was busily employed in removing her gloves, in order that they might see the fine diamond ring her dear husband had purchased for her, they exchanged gleeful glances behind her back.

In the meantime, Sir Reginald Bonython had seated himself between the two brothers and was chatting in a friendly manner with each of them.

"You look tired, Reggie," commented Joey and was advised that Trevu was the fifth house they had visited that day. "Luckily, we are off to the Roskilly's tonight to attend a choral recital. I know William will have some card tables set up for those not of a musical persuasion; if Rodda and Harvey are there, Denzil and I will be able to make a four and have some decent entertainment."

"We will be taking tea soon, Sir Reginald, I do hope her ladyship and yourself will be able to stay?" asked Paul, politely.

"Love to, old chap," smiled Bonython. "The wife wants to go on to the Trestrails, but damned if I'm gadding off for another visit at this time of day. Your cook, Paul, makes the best scones in the county and I'm determined to taste them before I have to move on," he announced. He then raised his voice and informed his wife that he had accepted an invitation to stay for tea. Joanna's bosom swelled indignantly, but her husband raised an eyebrow and gave her a stern look. She acquiesced at once, and smiled at Chloe as she said that tea would be quite delightful, for she could continue to tell her of the adventures she had experienced abroad.

"That was masterful, Reggie," admitted his admiring son-in-law.

"Well, I've known the lady who has become my dear wife for many years. I discovered it to be prudent to make my wishes plain before she has a chance to countermand them. Needless to say, this strategy does involve taking her to the jewellers or dressmakers and telling her that I've seen the very thing that will suit her and no other, but I consider that a small price to pay to be master in my own home," he intimated to them, a smile on his lips. From across the garden, Melior beamed back at them, not missing a word of what had passed between them.

They sat and chatted companionably until it was time for them to go in and partake of the tea, which had been laid out for them in the withdrawing room. Paul rose to his feet immediately and went to escort the ladies into the house, along with Sir Reginald. Nicholas, still holding little Leah, offered his arm to Melior, who beamed at him and let him lead her towards the house, whilst Alice dutifully followed in his footsteps, Lady Bonython's parasol still clutched in her hand. Her brother, Sam, walked at her side, trying to fit his large stride in step with her more feminine one. The youngest boys got to their feet, but put their heads together as Zacky, always the ringleader, appeared to be whispering instructions to them. Finally, Nathan and Treve headed slowly across the grass in the direction of the house, but young Zacky ran towards his father and asked if, after their tea, the boys could go down to the river to try to catch some fish.

"We'll see," Joey advised him and immediately, Zacky began to pout. "You always say that!" he moaned. "I bet Uncle Paul will let us if we ask him nicely," he again attempted, determined to get his own way. His father raised an eyebrow and tousled his black curls affectionately. "Well, I'll 'ave to see if you do..." but he was interrupted by his son, who sighed loudly and announced, "I know! 'If I do behave myself'," and not waiting for any further comments, he ran to catch up with Nathan and dashed through the open doorway, his older cousin skipping happily at their side. Joey Bolitho watched them disappear into the withdrawing room. The sight of his son, holding firmly to Nathan Nairn's hand, made him cast his mind back to his youth. He saw again the young coloured boy who had grinned at him so mischievously when, with

Redvers' help, he had escaped from the irate baker. If his life had been different, then perhaps he could have bonded with Paul from an earlier age and they could have experienced the friendship that his son shared with Nathan. Looking back, there was much he would have wished to change, but circumstances had decreed otherwise. He had found happiness with his beloved Sarah-Jane, only to lose it again. But now, despite knowing in his heart that he could not love his new wife with the same passion, Melior had made him far happier than he could have believed. Joey caught sight of his wife coming out into the garden and stepping towards him. She had blossomed since the birth of her daughter and it pleased him to think her happy, for she always seemed to be smiling. Unconsciously, he smiled back at her and then thought to ask the question that had been at the back of his mind for the last few days.

"Are you with child again, Melior?" he asked.

"I might well be!" she told him archly, her eyes twinkling with devilment.

"And when will it please 'e to tell me?" he asked, raising an eyebrow.

A tugging on his coat made him glance down in surprise. Zacky looked back up at him, his green eyes looking most serious. "Dada!" he enthused, "Uncle Paul says we can! He says we can go fishing!" Joey sighed and caught hold of his son's hand, then linked arms with his wife and started to walk towards the house. Turning his head, he mouthed to Melior, "Well?" still determined to get an answer to his question.

Melior giggled and said, "I'll tell you tonight, dear husband," and then added with a wicked laugh, "When we are abed!"

"Strumpet!" he called her and she hooted with laughter at the word.

Too late, he heard a young voice at his side ask, "Dada? Whas' a...a st...stumpet?"

Joey sighed and gave in as gracefully as he could. "If Uncle Paul says you can go fishin', then I won't argue with 'im. Mind you d' take Nicky an' Sam with 'e. I wouldn' want 'e fallin' in!" he added for good measure. He then gave his son's hand a gentle squeeze, pleased with himself that he had, in his opinion, handled the business quite successfully.

A replica of Joey's mischievous smile crossed his little son's face, but his father was smiling at his wife and did not see it. Joey Bolitho was only just beginning to discover that his boy was as cunning and resourceful as he was himself. Young Zacky looked towards the house and, catching sight of his best friend executed a nod of his head and an exaggerated wink. Nathan Nairn, watching from the doorway, grinned back in delight when he saw the sign. Turning his head, he nudged the older boy in the ribs, "Treef! Treef!" he whispered conspiratorially to Paul's youngest son, "Zacky 'ave got 'en say yes!" He chuckled gleefully and then announced, "Now's your turn. You ask your Dada if we c'n go fissin', an' don' forget say your Uncle Joey don' mind!"

Printed in the United Kingdom
by Lightning Source UK Ltd.
119882UK00001B/244